· BETWEEN THE FLOWERS ·

BETWEEN THE FLOWERS

Harriette Simpson Arnow

MICHIGAN STATE UNIVERSITY PRESS
EAST LANSING

PS
3501
.R64
B47
1999

Michigan State University Press
East Lansing, Michigan 48823-5202

04 03 02 01 00 99   1 2 3 4 5 6 7 8 9

Library of Congress Cataloging-in-Publication Data

Arnow, Harriette Louisa Simpson, 1908-1986
    Between the flowers / Harriette Simpson Arnow ; edited by
Frederic J. Svoboda.
    p. cm.
    ISBN 0-87013-535-X (alk. paper)
    I. Svoboda, Frederic Joseph, 1949- II. Title.
PS3501.R64B47 1999   99-6812

    813'.52—dc21   CIP

Cover design by Ariana Grabec-Dingman
Book design by Nicolette Rose

Visit Michigan State University Press on the World-Wide Web at:
www.msu.edu/unit/msupress

·   Acknowledgments   ·

Michigan State University Press and Frederic Svoboda would like to acknowledge the support granted by the Office of Research of the University of Michigan—Flint, the assistance of the Special Collections and Archives of the University of Kentucky's King Library, and the hospitality of the University of Kentucky's Gaines Center for the Humanities. Haeja Chung provided valuable background information, and Pat Arnow cogent suggestions regarding my introduction to the novel.

· Introduction ·

Frederic J. Svoboda

Harriette Simpson Arnow received acclaim for her five novels and four histories published from the 1930s through the 1970s, but one worthy novel written early in her career she abandoned to a drawer. *Between the Flowers* was written after successful publication of *Mountain Path* in 1936, but the author found herself frustrated in her attempts to revise the work to suit the demands of a publisher sometimes ignorant of the mountain life she portrayed so accurately.

Hearkening back to a way of life so different from today's—even in rural Kentucky where the book is set—the themes of the book also resonate to contemporary concerns. And because there is continued interest in the author's work more than a dozen years after her death, publication of this sixty-year-old manuscript is appropriate and timely.

Harriette Simpson, a young writer from Kentucky, submitted her first novel to Covici-Friede publishers in New York City after being encouraged by editor Harold Strauss, who had read her story "A Mess of Pork" in the journal *The New Talent*. She already had written one, the story of a young woman who becomes a teacher in a remote Kentucky mountain school. It was based in part on her own experiences. When he read "Path," which previously had been rejected by Macmillan, Strauss recognized the quality of the work. However, he advised Simpson that it might be wiser not to publish it but to develop a more "dramatic" and commercial novel.

Strauss desired to develop her as a star for the company, perhaps a parallel to Covici-Friede's other rising young novelist, John

Steinbeck. He bowed to her wish that the novel be published despite contrary opinions from other Covici-Friede editors and several literary critics to whom the typescript had been sent.

It appeared in 1936 as *Mountain Path* and was well received by critics. It also was named a Book of Month Club Alternate Selection. Simpson was living in Cincinnati, having worked as a waitress and in similar jobs at the beginning of her five-year plan to become a successful author, then working for the Federal Writers' Project.

Simpson soon turned to her next novel, submitting an early version of *Between the Flowers*. This was the tale of an idealistic young mountain woman married to an abusive man. It contained many of its themes in melodramatic form—including a scene, for example, in which after a quarrel the woman looks at her sleeping husband and whets a knife. It also repeated the rural Kentucky setting of *Mountain Path*, something Strauss had advised against because of the tendency for that subject matter to be viewed in terms of hillbilly stereotypes. This may have been commercially sensible advice, but it ignored Simpson's powerful imaginative link to her home.

Strauss gave considerable advice on the new novel, particularly suggesting that she make the husband as realistic a character as the wife instead of the two-dimensional and unsympathetic man she had portrayed. The novel's moral conflict would derive not from cruelty, but from the characters' contrasting desires in life. As Simpson developed this version, Strauss sought advice from multiple readers.

One reader's report illustrates great misunderstandings. He faulted her characterization as "sheer baloney" and misread the facts of farm life she presented. The reader did not understand a violent outburst from the husband about his wife's independence, unparalleled in their traditional society; and he did not even realize that for farm folk "dinner" was the noon meal.

Arnow's bitter disappointment at this unsympathetic reception is palpable in her marginal notes on her editor's letters, as is the frustration in her attempts to meet Strauss's seemingly shifting requirements. She was struggling to find the appropriate ending to what had become a novel of dual protagonists, the idealistic young woman and her husband, now both sympathetically seen. Eventually she wrote, ". . . the more I saw what I was up against, the more I knew that [the husband] was lost and hopeless and I had no heart to go hunting words. Just now I feel as if I never wanted to write again. . . ."

Late in 1938 Strauss explained to Simpson that despite his personal opinion of the book, the editorial board had rejected it. She continued revising, but Strauss lost his position at the foundering Covici-Friede and took a job with the Federal Writers' Project. While Arnow continued in Cincinnati he attempted to place her with other publishers, submitting *Between the Flowers* to Knopf and to William Morrow & Co. Both rejected the novel, and early in 1939 Strauss was advising her against trying to publish the book herself. Simpson soon would return to rural Kentucky—and marry Harold Arnow, whom she had met through the Cincinnati Federal Writers' Project.

The attempt to publish *Between the Flowers* had come to an end. It would be a long wait for her next novel. *Hunter's Horn* (1949), published under her married name of Harriette Simpson Arnow, would be even better received than *Mountain Path*. It was listed as one of the ten best books of that year by the *New York Times Book Review* and named book of the year by *Saturday Review of Literature*. Arnow would build a distinguished career as novelist and regional historian, achieving her greatest fame with *The Dollmaker* (1954), the story of Kentuckians uprooted morally as well as physically by their migration to work in the factories of World War II Detroit. That novel would particularly be marked by the conflict between Gertie Nevels, a woman who loved and lived for the land, and her husband Clovis, a man most at home wherever a machine needed repair.

At Arnow's death in 1986, she had lived in southern Michigan for much of her adult life. That Michigan connection led The Michigan State University Press to explore publication of works by and about her. Knowing my interests in twentieth-century American literature and textual editing, the Press asked me to examine the typescript of *Between the Flowers* that survived among her papers. What I found was not the stereotyped book that the 1930s reader's report might have suggested, but a novel of moral conflict deriving its tension from its dual protagonists' ultimate desires. It was precisely the novel that Harold Strauss had asked Harriette Simpson to write so many years ago.

I recommended publication. I worked with the novel with a light touch of the editor's pencil, making only a few cuts where Arnow struggled with the ending. *Between the Flowers* is a work of art and it deserves to be seen in its original condition.

The title *Between the Flowers* accurately suggests the book's lyrical and realistic qualities. This is a novel lived in the natural world, from season to season and year to year. And the moods of the book change and evolve from chapter to chapter. The closing of the novel echoes its beginning at a Memorial Day observance, as a young man, Marsh, first comes to a rural community and meets the spirited young woman, Delph.

One of the editors who regretfully rejected *Between the Flowers* in the late 1930s wrote of the novel as offering "a sensitive, authentic story of farm life . . . that goes beyond the ordinary values of these so-called "soil" novels. . . ." Today's readers will find in it an honest yet touching exploration of the joys and compromises and everyday textures of married life. It is a novel of adventure and lyricism and psychological depth. And now it is available, as by rights it should have been some sixty years ago.

Flint Michigan
July 1999

· 1 ·

MRS. CROUCH stood on the porch under the weather-beaten sign, Costello's Valley, Ky. U.S. Post Office, and looked up the steep stretch of narrow hill road where August heat waves trembled above the sheep-skull rocks and uneven chunks of blue-white limestone. The sun glare hurt her eyes, and she rested them with a slow glance over Costello's Valley—the sloping sides of wooded hills leading down to a gently moving creek bordered with willows and sycamores, the wooden bridge across the creek, and the great beech trees that grew on the bit of level land on either side of the road. The trees, the road, the creek, and the white-painted, high-porched building in which she lived and tended the mail and a general store, with plenty of time left to care for a plot of vegetables and flowers, made up Costello's Valley.

She heard from somewhere down the creek the soft clinking thuds of pitched horse shoes and low easy murmur of hill men's voices, and now and then from the heavy shade of the beech grove a squirrel's bark or a trinkle of bird song; but still there seemed less sound than silence. The heavy breathing of Old Willie Copenhaver on the other end of the porch came so loud that she turned to look at him. He sat as he had been setting for the last hour, his bark bottomed chair tilted against the house wall, his head dropped forward with his bushy gray beard spread over his chest; one knobby, blue-veined hand on the Bible in his lap, the other on a hickory sapling cane.

His son, Young Willie, a tall, stoop-shouldered bachelor in his late fifties, sat a few feet away. Mostly he watched the other occupant of the porch—a little old man with thin white hair and bright

1

blue eyes—carve a hazel nut basket, though sometimes he glanced concernedly toward his father. Mrs. Crouch, when she had studied the old sleeping man for a time, said to Young Willie, "It's a mighty hot day for a man old as your paw to be ridin' around."

Young Willie shifted his tobacco and spat into the yard, then smiled on his father. "Nothin' 'ud do him but he must come. He's not missed a Memorial Day up at Big Cane Brake in more'n fifty years. I wisht I could ha' gone with him but I've got that mail carryin' job. I'm hopin' though that Juber here'ull kind a look out for him."

The little man twisted about on his nail keg seat, and looked down through the beech trees to a slender legged bay mare tethered to the low boughs of one. "Pshaw, he'll be safe as a baby in its cradle a ridin' his Maude, an' anyhow I'll be gittin' on back to church pretty soon, Delph or no Delph. Today's th' day fer her magazine, an' nothin' ud do her but she must have it. I'll ride along with yer paw an' look out fer him."

The postmistress waited until Juber had finished his talk, then turned to search the road again. She was a big hill woman of middle age, wide faced and blue eyed with a twist of sand colored hair and a generous sifting of freckles across her nose and along her muscular forearms. She stood a moment and fanned herself with slow flaps of her gingham apron, then turned wearily to look at the flowers she had cut from her garden. She touched a drooping ladyfinger, and felt the coldness of the water in the pail that held snow-on-the-mountain and dahlias. She sighed and turned back to the road. "I wanted to have 'em fresh like an' pretty," she said, "but Lord that mail'll never get here so I can lock up an' go. Th' mornin' service it'll be over an' I'll hear none a th' singin'."

"It must be th' catalogues a keepin' him," Juber said, and added cheerfully, "Permelie, you've been tendin' th' mail long enough to know that Memorial Service or election day, rain or shine, it's all th' same to Sears Roebuck catalogues. They come an' a body cain't help it."

"An' while he's stoppin' at ever fence an' holler to hand 'em out, my flowers 'ull wilt an' die."

Juber smiled on a pale yellow gladiola. "Lord, it makes no difference to th' flowers when you put 'em on your graves. They'll be wilted dead by sundown anyhow."

Mrs. Crouch walked restlessly away to the end of the porch where she stood on tip toe and watched the road. But the road remained empty as ever; a hound dog trotted down from the poplar trees on the hill side, while one of the postmistress's hens led a bevy of half fledged chickens in a search for grain some waggoner had spilled among the stones. She watched the hound dog with narrowed mistrustful eyes, but when he paused to nose inquisitively at a small chicken strayed a bit from the others, the dominecker mother hen came at him with such a clucking and clacking and lifting of her feathers that he hurried on. "Here comes one a Old Willie's hounds a huntin' him," she said to no one in particular.

Juber cocked his head to one side and studied the dog. "That's no hound a Old Willie's. He'd never let a hound dog get so fat. Must belong to one a them strange oil men over on th' Long North Branch."

"I never heared of a oil man stayin' in one place long enough to keep a dog," Mrs. Crouch answered.

The hound settled the argument by coming up to Old Willie and sniffing his feet. The old man opened his eyes, patted the hound, then seemed to fall asleep again. "It's paw's all right," Young Willie said, "but it's hardly ever about th' place anymore. Took up with that nitroglycerine carryin' man that batches up on th' ridge above our place—an' he's feedin' it to death."

"Must be a funny oil man," Mrs. Crouch said, and after failing in an attempt to count her chickens, turned and watched Juber as he bent to the painstaking carving. "Always whittlin' things for them Costello youngens or growin' flowers for Delph," she said, and added, half teasingly, half sadly, "You ought to a had some a your own, Juber, an' not be tied hand an' foot to John Costello an' his breed all your days."

Juber straightened his back and studied the postmistress. "You're in a bad humor today, Permelie. If I'd a had children they'd a been dead or gone like yours an' ever'body else's in this Little South Fork Country. An' th' Costellos are better to work for than most. Not many like 'em left that foller th' old ways."

"Foller th' old ways is right. John's bringin' up Delph tighter than they raised girls in my day."

"Don't be too hard on him, Permelie. He's done what he could.

He wants to raise Delph right. Look, how hard he worked to git 'em to put this high school out here. Mostly on Delph's account he got it done, I know."

Mrs. Crouch sniffed. "An' that was all a mess of foolishness. Th' pore girl went through th' eighth grade three times while she waited fer th' school, an' anyhow what good'll this three year high school do her if he won't let her go to th' one in town to graduate?"

"Now, Permelie, don't be too certain about things you don't know. Lord, they've had it up one side an' down th' other this summer, her on one side, an' John an' Fronie on th' other. 'Pears like they'll have to give in." He sighed and bent again to the carving. "I wisht they would. T'other day I found her a cryin' in th' hay loft. Delph was never one to let a body see her cry."

Mrs. Crouch gave her apron an indignant flap. "That Fronie's so wrapped up with th' angels she can't have any heart for her man's own blood kin he took by force to raise. Th' other day when I saw her up at Hedricks', I says to her, "Well, I reckin you're aimin' to send Delph away to Town to th' County High School this fall.""

"An' she rung in Jake Barnes's oldest girl, I reckin," Juber said.

"Jake Barnes is right. Soon's I mentioned Delph why Fronie started rollin' down her eyes an' actin' pious. 'Look what happened to Jake Barnes's oldest girl when she went off to Cincinnati,' she whispers to me. 'I've tried hard to raise Delph right, an' get her to join th' church an' give her heart to God,' she says. 'But sometimes I think my pains'ull be fer nothin',' she says, an' whispers on, a noddin' that red head a her'n so broken hearted like. 'You recollect Delph's paw, an' you know th' stripe her maw was cut frum, marryin' agin an' leavin' th' country when her man was hardly two years in his grave.'"

Old Willie rattled his cane and opened his eyes. "A better man never lived than Reuf Costello. He was a man, if'n he did shoot up th' country, an' git hisself killed before he died," he said in a loud argumentative voice.

"'Delph's a good girl,' I says," Mrs. Crouch began, but stopped abruptly with her mouth open and her head tilted in an attitude of listening. "Ain't that wheels comin' up on th' other side a th' hill?— No wonder th' mail's late if he's tryin' to make it in a wagin."

Juber listened, too, with his knife suspended above the hazel nut basket. "It's wheels all right, but sounds uncommon light fer a wagin."

Young Willie cupped a hand to one ear, and the hound dog lifted his head, looked up the road, then got up and trotted toward the sound. "Must be that well shooter an' his cart, frum th' way Colonel Lee's actin'," Young Willie decided.

Mrs. Crouch looked both frightened and curious. "He shorely wouldn't come down this way with a load a nitroglycerin, when th' nearest wells are better'n four mile away."

Young Willie quieted her fears. He believed the cart to be empty and reckoned the nitroglycerin man was just driving by, maybe going to the Memorial Service at Big Cane Brake three miles on the other side of the creek.

"He's got no dead in this country. What business would he have a goin' up there?" Mrs. Crouch wondered, while Juber reckoned aloud that any man who did such dangerous work must be an awful fool.

"They's good money in it," Young Willie said, and added, "He's dropped by our place three, four times, an' a body can tell he's got plenty a sober sense by th' looks a him."

"He looks too damned sober to suit me," Old Willie called. "Reminds me uv a mule a holdin' itself in. An' gittin' a word out a him is like pullin' a penniwinkle out a its shell—less'n he's swearin' an' then it's pure sin to hear him."

"Well, sensible or foolish I cain't see th' good a money when a man's blowed to Kingdom Come, an' as long as he does that kind a work he cain't ever marry an' settle down like a man ought. I've heared say they won't let married men haul nitroglycerin," Mrs. Crouch said.

Juber smiled at the postmistress's foolish ideas on oil men. "Who ever heared uv a oil man a settlin' any place long. They ain't built that way, else they wouldn't be oil men," he argued, and got up to get a better view of the light nitroglycerin cart with its driver, and drawn by two big-bodied horses, just clearing the crest of the hill.

The outfit was coming on at a smart pace, when Mrs. Crouch gave a troubled cry of, "Lord, Lord, look at that fool hen. Leadin' th' chickens right in th' middle a th' road. That Logan Ragan flyin' around in his car just missed killin' one this mornin.'"

"It 'ud be just like a oil man to come smashin' right down over 'em," Juber said, and all were silent as they watched the oil man and the badly flustered mother hen dispute for supremacy of the road. He pulled his team to a slow walk, and when the hen continued to go clucking straight ahead with her chickens scattering on each side, he halted and sat a time and looked at them.

Mrs. Crouch sighed with relief. "He's got a heart in him," she said, and when at last the hen and her sunburned chickens were safely out of the road, and the cart was coming on again, the post mistress picked up the zinc water bucket by the door, emptied it of its stale water and hurried in back for water fresh from the well.

From his seat in the cart the driver appeared to be a youngish man of medium build and medium height, straight-backed and square-shouldered with a body sparsely covered with flesh as that of a hill man. His gray eyes, however, and the little of his bright pale hair that could be seen from under the battered black felt hat he wore, marked him as a stranger to the Little South Fork Country. "He's a quair mix up, but he's got a pretty team," Juber said in a low voice, and wondered why he had come this way and where he was going. Certainly not to church, for he wore an old blue cotton shirt, thread bare at the elbows, faded with sun and sweat across the shoulders. His dark brown corduroy trousers were little better than his shirt, and a few days growth of whiskers, the same bright color as his hair, made the hill men fresh from Saturday shaves and in clean overalls seem well dressed by contrast.

His team was sleek and well fed in oiled and polished harness, and the plaiting of the horses' tails and smoothness of their manes showed signs of unusual care. He turned from the road and drove down among the beech trees where the saddled mules and Maude were tethered, and selected a well-shaded spot for the cart. The men on the porch continued to watch him as he unhitched and led his horses to the creek for a drink. They drank slowly, pausing at times to lift their heads from the water and blow windy sighs through their nostrils, while he stood patiently in the hot sun with their bridles over his arm. When they were finished at last and he had hitched them in the shade, he did not come immediately to the post office, but stopped to examine his lead horse's left hock, that showed a slight thread of red like a scratch from a nail or sharp bit of limestone.

He came on then, but stopped uncertainly at the edge of the porch with his hat in his hand. The sunshine on his hair made it bright like red tinged silver, but the light seemed not to touch his eyes. They were gray with something of the sheen of a slate rock in the rain, dark and quiet under stiff short black eyelashes, and contrasting sharply with the brightness of his hair and whiskers. He was a square faced, straight-mouthed man, with a jaw that, though not unduly large, hinted that it was made of bone.

Young Willie and Old Willie nodded in greeting, while Mrs. Crouch pointed to the sweating water bucket and invited, "Come have a drink."

"Thanks," he said, and Young Willie, watching him, asked when he had finished three dippers full, "Your lead horse get a scratch?"

He flung drops of water from the dipper, and answered in a low quiet voice that matched his jaw and his eyes, "That damned fool of a Logan Ragan scrouged me out a th' road comin' up. If it hadn't a been that my horses will stand up to anything I'd a had a runaway.— He was gone 'fore I could get at him."

Old Willie came to sudden life, sputtered and pounded his Bible then cried, "Since that one of th' Ragans got that fine job with th' Standard Oil in town where he can keep hissef clean an' tell other folks what to do, he goes larrapin' around like a addled somethin'— scarin' hosses."

"Somebody ought to take him down a peg," the oil man said, and went to sit on the edge of the porch near Juber.

Mrs. Crouch studied him with kind, concerned eyes, "He mebbe meant no harm, jist hurryin' to see Delph Costello. Nearly killed one a my chickens—but well—if I was you I'd jist forget it."

Juber and Young Willie nodded. "He's one a th' Little South Fork Ragans, a triggery breed like th' old Costellos—got three brothers," Juber said, and gave the oil man a sidling speculative glance.

The stranger eased his back against a porch post and glanced toward his lead horse with darkened, narrowed eyes. "I can use my fists," he said.

"Boy, they'd never give you a chance to use your fists," Young Willie warned, and added soothingly, "That looks like a little scratch, an' to my mind won't make a scar."

The front legs of Old Willie's chair came down with abrupt violence, and the iron shod tip of his cane rang on the floor. "Pretty soon nobody in this country'ul keep horses any more. My Maude an' John Costello's Silver are about all th' good ones left, an' then they run us out a th' road. Th' ones that git any money from oil or timber they go away, or else they buy 'em cars an' go fistin' around where th' roads are good like that Logan Ragan."

Young Willie pulled his father's coat sleeve. "Now, Paw, you'll have a coughin' spell, gittin' so excited like."

And the oil man turned to Old Willie and comforted, "There'll always be horses in th' Bluegrass country." His eyes glowed as if he smiled, though his mouth did not change. "Th' thoroughbreds around Lexington, they're pretty things," he said.

"We've never had that kind in th' Little South Fork Country," Juber answered, "but I'd jist as soon or ruther have a good hunter of a five gaited saddle mare that 'ud take blue ribbons at th' fair.—Delph, she's th' niece a th' people where I live, she had one like that about two yer back, but her Uncle John sold her. Delph rode her so wild, a jumpin' fences like a heathen an' a lopin' down hills. We was afraid she'd break her neck."

"I'll bet th' girl hated it when they sold her mare."

"Aye, she was mad a plenty an' give 'em a piece uv her mind, but I don't think it was th' mare she loved so much as th' runnin' an' jumpin' uv her."

Mrs. Crouch turned from her business of watching for the mail. "That's always been Delph's trouble. If she'd cry an' beg to John 'stead a talkin' up to him she'd mebbe git more a what she wants."

Juber polished the hazel nut basket with slow strokes against his knee. "Th' ones that naiver let on, them's th' ones th' world cuts deepest," he said, and added sorrowfully, "so many times she says to me, 'Juber, I wisht they'd let me go away an' learn things like singin' an' such.'"

Mrs. Crouch smiled as over the foolish whim of a well-beloved child, "Pshaw, like as if she needed to learn to sing, when she's th' best soprano they've got up at Big Cane Brake. I've heared Preacher Dodson say many a time he'd taught her about 'bout all he could, an' he's one a th' best singin' teachers in th' county."

"She don't want to sing jist church songs. She wants—." But Juber stopped abruptly, and seemed like a child caught in the crime of giving a secret away.

"What does she want to learn? Dance tunes?" Young Willie asked with a note of condemnation in his voice.

"An' supposin' she does want to learn dance tunes?" Mrs. Crouch demanded with a belligerent out thrusting of her chin toward Young Willie. "I square danced when I was a girl—an' turned out decent—but thank God I was never raised by a Fronie Butler Costello. But if Juber, here, don't quit fiddlin' dance tunes for her when John an' Fronie's not around, he'll be puttin' notions in her head."

"But she likes th' lively music so," Juber answered, and stared out through the grove of heart and initial scarred beech trees.

The oil man followed his glance and studied the trees. The initials and hearts cut into the smooth gray bark were grown high into the limbs and so enlarged and distorted by the swelling growth of the trunk that they seemed to have sprung from the ground with the tree. He twisted his head in an effort to read the initials, but stopped when Young Willie said, "Aye, you'll never make 'em out. No stranger ever could. Lots a people frum away off, th' ones that have gone away, they come a lookin' in th' beech trees same as they go a lookin' in th' graveyard. Th' last time Dorie Dodson Fairchild was down this way she stopped an' walked all through them trees a tryin' to see where her man, he's dead fer more'n a dozen years—died uv drink an' goin' wild—had cut his name an' hers up in a heart on a beech tree mor'n forty years ago when they was young like an' he was visitin' here."

The oil man smiled, a slow bright smile that touched his eyes, "I'd like to see Old Dorie. Not many can beat her at farmin'."

"She's never fergot her raisin'," Juber said with pride. "Them thirty or forty miles 'tween here an' Burdine never keeps her away from Big Cane Brake Memorial Day. You know her? You ought to go on up to th' church an' have a bite a dinner an' speak a word with her. If she liked ye onct she'll allus recollect ye. She's a Dodson through an' through."

"I saw her not long back on my way up here to work. Sometime in th' spring it was. I recollect th' black locust bloom in her back yard. I don't know her so well, not th' way you do. I stayed with her a time six or seven years back when I was drillin' down by Burdine."

"Better come an' go along with us," Juber advised, and got up and squinted at the sun above the beech trees.

The oil man thought he'd wait until the mail came, but after much advice from Young Willie to Old Willie concerning such matters as keeping out of the sun and over eating, the two older men rode away, but at the bridge Juber must turn back to call, "Permelie, if'n anybody comes up this way recollect to send Delph's mail, less'n you want to be bothered with it."

"I'll take it," the stranger suggested to Mrs. Crouch. "I know her.—I mean I've seen her a few times in town."

The post mistress studied him, then asked with a sly pleased smile, "I wonder now is that what could be takin' you up to Big Cane Brake?"

"Hell, no," he said, and asked abruptly, "I wonder is there any mail for me. I—I've sort of been expectin' some. Marshal Gregory is my name."

Mrs. Crouch shook her head. "There's not been a strange letter in this post office for weeks."

"It wouldn't a been a letter."

"Well, soon's th' mail comes—if it ever does—I'll unlock an' have a look through th' stuff I ain't handed out. Mostly advertisin' stuff or old election candidate trash. I don't generally hand that out, till th' election's over. Th' August primaries always cause too much trouble anyhow, an' men like John Costello go around for weeks with nothin' in their heads but politics. You interested in politics?"

He shrugged uncomfortably. "I hardly ever stayed in one place long enough to vote."

"You a native born Kentuckian?"

He nodded. "I was born up in th' Bluegrass."

"Your people still live there I reckin?"

"They left when I was little like, an' mostly they live all over.— I think I'll go down an' look at my horse's hock again," he said, and got up and walked quickly away.

Not long after the mail came; a battered Ford truck loaded down with boxes of empty fruit jars, sacks of sugar, and sacks of mail fattened by catalogues. The driver, a thin, sun-burned young man with a rakish tilt to his hat was heard to be delivering his opinion of the Little South Fork Country women who ordered goods from Sears to come by mail, and so received catalogues as a further burden on the mail. His most pungent remarks, however, were reserved for Fronie Costello who, because the summer's fruit harvest was an abundant one was apparently not content to can for a winter only, but from the dozens of fruit jars and hundreds of pounds of sugar he had hauled and was hauling out for her, she was evidently canning for the next dozen or so years to come.

The oil man came and helped the horse shoe pitchers and Young Willie in the unloading of the mail. That finished, he went inside to stand by the wicket gate that separated the post office from the store, where several other men had gathered for the sorting of the mail. Mrs. Crouch finished the letters quickly, for the bundle was thin, then glanced about the room and said, "None a you all got any letters, 'ceptin' Mrs. Willie Burnett, an'," she turned to a slender rabbity eyed young man with flax colored hair who had stepped expectantly forward, "No, Willie you're not takin' it. Ruthie told me she didn't want you bringin' any more a your mail. You're liable to lose it like you done that last.—Wait, don't none a th' rest a you be leavin' either. I want to get rid a these catalogues."

The stranger stepped from between a stack of meal and a case of shoes and edged nearer the window. "Recollect, I'm Marsh Gregory," he said in a low voice. "What about my mail?"

"I know there's nothin' for you else I'd a remembered that strange name," Mrs. Crouch said, and added without looking up from the catalogues she sorted, "Now, don't go runnin' away. There's Costello's mail."

"My mail wouldn't a been a letter or a catalogue, either," he insisted.

"I'll have to sort out all this mess a catalogues," she said, and began calling in brisk tones, "Armstrong, Barnes, Burnett, Costello— here you are, oil man, a catalogue, an'—don't go runnin' away. I think one a these magazines is Delph's, an' Fronie's *Bible Quarterly* ought to be in today. Most generally I look it over to see what sort a doctrine she's up to, but I won't bother today. Wait. I'll look."

She handed him soon a *Bible Quarterly* and a tightly rolled brown parcel that looked to be a woman's magazine. He hesitated by the window until she glanced at him and said, "That's all th' Costello mail."

"But mine?" he asked.

She rummaged through the papers scattered on the mail shelf and on the floor, squinted over this and that until she found a small stampless envelope that might have held a bulletin of less than twenty pages. "Here's somethin', but it's nothin' but gover'ment foolishness—some bulletin from Washington tellin' a man how to farm like as if they knowed in Washington. Farmin' with their mouths, I call it," she went on, and Marsh felt rather than saw the smiles of the hill men.

He took the bulletin, shoved it hastily into his pocket, and turned toward the door in time to see the boys lounging by it make way for Logan Ragan, the man who had forced him out of the road. He was a tall, slender young man with black hair and blue-gray eyes, handsome as the hill men were sometimes handsome when they lived in town a time and learned to wear good clothes with the same careless grace they wore their overalls. He glanced at Marsh in cool-eyed appraisal, then turned to Mrs. Crouch and smiled and said, "Miss Costello sent me down for her mail. She's expectin' some, I think."

Marsh heard the sudden silence of the room, but Logan noticed nothing. He came and leaned by the mail window and waited. The postmistress turned a catalogue end over end and seemed unable to find the address. "I give it to this oil man here," she explained after what seemed an uncomfortably long time. "He was goin' up that way."

Logan turned quickly and held out his hand to Marsh. "I'll take it an' save you th' trip."

"I'm makin' it anyhow," Marsh answered, and studied him with narrowed eyes.

Logan laughed. "Don't be silly. Miss Costello sent me for it special. I'd get there quicker—with a car."

"I notice you go around damn quick in that car. But I'm takin' what I've got here," Marsh said, and walked toward the open door.

Logan turned and with two long strides was in the door. He stood with his back to the porch and looked at Marsh. Now, he was less the handsome young man polished a bit with some life away, than a cold-eyed hill man with spots of red on his thin cheek bones.

Marsh took a step nearer, and Young Willie whispered, "Better look out, Nitroglycerin Man." And some one else said, "If he ain't got a gun he'd better git out a th' door. That oil man's got a temper like th' load he carries."

Marsh dropped the mail to the floor and looked at the other's chin, and wondered through the unreasoning fury that choked him why he was making a fool of himself—because of a scratch on his lead horse's leg or over a girl he had scarcely seen.

Mrs. Crouch jerked open a drawer under the mail shelf, snatched up an antiquated forty-five, and pounded with the butt of it on the mail shelf while she boomed, "Logan Ragan, git out a that door. I give him leave to take that mail. You're standin' in his way. Obstructin' th' mail an' fightin' on gover'ment property is a federal offense. Git goin' 'fore I send you to Atlanta."

Logan turned abruptly away, strode across the porch, sprang to the ground with no bothering about the steps, and went to his car. Marsh felt a curious disappointment mixed with shame, and only remembered the mail and the excuse for his anger when the rabbity-eyed man nudged his elbow timidly and said, "Here's your mail, Sir."

Young Willie shifted his tobacco in his cheek, spat into the cold stove hearth and said, "Them Ragans was never any hands for fist fightin'—but all th' same they can fight."

Mrs. Crouch came out of the mail corner with a slamming of the slat gate. "Young Willie, you'd better be a takin' up your saddle-bags an' mail an' gettin' 'em on over to Holly Bush, stead a try to skeer him. It's good for them Ragans to learn once in awhile that they don't own th' world," she said.

Marsh saw admiration in her eyes and some of the others. He hated it. Any half-witted roustabout could have done what he had just done, only the roustabout would maybe have been quicker and knocked the man down. He waited by the door until the black roadster of Logan's had gone chugging over the bridge, then went to his team. As he hitched the horses to the cart, he paused for no reason and fumbled a bit with Jude's throat latch, and slapped Tim on the shoulder. He liked to feel their sleek short hair and solid muscular flesh smooth under his hand. Many times he stroked his horses so, talked to them even, when he loaded his cart with nitroglycerin. He did not talk today. He was conscious of the men on the porch watching him, and his words to his horses as well as the government bulletins he collected and read were things belonging to himself alone.

He did not know whether to be pleased or sorry when, as he was driving away, a teen-age boy with his arms filled with flowers came running and calling to him, "Mrs. Crouch said could she please go along with you. She's borried a horse special, but she thought it'ud be easier to ride with you she's got so many flowers."

· 2 ·

THE CART bounced at a smart pace up the rough hill roads while Mrs. Crouch clutched at the seat with one hand and fanned herself with a hymn book in the other. Now and then she glanced at her flowers, and often at Marsh, but each time found him straight mouthed and hard eyed. He commented on nothing, though his deep gray eyes, swinging slowly from this to that, missed nothing by the road; a clump of purple ironweed in some grassy space, the white and pale lavender of the wild asters scattered here and there among the trees, clusters of beech nuts that hung sometimes above his head, and the sky—a high blue August sky where a few powdery white clouds drifted.

"I always rest my horses at th' top of a hill," he explained in a half apologetic, half defensive tone as he stopped his team in a shady spot at the top of the high land that divided Costello's Valley from the Little South Fork Country.

"I noticed you was an uncommon careful driver," the postmistress answered, and smiled to see that her flowers had lost few petals on the way.

"You get careful—haulin' nitroglycerin," he said, and was silent then while he sat and looked down into the Little South Fork Country. He saw a broad sweep of level farming land, cut by a creek, and encircled by high but gently sloping hills, some wooded, some in corn, with here and there a rolling pasture field dotted with sheep and cows. The floor of the valley was given almost entirely to cane and tobacco and corn. The corn stood high and a rich dark green with its spreading tassels shining golden brown. The few log or

15

frame houses, surrounded by orchards and log barns, were mostly on the lower slopes of the hills, set in wide yards where sometimes a horse or calves grazed; and over the whole of the valley there was a peace and a quiet and a dreaming like that of an old man sleeping in the sun.

"It's a pretty farmin' country," he said, without taking his eyes away.

Mrs. Crouch nodded. "Aye, but you ought to see it in th' fall. There's somethin' so quiet an' safe like about th' fall—specially after a good crop year like we're havin' now."

"Yes. That would be a pretty time." He looked across the valley, up through a grove of trees, and above the trees he could see bits of a great gray-white house, flanked by weather stained rock chimneys surrounded by barns and smoke houses, and towering above it all was the wide sweep of a high hill pasture field. He nodded toward the farm. "Whose place is that?"

"Costello's," Mrs. Crouch answered with a short, hard emphasis on the name.

"Is that where Logan Ragan's girl lives?"

She nodded so violently that the purple pansies on the black straw sailor jiggled. "Yes. It is.—Now don't misunderstand me. I was never one for meddlin'.—But if you're got any sense you'll give that mail to Juber when you get there an' stay away from th' girl. She's somethin' like a load a dynamite anyhow."

He turned to her and smiled, a quick flashing smile that bared his teeth and showed them white and fine with a pointed tooth on each side. "I'm a good hand at haulin' nitroglycerin."

"If'n Logan an' all his brothers turned loose on you, an' then her Uncle John found out his Delph was so much as castin' sheep's eyes at a stranger your nitroglycerin would seem like clabbered milk alongside of it all.—You'd better stay by me, an' not go mixin' 'round her."

He laughed and started his team. "I only meant to see Dorie—an' well—I'd like to hear this girl sing. I've heard about her singin'."

"Listenin's all you'd better do. John went to law an' took her from her mother—th' Costellos can win any law suit in this county—when she wanted to take her to Oregon where she went when she married again. An' he's not aimin' for nobody to take her away from him."

"She goes with this Logan," he insisted.

Mrs. Crouch shook her head. "That's different. Th' Costellos an' th' Ragans have always been friends. I reckin they fought together in th' Revolution, an' again in th' Civil War, an' mebbe in th' Spanish American. They've fought in all th' wars that ever was, an' that was how they got their start a land."

"This girl's uncle own a lot a land?"

"Not anymore. I'll bet John Costello don't have more'n six hundred acres countin' his timber, but in th' old days th' Costellos owned all th' land that you could see on both sides a that high spot where we stopped. It went like all th' other big holdin's in these hills. Th' generation got bigger, an' they divided an' kept sellin' out an' a goin' away till John's all that's left."

Marsh asked no more of the girl. As they drove through the valley his attention seemed mostly for the crops behind the rail fences that bordered either side of the road. They came at last to Big Cane Brake Church near the head of the creek, a fair-sized building for the hills, painted white, and set in a shadowy, tree-filled yard. Sounds of singing came through the open doors and windows while the crowd of men and boys close-packed about the doors were still with listening, and the bare-footed children who played a game of needle's eye in the shade of a twisted white oak tree sang, "Many a beau have I let go because I wanted you," in soft hushed whispers.

Farther from the door, men sitting with their backs against the trees whittled and talked in subdued tones, with now and then a glance toward some straw-filled wagon where a baby slept, often times in company with baskets and buckets of food. A group of young boys played a quiet game of marbles in the shade; and they, with the singing children and whittling men, gave the place more an air of quiet holiday than of sorrowful service for the dead.

Marsh hitched under a black locust tree near the road, and offered to watch the food and flowers while Mrs. Crouch went to attend the services, but the postmistress insisted that the flowers would be safer than he. Though he had no wish to enter the church, unshaved and dressed in such poor clothing, he argued the matter but little, and stood untroubled by the craning heads of the hill men under the trees. Mostly, he listened to the singing. He thought he heard the girl's voice rising above the others, high and clear it was, but sad somehow, sadder even than the words of the song, touched with some great hunger, as if under the words and the music her thoughts were much like his own. He listened a moment longer, then said, "Sure, I'll go inside."

Mrs. Crouch pointed to the mail he carried and whispered, "You'd better give that to me. I'll see she gets it."

He shook his head, then walked with her through the yard, careful to keep his eyes straight ahead as he went down the narrow lane the crowd by the door opened for them. He went inside and felt himself the mark of many eyes, and flushed when a small girl with tight pig-tails tied with gingham strings giggled and said in a shrill whisper, "Look at a stranger man comin' through th' woman's door."

Mrs. Crouch, as if to conceal him as much as possible, sat him on the inside corner of a back bench with a window on the one side of him and herself on the other. The small girl tapped his shoulder with the palm leaf fan then handed it to him, while a round brown arm in front reached backward and dropped a hymn book into his lap.

The church was one large, high-ceilinged room, boarded and ceiled with lumber whip-sawed and planed and tongued and grooved by hand. It was easy to believe Mrs. Crouch when she turned to him and whispered with pride, "This church was built better'n a hundred years ago." The nine poplar pillars that supported the ceiling were golden brown with age, and the wide-seated, high-backed benches, fashioned of wide, four-inch-thick planks, were worn smooth and round in front, but much initialed on their backs by the generations of knife carrying men and boys who had worshipped there.

Marsh, conscious of being watched, studied the church as long as he was able, but soon his glance wandered to the pulpit where several preachers sat near the water buckets and behind a Bible stand banked with flowers. He tried to look steadfastly at the preachers, but from the corner of his eyes he could see Delph in the front row of the choir. He heard her and the other sopranos sing, "In that sweet by and by," dwelling on the high throbbing sadness of the long drawn "sw-e-e-e-et," while the bass growled in with quick deep "by and by"s. It seemed to him that for Delph the words had a meaning all of their own that had nothing to do with the departed dead or God or that rich heaven of purple and gold across the jasper seas of which the hill women loved to sing. There was in her voice no supplication nor worship, more a straining and a yearning as if she would on the instant go in search of the promised land; take it in life with no waiting for death.

Then suddenly her voice was not enough and he must look at her, stare with his shoulders thrust forward, while the forgotten hymn book and fan slipped between his knees. When he looked at her he thought of curious things, foolish nothings he had never had, a mountain top dark violet in a blue twilight, the smell of clean oak wood, the stars—memories of many things he had rooted away in his mind to keep. Other girls, pretty now with round cheeks and soft curving flesh, would in time grow old and fat and ugly, but not the girl in the choir. Her beauty lived in her strong straight body, her eyes, and the bones of her face, the proud free tilt of her head, and some air of expectancy or of waiting that gave her a look of eager aliveness even while she sang.

He liked her dark brown hair, the heavy braids of it wound about her head, with loose half-curling tendrils of the fine dark stuff slipping about her ears and forehead. And when she moved her head, lights and shadows glinted on the braids, and other lights and shadows flickered through her eyes. They were a hill woman's eyes, a deeper blue than most, snow water clear and forever changing, like deep lakes or rivers, darkening and brightening as clouds raced across the sun.

Mrs. Crouch nudged him violently with her elbow and whispered heatedly, "You're a lookin' in th' wrong direction. There's Dorie Dodson Fairchild over by that post." Marsh roused, and remembered dimly that Dorie was his excuse for coming to the church. He found her by a pillar near the front as the post mistress had said. She was a hill woman in her middle fifties, but her face in repose seemed older than that, brown it was, and wrinkled with sun and wind and squinting at the sky for rain, not a pretty face, unadorned with even a wisp of her iron gray hair, gathered in a knob at the back of her head and skewered with what had always seemed to him a dangerously small number of pins. She sat now and looked about the room, her large, blue-gray eyes traveling slowly from this to that, measuring all things and questioning most. "She's as hard-boiled lookin' as ever," he whispered to prove that he had seen her, and then turned back to Delph.

"Could you manage a six hundred acre hill an' river bottom farm, a drunkard for a husband, raise seven good children by a God-awful lumber town an' still be tender?" Mrs. Crouch wanted to know in a hissing whisper.

But Marsh was taken up with Delph. He thought it was maybe because her brows were so dark and her eyelashes heavy and black that her eyes seemed so blue. He studied her eyes, but they never noticed him. Now that the hymn was finished Delph sat and watched Brother Eli as he prepared to read the letters of the ones away. He was an elderly man with a whiter fuller beard than Old Willie's, but he was sprightly for his years, and with a habit of looking first at the ceiling then at the floor, dwelling briefly on his audience in between times so that his beard was in constant motion. He was native to the Little South Fork Country, but like Dorie now lived by Burdine on the Cumberland where he farmed six days each week and preached on the seventh.

There were many letters. Minnie Copenhaver, a farmer's wife in Kansas, wanted to give greetings to all her distant kin and former neighbors, and asked them to pray for rain in Kansas. Roy Belle, a bartender in Seattle, asked that someone please put marigolds on his grandmother's grave. Emma Fairchild, daughter of Dorie, sent greetings from Chicago and money for the upkeep of the church. Eulie Saunders, a missionary in China, asked for money and prayers for the heathen.

Marsh heard the drone of Brother Eli's reading, but had thoughts only for Delph. She was still with her hands folded in her lap, her eyes fixed on Brother Eli and the bits of paper in his hands, and when he had finished a letter she bent forward with eagerness until she learned from whom and where the next one came. After the reading of the letters she showed little interest in Brother Gholston's sermon that followed, but saw with her black lashes low and meek above her eyes and seemed to dream of some pleasant thing. She did not smile, but her face seemed more gentle with less of the impatient hunger that touched it when she had listened to the letters.

Gradually, however, as Brother Gholston's shrieks for the unsaved grew louder, and more thickly interspersed with gasping "ah"s for breath, Delph looked more steadfastly at the preacher, and her eyes from being warm and bright grew stony cold. When Brother

Gholston stopped for lack of breath and commanded that an invitation hymn be sung, though her face showed nothing but its coldness, it seemed to Marsh that when she arose to sing her shoulders had stiffened and her head was higher and prouder than it had been.

The choir broke into the wailing strains of "Ye who are weary come home," and Mrs. Crouch fidgeted and looked out the window, then whispered, "I was hopin' I could come to this church once without bein' cried over—but I reckin if Delph can stand it I can."

"What—What's Delph done?" he asked in a troubled whisper.

"We're both unsaved—th' only wonen in th' whole country," Mrs. Crouch whispered through set teeth, then bowed her head and looked at the floor as a tall, red-haired, deep-bosomed woman with a fat baby on one arm forced her way between the benches. "Oh, Permelie, won't you ever give in an' offer your stubborn soul to God?" she began in a sobbing voice with tears streaming heavily down her round red cheeks. "Tomorrow it may be too late, ever lastin'ly too late," she shrieked, and collapsed with her head on the post mistress's shoulder, and held it there while she sobbed long and violently. The blue-eyed bald-headed baby seemed in no wise distressed by the situation, but smiled pleasantly at Marsh and seemed of half a mind to finger his hair.

But Marsh was too troubled for Delph to notice the baby. A short fat woman stood on one side and patted her on the shoulder and begged in a low voice, while a tall elderly woman in a black sunbonnet stood in front of her and cried. Delph lifted her head and looked at the ceiling and sang. She continued to sing when the red-haired woman left Mrs. Crouch and went to her and cried and begged more violently than over the post mistress. "That's her Aunt Fronie—th' woman th' pore girl has to live with," Mrs. Crouch whispered, then bowed her head again.

Delph continued to sing, standing still with her aunt's head on her shoulder while she glanced with something like defiance out over the heads of the congregation. Her ears and cheeks and neck were red with embarrassment, and her eyes blazed a hot bright blue that could have been shame or might have been anger. Marsh knew he ought to look away. She would find him gaping at her, and her eyes would crackle with defiance for him as for the others. But he could not look away, and in a moment her glance swept over him.

Their eyes met, and it seemed a long moment that just she and he were in the church with their eyes meeting, and then her glance had gone on to the quivering leaves of the black locust tree by the window.

When not long after there was a stir in the house and murmur of voices, he roused to learn with disappointment that the morning service was over. Mrs. Crouch caught his elbow, and though she whispered, she spared no pains to show her opinion of him. "I know Delph's a pretty girl, but Lord you've been all over th' world, an' will be again most like. You'll see just as pretty in your time, an' can stare 'em out a countenance without runnin' th' risk a bein' bush-whacked."

"I mean to give her this mail an' speak to her," Marsh answered.

Mrs. Crouch turned away in disgust. "Ask Dorie an' see what she says. If I can't talk sense into you, mebbe she can.—But recollect, don't go off 'fore I give you somethin' to eat."

He waited by the bench and watched the people come down the aisle. They came slowly in little groups, never alone, and always there was much talk and shaking of hands. A child in a candy-striped dress came with her finger in her mouth and stared at him a moment in wondering silence before she ran away. Colonel Lee, the hound dog came, and sniffed at his trousers and his hands, and when he learned there was no food, walked on. Marsh didn't blame the dog. His clothing always carried a smell of crude oil, and sometimes he was grateful that the dog even deigned to visit him for food.

A young man, hardly more than a boy, and plainly a stranger to the hills with his careful white flannels and buckskin shoes, stood ill at ease by a bench across the aisle. Old Willie Copenhaver came down the aisle leaning heavily on his iron shod staff, and deep in conversation with Brother Eli. The old men stopped and stared at the young one, studied his nose and mouth and eyes, the way his hair fell back from his forehead, glanced at his feet and seemed to ponder on the shape of his hands. Finished with the examination, Old Willie and then Brother Eli each extended a hand. "You've some of Peter Chrismann's blood else I've gone blind," Old Willie said.

"He was my great grandfather," the young one answered, and went on to explain while the old men nodded and smiled, "I never saw him—my mother left this country when she was small, but she used to tell me stories." They walked on with Old Willie stopping first one and then another to say, "Here's some a Peter Chrismann's kin come home."

Others passed Marsh. A few glanced in his direction, but after one appraising glance they knew him as a stranger to their blood and walked on. It was Juber who came hunting him, thanked him for bringing Delph's mail, and suggested, though somewhat hesitantly, that he come share in the dinner. "I'm not hungry," Marsh answered, and added defiantly, "All I want to do is speak a word with Dorie, an' give Delph her mail."

Juber studied him uneasily, "Mebbe it's better anyhow that you don't come to th' Costello's end a th' table. Logan, he'd be there.—I heared about th' scrap you had."

"I've done him no harm," Marsh answered stonily. "He stood in my way, an' if he hadn't a got out I'd a knocked him down."

Juber smiled his gentle smile. "An' do you allus go around knockin' ever'thing down that comes in your way?"

Marsh nodded. "I've worked in th' oil fields since I was six-teen—before that I lived with my people. After I could recollect they were renters—always on th' go. I've learned a few things from them an' th' oil fields."

"I wondered how a oil man could handle a team so well."

"It was born in me to handle horses," he answered with a hard-ening of his jaw. "But what I learned was that there's bound to be a lot a knockin' in th' world; it's better to knock a man first so he can't knock you."

"But allus recollect, Boy, they use guns in these hills—fer strangers that come meddlin'.—Ever hear a bushwhackin'?"

"Mrs. Crouch was speakin' a somethin' like that."

"Well—bushwhackin' is somethin' a man—a stranger like you— has to take on faith, like th' thief on th' cross. He's never been back to tell us he went to heaven, no more'n there's ever been a bush-whacked man come back to tell who got him.—An' if he did most likely he wouldn't know." Juber lingered a moment to see the effect of his words, and when he could find no effect, walked on.

When he had gone Marsh went down the uncarpeted aisle of the now almost empty church. He saw Delph, and so much were his thoughts and his eyes for her, that he scarcely noticed she stood near Dorie Dodson Fairchild, the woman he said he had come to see. He saw Logan standing by a window, and though his body looked long and lax and lazy there was a taut look in his eyes. Marsh met his glance, and nodded, and wished again he had struck the man. There was contempt rather than hatred in his cool unflickering eyes.

Delph stood on the outer edge of a little group of people gathered about Brother Gholston, and the tall, blue-eyed, wide-shouldered hill man whom he knew was her Uncle John. He saw Fronie patting her baby on the back and raptly attending to some talk of the preacher's. And because they were Delph's people they seemed important to him, and he wished he had shaved and worn his new suit.

Fronie saw him first, and stared at him a moment in a wondering puzzled way, until she saw the catalogue and brown roll of the magazine. "Oh, you've brought our mail," she said, and reached for it. He was conscious of the silence of the others while they looked at him. All but John and Fronie knew most likely that he had made a fool of himself over Delph, but the thought didn't trouble him. He wondered instead if she remembered the day he had seen her in Town, and he wished she would look at him. He forgot it was Dorie he had come to see until she was seizing his arm and exclaiming, "Why, Marsh Gregory, just this mornin' when I was gettin' ready to come, Katy an' Poke Easy were talkin' of you, a thinkin' you'd like to see th' tobacco now, an' wonderin' if you'd be down soon."

Then Fronie, less frigid after Dorie's greeting, was taking the mail and thanking him, and Dorie was explaining to the company, telling of how that year—and here she must reckon on her fingers—the year before she got her bull Solomon and while Poke Easy was still in the grades—and the summer before Rachel ran away to be married—seven years ago—the year they had had that oil boom about Burdine, this Marsh Gregory he was a driller then and—

A cry of "Law, law if it's not Dorie," followed by Dorie's cry of, "Why, Permelie Crouch, I was wonderin' if you were here," switched the conversation from Marsh to girlhood reminiscences, while Fronie, mindful of all the Costello dinner baskets to be unpacked, excused herself and left with her family. Though Marsh wriggled masterfully, Dorie, deep in conversation with Mrs. Crouch, did not loosen her grip on his arm, and he stood disappointed and angry, but powerless to do more then watch Delph as she walked away with Logan.

The two women talked on this and that, mostly of the old days and their children away, until both realized with a start that the church was empty and the preachers would be saying grace and their food not on the table. However, Mrs. Crouch must take time to relate Marsh's misdeeds, smiling as she talked and declaring he was just like her boy Les. The women turned upon him then as if he had been some small boy, stubbornly risking his neck in a hazardous game. Dorie wanted to have a talk with him and tell him about her farming, and Mrs. Crouch wanted to see that he was fed and treated properly.

After much talk it was finally agreed that since it might make trouble and since he had no wish to eat with the others anyhow, it would maybe be better for him to take a bundle of food to the grave-yard—the old Costello burying ground was the nicest spot—and wait there for Dorie. After dinner she would like to sneak away to a nice quiet spot and have a Bull Durham cigarette. She'd have to do it on the sly, for in the Little South Fork Country the only thing that a decent woman ever smoked was a pipe.

Marsh, when he had been loaded with food and directed where to go, crossed the road and climbed the graveyard fence under cover of a clump of holly trees. He found Costello's graveyard as they had said; an older quieter world of the dead, surrounded by a high iron fence and hidden by great, close-growing cedar trees. The graves were covered with short brown cedar needles, and submerged in a deep blue green twilight with no pattern of sunlight and shadow filtering through. Neither grass nor flowers grew in the heavy shade, though today the graves were bright with flowers, great red and yellow dahlias, the fiery flames of zinnias and bright gold of coreopsis. Strange flowers for the dead, and he wondered if Delph had not put them there.

He walked about and read the names, and always the last name was Costello, when it could be read at all. One, a great mound of flat gray limestone, bore nothing, and it seemed to be the oldest of all. Leaves and cedar needles had drifted into the crevices between the top stones, and a saw briar and a wild grape vine grew there with their long runners, pale for lack of sun, trailing down across the stones. The finest flowers of all, great twisted petal dahlias large as a plate, lay on the heap of stones. Others of the graves were curious things, like boxes of stone laid on the ground, and two were foot thick slabs of stone flat above their graves long as a tall man, and cut with square heads and wide shoulders tapering down to feet.

He sat on one and ate some of the fried chicken and other good food with which Mrs. Crouch had showered him, but he ate slowly with little thought for the food. Dorie came before he was scarcely finished. "Lord, it's a lonesome place to have a smoke," she said, and sat with him on the man shaped stone, and rolled a cigarette.

Marsh glanced about at the old protected graves. "It's a nice way to be buried, though. Whole families together like this," he said, and after a pause added slowly, "An' when th' ones livin'—die, I don't guess they mind it so; knowin' how it'll be."

Dorie pulled the string of the tobacco sack tight with her teeth and studied him. "Marsh—you don't look so young like as you did in th' spring.—You'd better quit this work you're doin'. Somethin's unnatural when a man talks so a dyin' when he's not out a his twenties like you."

He locked his hands between his knees and looked at them. "It's natural—that is when a man hauls nitroglycerin—for goin' on four years."

Dorie blew a smoke ring and squinted at it. "You'd better quit it then—quit th' oil fields an' marry an' settle down."

"It takes money to settle down."

She looked at him in some surprise. "You've got money saved. Least ways you ought to have."

He continued to study his hands, and his face wore a guilty look. "Some I've got—but not so much as I ought," he said, and went on in his low level voice. "Used to be when I was a driller I'd wonder why th' big money-makin' nitroglycerin mixers an' shooters went on so many sprees an' spent so much, gamblin' an' drinkin'. Well—I know now."

Dorie nodded slowly, and her face showed understanding and pity not untouched by impatience. "I know. One a these days you'll be old, if you don't get blowed to pieces before then, an' you'll be like Dave only worse. Lord, how well I know. Ever' spendin' spree will be a little more drinkin', an' you'll have less an' less. Then one day you'll be wore out. They won't need you any more. You'll be like these factory workers that go out from these hills. When th' factories have had their fill of them, they come back, used up, to squat in th' hills till they die. You'll—."

He turned on her and his eyes were narrow black instead of wide and gray. "You don't have to say that.—I know it all an' a damned sight more. I—."

"Well, for God's sake, Marsh, do what you want to do. I've preached it to you ever' time I saw you for seven years, wrote you letters even."

He got up and walked restlessly away, talking as he walked. "I'll never risk goin' in debt. Another couple a years an'—well, I've been sayin' that since I was born. But I'll never bite off more'n I can chew an' risk losin' ever'thing like my old man did. He'd be alive an' ownin' a farm most like today if he hadn't a gone crazy through th' war an' gone in too deep."

Dorie gave a short impatient sigh. "Lord, Lord don't be so cautious like."

"If I hadn't a been cautious I'd a been dead long ago.—Your children all well?" he asked, sick of the wearisome conversation.

"Well as they'll ever be, I reckin," she answered shortly.

"Poke Easy, I guess, he'll about make up his mind this summer to farm when he gets through college?" he asked with an eagerness like a hunger in his eyes.

Dorie looked suddenly old with all the fight gone out of her face. "Aye, they'll all go like Sam. Maybe never so far in th' wrong direction. Poke Easy he'll end up with Joe in Chicago. Joe's makin' money an' gettin' himself a name—criminal law's big money they say."

"But Katy—she's one that'll never live in any city."

"She'll never die without seein' th' world." She gestured impatiently with her cigarette and turned on Marsh her hard angry eyes, "Who that's young an' strong an' smart like mine wants to spend their days on a river bottom farm by a dyin' lumber town? Burdine's dead. They've got th' coal an' th' oil an' timber out a these hills, th' money's gone, them that got it went away, th' land's washed out, an' what's to hold th' children?"

"There's good farms like yours by th' rivers," Marsh said, and added without looking at her, "It would be th' best kind a farm in th' world—a river bottom farm like yours—or that old Weaver place. How're its renters makin' out?"

"Takin' all they can take," she said, but the anger was gone from her face and her eyes were gentle with memories. "Sam he used to love that farm, an' talk th' way you do. 'All kinds of land we've got right here,' he'd say, an' then he'd go on.—Aye, Lord, it's a one-sided world. When I think a them, first Sam an' then Emma. Ethel an' Joe an' Rachel didn't matter so, or else I didn't mind by then, but Sam he could ha' done so much. Th' land could have a few, Marsh. It needs good heads more'n strong backs—but they all go away to live they—."

The gate clicked, and clicked again in closing. Steps sounded over the stones by it, then died as they came to the carpet of cedar needles. Dorie hastily handed her cigarette to Marsh, and began chewing a sprig of mint she had brought. In a moment Delph's blue linen dress showed between the cedar trees. She stopped uncertainly on seeing Marsh, but came on when Dorie called heartily, "Come on over, Delph. I've been wantin' to have a word with you anyhow. This is Marshall Gregory—don't mind him. He's like one a my family."

Delph smiled at Marsh, a polite good-child's smile, and said, "How-do-you-do, Mr. Gregory. I saw you in church," she went on hesitantly, "an' I wanted to thank you for bringin' my magazine—but I couldn't. I—I wondered if you had anything to eat."

"Mrs. Crouch took care of him," Dorie answered in his place. "Come on an' make yourself at home."

When Delph had taken a seat on one side of Dorie and Marsh had resumed his place on the other, Delph asked the question with which most greeted Dorie Dodson Fairchild, "Your children all gettin' along fine, I guess?"

And when Dorie only nodded and showed no inclination to speak of her children, she tried another timid, eager question. "How is Sam? I—I've read of him in th' papers a long time ago, an' I've well—wondered lots a time how it would be to do what he's done, be so smart an' win scholarships an' such." She seemed not to notice Dorie's moody silence, but hugged her knees and smiled at the cedar needles with bright dreaming eyes. "Oh, it must be fine to go away like that an' learn so many things—an' then to have a job by New York City."

Dorie grunted, "Well, from all I hear there's nothin' to keep you from finishin' high school an' then goin' on to college an' workin' away like mine."

Delph lifted her head and studied Dorie. "I wonder if I'm smart enough—or if I could learn all th' things that others learn in college. I'd—I'd give my heart to try. But if—if—."

"Now what's th' matter?" Dorie wanted to know when Delph had sat a time looking at the ground with troubled eyes.

Delph sat suddenly erect with lifted chin. "Nothin's th' matter. Not a thing," she answered and clasped her hands tightly in her lap, but while her mouth smiled her eyes begged something of Dorie. "I—I've been wantin' all summer to talk to you—a little about, well, about speakin' to Uncle John." She drew a sharp hard breath. "I'm still not certain he'll let me go, just to Town to take my last year of high school. Th' little one on th' other side of th' post office gives only three. Uncle John respects you so. 'Dorie Dodson holds by th' old ways,' he always says.—An' your children they went away—to college even—an' I—I can't live all my days in this back hill country wonderin'—."

She stopped, and sat flushed and angry eyed staring at the toe of her shoe. "There's no harm in your goin' away to school that I can see," Dorie said after a moment's silence, but her voice was doubtful and uncertain as she added, "But I never mix in family matters."

Delph's tightly clasped hands slowly loosened as her fingers relaxed their hard hold, and Marsh looking at the hands, brown and strong and slender like the rest of her, found them lax with a look of emptiness and of despair strange in things so young. He glanced up and met her eyes, and in their smoldering hunger he saw himself, straining always for the things he never had. Delph flushed and looked away, and he felt a curious sense of shame as if he had seen more of her than she would have any one see. "You two talk, I'll be gettin' on," he said, and got up, but stood hesitant with no wish to go away.

Dorie looked longingly at the half smoked cigarette, and then glanced appraisingly at Delph. "Mr. Gregory here," she said after a time, "has been askin' me about th' early generations of your family, but I couldn't tell him anything. You ought to tell him about Ole Azariah. Your father thought more a him than all his other blood-kin.—I'm sorry I can't stay. I want to see th' dates on ole Peter Chrismann's grave, an' look in on th' Dodson dead," and Dorie got up and walked away into a deeper tangle of cedar trees.

Delph looked somewhat startled at being left alone with a strange oil man, such a wild one at that, for though she had scarcely seen him until now and had never heard his name, she, no different from the rest of the Little South Fork Country, knew him as the man who batched alone because no one in the country would have a nitro-glycerin outfit near, had heard of him who could swear as men in the old days swore, only wilder with black heathen oaths. She was surprised and half disappointed when he touched a red dahlia on old Azariah's mound of stones and said, "Somebody in your family has a hand for growin' things."

She smiled but would take little credit for the flowers. She and Juber raised them together; sometimes he hoed them and sometimes she, but they both liked flowers, especially the big bright ones. "I thought," she said as she came and stood with him by the grave, "that most of th' old Costello dead, especially Azariah there—that's just a marker for him, we don't know where he is—would like bright things like old maids an' dahlias better than pale puny ones like baby's breath or snow-on-th'-mountain.

"Azariah was th' first of us all," she went on to explain when Marsh showed the interest that Dorie said he had. "He never lived here long. He was never one for stayin' in one spot like a knot on a log. He never even stayed to finish th' Revolution—he left that to his boys—he came sometime in th' late seventies, about a hundred an' fifty years ago, an'"—she lifted her skirt slightly, and the next instant stood on top of the mound of stones. "You come up, too," she invited, "an' I can show you as I tell."

Marsh stood with her on the mound of stones among the wilting flowers, and looked where she pointed and saw a spot he had often noticed while driving over the country; a high, flat-topped knob of stone, higher than the surrounding hills, that stood like a sentinel at the head of the valley. He knew its name, "The Pilot's Rock," but he had never climbed it. Delph told him of its height, of how one could stand on its top, and see into both Virginia and Tennessee. Old Azariah had stood on the rock and looked down into the Little South Fork Country, and liking it, he had gone back to North Carolina for his wife and sons—grown men they had been for Azariah was then past middle age.

They had settled in different valleys, with Azariah taking up the whole of the Little South Fork Country—a land grant given him for service against the Indians. But he had stayed only a dozen years at most, and then gone west into new wild country, leaving his wife and children with directions to care for his land and hogs and mules. They never heard from him again, and when Jane—that was his wife—died she asked her sons to make this grave for him; a proper grave for a man dead in Indian country.

Marsh listened to Delph's eager talk of the man dead all these years, and gradually the dead came alive and he could see him as Delph said, "taller than Uncle John, quieter, too, I guess, an' his eyes blue as corn flowers, strange far seein' eyes he had like all great hunters in th' old days, an' his hair was black as a coal, an' long down to his shoulders," and she talked on of what a man he was, never afraid, and always hunting in new strange country, not a bit like John.

"He was like you, I guess," Marsh said, and Delph flushed, and for the first time seemed to see him instead of Azariah.

"My eyes are not so blue," she said, and added with a smile, "but I'm plenty brown enough to be a long hunter." She sighed, but with little trouble in her sigh.

"Aunt Fronie fusses sometimes, but it's more fun workin' out with flowers an' such, or even helpin' in th' hay when Uncle John's not around than working' in th' house."

Marsh broke a spray of blue berried cedar and looked at it. He wished he could make her see him, understand that even strange oil men were men, more alive than her dead of a hundred and fifty years ago. Or maybe men like himself who had worked by days wages and known what it was to be bound and bossed and shaped and afraid—seemed mere shadows of men to her who was so alive. Strong she was, and almost as tall as he, and all as nature made her with never a smudge of paint, a store-bought curl, or bob, blood and bone of the old free dead, tinged with earth and sweat and rocks and sun and wind, a faint sprinkling of freckles to add interest to her nose, her hands brown, not pinky-white play things, but a woman's hands.

Then she was whirling away and springing from the grave like a startled deer when a woman's voice came calling through the cedar trees, "Delph-i-i-ne."

"It's time for th' afternoon services," she explained, and hastily smoothed her dress, and patted her hair.

He, too, jumped to the ground and stood a moment and begged her with his eyes not to go away so soon, and maybe she read his eyes for she stopped and studied him and said, "I don't guess a man like you—one that's been around a lot—would think much of comin' to church here, but early in September th' revival will begin, an' you must come sometime."

"I will," he said and when he had followed her a step or so through the cedar trees, touched her braids and said, "You can't go singin' in th' choir like that with cedar needles on your hair."

"Where?" she asked, and he said, "There," and flicked a bit of cedar from her hair.

"Thanks," she said, and was gone, running away across the graves.

· 3 ·

THE FIRST week of September came. Marsh as he hauled nitroglycerin to the wells in the high back hills found signs of fall in the blood red leaves of black gum bush, and a few slender fingers of flowering goldenrod. The hazelnuts were ripening, and he would sometimes hear the falling thud of a worm-bitten hickory nut.

He would listen intently, and then drive on; his thoughts not on the nut that fell but of the winter that seemed gathered in the sound. And as always there was the wonder of where he would be. His work by the Little South Fork Country was mostly done. There were days when he did not have to touch the nitroglycerin, and though he hated the loss from his wages, he now looked forward to such times. Once, free days had meant only that for a little while he could be free of the long fear and the long wonder that had like slowly revolving screws twisted deeper year by year into all his conscious thought. But now they were given an added brightness; if he managed just right he could maybe see Delph.

On the mornings of such days he fed his horses first as always, but different from other times he remained a while and watched them eat. Sometimes he quarreled a bit with Jude. He was certain that Jude had not forgotten the big barn and the river valley farm on the Cumberland that had been his home until last spring. Jude was always, especially in the mornings, a bit remorseful, a bit disdainful of his pole and pine bough stable with living pine trunks for its corners.

"I'll sell you in th' late fall," Marsh said one morning when there was no work to do. "You're not th' oil fields kind anyhow. Luke there he'd soon spend his days haulin' nitroglycerin as plowin' corn, but you, you fool, you're different," and he talked on so for a moment, softly, leaning against the poles, looking sometimes at the horses, now and then glancing away at the rising sun that hung like a red enameled pie pan against a gold and purple wall of early morning cloud. The big horses ate quietly of the oats he had given them, lifting their heads at times to glance at him. And in the red sunrise light their eyes, he thought, were kinder, more filled with understanding than at other times.

When he had cooked and eaten his breakfast which, no matter what time and care he gave to its preparation, never seemed either better or worse, he returned and curried his horses, slowly and with particular pains as if he might that day take them to a fair. It was some little time before the horses were finished to his liking, and even then he must stand a time and study his work and try once more to subdue an especially unruly patch of hair on Jude's left hock.

It was Jude, the unruly, scornful one, that he always rode, for he, unlike Luke, could not be led to graze in the woods. In the last two or three weeks the horses had grown more or less accustomed to his far flung search for a grazing ground when there were grass filled open pine woods within a stone's throw of the cabin. Today they followed much the same route they had followed on other days, keeping clear of roads, fording the creek, and wandering with apparent aimlessness until they came to a stretch of burned over ridge side where the purple blossoming beggar lice and a variety of wild yellow-flowered sweet clover grew lush and thick. He hobbled Jude and left Luke free, and Jude as always showed signs of surliness at the ways of a world that hobbled its leaders.

He left the horses to graze and went to sit by the roots of a thick black oak tree, a distance down the hill side. He drew a government bulletin from his pocket, smiled in a sheepish sort of way at the title and began to read. His reading, however, went slowly. Sometimes he paused to look at his horses, but most often he would turn about and look toward the faint trace of an old ridge road that twisted between the pines on the ridge top.

The morning lengthened, the dew dried, and in the heat the pine smell came strong and sharp, but still the road lay empty. He heard the slow ringing of Big Cane Brake church bell, calling all people to the morning service of the revival meeting. He continued to listen until the last faint hum of echo died. He sat a time longer, then put the bulletin on clover in his pocket and started slowly toward his team.

He stopped abruptly as he heard the faint sound of a horse's hooves beating over the sand on some stretch of the road he could not see. He hurried up the hill, and waited with his back against a tree. He soon saw Delph on Tilly, the big-footed gray mare John gave her to ride. She rode lightly, no bridle in her hand, for her hands were occupied with other things; a bunch of red and yellow dahlias in one, her hat in the other, and tucked under one arm was a good sized leather bound Bible, its gold edges flashing in the sun, while something that looked to be a bundle of clothing bounced at the back of the saddle. She saw him, waved her hat, smoothed her wildly blowing dress down over her knees, and came on at a more dignified pace.

"I was beginnin' to think you'd gone with th' others down th' main road today," he said when she came up to him.

She stopped Tilly, and smiled her quick bright smile, and gave no sign she knew the oil man lied. "I see your horses have run away again," she said. "An' you had to follow all th' way over here. Pshaw, I wouldn't have such horses."

"They're no worse than your big-footed Tilly you're ashamed to ride down th' main road to church," he answered teasingly, for that—with Fronie's disgust for young women who galloped their horses on public roads where all could see—was Delph's excuse for following the old ridge road.

No matter what they said in their stolen meetings; words of the weather, or Marsh's brief answers to the many questions she put to him about the places he had been, Delph was most often shy and ill at ease with a guilty look in her eyes that made him hate her family. It was a pretty pass when a girl couldn't speak to a man without breaking some law laid down by her people.

But today she sat and smiled at him, less mindful of the rules she broke than yesterday. Some gay eager excitement quivered in her face and made her eyes bright blue and warm with her lips redder and brighter than the dahlias. "How's th' revival?" he asked, and came nearer and smoothed Tilly's mane.

She tossed her head and something like defiance shadowed her eyes, and then they were gay again, taken up with other things, "I think there's about a dozen mournin' on th' bench, but so far nobody's got saved that I know of," she answered, and smiled at him, impishly, her thoughts a thousand miles from the mourners. "Somethin' good's happened to me," she burst out suddenly.

"You an' Logan aimin' to get married?"

She flushed, then smiled over Logan as she had smiled at the mourners. "Pshaw, no. I'll not be married for a long while—now." She leaned forward with her hands dropping on Tilly's mane near his own, and her eyes laughing down upon him. "Uncle John's goin' to let me go to Town an' finish high school. I never thought he would—an' when he told me last night I felt like flyin'."

She sat back and waited, smiling, for his congratulations. "That's fine," he said at last. "It'll mebbe take a while—but one a these days you can blossom out with a career an' all—mebbe be like th' women you read about in your magazines."

Her smile faded, and she sat remote and drawn unto herself, staring at the black velvet ribbon on her white straw hat. "But I thought you'd be glad to know," she said at last in a tight hurt voice, "that—that somehow from th' way you looked, you'd understand better than th' people here, better than Logan even, what this little beginnin' means to me."

His tongue seemed suddenly to have a will of its own, not sensible like the rest of him, remembering always that he'd most likely never see the girl again come fall. "You're mighty nice th' way you are," he said, and stood looking at her hands.

She tapped his bent head playfully with the dahlias, and he felt their yellow pollen on his nose. "It's such a little beginnin'. You needn't be worried. I'll stay with Cousin Emma Chrismann on Fronie's side, an' I won't be exactly seein' th' world, but at least I can get a little more of it in my head. Get ready to go to college—maybe. I can't begin to think how that would seem."

He looked up at her, but she was staring past him through the trees. Her lips were parted, and her eyes were free of hunger, feasting on dreams and visions instead of trees. He felt a hot unreasoning thrust of jealousy; the world she saw was finer than any man—or world—could ever be.

Tilly, impatient from standing still so long, rattled her bridle and Delph came back to realize that she was riding to church. She looked at Marsh's gloomy face and sighed. "You're kin of Aunt Fronie's, always so sober like," she said, then laughed again and bent and whispered quickly by his ear, "Tonight I'm celebratin' all th' same. I've fin'ly persuaded Logan an' th' Hedrick girls for us all after church to run away to that dance they're havin' at Joe D. Martin's."

Marsh frowned more darkly still. "Now I wouldn't do that. If your Uncle John found it out he'd never let you go to school."

"Pshaw, who'd be mean enough to tell him? I'm stayin' th' night with th' Redrick girls, an' Mr. Hedrick he's stayin' at our place with th' preachers, an' Mrs. Hedrick she'll most likely pray all night with Lucas Crabtree."

"Somethin's bound to slip," he insisted. "There'll be a wild crowd up at Martin's. An' if you must go you'd better have some-body else around. I've seen your Logan Ragan drunk as a Lord in Hawthorne Town."

She wrinkled her nose and prodded Tilly into motion with her heel. "Juber, he'll be there, an' anyhow Logan would never start drinkin' when he's out with me," she said, and added in mock scorn, "He's not a wild drinkin' oil man."

"There'll be one a them at that dance tonight, so save a few dances for him," Marsh answered.

"Recollect Logan he'll be there, an' I know now about that fight you almost had with him," she called as she rode away.

"An' you're not mad about it?" he wanted to know.

She answered nothing to that, but he smiled to see her neck and her ears red. It had taken some little time, but she had done what she set out to do, invite him to the dance. He watched until she was swallowed in the trees, then walked restlessly over the ridge side. The bulletin on clover stayed in his pocket, forgotten, while he looked sometimes at his horses, sometimes at the sky, and smiled with his eyes. And as he rode Jude home, Jude took advantage of his master's dreaming ways that left the bridle loosened on his neck and wandered two miles off their course before Marsh noticed where they were, and then he only gave one short easy oath.

Once home, Marsh cleaned his shack, carried all his clothing and bed clothing and spread them on the pine bushes for an airing. He often did that with the hope of taking the oil smell away, but it always seemed to him that he never quite succeeded. Later in the day when both he and his place were clean and straight, he went down to Copenhavers, his nearest neighbors, on what he feared was a useless errand. Still, it would do no harm to ask.

On the front porch Old Willie greeted him, and Maude nickered from the yard; a pretty thing she was with a white starred forehead, a shining mane and gentle eyes. "Aye, she's mindful as a woman with th' flowers," Old Willie said when Marsh praised the mare. The old man smiled and fondled her with his dim eyes as she grazed in the wide sweep of hill yard, filled with flowers and apple trees where the scent of overripe apples left to rot, and the marigolds by the log porch steps, blended in a sharp winey sweetness that drew the bees from their hives in the orchard.

Marsh lingered a time on the vine covered porch and stroked a hound dog lazily, and listened to Old Willie talk. He talked of horses and hunting and fiddles and hound dog tunes; and sighed for the old days when guns were guns and men were men, and the timber was fine and tall and filled with game. The guns were better then, truly rifled and truly put together, heavy, and of a length to suit a right sized man. "When th' old Costello breed a men died out or left th' country, we lost th' ones that knowed good guns an' loved a good horse an' could set all night on th' Pilot Rock an' listen to hound dawg music," the old man said, and spat contemptuously into the yard. "That John takes after his maw's people—sober like in his ways, but, Lord, his brother, Delph's paw—women or God couldn't keep him under. Too bad Delph's a girl."

"I wouldn't call her exactly a failure," Marsh said.

Old Willie sighed. "Blood's blood an' it'll tell. I look at her in church sometimes—a singin' away an' a cryin' in her eyes. They've held her in too close, brought her up so pious like an' still. An' she's th' old Costellos through an' through." He spat again with angry vehemence. "But she's a girl. When she marries into them smooth mouthed Ragans she'll go by their ways."

Marsh got up with sharp abruptness. "I've got to be goin' on," he said, but paused and looked down through the yard; the lower half of it in hill shadow now. The bee hives were filled with a soft sleepy droning, surrounded by clouds of homecoming bees sinking out of the sunlight into the shadow, and as each bee dropped near the hive it seemed to lose a burden of golden light and be but a small dark dot going home. Below the yard were the acres of bottom land corn, its lower blades in fodder now. Soon there would be corn cutting time, and time to sow the rye, and dig the sweet potatoes and put the apples away, then corn gathering time and wood getting; then winter when the bees were still and Old Willie sat by his hearth and whittled the endless balls in chains and chains through balls with which old hill men whiled away their winter hours. And through it all there would be no fear of death nor change nor wonder of how the next year would be.

He thought of all that, and he thought of Delph's eyes when they looked past him and saw visions he could not see. Somebody ought to have something. He wished he had shown some gladness when she told him of getting a thing she wanted. He would tell her tonight, say he was very glad. He remembered his errand, and stopped on the top porch step and looked at the corn as he said, "It'll soon be corn cuttin' time. My work's slack now.—How about me comin' down an' helpin' some?"

Old Willie smiled. "No oil man would want th' little wages we could pay."

"Th' pay wouldn't matter so much."

"Why, you'd mebbe cut your leg on a corn knife, an' it 'ud be hard fer you.—Easy work but all in knowin' how," the old man said.

"I know somethin' a farmin'—a little," Marsh explained hesitantly. "I was raised on one—well, more than one. In Missouri we raised corn. I know how to cut in case your son needs a hand."

Old Willie spat over the porch steps, then boomed, "Aye, there'll never be need for a money makin' man like you to fiddle with a corn knife, but if I was you," he went on after a long survey of Marsh's clothing, "I don't know but I'd take a knife or a pair a knucks if you're goin' where I think you're goin'."

Marsh smiled. "An' where would I be goin'?"

"I'm wonderin' myself. What I'm thinkin' is that there's talk that Delph Costello's been sort a castin' her eyes after you—sickened a Logan so I've heared—but recollect he's still her beau," Old Willie said, then dropped his head against the back of his chair and seemed to fall asleep.

"You oughtn't to tell such tales, Old Willie," Marsh scolded. "Why Delph's Aunt Fronie wouldn't let her look at a wild oil man."

Old Willie smiled in his beard without opening his eyes, while Marsh hurried down to the waiting Jude. Twilight lay blue on the valley road, though the taller pines and poplar on the hills were tipped here and there with a bit of red gold sunset fire. He galloped down the clay and limestone road; sometimes he glanced at a field of ripening corn, or snatched at a cluster of hazel nuts, but most often he looked straight ahead, and when Moses Sexton who lived where the toll gate used to be called to him, "I never saw you ride so careless like an' easy," he answered, "I feel careless," and rode on with never a glance back at the Sexton cows walking up to the barn for milking.

He stopped at the post office and ordered pork and beans and crackers and cheese from Mrs. Crouch for his supper. She glanced suspiciously at his fresh shave and good clothes, but said nothing. A batch of short-core jelly she was then making was just at that moment smoking its pipes, and she in fear that it would overcook took no time out for conversation.

He went to sit by the creek, where he ate, hardly knowing what he ate. He watched the darkness deepen and heard the first faint croakings of frogs and saw the fireflies go in and out among the beech boughs. He listened then to the conversation of two whip-poor-wills farther up the creek above the bridge. One seemed to be trying to comfort the other, but always failed, for each time the other would answer just as sadly as before, "Whip-poor-will," with such sadness on the will, that gradually the more cheerful of the two agreed that for some things there was no comfort, and cried his knowledge long and sadly through the darkness.

A rising night breeze rustled in the beech trees and whispered through the corn in Mrs. Crouch's garden. The wind carried a faint smell of earth damp by the creek, that hinted of some fainter, farther smell Marsh could not name, maybe leaves or trees or decaying wood, more like the memory of warm spring rain on fresh plowed ground. The smell was familiar as a suit of threadbare clothes. Yet always one quick first breath of it could cause a sharp thrust of what in another might have been homesickness, but since he had never had one certain spot for home he knew the earth smell could not bring that. Times like tonight it stirred a hatred of his wandering way of life, and pricked him, too, with something like regret or shame. He sat a time and figured in his head the money he had spent foolishly within the last year, but it was a hateful business, and he was glad when Mrs. Crouch called for her bowl and spoon.

He went to her dwelling quarters behind the store, knowing full well it wasn't the bowl and spoon she wanted, but mostly information as to where he might be headed. Since the day he had driven her to Big Cane Brake Church the postmistress had stood to him as something like a guardian angel, not only that but now and then she let out helpful hints such as, "Juber was tellin' me Delph was aimin' to ride down here to see what I had in th' way a gingham, tomorrow afternoon," or, "Boy, you mustn't ever dress up to go courtin' in these hills. Some a these men with young girls'ull mebbe be thinkin' you're out tryin' to spark 'em."

Though he disliked the lie, Marsh felt that the postmistress would be easier in her mind if she thought he was headed for Holly Bush eight miles away instead of Martin's dance, and so he gave that as his destination when she asked him where he might be going. She, in accordance with her usual custom of late, complained of having too much food and never being able to cook for one, and so begged him to eat of the hot fried ham and other dishes on the table. He was not hungry, but ate a bit, while she as always watched him and smiled, and talked of her own boys scattered in northern cities, and wondered if they had had good suppers that night. Sometimes she showed him their pictures, bringing the cheap shiny photographs from the massive folding bed in the side room, holding them carefully in one corner of her apron so as not to spot them with her dishwatery hands. They were all wide-shouldered, stalwart hill men, with something roving in their eyes that made him think of Delph.

But tonight Mrs. Crouch said nothing of her children, and never invited him to sit a time on the front porch as she usually did. She seemed in a hurry to finish the dishes, and Marsh noticing that under her wide apron she wore a dress different from her everyday ginghams and that her hair showed signs of curling irons, suspected that she as well as Delph might have a beau. He rode away in the direction of Holly Bush, but when he had topped the first hill, dismounted and sat on a fallen log until he heard Logan's car go up the road on the other side of the bridge that led to Martin's.

He rode again then, following a narrow, little used road that kept to the twisting ways of the ridge. He was in no hurry. He on a horse could get there quicker than Logan chugging over limestone ledges and creek bottoms. Now and then he stopped to watch clouds play hide and seek with a rising moon, or listen to the southwest wind in the pine trees.

Joe D. Martin's log house lay in a lonesome spot, a cove at the head of a narrow creek, well away from a main road or other houses. Though tonight the place held no air of lonesomeness, but was bright with lanterns and carbide lights hung on pegs on the log porch and on the gate posts. He lingered a time in the shadowy yard and listened to the low talk and lower, almost soundless, laughter of the hill men. The dancing had not yet begun, but from the big house room there came short wails and cries from fiddles being tuned, with now and then a lively twang from a guitar or banjo.

Soon after he heard the shuffling, stamping feet of the dancers, and felt a curious lonesomeness, unusual with him. Delph would be dancing now with Logan's arms about her waist, her mind on a million things other than a roving oil man. He worked his way through the crowd on the porch, and stood with other men in the low wide door and looked into the room. The musicians, including Juber, sat on the hearth in front of the empty fireplace, while the dancers, many girls in gingham dresses and men in overalls, held the center of the room. Big Foot Armstrong stood on the top step of the three steps leading to the loft room door and called the sets in his booming voice. Men lounged by the walls and in the windows. Women with babies in their arms and young children leaning by their knees sat in hickory bark bottomed chairs or makeshift benches by the wall, and listened to the fiddle tunes and watched the dancers with their deep quiet eyes which seemed shadowed by some memory of sorrow or foreboding of trouble and pain. The hands that waved the palm leaf fans seemed tired and slow, and the thin, stooped shoulders looked old for women giving suck to young. Marsh looked at them and was glad that Delph was going away to finish high school. Still, the women came from people different from her own, wives of poor back hill farmers and moonshiners, not of men with money in the bank and acres of timber and farm land.

He looked for her among the dancers, but found her instead sitting quiet and still between Logan and Mrs. Crouch in a shadowy corner of the room. He caught the postmistress's eye, but she looked at him in such fierce surprise that he stayed where he was, and hoped that Delph would look at him. She, however, listened to some talk of Logan's with her dark brows lifted a bit and her shoulders too stiff and still. Soon she turned abruptly away and watched the dancers, and though Marsh looked fixedly at her she saw nothing but the bowing swaying figures.

He watched her fingers tap the time on her knees, and then her feet, slyly without her knowing, beat the tune on the floor. Logan glanced at her moving feet, and then at her. She flushed and held her feet and her hands carefully still. Marsh looked at her quiet feet and her quiet hands a moment longer, and then went up to her. Mrs. Crouch saw him first, and the wavings of her fan from being long and leisurely with pauses between each wave, grew suddenly short and agitated, though her voice was calm enough as she said, "Good evenin', Mr. Gregory. I thought you'd be goin' out to Holly Bush to th' shootin' match."

"Not when there's a square dance on hand," he said.

Logan turned and looked at him, and smiled his frosty hill man's smile. "How come you're not dancin' then?"

"I've not found a partner to my likin'," he said, and watched Delph's ears redden and wished she would look at him.

"I see no sign a one in this corner," Logan answered, while Mrs. Crouch got up with a nimbleness surprising in a woman of her age and size, seized his elbow, and said all in a breath, "I've been noticin' one a th' Branchcomb girls lookin' after you all evenin'. She's over there by th' bed—a pretty girl with red hair—I'll take you over an' make you acquainted. She's a might good dancer an'—."

Marsh disregarded her not so gentle pull on his arm. "What about De—Miss Costello? Doesn't she dance?"

"Yes. I mean no, she—," Mrs. Crouch began in a feeble voice, but Logan cut her short with an icy, "No, not in this rough crowd," while Delph said nothing as she got up, dropped her cardboard fan across Logan's knees, and took Marsh's free arm. "Yes Delph dances," she said to no one in particular. "She didn't come to sit around like a deacon's wife—an' Logan."

Logan sprang up and stood staring at her with open mouth, and surprise and anger struggling in his eyes. "Delph, you can't go runnin' around with a stranger in this rough crowd—a man you never hardly saw in your life."

"She'll not be runnin' around. She'll be dancin'," Marsh answered, and led her away with no looking back. He was conscious of the eyes in the room, searching his face and his back like fingers feeling cloth to learn its worth.

"I guess I've made a fool a myself," Delph whispered as they joined the lines of dancers.

"You're awful pretty when you're bein' a fool," he whispered back, and laughed down into her eyes where all the frolicsome fiddle tunes seemed gathered in a flickering, dancing, laughing world of light and shadow.

Delph danced and never thought of Logan, only noticed in an absent minded sort of way that he made frequent trips to the back porch where she guessed young John D. Martin was doing a thriving business in white corn liquor. If he wanted to make a fool of himself because she danced, she didn't mind. She didn't mind anything. She saw Juber with his fiddle under his chin and eyes and heart for nothing but the leaping bow in his hand and the strings quivering under his fingers. Juber loved the music so—maybe it was the only way he knew of going away. The fiddle and the bow, she knew, were finer to him than they really were. Sometimes while he helped her in the flowers or at night when he milked in the barn, he would talk in low broken whispers of the fiddle and bow he would like to have, a bow tipped with silver and a fiddle trimmed in gold, and of some wondrous sweet singing wood that was mellow and old with no harshness and no twanging.

She would never be like that, dreaming and dreaming her life away, never having, never knowing, never feeling the world. She would never be like Mrs. Crouch living away in a low lost holler and wondering after and sighing over her man dead and her children gone away. She wouldn't be like that thin stoop-shouldered wife of a poor hill farmer with a fat baby tugging at one blue veined breast and another sleeping by her knees. Marsh's hands clasped her waist, and swung her high and free. She looked up and smiled into his eyes, and her thoughts of the life she would live dissolved. Life for the moment was enough. The line advanced, she bowed, then straightened, and saw Logan by the mantle. His nose was white and his cheeks were red. He'd started drinking, she guessed. That meant that Marsh would have to see her home, but she didn't mind.

Becky Daughtery, the hill farmer's wife, shifted her baby to the other breast, and whispered to Mrs. Crouch without taking her eyes from Delph, "Lord, don't she make a body feel young agin. I'm glad she took th' bit in her teeth an' danced."

Mrs. Crouch nodded, and waved her fan in pleased acquiescence to the situation. "I hope that fool of a Logan Ragan gets so drunk he can't start trouble. I never had a girl a my own, but I always thought that if I had I'd a let her have a little fun—harmless like this with older folks lookin' on. A woman's dancin' days are short an' mostly things for her to recollect anyhow."

The hill farmer's wife sighed, and shook her head slowly as she smiled on Delph. "Aye, an' if she never dances th' youngens an' th' work an' th' fetchin' an' tendin' fer a man they'll come no easier anyhow."

And Juber, lost as he was in his fiddling, glanced at Delph and whispered to his fiddle, "She's havin' th' time of her life."

Big Foot Armstrong, caller of the sets, complained that his throat was dry, and one of the Martin boys brought in a jug of raw corn liquor, from which Big Foot helped himself. Then each of the musicians took one long drink, even Juber who shivered and batted his eyes as the drink went down. After that the music quickened and the feet and bodies of the dancers matched it with whirls and leaps and lively steps. The wide heavy planks of the big house floor bounced and swayed and creaked, while puffs of dust undisturbed for fifty years danced into spurts of sudden life between the cracks. Hound dogs visiting from miles around pressed between the legs of the watching men, and looked and listened to the goings on with glistening wondering eyes.

The more sober minded of the women began to grow restive and whisper to each other that it was getting late and time to start home. Each agreed that she had come only to hear a bit of music and not see all this sinful dancing with maybe Big Foot Armstrong and the musicians drinking on the sly. Of course it was only water in the jug, the men would never dare to drink so openly.

The older women were not the only ones worried by the gay turn the party had taken. Now and then one of the Hedrick girls tried to whisper to Delph that it was time to go home, but Delph never listened, and danced as if there were no world before and no world after, only the dance. Her cheeks were pinker than when she came, and her eyes were brighter, bluer, with all the smiles that touched her mouth living in them too.

At first she only smiled like a woman in her sleep when Logan took advantage of a pause in the music to come to her and say in a loose sleepy voice, "Delph, we'd better go home."

She studied him with angry narrowing eyes, then moved a step or so away. "You're drunk," she said.

He made an exaggerated motion of straightening his shoulders. "Not so much but I can drive you home—now."

Dolly Hedrick nudged his elbow and whispered, "He's drinkin' an' we'd better all go. He might start trouble."

But Delph only studied Logan and gave no sign she heard. "Come on, let's go," he insisted, and she understood that he was less drunk than angry.

She was still a moment, bewildered by a curious feeling, less of anger at his domineering ways than of surprise at herself. Yesterday or even while they sat in the corner and quarreled, Logan had mattered more to her than anyone. The prospect of school in Town had been sweetened by thought of seeing him. Now, suddenly, his anger or his pleasure didn't matter. He was only a bit of the Little South Fork Country—someone like Fronie to shape her in a pattern she had never chosen.

She glanced at Marsh and saw his eyes, gray slits in his face, and his mouth a straight colorless line. All at once it mattered very much that nothing should happen to him. He stood there, ready to use his fists, and most likely never knew that Logan had a gun.

"Delph, don't stand there wool gatherin' all night. Let's go," Logan said, and took her arm.

She felt his hot big hand through the sheer stuff of her dress; the touch sickened her, and she jerked herself free. She heard the ripping sound of her dress sleeve in the too quiet room, and was conscious of the faces watching her, worried and disapproving faces that held her up to shame. She saw Logan and the bewildered look in his eyes. He didn't understand. He thought she was teasing him with the oil man. He looked foolish with his jaws working twice before the words came out, "You—you needn't jump so. I'm not poison.—You've let plenty others hug you tight all evenin'."

She flushed and said in a choked dry voice, "I danced like th' others. I've done no wrong."

"Well, soon's I get you safe back to Hedricks I'll not be botherin' you. I brought you here. I'll have to see you home," he said, and stood waiting for her to come with him.

She stood with clenched hands and tried to look at no one. Her throat ached, not so much from anger as from a sense of loss; all the fun of the evening broken like a bit of bright glass. She had a sudden fear that she might be going to cry with all the people looking on. She had committed no sin, only danced; and now they looked at her as if she, and not Logan, were the guilty one. "I'll go home—," she said without looking at Logan. "But not with you. Not with anybody." She started toward the door, trying to walk slowly and never show how anxious she was to be rid of the watching eyes.

Logan followed her a step or so, then whirled about when Marsh said, "Leave her be."

"Listen you—you good for nothin' roustabout—you've caused enough trouble for one evenin'. You've no right to come nosin' where you're not wanted," Logan called over his shoulder.

"Nobody gave me cause to think I wasn't wanted," Marsh answered in a flat low voice, and stood with hands loose and easy by his sides and his feet spread a little like things rooted in the ground.

Logan looked at him in silence and so did all the others in the room. Only Juber stood on tiptoe and craned his head to see and muttered, "Easy now, men, easy. John'ull get wind a this an' it'll be good-bye to Delph's goin' to school," but no one noticed Juber.

"Th' bit a notice Delph gave you has gone to your head," Logan muttered, and backed slowly toward the door with his eyes on Marsh.

"You could be civil," Marsh said, and followed him.

"You've no need to come after us," Logan commanded, and went through the door.

"I go where I please," Marsh said, and walked on, careful to keep his eyes on Logan's hands.

There were others who watched Logan's hands, for the Ragan men were noted for their quick light hands as well as their soft-spoken, smiling ways.

He disappeared on the porch. Marsh followed him and stood for an instant sharply silhouetted in the lamplight falling through the door. He couldn't see Logan on the porch for his body was hidden in shadow, but he heard Delph's wild cry. He saw Logan's face then, a white blur by a tangle of vines on the porch edge. He saw Delph's dress, the white spinning cloud of it when Logan gave her a violent shove.

He jumped sideways and cat like as he had learned to do in his drilling days when the bull wheels burst or a cable broke. A bullet whined and splinters flew from the door jamb while a gun popped, softly, he thought. The way Logan talked. He heard Delph's scream of "Oh, you fool," and saw the whiteness of her dress again between him and Logan; saw it whirl and sway like a wild thing as she struggled for the gun.

He leaped and jerked her away, and caught Logan's hands. A hot something like splashing grease touched his arm as he heard another shot right by his chest it seemed. The gun clattered to the floor, and something inside him laughed at the helplessness of men like Logan without their guns. He stepped back, and while Logan stood bewildered, stooping a bit to see the gun, Marsh straightened him, lifted him with a blow under his chin. When Logan wavered, perfectly straight, immensely tall, he knocked him through the screen of vines, so that he fell with his head on the ground and his heels trailing in the vines.

He was suddenly conscious of the pain in his arm, and the worse pain in the knuckles of his right hand; of women screaming behind him and men crowding around. But they were dim and of no account when there was Delph's hand on his arm, shaking him while she begged, "You're not hurt, Marsh? Please, you're not hurt?"

He flipped hair from his forehead and smiled. Then he was ashamed and sorry. This fracas would most likely cost Delph her chance to go to school. Still, it was sweet to know that she stood there, not thinking of school, but saying over and over, "Please, Marsh, are you all right?"

· 4 ·

THAT YEAR more than one in the Little South Fork Country marveled at the beauty of the fall. The early frosts were light and the days clear and still, roofed by high bottomless skies, cloudless and intensely blue. Sometimes with only Tilly for company Delph went on long hunts down the pine ridges after wild grapes and chestnuts. Mostly she would come home empty handed, a few chestnuts in her sweater pockets or grape stain on her fingers. She would stand silent under Fronie's tearful lamentations, and never answer her aunt's eternal, "What ails you anyhow, Delph?" and never defend herself when she said, "You know no woman's reputation can stand runnin' around in th' woods by herself.—An' th' Lord knows yours is bad enough as it is, after runnin' away to that dance, an' causin' a fight by dancin' with a strange oil man."

Delph never told her aunt or even Juber what it was she hunted in the woods. She didn't know. Sometimes she would sit motionless on Tilly for minutes together and watch a single yellow poplar leaf rise and rise and linger for one moment high and bright and gold against a great blue sweep of sky, then turn and fall in long cascading spirals, its brightness lost in shadow, and settle at last only another leaf to rot and die. Something would ache in her throat and smart in her eyes, but she never cried. The sky and the leaves and the earth cried of change, and the honking call of the wild geese flying in a high vee was a challenge to go away.

And more than these were Marsh's eyes when he looked at her, and smiled, with little joy in his smile. Each day of fall brought the winter nearer, a time when he would be like the leaf and the wild

49

goose call, a memory of something that went away, They met often in the woods, sometimes in Mrs. Crouch's kitchen, but Delph seldom chattered gaily or teasingly as she had used to do with Logan. Marsh thought there were many who said he would be safer out of the country, tried not to think of the winter and of going away. The thought hurt when he walked through Old Willie's fields and smelled the ripened corn, but it was something worse than simple hurt when he looked at Delph. Sometimes he tried to tell her how sorry he was he had gone to the dance and had a fight with Logan of which the whole country, including her Uncle John, heard. But Delph would only interrupt to say, "Pshaw, if it hadn't a been that it would ha been somethin' else.—I guess I was never meant to go away," and she would look at him and smile with sorrow, but no blame in her eyes.

Many, especially Mrs. Crouch and Juber, marveled that Delph took John's refusal to let her go to school with such seeming unconcern. Delph herself wondered sometimes why it was that school and the mysterious world that books could open for her no longer seemed important—or even interesting. Marsh alone kept life from being empty and flat and dull. New magazines with their tantalizing smell of ink and fresh shining paper were irksome, and the endings of the continued stories no longer mattered. The letters that Logan sent filled with apologies and asking her forgiveness were bits of paper and nothing more. Fronie talked of dresses for the winter, and John, kind as always in spite of his sternness, bought her a blue tweed coat with a red fox collar—the nicest coat she had ever had and fine as any in Town—but she didn't want the coat. She didn't know what she wanted.

Nights when the west wind came softly up at dusk and brought a smell of smoke and ripened corn, and hinted too of some farther world, a land behind the wind, she would be restless, fidgeting with her sewing by the fire, and often seizing a water bucket from the kitchen and running to the well on the pretext that she wanted a cold drink.

She liked to stand by the well on a windy moonlit night, hear the soft, sad moan of the white pines by the gate, the whine and swish of beech twigs in the grove, and the deeper, farther wail of the wind in the high back hills. The world was a pattern in black and silver with shimmering pearl-gray clouds racing faster than the moon. On such nights something in her blood raced with the wind, and the nameless wanting was like a live thing stronger than she. Somewhere there was a life to match the wild free beauty of the night, a something that would make her rich and full and satisfied, not leave her like a daft thing staring at the moon.

It was on nights in fall like these that Azariah and the ones before him came alive, as if she had only to blow the old hunting horn and they would come. She had heard many tales of the ones before Azariah and the ones who came with him, stories handed down for three hundred years and joining many countries. Never tales of heroes, sometimes of women, but mostly of men, tall, blue-eyed, black-bearded men who chewed tobacco and swore long oaths, men who could shoot and ride and fight, men with great shoulders and mighty hands that could heave a cannon from a mud hole or set the timbers of a stockade into place.

Men who were ever restless, great hunters who bred children to go west and north and south. There were those out of Ireland who had sailed down Shannon Bay in 1665. What was it they had wanted or hunted when they broke with their King in England, went first to Scotland, then to Ireland, out of Ireland into wild unsettled Virginia, with children and grandchildren scattering in North Carolina, fighting at King's Mountain in the Revolution, and then, first Azariah alone, later a handful of others coming through Cumberland Gap into Kentucky? And those out of Holland, why did they leave Holland for New York, their children leave New York for the backwoods of Pennsylvania, some leave Pennsylvania for the Revolution and finished with that, take a flat boat down the Ohio, and at some nameless point on the river strike out east for the backwoods of Kentucky? Why did some, forced out of France, go first to Canada, push down into Vincennes in Indiana, and from there come down to the hills? What was it they had wanted? Not the rich fat cane brakes by the creeks and rivers, or the wildness of the hills. Or had they thought that here in the Little South Fork Country they might find the things she wanted now, the things that others went out from the hills to find—not land or timber or game, possessions to hold in their hands and say, "This is my own"? They must have laughed at the simple having, else they would never have gone on.

Maybe they had wanted only to live as they pleased, or maybe they had simply wanted the knowing, had been forced onward always by the wonder of what lay over the next hill. They must have stood and sniffed the west wind and dreamed of another life and another land, not old and stale and tight with all the brightness gone like this.

Then Fronie or Nance, the middle aged hired girl, would be calling, "Delph-i-i-ine, you'll catch your death a cold a standin' in th' wind," and she would go, slowly with the brimming pail, back to the house, but linger maybe on the back kitchen porch until someone called again.

The family would be sitting in the front room next to the parlor, about a low fire that seemed like the rest of the place, dead and quiet and old. Nights, Fronie and Nance pieced quilts or mended while John read, usually the Bible or some political pamphlet. His four young sons, though noisy enough outdoors, were always quiet, good like sober-minded little men when under their mother's eyes. Even the baby, hardly old enough to walk, seemed quieter than a baby ought to be.

After the outdoors the room was chokingly warm and still, with the lamplight thick and ugly as compared to the light of the moon, and the slow heavy ticking of the front hall clock more like deepening notes of silence than sound. And the faint cry of the wind in the high back hills was smothered and far away.

Sometimes there was scant slow-worded conversation, bits of gossip about the neighbors, talk of roads, and politics, and religion, and the weather. When in John's presence Fronie never mentioned Delph's misdeeds for John, though given to stern ways and quick outbursts of anger, had no love of quarreling. Many nights he tried to talk with Delph about this thing or that, but usually his conversations began and ended with the weather. "We'll have a hard killin' frost one a these nights that'll catch all your flowers, Delph," he would say or some such, and Delph would answer, "I'll be watchin' an' cut 'em all before they die."

She saw the doom of her flowers one night when she climbed the pasture hill on pretext of hunting the cows. The sunset was clear, shading through a band of yellow light flung like a scarf over the farthest hills, rising up through blue-green waves into a blue that was neither dark nor light, but that still deep blue that belonged to a frost promising sky.

She lingered a time, and stared at the indistinct ribbon of whitish limestone road that ran along Little South Fork Creek. She watched the road without taking away her eyes, hardly conscious that moment by moment it darkened, until a sudden whispered wail of wind in the one oak tree on the hill caused her to raise her head. When she looked again the road was faint and dim like a thread of gray smoke against a gray sky.

She had always liked to watch a road or path, hoping that something strange or new would pass, but of late when she saw a road she thought only of Marsh. There was always the chance that some errand or excuse would bring him down into the Little South Fork Country, or maybe up the hill by Costello's place.

When the road had faded and there was no longer hope of his coming she continued to look at the hills; dark mysterious things marching into the west, like Marsh going away. He was out there somewhere and she wondered when she would see him again. Three days now since their last meeting, and the time seemed long, endlessly stretching away like the hills behind the hills and the bottomless sweep of the sky.

Here on the high knoll, nothing hemmed the sky or rose against it; the hills and nearer trees were dark puny things against the high blue-green roof that, like some great crystal, held still the last brightness of the sun. She looked up into it and felt a moment's understanding of the bigness and the wonder of the world. It was there while she wasted her days on a hill in the back country, where the seasons and the weather marked the difference in the days, and living men clung to the old ways of their dead; a place where small things made a life, and mere nothings like the coming of the hard frost and cutting of her flowers seemed tragedies.

She ran down through the pasture, and there were tears in her eyes that had nothing to do with the frosty cold—and not at all tears for the death of her flowers. She laid up the top bar across the lane, and turned toward the yellow glow of lantern light that marked a cow's stable in the barn. Juber was milking in the stable; his hands moving in time to the slow words of the old tale he told seven-year-old Jobe, second oldest of her cousins. It was the story of the big white rabbit that led all good dogs to their particular heavens when they died.

She had heard the story numberless times since she was four years old and Juber had comforted her with it when Lee, her father's blue nosed fox hound died. She had needed comfort then, for that was the fall after her mother went away, and the autumn rains that year had seemed like tears trickling from some sad faced sky. Now she stood in the stable door and listened, and it was much the same; the child and man dressed much alike in blue shirts and copper-riveted overalls and unpolished raw hide shoes, the lantern flame weaving gently within its smoke-encrusted globe, and Daisy, the red cow, turning her head toward Juber with a look of listening in her gentle eyes, as if she liked to hear the words accompanied always by a solemn shake of the teller's head, "An' they never catch him, an' he never runs away so all they do is foller."

And Young Jobe asked, as she had asked, "An' where does th' rabbit lead th' good dogs when they die?"

Juber answered as he always did, "Ain't that heaven enough for any dawg, always chasin' a big white rabbit that leads him along through prettin' huntin' country?" He saw her in the door and asked, "Delph, it feels like frost in th' cow's teats. What do you think?"

"It looked it in th' sunset," she answered, and knew that he was thinking of the flowers. He stripped Daisy slowly with the absent-minded motions of a man trying hard to make up his mind. At last he said, "You'd better cut 'em, Delph. I reckon their time's come."

It was hardly light enough for walking on strange ground, but the flowers shone faintly as if they had caught a bit of the sunset and would not let it go. In the still air the scent of the chrysanthemums came sharp and stinging like a part of the cold against her face. She liked that sharpness better than the sweetness of roses or of iris. It made her think of spice, and folds of red silk, crisp and rustling, and rich mysterious countries where the ways of life were different from her own.

She cut until her arms were filled, and carried them across the front porch and into the seldom used parlor, and there laid them on the cold hearth by the potted touch-me-nots and maiden hair fern. She shivered and hurried from the ghostly shadowy place with its curious smells of old wood and old horse hair in the sofa. She sometimes thought it was the fault of the parlor and not entirely that of the organ which, no matter how fast she pumped or hard she pounded, could never be made to play a tune livelier than "The Drunkard's Grave."

She ran to cut the cosmos by the well, and the late blooming dahlias and marigolds in the garden, but stopped for a last look at the still, red-flushed sky where one large star looked lost and pale against the angry glow. The one star in the empty, frost-promising sky seemed old and familiar. Last fall she had cut the flowers in a cold clear twilight like this and the fall before, and maybe the fall before that—she couldn't remember. And each time the flowers had made her sad. Next fall she would cut them again, and be sad again, and then the fall after, and on and on. Her grandmother Costello had cut chrysanthemums in this same yard for more than fifty years, the same flowers growing in the same places, and each time she must have thought of the fall before and the fall to come after.

She thought of those others, now dead, and it did not seem that it was she, Delph, who had cut the flowers, but her grandmother, or her great-grandmother, some old, old woman who had lived beyond her time, always here and always cutting flowers that never died, but once between the cuttings she would die. And that would be all.

She whirled and ran blindly through the heavy twilight, but stopped abruptly when she almost ran against John as he came in from the garden with baskets of green tomatoes and peppers. "You scared, Delph?" he asked, and looked down and tried to find her eyes.

She shook her head. "N-o-o. I was just runnin'."

"You sound like you're cryin', Delph," he went on in the gruff tone that was his nearest approach to gentleness.

"A little bit—maybe. It's kind of sad to cut th' flowers—an' a sky like th' one tonight gives me a funny feelin'."

He nodded and looked at the evening sky, then smiled his slow stiff smile. "It does when a body's young," he said. "Used to be when th' older boys had all gone west an' just me an' your gran' parents I'd be like you—lookin' out after them th' way you do on th' high knoll—but you'll get over it," he comforted, and patted her shoulder awkwardly, the only form of caress she could remember ever having had from him.

She went into the house and lighted the parlor lamp with its circles of fat owls on its fat globes, and put the flowers in water. Finished with that she took the county paper, and slipped up the front stairs to her own room; a place that had long scandalized Fronie with its bright cushions and curtains and red hearth rug that gave the old solid black walnut furniture a rakish, tipsy air.

She sat in her red cushioned rocker, and searched through the county paper without reading any of the news until low in one corner of the front page she found an item which she read, then took scissors from the center table and cut it out, after stopping to read it a second time. She didn't know the girl of whom she read; but she was a girl from Fincastle County who had gone away and done something. That was enough. Her name was Minnie Weaver, and she had taken nurse's training at a hospital in Louisville, and had finished second highest in her class, and now had a position in a clinic, the paper said.

Delph went to the marble-topped dresser and from a bottom drawer took a tube of mucilage and scrap book filled with reports of those who had gone away. There were many of them; failures whose going was chronicled once and forgotten; successful ones who became doctors and lawyers and preachers in cities, and wrote letters to the county paper saying how much they would like to visit in "dear old Fincastle County."

First in the scrap book was Samuel Dodson Fairchild, son of Dorie. Tonight, Delph held the page close under the lamp and studied it as she had done many times. The picture was dim and blurred on the cheap paper, beginning to yellow with age, for Fronie, always a great respecter of Dorie, had cut the clipping a long while ago when Delph was too small to think much of such things. Sam looked young, hardly more than a boy, and though his mouth was closed, he seemed to be laughing at something. The puzzle of his laughter would hold her for minutes; she thought sometimes that maybe Azariah had laughed that way when Jane, his wife, had wanted him to settle down and farm. She wished Sam would write a letter to the paper or to the church on some Memorial Day; but she guessed he never would. Among all the names and faces in the scrap book, his she thought had gone the farthest and seen the most. He had been written about in the Lexington papers, too; how smart he was in college, and the scholarship he had won in chemistry—his picture was with that. There was another clipping about his having gone to Heidelberg to study, and a later one saying that he had accepted a position in a small town near New York City.

Chemistry and New York City; they were such exciting words; one, all that was fine in the cities of the earth; the other, name of a mysterious learning of which few in the Little South Fork Country had ever heard, something difficult that only those with brains could learn. She would have studied chemistry, learned at least what it was, could she have taken her last year of high school. Now, most like she would never know. She thought of Marsh; chemistry didn't seem to matter—now.

Fronie called her to supper, and she went down, sorry to leave her room and mingle with the rest of the family; Marsh seemed nearer when she was alone. The talk at supper was mostly of the sharpening cold and coming hard frost, with Fronie planning to make green tomato ketchup from all the odds and ends of green things taken from the garden, while Juber sighed for the Hedrick cane. Hedricks were still at the molasses making, and cold weather had come to catch them with a great mound of cut but unstripped cane.

John set down his coffee cup and looked at Delph. "Permelie was sayin' when I was down at th' store that Hedricks aimed to have a little cane strippin'—sort of—tonight. Whyn't you an' Juber go an' give 'em a hand."

Fronie opened her mouth for disapproval, but closed it again when John continued to Delph, "You ought to be neighborly."

"Standin' out half th' night is liable to give her cold," Fronie objected, while Delph was silent, waiting until they should agree. She didn't care whether she went or stayed. Marsh wouldn't be there. He'd never risk coming on this side of the creek—certainly not to a place like Hedricks' where there were young girls—and old Sil Hedrick hated oil men as much as he hated non-believers in his faith. The people there would look at her, then whisper to each other with their eyes. Some suspected that she met the oil man in the woods. But she wasn't ashamed. She knew she did no wrong.

"Tilly's got a loose shoe, an' I can't go," she suddenly said, after thinking a moment of the eyes.

"You could ride one a th' mules," John insisted, and Fronie wailed, "John, John don't have her doin' that. There's nothin' looks worse or trashier than a woman ridin' a mule. I'd as soon see her on that half wild stallion."

"No woman could ever manage Silver," John said, and Delph was immediately eager to go, rushing upstairs for her wraps, rushing Juber away to the barn the minute he finished his pie and second cup of coffee. When he had saddled the mule he always rode, she pointed to John's heavy saddle and said, "Now put that on Silver."

Juber strangled over the tobacco juice he unexpectedly swallowed. "God, Delph, you can't ride Silver. If he didn't run away an' break your neck—we'd be kilt all th' same by John for lettin' you try it."

She tossed back her hair and reached for the saddle. "I mean to ride him. I thought of it at supper.—Just once in my life I'm goin' to do somethin' I want to do." She lifted the saddle from its peg and staggered under its downdropping weight. Juber hurried forward and took it, but when he turned to rehang it on the wall, she caught his wrist and repeated through set teeth, "Juber, I said saddle Silver."

He stopped and studied her, then slowly took the saddle from the wall, and sighed,—"Delph, it's a mighty good thing you didn't live back in th' old days. They'd a hung you for a witch sure from seein' th' hell fire a blazin' in your eyes."

She laughed at that and spun on her toes. "It'll be fun ridin' Silver, jumpin' him over Hedricks' five barred gate like I've always wanted to."

"Your wild ways 'ull be th' death a you," he said, and hesitated like a man caught between two fires. "Delph, please—he's hard mouthed as a mule an wild as a buck in th' spring—Jumpin' over little ditches 'stead a steppin'. Why, you know I'd never risk him myself."

"You're you an' I'm me," she said, and pushed him playfully toward Silver's stall. "We'd better be goin' 'fore Uncle John comes out to make his round a th' barn. I'll watch an' if I hear him I'll whistle."

Juber came at last; his hat off and his usually smooth hair in uneasy rings and strands, and his shirt tail pulled out from his overalls by his strainings and strivings to get the big horse saddled. Delph had to laugh at Juber. It was more as if Silver led Juber than the other way around, for though Juber came with one hand on Silver's throat latch and the other on his cheek strap, the rearing plunges of the white stallion lifted him now and again from the ground. Delph's eyes glistened as she looked at Silver, seeming bigger and whiter and wilder than ever by moonlight. She watched the drawing in and out of his nostrils, the cold fire flash of his eyes, then called to Juber, "Wait," and ran and opened the big road gate, and came running back, laughing, flinging her hat over Juber's bare head. Silver plunged and snorted at the hat falling so near his nose. "Snort on," Delph said, and caught the pommel of the saddle. Silver shied away in a rearing plunge, but Delph leaped, and clung, one foot in the stirrup and the other, careless of her flying skirts, cutting a wide arc in the air.

Then she was on and saying to Juber, "Give him his head," but Juber clung to the bridle and moaned, "God you'll never manage him, Delph. Try to wait for me."

"I don't mean to manage him," she said, and jerked the bridle free. They were away then, through the gate and down and around the hill.

It was dark on the hill road, but Silver was never one to be afraid of the dark. The great horse seemed a part of herself, something that felt the promise of change in the frosty cold, felt the foolish hurt and sorrow at the death of the flowers, saw life as a long straight road through a prison yard with a door marked death at the end, and the door a stranger, brighter thing than the road; and so they would run away from it all.

His iron shoes rang sharp and clear on the rocky road like bells in the frosty air. Now and then he favored the edge of the road, but Delph crouched low in the saddle and only laughed when the beech boughs whipped through her hair and pulled the smooth neat braids out of place. They reached the floor of the valley and rode between John's fields of bottom land corn where the great fodder shocks stood like fat contented men, each with a round of black shadow like a carpet by his feet.

They forded the creek with no foolishness and no lagging back, but plunging right in, never minding the showers of flying drops and spray from Silver's hearty lunge.

Delph drew her breath in a long happy sigh when they had crossed the creek, and reached the valley road that lay empty and white and smooth like a challenge to Silver to show what he could do. She had no switch, but when she dug her heels into his sides that was enough. He took the bit in his teeth and ran, stretched his neck and lengthened his stride, until Delph felt the night wind whistle by her ears and Silver's flying mane tangle with her own hair and lash against her face. And the shadows of the trees that grew along the road seemed flying bands of darkness, no sooner in her eyes than gone.

She wished the road would last forever, or that she could follow it to some new strange place where all would not know her as Delphine Costello, the only Costello, save John, who hadn't gone away, but one that would go when she was twenty-one and so run no risk of being brought back. Still, the ending of the road was pleasant to think upon. At least she could jump the Hedrick gate before she went to work quietly with the others about the bonfires among the piles of cane.

She wondered a moment if she could turn Silver into Hedrick's lane, or maybe he would go dashing on, over the bridge and past Mrs. Crouch's store. She wondered if he would really jump the gate or shy and whirl away when he came upon it, or maybe stop suddenly and fling her over his head. But whatever he did, she didn't mind. They neared the lane, and from somewhere near the end and by the gate, a horse neighed loudly in greeting, and Silver turned as if by his own free will.

Delph could not bother to wonder over the horse by the lane; its neigh had a familiar sound. The gate was there, rising dim from the shadow of a walnut tree by it. She lifted the reins and leaned back low in the saddle, and for a split second Silver seemed to hesitate, then she felt him rise as if he flew, and it was fun to see the gate flying under her, and then the black shadow of it, rising as if to strike her. She felt the shock of his landing, and there was a moment when he wavered as if he would pitch on his knees, then he was up and she had an instant's taste of triumph in knowing she had jumped the five barred gate.

The white back of a badly frightened cow loomed suddenly under Silver's nose. He snorted and whirled and bucked like a thing gone mad and flung Delph from him as easily as he had cleared the gate, then circled wildly about the barn. Delph landed cat-like with both feet on the ground, and stood looking dazedly after Silver and was unable to answer Marsh's frantic calls from Jude by the lane, "Delph, you all right? Delph?"

He swore at the tricky gate, mastered it at last, and rushed through, leaving the gate to swing free. He glanced wildly about the barnyard, until Delph found her tongue at last, and said, still looking after Silver, "He—he got away."

Marsh ran to her and caught her shoulders, still asking, "You hurt, Delph?"

She laughed to hear the old man terror in his voice, afraid for her as Juber was afraid. "Delph, I thought you'd broke your fool neck," he whispered, and all at once she felt weak and timid, glad Silver had not broken her neck, almost afraid to ride him again. Marsh was kissing her, and his kiss more than the wild free ride on Silver cleared all sorrow and hunger and emptiness from the world. She was still a moment in his arms, then struggling, laughing, remembering in a thousand ways that she was young and strong, and life was good.

"You'd better go shut th' gate," she said, and teased, "Th' Hedrick cows are all runnin' down th' lane."

He looked over his shoulder, but did not move. "If there's cows in th' lane, they're colored like th' wind," he answered, and turned back to her.

"What is a wind colored cow?" she asked, and knew she must send him after Silver, but wanted this bit of time so close with him to last a moment longer.

He smiled at her, but with something stern and sober in his smile with his eyes black in the moonlight, and his chin outlined sharply like a chin cut in stone. "It's th' kind a cows my people had. My father had a sayin', 'Our fine blue-blooded horses an' our big fine cows are in our big fine barn but they're colored like th' wind—.' What in th' hell do they mean lettin' you ride a horse like Silver?"

She laughed and tried to draw away. "I just rode him—for fun."

"Promise me you'll not be up to such foolishness again," he begged, and gave her hands a gentle shake.

She smiled at that. "I hate promises.—Think if I'd promised th' church an' joined. I could never a run away to that dance."

"You're stubborn," he said, and kissed her again, then turned quickly away after Silver, who was at the other end of the barn, quietly helping himself to fodder intended for the Hedrick cows, no longer frightened as he had pretended to be, but suddenly tired and tame.

Since it would never have done for Delph to ride alone to the cane field, a good half mile away, and since Marsh could not take her there, the only thing that they could do was sit on a shadowy corner of the fence and wait for Juber. It was some few moments before Marsh recovered his wits enough to remember his reason for coming. He burst out with it while Delph was laughing at his cunning in persuading Mrs. Crouch to persuade John to send Delph down to Hedrick's. "I won't be goin' away 'til spring, Delph," he said, and added confusedly, "I—I thought you'd like to know."

All Delph's fear of a long quiet winter dissolved like mists before a sun. She was quick to reassure him when he spoke of doubts that his was the proper plan. He had asked for and been given the job of pumping and looking after the wells drilled during the summer. The pay would be small, good enough for some, but little compared to what he had been making; still, he would have plenty of time left for doing all the things he liked to do—especially for exercising Jude in the woods, he whispered to Delph.

She was of the opinion that Tilly would profit by long winter rides over near the wells, but thought that maybe at least by Christmas Time she could persuade John to let Marsh come visiting her as Logan had.

· 5 ·

THE COLD snap that Juber said had come only to ripen the corn was past. It was November, a time of leafless trees and languid yellow light falling lazily onto the hills that lay as if asleep under a faint blue veil of smoke. The sun seemed slyly dying day by day, the flaming dawns of early fall were gone, and in their place came the sunrise, pale blue and gold; sad it seemed to Delph. The sunsets, too, were dull and dead, endless banks of clouds above the rows of marching hills.

There were long days of slow cold rain that never sang or hummed like the spring rains or summer thunder showers, but fell straight down with a lifeless regularity that changed the barnyard and the bottom fields into seas of mud and left the last of the yellow beech and poplar leaves gray and flat and sodden. Delph had always loved the rain; had liked to see it ride over the hills, and enjoyed the bit of variety it added to the weather, but now she hated it. Rainy days could not be brightened by thoughts of a chance meeting with Marsh. Fronie would have been scandalized at the thought of any woman walking or riding in the rain just for the walk or the ride. It was bad enough for Delph to ride about so much on fair days, but to have let her go off in the rain would have set all the neighbors talking.

So Delph sat by the fire and sewed, or rummaged in her own room trying to find a book she had not read, or spent long minutes by her front room window that opened on a wide view of the hills. She knew she could not see Marsh through the walls of mist and rain that wrapped the Little South Fork Country, but he seemed nearer when she stood by the window than when she sat by the fire.

Fronie found her so early one afternoon, and grumbled at her lazy, day-dreaming ways, and wondered why she didn't read a good book or some of Tennyson's poems or sew. "Why don't you get out that dress pattern a blue wool John bought last time he was in Town. It'll be mighty becomin' to you."

"What's th' good a lookin' pretty here?" Delph answered shortly, and Fronie turned away in disgust.

When her aunt had gone, she walked restlessly about, took books from their shelves by the bed, opened first one and then another and returned each to its place; they were all so old, so solid, smelling of dust and saddle leather and she had read them all, just as her grandfather before her had read them; Thackeray, Emerson, Swedenborg, W. O. Barnes. She stopped and looked at a dog-eared copy of Tennyson, once the property of her mother. She opened the book, and the pages fell apart to a much thumbed spot, and she read:

> On either side the river lie
> Long fields of barley and of rye,
> That clothe the world and meet the sky;
> And thro' the field the road runs by
>   To many-tower'd Camelot;
> And up and down the people go,

She closed the book swiftly and shoved it on the shelf. She would never be a Lady of Shalott, feeding herself on pictures when just past her was the world.

She went to the window that opened on the side yard, and opened it and leaned far out, and let the rain fall on her hair, then turned and let the drops strike her face and splash into her eyes. She amused herself a moment with staring up into the sky; a thing she had done as a child when she had stood on tiptoe and strained her eyes until the blue glimmered like mother-of-pearl, and still there was never that finding of the top of the sky. Juber and Old Willie had used to tell her stories of the beings who lived there, and she had believed and gone hunting the top of the sky.

"Hey, Delph."

She turned quickly and waved to Juber calling from the barnyard. "You workin' hard, Delph?" he asked, cupping his hands and seeming eager to make himself heard by her alone.

She shook her head and dropped her hands to show their emptiness. "Come out to th' barn. I've got somethin' to show you," he called in the same guarded way.

She threw an old coat about her shoulders and tip-toed down the back stairs and through the empty kitchen. "It's come," Juber cried when she came up to him. He hugged his jumper about his meager chest and smiled a delighted unbelieving smile.

"What's come?" she asked, and teasingly tried to pull open his tightly clasped jumper.

"Don't tell me now you don't recollect when you made out th' order an all. It's th' book of song ballads we ordered with thirty-five cents an' coffee coupons. Recollect? I'd give it up for lost. It's got 'Lorena' an' 'Frankie an' Johnnie.'" He opened his jumper slightly. "Look, a finer lookin' book you never saw, all covered in yeller paper—but I dasn't take it out here in th' rain. Soon's th' mail come in Permelie sent it up to me. Wasn't that nice a her?"

"Who brought it?"

He smiled slyly. "That oil man. He's at th' other end a th' barn now tryin' to count Linnie's pigs.—Wait don't go runnin' away. Soon's I git in th' dry I'll let you see.—I want you to hum some a these fer me while I try to foller 'em on my fiddle."

"Come on, I'll hum," she called over her shoulder, but Juber, all forgetful of the rain, came walking on with his eyes on the book and could not keep up with her.

She tip-toed down the long barn hall, noiselessly opened the stable door that led to Linnie's pen. She saw Marsh with his hat pushed to the back of his head, and his elbows on the low partition separating the sty from the rest of the stable. He had a big white ear of corn in his hands from which now and then he shelled a few grains and flung them into the pen. He and Linnie seemed to have been having a quarrel. The great sow lay and looked at him and batted her eyes and grunted now and then in a half quarrelsome, half contented sort of way, as if to say she would continue to quarrel if he wished, but it was useless because she had the best of him.

He flung another handful of grain enticingly near her nose, and tried again. "Come on, Linnie, roll over, get up, move. I want to count your pigs," but Linnie only grunted again, more agreeably than before. Her pigs except two that tried in vain to reach her teats lay sleeping at her sides with their black noses, black feet and white tails so tangled and mixed that there was no counting them, "There's twelve," Delph called, and both Marsh and Linnie jumped and looked in her direction.

Marsh hurried forward, but guiltily, as if half afraid that Delph would scold him. "You don't mind—just this once, comin' to your house. Permelie would have me bring Juber's song book—an' so I thought I'd wait a spell in th' barn till th' rain slacked. They surely won't mind—this once," he begged, and came and caught her hands.

"They'll never know," she said, and felt his hands and wondered how it was that a few minutes ago the day had been dull. "It was nice of you to bring Juber's song book," she went on, when it seemed that they had stood too long silent, saying things with their eyes that neither of them would ever put into words.

"I asked her to.—There's somethin' I wanted to tell you, Delph."

"Logan after you?" she asked quickly.

He shook his head. "No worse'n common, I guess, but—."

Roll me over gently, roll me over slow,
Roll me over on my right side
Cause my left side hurts me so.

"How's that, Delph? I was never any hand at readin' notes," Juber explained as he stuck his head through the door. He looked at Linnie, closed his eyes, and marking the time with his right forefinger, continued to sing in his cracked old man's voice:

With the first shot Johnny staggered, with the second shot he
    fell,
When the last bullet got him there was a new man's face in hell.
He was her man, but he—

Delph caught his sleeve, and silenced him with a shushing. "You'd better not sing so loud. You know Aunt Fronie wouldn't like that song."

"It's a good song ballad, an' your Aunt Fronie knows I sing what I please in th' barn. Look, it's better even than I thought it would be. Notes it's got an' ever'thing." He wetted the tip of his thumb and pushed rapidly through the pages. "Look here's 'Shady Grove' an' 'Two Little Girls in Blue.' Lord, I wish I had time to fiddle that right now."

"If you'd go soft an' easy-like Fronie would never hear. Take time," Delph suggested. "There can't be any press of work in all this weather."

"There's loggin' harness to mend. Me an' John'ull be needin' it th' first hard freeze that comes."

"I've nothin' to do today. Let me mend harness, an' you fiddle, an' Delph can sing," Marsh said. He looked up at the hay loft and then at Delph. "It would be nice to be up there."

Delph hesitated, eager to be with Marsh, but afraid that John might come and find him. "Fronie wouldn't like it so well."

"She'll never know. Have a little fun before you die, Delph," Juber advised. "I'll play soft like an' you sing low. If she hears anything she'll think it's th' ghost of crazy Aunt Rhodie Weaver out agin an' singin' in th' rain. Look, here's 'Birmingham Jail.' I tell ye this book's got ever'thing." And Juber went humming away to get the logging harness and awl and leather thongs for mending. Delph wished Juber would not dart about so, and she and Marsh could be alone at least until she learned what troubled him, but Juber was back in a moment, reminding her to bring his fiddle from the crib wall.

They sat at the end of the hay mow farthest from the house, near a small window, high up under the eaves, through which enough of the rain gray light filtered for Juber to see to fiddle and Marsh to mend the harness. The hay was clover mixed with red top and timothy, unbaled and bright with a clean fresh smell that made Marsh think of a windy night in spring. The harness mending went slowly, often with little help from either his mind or his eyes. He saw Delph smile and heard her sing, softly with notes that seemed scarcely louder than the rain on the roof shingles. Juber was eager to try all the ballads in the book, so that she was kept skipping from one to another, patiently humming or singing a verse until Juber could follow it on his fiddle.

Now and then her eyes strayed into Marsh's, and begged to know what it was he had intended to tell her. Marsh would smile back, and try to reassure her that it was nothing very bad, but mostly he tried to avoid her glance for his eyes seemed no good at lying today. When Delph had sung until her throat was tired, Juber commanded a rest. "You two've been mighty good to me," he said.

"Marsh mends my harness an' Delph sings my songs, so I'll give you all a special treat—but first you'll have to hunt it in th' hay."

"A hen's nest with twenty eggs, I bet," Delph said, and sprang to her feet.

Juber shook his head, but Delph went hunting through the hay. Marsh dropped the harness mending and followed her. When there was a mound of hay like a mountain between them and Juber, he kissed her as she knelt searching elbow deep in the hay. He saw her eyes for an instant before she sprang up and started away, and he was less afraid to tell her what he had come to tell. "Don't run away, Delph," he whispered.

She stopped, but would not look at him. "Is—is that what you wanted to tell me?"

He flicked a dried clover blossom from her hair. "Somethin' like that," he said, and was silent then while he thought so hard on what he must say that he could not bother with words.

Delph felt his eyes caressing her face, looked up to meet them, and then looked quickly away. His eyes were gray and soft, shining in the shadowless rain gray light, but they were not happy eyes; and when she had looked at them a moment she knew what he had come to say. She heard the rain fall on the roof with a heavy leaden sound, and the coldness of it touched her as if she had stood naked under it. She drew a long shivering breath, clasped and unclasped her hands; looked at them while she said with more simple statement than question, "You're goin' away—soon, I mean."

He nodded. "It's partly Logan's doin'. He's a friend or kin of th' man that gave me th' pumpin' job.—Now they're givin' it to Logan's brother."

She tried to smile, but her mouth felt tight and cold. "Spring come—you'd a gone then anyhow—maybe—maybe—pshaw, I guess it's better that you go now before—before—."

"Before what, Delph?"

Her throat hurt, and she didn't want to talk. "Nothin'—th' longer you stay th' worse it would be—your goin' away I mean." She flushed at her loose-tongued, begging ways, and stood staring at one of her feet half hidden in the hay. She felt something on her cheek, and knew it was a tear, and feared to raise her hand and brush it off. He would notice her hand quicker than the tear.

"Delph,—I've been thinkin'." He stopped because he didn't know what he had been thinking. All his thoughts could not change the two facts in his head; he could not forget Delph wherever he went, and he couldn't offer her the life the oil fields had to give.

The first tear fell on her sleeve, and he watched another take its place. He stepped nearer and put his arm around her shoulder. "Delph, I didn't come to make you cry."

"I—I'm not cryin'," she said, but would not lift her head.

"Delph—you've said lots of times you'd like to go away."

She nodded. "Always."

"Delph?"

"Yes."

"Would you be afraid to—?"

She waited and when he did not finish, only stood with his arm tightening about her, she asked in a low voice, "Of what?"

"It's hard to say. You're not very old—hardly eighteen. An' I guess you know me so little an' my people—they were—are renters—scattered now—with no land a their own—different from you an' yours, but maybe all th' same in their bones. They didn't want to be always on th' move.—But, Delph, there's no harm in tryin'. I didn't mean to when I come—exactly. I ought to keep still."

"Why?" she asked still more softly.

"Because—I can't ever forget you, Delph, an' it oughtn't to be like that. I mean I oughtn't to."

"An' is it a sin for you to like me?" she asked in a choked, half audible voice.

His tongue fumbled with words, and he shook his head impatiently. "No—but in a way—I guess it's like I'm already married except I'm not. But—oh, hell—Delph, would you marry me an' maybe go away from here an' not be afraid?"

"Why would I be afraid?"

"You know me so little—but would you?"

She moved her lips and wondered if he heard her "Yes," and knew as his body touched her body. "You wouldn't ever be afraid or sorry maybe, Delph?"

She put her hands on his shoulders and looked at him. "No. I wouldn't be—ever."

He drew her suddenly tight against him. "Delph—please, are

you certain? I mean—it maybe won't be easy. I've nothin' much to give. Different from what you've always had, an' hard, too, maybe."

She smiled, and her eyes were free of doubt. "I wouldn't mind—anything," she said, slowly as if she understood what it was she said. She struggled suddenly away like a frightened bird when Juber's voice came calling, "Come on back, you two. You'll never find 'em way over there."

"Wait, Delph," Marsh begged. "There's somethin' else. I—well you see I want to do it right—th' way a man here would do—so I mean to tell your Uncle John, ask him decent like."

She turned on him with frightened eyes. "Marsh, he'd never give his say. All at once, I mean. I could tell him—little by little an'—."

He frowned. "There'll maybe be no time for little by little. I finish my last shootin' job, next Thursday, an' then I'll speak to him."

Juber was calling again, more loudly than before. Delph in a flurry of fear that Fronie would hear, started over the hay, whispering breathlessly, "Marsh, please don't say a word. He'd say things to maybe make you hate him—he's quick tempered. Why, he wouldn't a let me a thought of—bein' engaged to Logan for a good while. Don't say anything."

"I won't go sneakin' around like a leper," he muttered, with his jaw looking hard, and his eyes turning black. "I'm not afraid of him."

She caught his sleeve, as Juber called again. "I know you're not—not afraid of anything—but wait—he's in a bad humor now over th' elections. At least wait till you're all ready to leave," she finished quickly.

Marsh chewed a strand of clover and considered. "All right—I'll shoot my last well next Thursday—but I'll ask him that very day."

Delph gave a little moaning shiver. "I wish you wouldn't. He'll have a fit."

"He won't kill me," he said, and laughed and caught her hand, then forgot to drop it when they came within sight of Juber, who smiled on then unsuspiciously, and scolded, "I never thought you'd take th' business so serus like an' go pokin' around like it's gold you're after. I've found 'em already."

Delph had scarcely a glance for the hired man's gift of pears nested in the hay. Juber took his pocket knife, and started a neat spiral of yellow peel, talking all the while. "Frum th' way Fronie took on when she couldn't find 'em in th' cellar, you'd a thought they was pure gold. She was a savin' 'em fer th' preacher's next fifth Sunday meetin', but there's nothin' Tilly likes so much as a good juicy pear all peeled an' quartered so she won't choke herself. I've got a bushel a th' finest winesap apples I could find put away fer th' others, an' Fronie an' Nance th'd die if they knowed it, but Delph here she's a good girl, an' won't let on. Will you, Delph?" he asked and lifted his head and looked at her.

"Oh, yes," Delph answered, and sat down on the hay and picked up the song book, and began to turn quickly through it.

Juber sat with his peeling-curled knife suspended above the pear, and looked at her. "What you mean, Delph, sayin' you'll give me away? What's th' matter anyhow? You seem plum out a breath an' all excited like frum huntin' in th' hay, with your ears red as fire."

"It's this new song ballad book," she said, and would not look at him when he handed her the pear, ready-peeled to eat, but reached her hand and took it blindly.

Juber glanced at Marsh sitting with his head slightly bent and his eyes on the pear he peeled. "You take mighty thick choppy peelin's to be such a savin' sort of man," he said.

Marsh continued to peel away as if he had not heard. Juber studied him a time, then looked at Delph, sitting too still, not eating, not reading, just sitting with a bite of untasted pear in her mouth and juice dribbling down her chin. "Don't you like Tilly's pears, Delph?" he asked.

"Yes, oh, yes," she said, and the song book slipped from her hands into her lap while she sat hugging her knees and smiling at the hay.

"I can see it's mighty sweet in your mouth," he said, slowly, and with a curious sorrow like a leave taking in his voice, that made him seem tired and old. Neither noticed when he took his fiddle and crawled up over the hay to the small window. Rain splashed against the panes, and the hills and creek bottoms and trees and fields seen through the rain wet glass looked crumpled and gray. He leaned his back against the barn wall, and with his head almost touching the rafters began to play softly:

I never knew what true love meant
Till I courted in the rain.

Marsh heard the tune, and smiled at Juber in understanding, and came and sat with him. But he was restless, fingering the hay, looking sometimes at Delph, then again at him. "Could I open th' window a little, or would th' dampness hurt your fiddle?" he asked after a time, and when Juber nodded, he unhooked the latch and propped the window open with a twist of hay.

The rain smell and the earth smell came sharp and clean. Juber paused in his fiddling, and drew a deep breath and said, "It makes a body think a spring an' plantin' time."

"Yes, it does," Marsh said, and looked at Delph, and begged her with his eyes to come sit by him.

She came, and smiled at Juber's song, but when he asked her to sing it, she flushed, and seemed suddenly the way Fronie would have her be—shy, and still, and with the wonder of some great understanding wide in her eyes. "I wouldn't sing it, either," Juber said. "Anyhow not th' part that says:

I never knew what trouble meant
Till I courted in the rain.

· 6 ·

JUDE'S FEET rang loud and hollow on the frozen road, and Marsh as he topped the hill saw the post office, wished he had not hurried so. John would most likely be there instead of home. At least he would have to stop and see; for it was Thursday afternoon, and he had finished his last well. He hitched Jude to the low limb of a sycamore near the creek, and paused and stroked the horse's shoulders, slowly with hard, heavy strokes. Jude turned and looked at him, and he asked softly, "What if he's in there, an' I ask him, an' he won't give in?"

Jude arched his neck, and gave a windy snort that was like a laugh to all the world. "You mean you'd take her anyhow, or do you mean I'm a fool for even thinkin' on it?" Marsh asked, but turned away without giving Jude time to answer.

He walked on, under the leafless beech trees and up the porch steps, encrusted with frozen tobacco juice and frozen mud. He heard men's voices on the other side of the plank door, easy and pleasant they seemed to be, but quiet and contained, hill voices under the pleasantness.

He pushed open the door and was still a moment, hunting out first one face and then another in the smoke filled twilight of the room. The conversation stopped abruptly while men craned their heads to look at him. Young Willie Copenhaver, sitting on an upturned dynamite box, called a greeting, and so did some of the others, but most, including John Costello, simply glanced at him, in brief appraising silence.

Mrs. Crouch came from between the curtains that separated her living quarters from the store, and called, "There's nothin' there for you to set on. Come an' take this chair."

"I won't be but a little while an' I'd just as soon stand," he said, but as she started with the chair he went back to her.

She seemed to have forgotten the chair, but stood fingering the curtain and looking past him at the crowd. "I wouldn't speak to John," she said. "Delph told me you had it in your head, but you'd better write him a letter."

"I want to do it right—th' way a man here would do it," he answered.

She continued to look past him and frown, then said resignedly, "Talk if you will, but I'm tellin' you he'll fly to pieces. You'd better do it outside. I'm not wantin' trouble here on gov'ment property.— That's one a Logan's brothers a settin' close to John. Don't be lookin' around now." She sighed and smoothed her apron, then smiled at him. "Lord, but you're like my boy Les. How that child did love trouble.—If I was religious I'd pray for you, I reckin. You'll need a lot of prayers I'm thinkin'." But she looked at him as if she thought he might get by without her prayers.

"Thanks," he whispered, and turned away, but a shrilly whispered, "Lord, you've forgot your chair," caused him to turn and seize the chair in some confusion. The men were watching him now. He felt their eyes slip away from his face when he walked up and sat down near Willie Copenhaver and on the other side of the stove from John.

He sat still, trying to hold the words he had gathered neat and straight in his head, but they kept slipping away, scattered by the bits of conversation he heard, mostly on the tobacco market, just opening at Lexington. He heard John's deep, almost toneless, voice. "Me, I'd never fool with tobacco. It's too much like gamblin'."

Sil Hedrick nodded, spat into the stove hearth, then turned to John and answered, "Last year white burley brought next to nothin'. This year them that has a good crop will be gettin' rich."

Young Willie Copenhaver pulled a square of mahogany colored chewing tobacco from his jumper pocket, cut a fair sized plug, and offered knife and tobacco to Marsh. "Chew?" he asked.

Marsh shook his head. "You don't smoke neither," Willie observed.

Marsh shook his head, more impatiently, and sat forward on the edge of his chair in order to see around the stove to John and the Ragan boy. Willie nudged him again. "You'd better take a chew a my tobacco. It's home made, ever' leaf smeared with honey and sprinkled with whiskey 'fore it was pressed more'n a year ago. One chew 'ud put heart in a daid corpse."

"I've got heart a plenty an' to spare," Marsh said under some booming talk of Sil Hedrick's.

Willie nodded toward John. "You'll need heart an' more when you talk with him—like I think you're aimin' to."

Marsh looked into Willie's eyes, then glanced slowly over the faces of the other men on his side of the stove. Some looked at him, and some looked carefully past him, but in all the faces there was the same thing, a look of expectancy and of non-committal silence. Logan's younger brother flicked him with his eyes, then glanced at the busily talking John, and smiled, a slow secretive sort of smile. Marsh saw Sil Hedrick shift uneasily in his chair, glance in his direction, then back at John, absorbed still in the talk, and gesticulating with his pipe. It seemed that John, alone of all the company, was ignorant of what had been shaping between the oil man and his niece through the summer and the fall.

Marsh got up and went to the other side of the stove, and stood with his back to the fire directly in front of John, and looked at him in the hope of catching his eye. When at last it seemed that every man in the room sat holding his breath and waiting, except John, the Ragan boy yawned with a lusty stretching and said, "This place is makin' me sleepy. I think I'll be gettin' up th' road." He looked at John, and asked with undue loudness, "Comin' along, Mr. Costello?—I think this oil man here wants a word with you."

John glanced at Marsh, puffed once on his pipe, took it from between his teeth, and asked, "Is it your team you're wantin' to sell me?—I've heared you're leavin' th' country."

"No. I'm not ready to sell my horses."

John puffed his pipe again, blew out a slow drift of smoke, and considered Marsh with his calm eyes. "What is it then?"

"I'd rather speak to you outside."

"Trouble?—If it's come to a scrap with Logan Ragan I'm no hand at takin' sides," John said, and looked neither troubled nor inquisitive, only dead calm, with his eyes cold as quartz in a frosty moonlight.

Marsh stiffened his shoulders, and stood more on his heels than his toes. "I was never one for makin' after help in trouble—that is fightin' trouble."

John continued to study him. "You look like you might be in trouble now—or mebbe drinkin' from th' shine of your eyes.—Speak up, these men are my neighbors. I've been with 'em all my life."

"I'm dead sober, but—please—I'd take it as a favor if you'd step outside a minute.—That is if you're not afraid."

"I don't know what you're drivin' at, but least way it'll do no harm, since you ask me civil like," John said, and got up and came and knocked his pipe against the stove hearth.

In the room of silent, watching men, the sound was like a loud clanging. Marsh jerked his head in a startled way, and the Ragan boy laughed and said in a low voice, but loud enough for him to hear, "Whatever th' oil man's business is, it's a makin' him nervous."

Marsh glanced back and saw Young Willie watching him, and then Mrs. Crouch twitching at the curtain and following him with her eyes. He opened the door, and John inclined his head slightly and said, "After you, Sir."

He led the way to the end of the porch and down the steps, but John halted on the top step and said, "Whatever your business is, it can't be so private but that this is far enough to go.—Well?"

Marsh struck the palm of one hand with the fist of the other, looked first at the ground, then up at John. "It's—it's about Delph."

John's Adam's apple jumped as if it had a will of its own, and his eyes lost their look of fixed calm. "Delph?"

"Yes."

"Why in thunder would you be talkin' to me about Delph?—You wantin' to come courtin' her one a these days. Is that what you're after?"

"N-o-o. Yes. I mean—I mean I'm askin' for her."

"Askin' for her?" John's pipe clattered to the floor, but he did not stoop to pick it up.

Marsh nodded. "Yes. I mean to marry her."

"You—you mean you're standin' there askin' me to let you marry Delph? Why—why you hardly know th' child."

"I know her better than you think."

There were four steps to the ground and John covered them in a stride. "What—what you mean you know her?"

Marsh slanted his hat to the bridge of his nose, and looked at the top button of John's shirt. John stood six feet three, and he'd be damned if he'd crane his head to look into his eyes. "What I say. I'd like to marry her. I thought I'd ask you decent like an' civil."

"Decent like an' civil—you—you good for nothin' trollopin' jack ass—you—you don't know th' meanin' of such words."

"I'm civil else I'd knock you down—now."

"You'll mebbe knock me down—I'm not sayin' you couldn't— you've got a chest like a rock breakin' convict's—but by God get this straight—I'll be th' last man you'll ever knock down. Civil? Does a man come askin' for a woman like a youngen out to bag a sack a meal. You could ha come to my house, like a honest man, dressed decent, stead a comin' in your filthy oil clothes, callin' me out from th' store an' talkin' such matters over in th' road. If it's jokin' you be, it's a poor joke."

"I never make jokes."

"More's th' pity. It's Delph I'm thinkin' on. I know she's full a foolish notions, but she shorely didn't put this in your head."

"I can't say that she did," Marsh answered, and waited. When John said nothing more and seemed ready to turn away, he went on. "I'd like your answer."

"You fool, you know what th' answer'ull be. I'd rather see her stretched dead in her coffin than married to th' likes a you, a man she don't know. You've mebbe got half a dozen wives for all I know. Not a roof to take her to, no job either—from what I've heared."

Marsh tried to keep his tongue civil in spite of the hot blood pounding in his ears. "I can get a job long as oil comes out a th' ground.—An' I've got money saved. Not so much as I'd ought—but more'n most."

"Money?" John spat the word in his face. "Money in th' bank never yet kept a man from bein' low down white trash. You can't buy her a decent name, or a place in th' world. You can't give her a thing she's not got already."

"I've seen better satisfied."

John snorted. "She's got a mind like a April wind. It's not been three months since she was dykin' herself out for Logan, then she was beggin' to go to school. Now, she thinks she maybe wants to marry you, an' spend her days gallivantin' over th' country or livin' in some tin roofed oil shanty."

"She'll not spend her days like that. I'll—"

"You don't know what you'll do. You'll have to go where a job takes you. An' one thing's certain. You'll never settle down. It's not in th' likes a you.—An' another thing is—I'd cut my tongue out 'fore I'd give my leave to this."

"That's all I wanted to know."

John took a step backward, looked straight into Marsh's eyes, and emphasized his words with short hard strokes of his hand. "Recollect, I've got th' say over her 'til she's twenty-one. An' if I see hide or hair a you about my place there'll be trouble. Recollect?"

"I'll recollect," Marsh said, and turned and walked rapidly toward Jude. He looked down, and saw his clenched hands, the knuckles blue and the fingers blue white. He stopped suddenly, torn by a hot wish to run back, knock John Costello down, choke him, break his nose, and blacken his eyes. An oil man with maybe half a dozen wives, and he'd never settle down.

He sprang on Jude, and the big horse, mettlesome from standing in the cold, swung away in a hard gallop. He heard the planks of the bridge ring under the horse's feet, and knew he was going to see Delph, John or no John. He wondered if he were riding in the wrong or right direction. He looked back once and saw a crowd on the porch, centered about John who stood stiff and straight like a man cut in stone with his eyes bright blue and burning in a face bleached with anger. "You'd never catch up on a mule," he heard Young Willie say, and he thought there was satisfaction in Young Willie's voice. He saw Mrs. Crouch in the door gaping after him. She looked immensely tall and wide as she stood on the sill higher than the porch. She smiled over the heads of the men, and made a shooing motion with her blue checked apron, as if he were some stray chicken to be hurried out of danger.

He rode on then, and did not stop to see if any followed. Jude's breath came in gasping heaves when they stopped at last by Costello's barnyard gate. Juber saw him and came quickly from the barn hall, and opened the gate and looked at him with troubled eyes. "I see you've asked," he said. "You're too quick like an' triggery to ever get along with people. You had ought to a handled John like a gun shy dawg, 'stead a that you must go bustin' down soon's you finished your work, I reckin."

Marsh dismounted and led the overly hot Jude to the shelter of the barn. "Mebbe John was civil when I talked to him," he said.

Juber shook his head. "Aye, God I can see th' treatment he give ye. It's writ plain on your mouth, an' your eyes black as coals. You come ridin' like a wild man with your chin all stuck out.—Delph's gone to hunt th' cows right now, an' to my mind you'd better speak a word with her an' let your horse rest a bit, an' then be gittin' out a this country—fer a spell at least."

Marsh turned away to go for Delph, but Juber halted him. "You'd better wait right here in th' barn," he said. "They can see ye on the hill from th' house. If she don't come pretty quick, I'll call her," he promised, and handed Marsh a grass sack to rub the mud and creek water from Jude. The old man went away, and except for Jude's breathing the great barn was still. Outside, the early autumn twilight was coming down in a slow gathering darkness like blue gray smoke dropping unseen out of the sky. High up in the pasture he heard the cow bells, and then Delph's calling, "S-u-u-uke, Bessie, s-u-u-uke," in high long notes, that rose and rose like birds crying above the hills.

Bessie must have heard and come for the call was not repeated. He watched through the wide barn door and saw soon the cows, and then Delph with a long switch in her hand walking behind. She stopped at the highest spot on the hill, and stood with head lifted and searching as if she hunted in the sky. The cows reached the barn lane, and began an impatient jangling of their bells, and still she stood, straight and sharp and dark, like a thing rooted in the ground and growing up against the sky.

Juber called her at last. Marsh saw the startled movement of her body, and wondered if the thoughts and dreams that held her so had been centered about him or the bright heaven built on poetry and women's magazines she called the world.

She ran down the hill and opened the pasture gate. The cows and yearlings pushed impatiently through, but it was not until she had closed the gate and given the always lagging Bessie a light cut with her switch, that she saw him impatiently hiding in the doorway of the barn. She dropped the switch and ran to him past the ambling cows. "I never thought you'd come so soon," she said, and caught his outstretched hands.

"Your uncle almost got me down," he whispered, and tried to smile.

"I was worried," she answered, and when he looked at her he knew her thoughts on the hill had been for him. Maybe it was because her cheeks were red from the cold or because of the dusky light in the barn hall, but her eyes seemed brighter, a burning blue like a high October sky at noon; eyes that would never be afraid.

"John will mebbe try to make you change your mind," he warned.

She smiled at his foolish doubting ways. "He'd have to kill me first," she said, and flung up her head. She was silent a moment with her smile slowly fading. She buttoned and unbuttoned the leather strap on his jacket cuff. "It won't be easy this winter.—I mean with you gone."

"What a you mean this winter with me gone?"

She glanced up, startled by the impatience of his tone. "You'll have to go away—at least a little piece. Maybe—maybe." She couldn't talk when she thought of his going away.

She felt the worn leather of his jacket hard and cold against her face, and his hands tight about her shoulders. "Listen, Delph. I'm no good at waitin'. I—I've got to be certain, Delph. I can't go away with things like this. Your uncle so set against me that he'll maybe—"

Juber called from the other end of the hall, "Lord, Marsh, please get goin'. I think that's John's mule comin' up th' hill now."

"Delph, I can't leave you here with nothin' certain. An' Logan Ragan, they want you back with him."

She sighed at his inability to understand. "But we're engaged.— I couldn't have anything to do with Logan when I said I'd marry you. We—we can't just pick up an' go. Uncle John he'd—."

"He couldn't do anything. We'd not be around to know. I don't want to wait an' go away never knowin'. Come on an' bring nothin' but th' clothes on your back."

"Now?" she asked, with a sharp excited breath, and was ready to gallop away behind him on Jude.

He hesitated. "I'll set a day to meet you, an' know first where I'm takin' you."

"Lord, Lord, you two. Save your huggin' an' bussin' till some more fittin' time. I can see him a comin' up th' hill."

Delph stirred in his arms, and wished he would take her—now, but Marsh stroked her hair and seemed to ponder. "I'll write—let you know in a week or so. Mrs. Crouch she'll—."

"He's a stoppin' at th' front gate now. He'll be a callin' Delph, or a comin' out with a shot gun. Fer God sakes, man, git goin'."

"You'd better go," she whispered. She clung to him a moment, then pushed him away, but held him with her eyes and asked, "But where will you be—if—"

He backed slowly toward the stable door. "You mean you'll meet me when I say."

She nodded, but he continued to look at her a moment longer. She saw worship in his eyes, and hunger, too, and something else that made her think of Logan and his too-possessive ways. Then he was gone, and there was no place in her mind for thought of Logan. She wanted to run after him and learn where he would be, but he was on Jude and galloping away with no looking back. She stood still with her back against a stable door and tried to think. Juber came and shoved a milk bucket into her hand. "Be a doin' somethin', be a milkin'. If he don't start callin' you. He'll be comin'."

She followed him and was meekly still while he lighted the lantern and held it up to her face. "Pat your hair a little straighter, Delph. An' now git to milkin', but fer God sakes don't let him see yer eyes."

She began the milking of Flossie, but the dehorned Jersey was more unruly than common, tossing her head, wasting her bran from the feed box, moving about the stable, and at last kicking the milk bucket from Delph's unskillful hands. The racket brought Juber hurrying to the stable door. Delph sat on her heels and looked at the spilled milk, while Flossie stood in a corner and looked at Delph, then turned her great eyes on Juber and bawled in plaintive aggrievement.

"I don't blame ye a bit," Juber said. "This girl's addled. Delph, in case you ever come to enough to recollect, Flossie's got a three-week-old calf she's been in th' habit a lettin' suck."

"Oh," Delph said, and got up, but stopped and looked wildly at Juber when John's voice came thundering down the hall. "Juber, whatever have you got Delph at th' milkin' for anyhow? Can't you milk four cows?"

"Th' rheumatism in my shoulder has got down into my hand," Juber answered, and went for Bessie's calf.

Delph smoothed her hair, and thought of Juber's advice about her eyes. She saw John's shadow fall on the stable door, and the shadow covered her, and she knew he was standing in the door. "Delph?"

"Yes."

"Turn around an' look at me, Delph."

She turned slowly with bent head and saw first his heavy boots laced with rawhide thongs. "Delph?"

"Yes."

"I reckin you know, if you've got any sense at all, th' answer I gave that fool oil man. He's been here, I reckin."

"He—just stopped."

"I 'lowed as much." He bent his head and stepped through the stable door, and glowered down at her in the same troubled, uncomprehending way as he had used to do when she was a small thing racing home from school with tangled hair and torn stockings. "Delph, get this in your head. It's th' last time he'll stop. There's to be no more a this hangin' around th' barn—or meetin' him in th' woods—if you have been up to such. Get that?"

"Yes. But—Uncle John he's not th' way you think. He's—."

He lifted his hand for silence. "You can't tell me a thing about him—You don't know anything. You couldn't.—It's shameful leadin' a fool like that on—makin' him think God knows what."

"I never thought of leadin' him on."

"You never think of anything. Th' night you run away to that dance I reckin you wasn't thinkin' what a scandal you'd cause an' hurt your Aunt Fronie's feelin's. Always runnin' after somethin'— an' this'ull might nigh be th' death a her. She's prayin' in th' parlor now." He turned on his heel, and stalked away, saying over his shoulder, "Now get on back to th' house where you belong—an' stay there."

She walked sedately down the barn hall, but once free of John's eyes, and under cover of the deepening darkness, she whirled twice on her toes, smiled on a startled shoat, and then ran humming to the back kitchen door. There, she stopped a time and listened to Fronie who had given off praying in the parlor for crying in the kitchen.

Delph heard her sobs and sighs as she unburdened herself to Nance. "I've tried to raise her more careful like than I would a girl a my own, bring her up to be a good Christian woman that'll never give reason for whisperin' behind her back, an' look at th' thanks I get.— Meetin' a good for nothin' oil man in th' woods—an' her not a knowin' one thing on God's earth about him—his people could all be idiots or eat up with bad diseases or—oh, Lord, Lord." And Fronie burst into loud weeping.

Delph listened and pitied her. She had so much and Fronie had so little—but then no woman on earth had as much as she had. She dreamed a moment of Marsh his eyes and his hair, and his hard square hands, gentle when they touched her, and the strong set of his shoulders, and—Fronie was flinging open the door and calling, "Delph-i-i-ne," in a ringing, quavering voice.

She answered, and walked into the kitchen with red cheeks and lowered eyes. She stood silent with bowed head under the tongue lashing that Fronie gave her, and such was its completeness that even Fronie grew tired and left off quarreling. And at supper she treated Delph with unaccustomed tenderness when she saw that her eyes were bright as if filled with tears, and that though she put food on her plate she ate nothing. Juber smiled to himself and marveled that a woman old as Fronie could so mistake the effects of love for a feeling of guilt and shame. He'd venture to guess that Delph remembered not one word of what her aunt had said.

He was thankful when, next day, the weather continuing cold, Fronie decided to have an early hog killing, and ordered two fat barrows killed. The extra work of grinding sausage meat and rendering lard kept Fronie and Nance so busy that they had little time for watching Delph, who sat mostly in her own room smiling at the fire, or spent long minutes on the high knoll on pretext of hunting the cows. He wondered why she stood there, when word had come by John from Mrs. Crouch that Marsh had left the country the day after he asked for Delph.

In spite of hog killing, logging, wood getting, and corn gathering, Juber found time for a daily ride to the post office. There, he would stand a time by the stove warming his hands, and passing the time of day with any who happened to be in the store. Mrs. Crouch would come to inquire of the health of the Costello family, and when he had talked with her a time he would ask in an off hand way, "I don't reckin there's any mail," and she would answer with a great rolling up of her eyes, "Pshaw, Juber, you know that ever since that fool oil man asked for Delph, John's been here waitin' when th' mail comes in. He took all Costello's mail."

And Juber would say, "But law, Permelie, you're so careless like you could overlook a letter." Mrs. Crouch would smooth her apron, and answer with a forbearing sigh, "Well, Juber, none of us is perfect. I'm not sayin' I couldn't overlook a bit a mail, but I'm most certain I didn't today."

Juber would warm again, and maybe talk a time before he went away. He would ride slowly home with his head hunched between his shoulders, and forgetting to play the French harp he carried for company. He would ride into the barn lot and on through the barn hall. In spite of John's command, Delph would most always be waiting there. She would look at him and he at her. The eagerness that flamed in her eyes would waver and fade, then flare with a sudden quiver of hope when he opened his mouth to speak. "There wasn't anything yet, Delph—But he'll write, never fear. He won't fergit ye."

Juber would watch her as she walked away. There was something too meekly patient in her shoulders, something about the way she carried her head that made her seem a woman grown with a woman's troubles; not the girl who had run away to a dance and laughed at her uncle's scolding.

Fronie scolded still, nagged over little things, such as the hours of foolishly painstaking work Delph had put into the blue woolen dress, trimmed on the cuffs and the shoulders with bright red embroidery. "A body 'ud think it was a weddin' dress th' way you've worked on it," she said one afternoon when the dress was finished except for buttons.

Delph smiled at the dress, and gently pulled a bit of lint from one bright shoulder. "I'd have to have a man, an' anyhow who'd wear a bright blue dress embroidered with red to a weddin'?" she said, and got up and stood before the mirror and held the dress up to her shoulders.

Nance stood behind her and looked into the mirror, too. "Lord, but that becomes you to a fare ye well. It makes your eyes fair shine, an' your hair shine, too. You know you're pretty, Delph, prettier than you used to be. Your eyes somehow. They make me think of th' angels lookin' into th' promised land—recollect that sermon Brother Eli Fitzgerald preached once up here a couple a yers back—well, that's th' way you look."

"Such talk, Nance," Fronie said, and made a clucking noise with her tongue. "Dorie Dodson an' some may hold by Brother Eli's milk an' water doctrine, but I never could—An' anyhow it wasn't th' angels that looked into th' promised land. What would a angel need with th' promised land. You'll have us all thinkin' Delph's goin' to die or somethin'."

"That's good talk. It 'ud please Brother Eli, I know. Mebbe Delph here has turned over a new leaf an' died to th' world of sin."

"She's flesh an' blood an' so can't die to sin till her spirit leaves her body," Fronie said with the finality proper to a deacon's wife and went downstairs.

"Delph," Nance whispered when Fronie had gone, "if'n you'd kind a—well, I mean humor her—beg her a little—an' make her think she's big it, stead a standin' off stiff necked an' stubborn as a mule, you'd get more a what you want. They're talkin' it over, an' I think they'll mebbe let you go to school after Christmas—if you do right."

Delph lifted her chin. "I won't get down on my knees an' beg like a slave for somethin' that's my due."

"You'd ought to learn to beg, Delph. It's somethin' a heap a women have to do a sight of before they die," Nance said, and sighed a bit over the dress as she carried it to the kitchen to press it.

The dress hung new and ready pressed in Delph's black walnut wardrobe for several days, and still Juber brought no word. One day when she had returned from a stolen meeting with Juber after his trip to the post office, Fronie looked at her and said, "You're lookin' peaked, Delph, all eyes. Th' next time John goes to Town I'll have him get you some medicine." She lowered her voice discreetly and studied Delph with searching eyes. "I know there's nothin' ails you, maybe a little touch a female trouble. If you don't feel it now you will some day—never wearin' enough underclothes, an' goin' around half naked—wearin' silk stockin's an thin shoes to church when it ought to be high shoes an' wool."

Delph looked at her aunt with an anger like a blindness in her eyes. "You're enough to make a woman hate her body, an'—." She whirled away and went upstairs. She hated the sound of her voice quarreling with Fronie, when all that mattered was Marsh. She walked to the calendar and counted the days, slowly going with her finger from one square to the next. Twice she did it, and each time the days were the same; one more than they had been yesterday, one less than they would be tomorrow. Yesterday there had been twelve; tomorrow there would be fourteen crawled away since she had stood in the barn and promised Marsh she would marry him.

She told herself she was not afraid, but that night she was wakeful with curious dreams. Fronie's eyes next day were kinder when they looked at her. Once, as they sat by the hearth tearing carpet strings, she said, "Delph, you ought to perk up a little. John's talkin' again a sendin' you to school."

"I'm all right. I'm fine."

"There's circles under your eyes. You eat hardly nothin' an' last night I heared you cryin' in your sleep."

"I was dreamin', I guess.—I dreamed of Old Azariah."

"Lord, Delph, he's been dead nigh onto a hundred an' fifty years."

"I saw him, though, th' way Granpa used to tell. He stood on th' Pilot Rock, an' all th' hills were covered with snow. I stood with him an' we looked an' looked an' couldn't see a bit a smoke."

"How did he look?"

"Just like he always did; thin an' tall with his eyes blue an' his beard black, an' his hair down to his shoulders. He had a long gun like them in th' attic. It was all so plain. I could see th' fringe on his huntin' shirt, but his cap I don't think was coon skin like granpa used to say—more like a fox with th' tail long an' wide down between his shoulders."

Fronie shivered and looked into the fire. "Don't talk on that way. You'll have me seein' ghosts. Dreamin' a th' dead is a mighty bad sign.—Did he talk or say anything?"

Delph pondered. "Never a word that I can recollect. That was why I cried, I think. I thought he might be dead; he stood so stiff an' still, just starin' out over th' country."

Fronie shuddered. "You ought to go for a walk, Delph. Visit somebody. John wouldn't mind. You can't allus set by th' fire like an old woman. You'll have people talkin' worse than if you run around too much."

"I'll go down an' visit Hedricks one a these days—mebbe stay th' night," Delph said, and tore carpet strings with eyes that were blind for the red dyed cloth.

She was tearing strings again when, two days later, she heard a mule's feet thud over the road, quicker than Juber usually came, but it was Juber. She heard his French harp, faint and shrill, like a lost breath of wind, but speaking clearly as if Juber had cried, "Delph, I've brought you some mail."

Fronie listened too. "I wonder whatever is takin' Juber over th' country so much. He's gone off somewhere's ever' day for weeks."

"Courtin' Permalie," Delph said, and added in slow careful words, "This room seems so stuffy like—I think I'll go for a little walk—not far."

Fronie nodded. "A breath of air would do you good."

She rolled the red strings neatly about the ball, and glanced swiftly at Fronie but Fronie seemed to have noticed nothing. The French harp came with a louder, gayer cry, and she laid the ball in the basket by the hearth and said, "I think I'll go now."

"Don't go without a coat, an' with nothin' on your head," Fronie reminded.

She walked slowly into the kitchen, and took the first coat and cap she saw. She was careful to close the back door with no hasty banging. She was careful to walk slowly across the porch, but once she had reached the dead, soundless grass of the yard, she ran to the barnyard, and after one swift glance back at the house windows, she opened the barnyard gate and dashed down the road to Juber. "Easy, now, easy," he whispered, and looked toward the house. "You don't want them to see."

She danced impatiently on her toes. "Give it to me, Juber. Give it to me. I'll go down in th' beech trees below th' road where they can't see."

"Lord, Delph, it's a good thing Marsh can't see you now. He'd have th' upper hand for th' rest of his days," Juber told her as he pulled the letter from an inside pocket. Delph snatched it and ran down among the beech trees with no answering and no words of gratitude. Juber sat his mule a time, and stared at the trees that had swallowed her. He glanced down at his French harp, raised it to his mouth, then changed his mind. He wiped it carefully clean and dry on his jumper sleeve, then stowed it in his jumper pocket. "Another one's gone out frum th' hills," he said, and rode on to the barn, slowly, and with his chin dropped forward on his chest.

He stabled the mule, and was gathering eggs when Delph came, running lightly on her toes, flinging her arms about his neck as she had used to do when she was a child. "Oh, Juber, I wish I could fly. He's got a job, Juber. That's why he was waitin' to let me know. He wanted to be certain, he said. He's all right. He's been stayin' at Dorie Dodson's. He has it all planned out to th' day an' th' hour how he'll meet me. His job's in South America—I never thought I'd live to go so far away. There'll be a man come with him to get me in a car. Oh, Juber, I can't believe it all."

"You're chokin' my Adam's apple," Juber whispered. "You'd better look out. They might be somebody around a listenin'."

"John's off huntin' quail. I've got to tell somebody. I wish I could see Mrs. Crouch. I can't go back to th' house an' be still by th' fire an' talk to Fronie about th' weather. I've got to do somethin'."

"Well, it's a plain fact you can't hep me gether eggs. Look, you've put in a nest egg two months old."

She smiled at him, but saw a thousand things instead of Juber. "It's th' strangest feelin', Juber. I don't think I'll ever want to eat or sleep again."

Juber sighed and went to another hen's nest. "Fallin' in love's a lot like dyin', I reckin. No two people ever act th' same way. Lord, I'll allus recollect th' night that Fronie an' John come tellin' around that they was goin' to be married."

"I guess they didn't laugh or seem—well, happy, even then."

Juber spat at a corn cob. "God, no. There was a big revival on, an' John he'd been squirin' her to church right regular. You'd a thought it was a funeral. Fronie was no spring chicken anymore, but she went around a blushin' an' a castin' down her eyes, an' your granma—if you recollect it was th' winter after your granpa died— she had 'em a settin' by her while she read th' Bible over 'em an' they all prayed an' cried together."

Delph fingered the letter, and looked at it while she asked, "Tell me, Juber—when my father brought my mother home how was it? Was she—well—so sober like an' still—an' did she seem afraid to be in love—an' ashamed—th' way Fronie says a good woman ought to be?"

Juber shook his head. "Your mother was cut of a different stripe from Fronie. No puttin' on or hidin' under about her." He picked up the basket of eggs. "Why don't you go after th' cows? Somebody's got to do a little plannin' on how to get your clothes out a th' house. Th' cows ud come by theirselves this time a year, but th' walk 'ud mebbe half settle your mind, an' keep you out a th' house a little longer. You can't go bustin' in to Fronie all bubblin' over like a jug a new made wine."

"I'll never let on," she answered, and went running away to hunt the cows.

Dark came and Fronie was out and calling. She questioned Juber when he went to the kitchen for milk buckets. "She's gone to hunt th' cows," he said.

"But I heared th' cow bells in th' lane more'n half an hour ago," Fronie answered, and stood in the kitchen door and looked up the pasture hill.

"Aye, I guess it is that Bessie. She is th' artfulest cow to wander off an' hide. An' she'll stand so still in th' brush a chewin' her cud with never a jangle from her bell. A body 'ud think she muffled it."

Fronie continued to search the pasture hill. "Looks to me like her a standin' by that black oak tree. She'll catch her death a cold a standin' so still.—Wool gatherin' as always, people'ull take her for a daft woman—Delph-i-i-ine."

Juber smiled at the indistinct figure. "She won't hear ye. She's a listenin' hard fer Beesie's bell, an' a buildin' castles in them clouds."

"She'd better build her castles by a good warm fire an' not be catchin' her death a cold. Delph-i-i-ine."

"Speakin' a colds that reminds me—Permelie's not feelin' so well. I was wonderin' if I could take her down a basket a turnip greens. Them seven tops in th' garden, I'd like to take her a big basket full. Some green truck 'ud do her good."

"What's happened that Permelie's got no greens a her own? Most a th' time she has greens when nobody else's got any. She bad sick? I've been layin' off to get down to see her one a these days. I might take 'em myself."

"No—no—I'll do it. Law, it 'ud be too unhandy fer you, carryin' a basket an' a ridin'. I'll take 'em down in a few days, an' mebbe a sack a apples."

"Don't tell me she's out a apples 'fore Christmas."

Juber nodded and sighed for the post mistress. "It's th' strangest thing. Her apples all rotted. I reckin Permelie's gittin' careless like or somethin'—folks 'ull be sayin' next she can't haf sort th' mail."

"Her eyes are plenty sharp for some things. Mrs. Hedrick told me that Mamie Hardgrove told her she'd heard it said that Permelie Crouch said that Delph was head over heels in love with that fool oil man—an' him a stranger she's not see half a dozen times."

"Lord, a body cain't be too careful a young girls like Delph.— Permelie was sayin' th' other day he'd better not be tryin' to write to Delph. She'd give th' letter to John quick as a flash, she said."

Fronie smoothed her apron and looked satisfied. "Permelie is a good soul. It's a pity she won't get saved. Take her down th' greens an' a sack a apples, too, whenever you have time. An' tell her soon as I make some hominy I'll either bring or send her a mess.—Lord won't that girl ever get on in—Delph-i-i-ine."

· 7 ·

TUESDAY, THE day that Marsh had set for the runaway, dawned gray and cold under low skies. A biting wind shrieked across the pasture, made a moaning by the house corners, and now and then flung scattering showers of fine ice-like snow. Mid morning found Delph watching Juber in the garden, as he gathered a bushel basket of frozen seven top turnip greens. Downstairs, Fronie rocked the baby and declared that Juber was either addled or head over heels in love with the postmistress, to go picking and carrying greens in all this weather.

Delph waited, and when Juber had gone to the barn, she slipped down the front hall stairs and ran after him. He was by the pig sty cautiously feeding handfuls of turnip greens to Linnie, the sow. "You'd ought to a stayed at th' house," he warned in a whisper. "If they're not onto somethin' from th' noise we made sneakin' out your things last night, they're dumber than I think they are."

"You're liable to forget somethin'," she argued, and would have climbed with him into the hay mow after her hidden clothing, had he not commanded her to stay below and watch.

"Put my shoes in th' sack that's to be apples," she called once in a loud whisper, but Juber had troubles other than the shoes. "I can't get in this little work basket your mother left ye," he called after a time.

She pondered with arms hugged tight to her shivering body. "Take out all a my winter underwear an' heavy stockin's. I won't be needin' 'em."

"It'll mebbe be cold in South Amerikee fer all you know."

"But there'll be nobody to fuss about my heavy underwear."

"There's no room for this big geography, Delph."

"Take it out then. I won't be needin' th' maps so much—now."

He came down not long after with a basket heaped with turnip greens in one hand, and the knobby sack supposedly filled with apples, on his shoulder. He smiled sadly at the sack as he stood it against the wall. "I think it'a a mess a punkins I'm takin' Permelie, 'stid a apples. They're awful big peculiar sized apples."

She patted the sack affectionately, and pushed a shoe heel into a less noticeable position. "It's crooked necked cushaws, I guess.—I hope you an' Permelie don't get in trouble over this."

"Never you mind. Nobody'ull be th' wiser. You'd better worry after Delph. To my mind this weather's so bad they won't let you go visit th' Hedricks like they promised."

"I'll slip off at dark then," she said, and ran toward the house, and wondered as she ran how she would spend the day. Her hands were cold but her ears felt hot and she feared that they were fiery red. Fronie and Nance, busy making souse meat from the second hog killing, might question why her ears were red or why she didn't sit still and sew, and so to avoid them she took the ten month old baby and three year old Jim up to her own room and played with them; Fronie would not come bothering her as long as she kept the children from underfoot. She would miss the baby, she thought, and once whispered to it that she was going away, but the baby only crowed and bounced on her knees.

She was glad when Fronie, after having waited dinner a time, called her to come and eat as she guessed John had ridden clear to the head of the creek and would not be back before sundown. Yet even with him gone, dinner was a long struggle to bite and chew and swallow food that choked and sickened her.

She was glad when the meal was finished, and she could return to her room. But once there, she only stood a moment by the hearth, and rushed downstairs. Nance was surprised when she jerked up a dishcloth and began drying the dishes, humming "Nine of the Bent to Over the Bow." as she worked. Nance thanked her, for helping with the kitchen work was a thing Delph seldom did; but when Nance's words of gratitude were said, Delph had the sudden terror that she might be going to cry, and after that it seemed an eternity passed as she dried the dishes.

She finished at last, hung the cups in their proper place in the cupboard, and turned to Fronie and said, "I think I'll get ready to go now."

Fronie had the baby cradled in one arm, and a cookbook cross her knees. "Wherever are you aimin' to go in all this weather?" she absent-mindedly asked, without lifting her head from the cookbook.

"You know. You mentioned it first a while back. This is th' day I'm goin' down to visit Hedricks."

Fronie glanced out the window where a few snow flakes whirled in the wind. "Law, I wouldn't think a walkin' out in all this weather.—Where is that fruit cake recipe, anyhow? Soon's we finish this batch a souse meat, I think I'll start on th' fruit cakes."

Delph untied her apron, and laid it over the back of a chair. "If you don't mind I think I'd better go. They're expectin' me."

Fronie considered with a forefinger on a page of the cookbook, "John mightn't like it now.—Nance, looks to me like you're puttin' an awful lot a pepper in that souse meat—but if you're dead set on it why go ahead. Maybe it won't kill you—you look better anyhow than a few days back."

"I'll be all right," she said, and ran up the kitchen stairs.

She dressed quickly, picked up her purse, took her mother's rings, the ladies' watch made to be worn on a breast pin, a locket, and other trinkets from her mother; too precious to be trusted to the sack of apples and basket of greens. She hesitated a time over her savings kept in an old hunting horn; more than a hundred dollars that John had made her keep from time to time; to teach her thrift he had always said. She thought of Marsh—what was hers should be his—and shoved the money hastily into her purse.

She stood a moment then and looked about the room, her eyes moving slowly from this to that—the hills out the window, the sticks of seasoned maple wood by the hearth, the books in the shelves Juber had built for her, the stacks of magazines, the boxes of paper dolls—her mother had cut some of those—and the bottom dresser drawer that held the scrap book. She opened the dresser swiftly, took out the scrap book, smiled a moment at the first picture she saw, the one of Dorie's Sam, then closed it and put it away. The scrap book and Sam's picture were like her books of poetry and the maps she had once traced out with her finger—going about the world with

Marsh, she would have no need of such things now. She opened the box of paper dolls, and tried to put a dress on a lady in a pink silk petticoat, but her hands were stiff and awkward, cold as if she had been playing in the snow, so that she never dressed the doll but laid it away with the others.

She walked slowly down the kitchen stairs, and stood a moment by the stove and pretended to warm her feet, careful to look at neither Nance nor Fronie. Nance was just finishing the mixing of a pan of souse meat, and stood now with her head tilted to one side and studied her work, while Fronie held a spoonful and made soft smacking noises with her lips and tasted critically. "Delph, I wish you'd see how this souse meat is anyhow. Nance thinks it's got too much sage," Fronie asked, and scarcely glanced at her.

She took a spoonful of the well peppered meat, looked at it a moment, then said, "It's just right."

"But you've not tasted it."

"I—I mean it looks an' smells all right." She swallowed the meat, but it was tasteless in her mouth, like dry meal going down. "It's awful good."

"An' you don't think it's got too much pepper.—What are you all dykin' out in your good new coat for? People'ull be sayin' next you're puttin' on airs. What about th' salt? I've smelled an' tasted till I can't tell a thing."

"Th' salt? Oh, it's all right. Fine. I thought—I'd wear this coat just for a change," she answered, and drew on her gloves.

"Your old one's nicer than most girls in this country have. Nance, you taste. I think it needs a touch more red pepper.—Delph, don't forget your overshoes. You think it's all right, Nance?"

Nance nodded over the souse meat, then went hurrying to the back porch for Delph's overshoes, which she insisted on warming a time before Delph put them on.

Delph buckled on the overshoes at last, and smiled at little Jim. "Kiss me good-bye," she asked suddenly, and held out her hands, but the little boy hung back, abashed by the suggestion.

She got up and stood a moment staring at the stove. "I'd better be goin'," she said.

"Have a nice time, an' if it turns warm an' rains don't try walkin' home tomorrow. Juber can bring Tilly after you," Fronie said.

"Tell Mrs. Hedrick I'll be down one a these days to help her with her quiltin," Nance said, and little Jim said, "Bye, Delph."

"All right—good-bye," she said, and opened the door, closed it quickly, and walked away without looking back.

Juber met her in the barn hall. His sparse hair lay in damp smooth strings across his head, and he wore the clothing he wore on his rare trips to church or Town; new overalls, a blue striped shirt, a red tie, and a black suit coat worn shiny at the cuffs and seams. "I'm goin' to walk a piece with you," he said, and took her hand and swung it as he had used to do when she was a little girl.

"You'd better not. John, if he ever learns all this, he'll turn you out a house an' home," she warned.

He shook his head and stared down at his neatly polished Sunday shoes, "I feel right now like I'm losin' th' most uv it anyhow."

"Now, Juber, don't be silly. I'll write. I'll send you postcards. Wouldn't you like to get a postcard from South America?"

"Lord, Delph, but it's so far away."

Her eyes glinted with excitement. "But we'll maybe go other places, too. Oil men go all over th' world, an' I'll mebbe visit back. Maybe we'll have a car, an' come drivin' in some Memorial Day."

"Mebbe so," he said, and walked with her through the barn and down the lane.

She stopped at the end of the lane, and looked up toward the high pasture hill. "Juber—I'm goin' th' back way, so could you walk around an' meet me on th' other side? I think I'd like to go up over th' hill—this once."

He nodded and walked on, and she climbed the hill. The brown grass and dead sweet clover caught at her feet and brushed against her ankles. Now and then she stopped and turned to look back. Each time Costello's place was smaller, the hills farther flung and lower lying. Then she stood on the top with all the world about her falling away. The wind whistled through the black oak tree, and lifted the brown frozen leaves with a little rustling.

She felt hot tears on her wind cold cheeks and knew it was the north wind in her eyes. She saw, looming above the other hills, the high mass of cold looking stone that was the Pilot Rock. She saw the road to school, and the one to church, and there was the Hedrick place. Past the Little South Fork Country, the frozen hills lay dark and cold and lonesome, with now and then a thread of smoke spiraling up against the sky. She had an instant's pity for the women sitting by the fires that made the smoke. Young hill women wanting to go away, older ones with their children gone, opening albums and taking pictures from cupboards and dresser drawers, showing them proudly to visitors, or just sitting and studying them. She would have more of the world than the pictures of those that went away.

She picked up a pebble and twirled it high and toward the Little South Fork Country, and then she turned and ran with no waiting to see where the pebble fell. She knew the long sweep of the pasture hill, and had no need to watch her feet. It was almost as if she played that game again, lived over the stolen fun she had had when she went to hunt the cows, when she ran with her eyes closed, down through the knee high grass, then fell in a heap at the bottom and opened her eyes and found them filled with sky, and lay and laughed and laughed, at the cows staring at her, at Fronie who would have scolded, at nothing, at everything, laughing that there was no one to see and ask her why she laughed. She reached the cup-like bottom of the pasture, and opened her eyes to see Juber waiting for her there. She caught his hand and tried to laugh, but could do no better than a stiff tight smile.

They stopped by the rail fence. She looked at him and wished her throat would stop hurting the way it did, but he looked so solemn and old—like some hungry troubled bird on the first day in winter. "You'd better not go any further," she said and dropped his hand.

"I won't. It'll soon be barnwork time, anyhow." He took off his hat and held it awkwardly in his hand. "I wish ye well, Delph. Mebbe—things'ull work out so—you'll hate me fer hepin' this on, but—."

She shook her head, and looked at him with warm eager eyes. "Things couldn't be that would make me sorry—ever."

He pulled a splinter from the rail and stared at it. "Aye, Delph, it's a long road you've got ahead. I can't see it, an' you can't see it, but it's there a layin' a waitin'." He looked slowly over her face; his eyes lingering on it feature by feature. "You know so little, Delph. I wish—now, I can sorta see why people cry at weddin's. It allus seemed foolish 'til now."

She patted his shoulder. "Pshaw, Juber, don't carry on so. Marsh, he'll take care of me—if I need anybody to do that."

He continued to study her; his face made her think of John's when he talked to the people in church, sober and filled with solemn thoughts. "Delph, I reckin you feel so, well—somethin' th' way Enoch felt when he walked with God.—But someday that'll wear off. It not in th' nature uv things fer it to last—th' way it is now. An' then—I'm not sayin' you'd forgit, ever—but then there may come times, mebbe—when you'll have to recollect an' remember always that you come a good blood, oldest an' finest to these hills—an' a body can't go back on their blood. Wildness runs in some a your kin mebbe—but not goin' back on promises—ever. An' you'll never need strange laws or people to tell you what's right an' what's wrong. You'll know."

"I'll be good. I'll write." She sat on the top rail and looked at him a moment longer, then sprang to the ground and hurried away. Once, she turned and looked after him, but he was walking up the pasture hill, his hat still clutched in his hand, and his white thin hair ruffled in the wind. She wanted to call to him that the wind was cold, but the words hung in her throat.

She walked on, through a clump of cutleaf beech and prickly holly bushes where the jagged leaves caught at her coat and hat. The path twisted suddenly, and there was Marsh, looking just like Marsh in his old leather jacket and the battered black felt hat twisted in one hand. "At first I thought it wasn't you so dressed up an' all," he called, and hurried up the path.

"I wanted to look nice walkin' to my weddin'," she answered, and tried to walk to him with proper slowness and decorum but somehow she was running and so was he, and she never knew whether she reached for him or he for her. It didn't matter. He was there and kissing her, telling her not to be afraid. "You've been gone so long—twenty days it was—yesterday," she whispered. "I was worried until I got your letter."

"Dorie was behind in her corn gatherin' an tobacco strippin', an' I had to wait for Roan. An' what's twenty days?" he said, and kissed her again and smiled but there was something somber, troubled in his smile. "You knew I'd come back. It was like th' head part a me— Oh, Delph, what's th' use a talkin'. Roan Sandusky is waitin' by th' road for us in his car. We'd better be goin'."

She made no move to go, but stood a moment longer in his arms. "Marsh, you're not afraid—or thinkin' maybe that—we ought to a waited."

He pushed her hat back so that he might better see her eyes. "No, Delph, I'm not afraid, of anything—now. It's just that I was worried you might be—an' sorry, too, sometime."

"Ever'thing will be all right. There's nobody out to see. I think Uncle John went cattle tradin' in th' other direction. An' it's so cold an' windy most people are sittin' by their fires—like them at home."

"Why, Delph. You're cryin'."

"No, I'm not."

He patted her shoulder, and when she stood with bowed head and made no move to wipe her eyes, he pulled a red bandanna from his jacket pocket, and dabbed at her face. The handkerchief smelled strongly of fresh raw tobacco, and the rank unaccustomed smell caused her to sneeze. "It's just that I'm takin' a little cold," she said, and managed a shaky laugh.

"You're a brave one," he said, and in spite of the rough brushy way they walked hand in hand. Marsh comforted her, talking in the rough excited whispers of a child. "Someday, we'll come back, Delph, an' mebbe even John he'll be proud you married me, an' not thinkin' as he thinks now."

She laughed and wondered how she could have cried. "What do you care about John?" she asked, and was eager again, looking ahead to see the car. She saw it soon, a badly outmoded touring car with a convertible top and windows of yellowed, crackled isinglass. Such an ugly thing, and she thought she would remember and love it always.

Her heart thumped in her ears and her scalp tingled with excitement, when Marsh bade her wait behind a tree until he should see that the road was clear. There were so many questions she wanted to ask him; where in Tennessee would they be married, and would this car take them there, or would they go on a bus or train? She wished for a peep at the wedding ring, and wondered if they would spend the night in a hotel. It would seem strange, sinful somehow, to stay the night with a man in a hotel, even though the man were her husband. Husband—she whispered the word and thought of Juber's solemn face, and tried to think exactly what it was he had said about always and never turning back—always—always—until she died—

that was a—. Then Marsh was motioning her forward, helping her down the bank, racing with her across the road.

A long brown bony hand opened the car door, while its owner said in the tone of a hill man speaking of the weather, "Well, I'm right glad to see that nobody's shot." He pulled his tall thin body farther over on the seat, smiled at her with calm brown eyes, and asked, "Is this th' girl?"

"Delph, this is Roan Sandusky, th' county agent over in Westover. I guess maybe you've heard of him. He's a friend of Dorie's an' went to school with Sam."

"I've read of you in our county paper," she said, and smiled. She hoped that sometime she might see him again, and he would tell her about his life in college, and the two years he had spent in Europe. The paper had told of that, though from the looks of him a body would never have known he had been any place.

Marsh sprang into the car, slammed the door while Roan began the business of getting out of a mudhole. Delph shivered and wished they would be gone. It seemed to her that the car made an uncommon amount of noise, and must be drawing the attention of all people for miles around—John might have ridden down this way instead of the other. "You stopped in a kind of unhandy place," she observed.

Roan sent a spray of tobacco juice out the window, smiled his brief crooked smile and said, "I parked in a mud hole on purpose; in case anybody come by askin' what I was waitin' for I could say, 'I'm stuck in a mudhole.'"

Delph started to answer, and could not when as the car made a sudden backward sally, her head was jerked violently forward. Roan stuck his head out the window, and with much twisting and turning of the steering wheel, craning of his head, consultations with Marsh whose head was out the other window, and indescribable squeaks, coughs, shivers, and gasps on the part of the car, they were at last free of the mudhole and bumping down the road. "That's that," Marsh said. He fastened the flapping curtain and turned to Delph. "Scared?" he asked, but she shook her head and smiled with warm eager eyes.

Soon the places she had known were gone, and they were on the county seat pike. Once, she tried to look back, but could see nothing through the yellowed isinglass. Marsh whispered, "We're safe now." She smiled, but it was strange and a bit disappointing to know that the runaway she had thought on and trembled over for days was finished so easily and so quickly. For the first time she thought of her clothing, but found it carefully stowed on the back seat. Marsh followed her glance, and apologized for the rumpled condition of her dresses, "But soon as you get to Dorie's you can straighten ever'thing out," he said.

"Dorie's?" she asked, while Roan laughed and said, "I take it she'll be in th' ceremony. You might tell her a bit a your plans."

"I meant it as a good surprise," Marsh answered, and squeezed her hand while he went on to explain, "Dorie begged me to bring you down, an' anyhow they've changed th' marriage laws in Tennessee, so wherever we went we'd have to have somebody to swear you're twenty-one. An' Dorie said she'd fix it up with th' county clerk." He waited, but when she had continued sometime silent he went on excitedly, "We'll be married in her house, Delph, with people we know—a little—almost like bein' married in a home of your own."

She nodded slowly, and looked steadfastly at the road. "Yes—it will be somethin' like bein' at home—I guess."

He gave her shoulder a quick hard hug. "Say somethin' besides 'Yes.' I thought you'd like it a lot. I—I somehow couldn't stomach bein' married in a courthouse by a justice of th' peace or somethin'."

"It will be so—so lovely," she said. "I hope we won't cause Mrs. Fairchild too much trouble, stoppin' with her before we go on," she said, and sat and watched the bleak new country and thought of Dorie Dodson Fairchild.

Instead of taking the roundabout way of the county seat pike by which they had come, Roan took a shortcut by a little used back road. They drove through the southeastern tip of Westover County, a poor land of low steep limestone hills, sparsely inhabited, with no wide bottom lands for corn, or smooth hill side pastures like those of the Little South Fork Country. The few houses along the road were small things, mostly of logs or poles, usually porchless, scant windowed, set on steep hill sides, and under many of the high cedar post foundations hogs grunted and shared their shelter with hounds and hens. "This place makes me ashamed to be out a th' hills,"

Delph said, as they bounced past one that looked to be little more than a roofed box of poles.

Roan eased the car into a chug hole and studied the house with something like despair or anger in his dark brown eyes. "Looks like a body could begin to see some change in one county where he's worked eight years, but God if I can—sometimes I think things look worse."

"Some a th' back hill people will hardly listen to anything," she comforted.

"They've never had many botherin' to tell 'em," the county agent answered, and frowned at a thin-sided, brindle cow in a muddy pole pen. The cow stared at them dully a moment, then went back to the few corn husks scattered in the mud.

"She's cold," Marsh said, and twisted around and looked at the cow's long coarse hairs lifted along her back against the cold, and the shivers that convulsed her hollow flanks and rib-ridged sides.

"She's lived through four winters in that pen," Roan said. "I guess in all I've spent a good week talkin' to th' man that owns her—begged him to build a pole stable, then begged him to let her range.— Too much trouble to hunt her, he said, an' he had no fence. Worst thing is that cow's got TB. Th' man's got four kids—an' what can I do? Nothin' by God."

They came to an especially rough bit of going, around and down a long ridge side that dropped into a narrow gulch-like valley, filled with slender second growth poplar and maple. Roan drove slowly with his eyes on the valley. "Look, Marsh, I can recollect when that was all burned off, clean as a hound's tooth, th' ground beginnin' to wash. In fifteen more years that'll be a pretty stand a poplar. I brought a bunch a school boys out to look at it—nearly ever' one went back an' planted some poplar on his own land."

"I wonder will they stay to see 'em grow?" Marsh said. He looked at the young growing trees, their blunt twigs faintly silvered in the deepening dusk, and his eyes made Delph think of Juber's eyes when he played his fiddle, gentle somehow and filled with an old man's dreaming; only Marsh was no old man.

The going grew gradually easier; lengths of wire fence flashed by the road, with sometimes a gate, a corner of a substantial barn or dwelling rising for an instant out of the darkness; enough to show that they were free of the back hills. Soon they were on a narrow concrete highway, unrolling over almost level farming country; a land of great barns and silos with fodder shocks marching away into the night, and here and there the dead suckered stubble of a last summer's tobacco field. They passed a filling station, then a small building, bearing a large sign, "Salem Ky. Post Office." A few minutes later Roan said, "Well, here we are," and turned into a graveled sideroad after pausing long enough for Marsh to spring out, and run to open a white-painted barnyard gate.

Delph caught glimpses of a low stone fence covered with myrtle and leafless honeysuckle vines, the trunks of white pine trees, and a black iron hitching ring boy with an iron wreath in each hand. Two wildly barking black shepherds rushed to meet the car, then went dashing back to Marsh who had remained to fasten the big gate. Roan stopped by the yard gate, and somewhere a girl's voice shrilled in high excitement, "Angus! they've come. He got her all right."

A tall young girl with a black wooly pup under one arm and milk bucket in her hand came flying into the band of light from the car. She tossed back her flock of poplar-leaf yellow hair, shaded her eyes with her hand, and came on, talking all the while. "We're behind with ever'thing tonight. Mama had to go down to look at one of th' renter's mules. They think it's goin' lame. I've been helpin' Angus with th' milkin', but th' barn's in such an uproar th' cows'ull hardly give their milk down.—Where are you all anyhow? I want to see Delph."

"I'm climbin' out of th' car," Delph called, eager to see more of the girl and go into the Fairchild house looming up in the early darkness. The porches were flooded with light, electric light such as city people had. She wished it were day, and she could see more of the place. The house looked large and fine with wide stone chimneys rising up against the sky, and the white columns of the front porch shining so proud and high. She thought for a moment of all those young ones who had lived in the house and then gone away—Sam in New York, Emma who wrote letters to the county paper and worked in Chicago, Poke Easy in college studying law, Joe a lawyer in Chicago, and two other girls married well off she had heard.

Then Katy and Roan and Marsh with the dogs were all crowding round, and Katy was dropping the milk bucket and shifting the pup to her other arm in order to shake hands, introducing Brown Bertha and Black Peter, the pup's mother and father, declaring that Caesar the pup was going to be the death of her.

"Now, what's my dog done?" Marsh wanted to know, and took the young dog, who thudded his tail excitedly and licked Marsh's chin and tried to get his hat between his teeth.

"He can't get over th' notion he's a Spanish bull fighter," Katy sighed, and plunged into a long recital of the trouble and excitement he had caused that afternoon. He had always been a mighty one to growl and ruffle his hair when Solomon the prize bull bellowed, but this afternoon what he had done had capped the climax. He had slipped off to the barnyard, and when Angus the hired man was driving out Solomon, Caesar had dashed between his legs and caught the bull by the tail. The whole barnyard had been thrown into an uproar, while Caesar rolled back his eyes and hung on and Solomon pawed and bellowed and pranced. Caesar had held until he could hold no longer, and then leaped away with Solomon's horns just missing his belly. Now Solomon was wild; just listen to him roar.

Delph tried to share the interest of the others in Solomon, but she wished they would go into the house. The long ride in the unheated drafty car had chilled her to the bone. Not only the ride was the cause of her shivers, but she, when dressing for her journey, had as one last gesture in defiance of Fronie, left off the winter underwear her aunt had made her wear. Now, as she stood in teeth chattering misery she thought of the discarded clothing with more longing than disdain. Though a northerly west wind tore through her tightly wrapped coat, she stopped with the others when Marsh sniffed the wind and said, "To my mind we can start strippin' tobacco again by tomorrow."

He stopped then to study the stars, pale tonight and smudged in spots by thin streamers of torn, gray-white cloud. The North Star was hidden, and the seven stars were dim, but there was the Big Dipper, and farther west and lower lying, a bright star burned, the evening star, he guessed it was. He felt Delph's hand, timid, yet somehow assertive as it touched his arm. "Don't you like to look at th' stars, too, Delph?"

She shivered. "Y-e-es, but they're not so pretty tonight—dim an' little somehow."

"I didn't mean pretty—but well—they're one thing a man can look at—an' know they'll never change an' never go away," he said in a low voice as if it were a secret he wanted to share only with her.

"But we'll see different ones in South America," she reminded him, and marveled that she was such a lucky one—to go so far that even the stars changed. She started to ask him exactly where they would go and when, but stopped, for he was talking again with the others. All were wondering if the wind wouldn't shift south as well as west and blow up a warmish rain—that would make fine tobacco stripping weather. Katy began begging Roan to stay the night and not drive on to his office and home in Hawthorne Town. Dorie would love to have him stay and take a look at the grading in the morning. Delph listened to it all in silence, and felt a prick of loneliness when Marsh turned away and went to the barn with Angus and Roan, talking with them of the tobacco market as if he had forgotten he had a bride.

Katy remembered her duties as hostess and led the way to the house, but stopped on the porch steps to listen again to Solomon's bellows from the barn. Caesar listened, too, and pricked his ears and growled low in this throat while the hairs on his neck rose like quills. "I guess it's a good thing we're givin' him to Marsh," Katie said. "No farm would ever be big enough for him an' Solomon."

"Marsh can't take a dog to South America," Delph pointed out, then sneezed, and Katy for the first time seemed to notice the cold. She hurried Delph into the front hall, considered a moment by the parlor door, and at last decided to take her there. The room, though large and high ceilinged, filled with finer furniture and rugs than any Delph had ever seen, was disappointing. In spite of the piano, the books, and electric lamps, it was much the same as the parlor at home. There was the same air of a thing carefully kept and little used, and the large old-fashioned pictures of people, now dead, might have been kinsmen of the dead that looked down from Fronie's parlor walls.

However, there were other pictures, in smaller, newer frames, scattered here and there over the piano and the tables. They were Katy's brothers and sisters, Delph knew, though it was hard to think that Katy in a serge skirt torn in spots and pricked with cockle burrs, a denim jumper and brass buckled boots, could be one of that group.

She sat now on the edge of her chair, and was silent until Delph, glancing at a picture in a fine silver frame, said, "That looks like your brother Sam."

"It is," Katy answered, and got up and brought the picture for her to see.

Delph studied it a time then said, "He looks like you."

"Mama says he's better lookin' though. His eyes are bluer, an' his ears are not so big as mine'll be."

Delph looked at Katy in some surprise. "Didn't you ever see him?"

Katy studied the toe of one shoe. "He never comes home like th' others—eight years it'll be this spring, an' I was five years old."

"I guess you get anxious to see him sometimes."

Katy pondered over the picture. "I don't know, In a way—he wouldn't be like my brother. Th' others change—some—an' they visit home a good bit an' are not so far away. I don't guess he'd hardly talk th' same."

"I know your mother's proud," she said, and sat a moment smiling at the picture, then both she and Katy jumped when Dorie's voice thundered in the hall, "Katy, whatever do you mean bringin' somebody same as a member of th' family into this cold graveyard of a parlor, an' lettin' her sit with her coat on. You might as well a left her standin' on th' porch."

"But, Mama, you had me build a fire. I thought it was for Delph."

"Katy, you get less sense ever' day of your life. That new preacher over in Burdine told Brother Eli he was aimin' to visit me today, tryin' to get up money for th' heathen, like as if we don't have enough needy right here, an' I thought if I put him in this parlor he'd cut his stay short, unless he's part Eskimo." Dorie strode into the room, pushed back the man's brown felt hat she wore, and after a moment's smiling appraisal of Delph, wrung her hand vigorously. "Well, I see you got here with no mishap."

"It was nice of you to let us stop over with you, an' I hope we won't be causin' you—."

"Pshaw, why my grandfather thought nothin' a stoppin' at your granpa Costello's for a week at a time, an' I know nobody offered him a cave of a room like this when he was tired an' cold th' way you must be. But come on, I'll soon thaw you out in th' kitchen."

"Aw, Mama," Katy wailed, "don't let's take her there—it's an awful place to take a young bride with maybe good resolutions about housekeepin'. I'll take her to her own room. It's nice an' warm," Katy continued, and without waiting for her mother's answer hurried to the foot of the stairs.

"Don't be stayin' all night. Supper's ready all but gettin' it on th' table, an' if th' kitchen's straightened you'll be th' Miss to straighten it."

"There's Bull Durham sacks an' books an' barn junk like calf halters all over it," Katy giggled when they had reached the top of the stairs. "Anyhow, I wanted you to see your room—it used to be Ethel's; she's married now an' lives in Detroit. She liked it, an' I thought you would, too, better than th' others. You can see over th' Big North Fork to Burdine, an' sometimes th' lights are kind a nice when it snows. From what Mama an' Marsh have said of you I thought you'd like th' lights."

Delph scarcely glanced at the room furnished in familiar black walnut and wild cherry, and warmed by a coal fire in a gray marble fireplace, but walked with Katy to the window. Katy drew back the curtain, and they stood together and looked down at Burdine, now no more than strings and clusters of lights scattered over the valley and the steep sides of the triangular hill that rose back from the spot where the Big North Fork joined the Cumberland. Delph, in spite of the cold, opened the window and leaned far out, and studied the town. "It's th' most lights I ever saw at once," she hesitantly explained when she had remembered her manners and closed the window.

Katy talked, pointed out this and that, so that Delph saw the town, fine and alive, covered by the darkness and colored with Katy's talk. The lights that were bright and low down near the rivers, they belonged to the lumber mills. Higher up were the stores and a few dwelling houses, then the lights that winked red and green they were signals by the railroad tracks, and the two real bright ones they were by the depot. Past those and higher the lights were scattered and less bright. That was the part of the town where the most of the people lived. The churches were up there, and so was the school. The best people lived on High Street, but mostly they were old and their children gone away. That and a few others were pretty streets, but down in the bottoms and by the river it was awful, the white trash, shanty people, and bad women lived there. Katy whispered the information about the bad women, then turned away to fix the fire. But Delph stayed by the window, asking about this light and that, and had the excitement of seeing a train, all alive with light, the engine wreathed in rose colored smoke, come flying out of the tunnel and across the high bridge, a passenger train with rows of twinkling, flashing windows. She hoped it would stop, but it went on, flying around a curve she could not see.

"That's number eight, th' Florida Belle," Katy explained. "Trains like that never stop in Burdine, anymore. But they used to when it was a boom town an' before th' road was made an' th' big busses didn't go through here.—Don't you want to come an' rest awhile?" she suggested after a time of looking at Delph's back, bent forward with eagerness to see things not shown by the lights.

Delph turned slowly away from the window. "It makes me think of a Christmas tree—one lit up with electric lights like I saw once in Town." She flushed suddenly, and looked into the fire. "I guess you think I'm silly carryin' on so over a few lights—but, well—you see I've stayed pretty close in th' back hills—until now—an' my county didn't even have a railroad."

Katy smiled in understanding. "Even Ethel when she comes home from Detroit she'll stand an' look at th' Burdine lights. 'I'll never see any that'll look half so fine as they used to look,' she'll say.—Maybe I'll stay home from school tomorrow, an' I'll take you down to Burdine. It's ugly as can be by daylight, though; they never did build th' bottoms back after th' 1913 flood. But maybe sometime we'll go in th' truck to Hawthorne—that's our county seat—an' it's lots bigger than this with railroad shops an' a refinery an' roundhouse an' lots of stores."

"I don't guess I—we'll be here long enough for that, but it would be nice to go."

Katy looked at her in some surprise. "Didn't Marsh tell you? He's not leavin' 'til sometime in January an' you all will be with us 'til then." She hugged her knees excitedly. "Mama says I'm already more excited over th' weddin' than if I was th' bride, but neither one of my sisters was married at home, an' you'll be takin' their place somehow.—I hope we get th' tobacco off a hand right quick, so you can have your weddin' soon."

Delph sat with her eyes fixed steadfastly on the ashes in the grate. It was not easy to keep Katy from learning that all these plans were new to her—and disappointing.

· 8 ·

THE WEST wind shifted more south than north, so that by morning there was damp heavy snow, and by noon time rain. The rain continued, a warm rain that made Dorie's fields of rye green as April, and in the damp air the tobacco was soft and springy to the touch, fine for stripping. Marsh stood hour after hour, stripping and grading with Perce Higginbottom, a red-faced, leather-necked giant of a farmer from Cedar Stump over the Cumberland. Sometimes Dorie or Katy came to help; now and then Delph stood around and watched, for she knew nothing of tobacco and Dorie would not risk a green hand.

Most often, however, the men worked alone. Sometimes there would be talk; Angus would say a few words concerning Dorie's crops or hogs or children, and Perce too, talked of land, and crops, roads, and county politics, but mostly of his wife Lizzie, whom he was fond of quoting, and of his four boys and a girl, "Th' spittin' image of her maw." But usually there would be long whiles of silence, broken only by the rain on the high roof shingles and the gentle rasping sound of tobacco leaf being torn from tobacco stalk. Now and again one of the three would hold up a leaf, smooth and flatten it between his palms and say, "As pretty a long bright red as ever I stripped," or "Look how light this lug leaf cured, an' thinner than silk," or some such like. Marsh listened and commented most often with his eyes alone.

Many times when the barn doors were open and he could see out and away through the thin white walls of rain, Angus or Perce might talk and he would hardly hear them, and work half conscious of the bright crumpled silk of the tobacco leaves in his hands. The back doors of the tobacco barn opened on a wide view of a field in winter. At one side of the field was a great brick house, white porched, many chimneyed, green shuttered, larger than Dorie's house, and rented now to Mr. Elliot, northern owner of the Burdine lumber mills.

Sometimes Marsh, after a time of looking at the land across the river, would say to his fellow workers in a halting apologetic way, "I think I need a bit of air not so tobaccery," and they would nod and maybe look after him while he went across the barnyard to stand by Dorie's back fence.

The wire fence marked the boundaries of upper Fairchild Place. The earth fell away in a stretch of steep, fern-covered rocky hill side that dropped down two or three hundred feet to the acres of flat river bottom corn land, the richest part of Costello's Place. Marsh could, when he leaned on the fence, look down and see Dorie's fields, see two small white-painted renters' houses near great barns where cows and fat chickens and fatter hogs ambled about and seemed to feed all the day long on hay and fodder and corn.

He would pause to smile briefly on Dorie's side of the river, then his eyes would go walking on, through a band of willows, over clumps of white limbed sycamores to the bottom lands that lay below the brick house and were a part of the old Weaver Place. The old farm was a world unto itself, a half moon of rich bottom corn land, hills and rolling fields above for pasture land, all bound by a river, a river bluff, and a creek on the other side of the river hill. Marsh had never seen the whole of the place except once seven years before, but he knew it well; had seen it many times through Dorie's eyes, and had listened to Roan's lament that it was another bit of good farming land being wasted by weather and careless renters.

Seven years ago Dorie had wanted to buy it, but her children objected, all except Katy, six years old, who had wanted to sit on the back porch with the field glasses all the day long and supervise the running of the new farm. He remembered the talk the Fairchild children who were home had had, hours of it, then Dorie's sorrow when the bank took it over and no real farmer ever came to buy it. There was that Sunday morning, he had been almost a stranger to Dorie then, when she had come with Katy to his boarding place, and asked him to set her over the river. She didn't want her own boys to know, she had said. They had slipped away like thieves, broken the lock on Poke Easy's skiff, for Dorie in her excitement had forgotten the key, and gone over the river and explored the farm. It was early April and on the river hill above the corn land the dogwood and redbud were in bloom, and the lilac flowers in the brick house yard had hung heavy and fragrant and sweet. All that was seven years ago. Land was high then, but money was cheap; land was cheap now, but money was high, hard to come by.

His eyes would travel slowly over this and that, the renter's house in the bottoms, a square gray ugly building it looked to be of six or seven rooms, porchless and paint peeling, standing bleak and ugly in a grassless, fenced yard. He could see a smoke house, chicken house, and tool house, and the door of the stone spring house under the hill. He remembered the spring cool, with moss covered walls and mint and blue-eyed water grass growing by its door. But everything was old and poorly kept, lost in the half moon shaped stretch of corn land, dwarfed by the great barn, larger than Dorie's cattle barn.

The fields ended at the foot of a steep river bluff, sheer crags of blue white limestone in spots, in others steep walls of ground where stunted cedar trees, mock orange bush and all manner of things grew. He would follow the rutted red clay road that twisted steeply up the less craggy portion of the hill, then led between the unkept orchard and the poorly tended pasture fields to the paved road to Hawthorne Town. He could not see where the farm road met the highway, nor the rough land past the pasture hill as it dropped down to the creek on the other side. He knew they were there, just as he knew that in the pasture there were wide acres of gently rolling land, limestone soil that would grow clover hay or rye or wheat or corn, if need be. He knew that in the orchard there were tall old pear trees and thick-trunked, crooked-limbed apple trees; Ben Davis, Winesap, and Horse apple, Early June, Golden Delicious, Limber Twigs, and Rusty Coats. Just above the banks of the creek he could not see there was a grove of sugar maple trees, some oak and beech and shag bark hickory, thickets of wild plum near the pasture, and over many trees the thick, rope-like vines of wild grapes grew.

The uncut fence rows were worlds unto themselves, jungles of sumac bush and blackberry briars, sassafras shoots and red haw bush with its thorn-like twigs. There were persimmons in the pasture, a grove of the small, deep-orange, sweet-meated kind near a clump of black walnut and butternut trees. The back boundary of the land followed a shallow stream, falling over wide ledges of limestone where watermoss and mint grew and periwinkle shells twinkled in the sun, or again caught into shadowy pools thick with minnows. The path of the creek turned and steepened into a series of cascades that carried the water soon to the river, and where the creek water touched the river the farm ended.

Marsh would stand for long moments with his fingers pulling and bending the tight squares of wire, his mind never knowing what his fingers did. Sometimes white fog would blanket the bottom lands and he could see no more than the comb of the barn or tip of the renter's house chimney, but the fog never hindered his slow searching glance nor covered the things he saw. Back in the barn, Angus and Perce would look at him, study his strong straight back, and the way he stood, squarely on his two feet with no laziness and no lounging. Perce might say as if to the air, "He'd make a good neighbor," and half an hour later Angus as he tied a hand might answer, "Pity he's got to go off to South America—go livin' by day's work in strange places."

Dorie, as well as Angus and Perce, saw Marsh sometimes as he stood in the rain and looked over the Cumberland. One afternoon when the tobacco was mostly stripped, and the rain was more foglike mist than drops of water, she called to him from the back porch, "What are you huntin' for over th' river, Marsh?"

"There's no huntin' to it," he called back without looking at her.

She threw a jumper over her shoulders and came and stood with him by the fence. "You ought to go over there one a these days, Marsh," she said, and glanced speculatively at him from the corners of her eyes. When Marsh remained silent she continued after a long survey of the farm, "That place is a cryin' for somebody to get it in shape."

He nodded to that, and she, after another sidelong glance, continued, "Bad as that pasture looks to be, there's still good grazin' with nothin' done.—Lord but it hurts to see a place mistreated so—ever year it washes worse."

He shoved his hands into his pockets and spoke with his eyes straight ahead. "Th' renter's house is in a bad way.—Reckin it could he fixed?"

"Pshaw, it's strong, th' roof's good, an' th' rails are sound. A good man handy with his hands—like you—could fix it up with a underpinnin' an' porches in no time. Lots live in worse.—Aye, but a body could raise fine clover hay up there above. Burn him a lime kiln and sweeten up the land—smoother an' better than some a my own."

Marsh cleared his throat. "Looks like a big rich garden there by the barn."

"But if somebody don't get to it one a these days that little spring branch will be th' ruination of it. It's a cuttin' a gully now. But it an' them gullies above could all be fixed with rock an' cedar brush an' grass sacks of dirt with sweet clover seed," Dorie said, and peeped at him from under her hat brim.

"They'd better mix a little red top with their clover seed, an' put out some Bermuda grass sod. Nothin's so good for holdin' as Bermuda grass once it gets a start." He hesitated, and would not look at Dorie as he asked, "I wonder now—is that limestone any good for buildin'?"

"Nothin' better. Makes good lime, too, an' a body could build with th' plain rock or break 'em up for strong cement. A workin' man strong—like you—could, with sand from th' river an' limestone from th' hill, make cement waterin' troughs an' put a cement floor in th' barn for might nigh nothin'."

Marsh nodded and pulled harder at the fence while Dorie continued, "He'd have that brick house to rent an' help him along with cash. Elliot'ull want it for three or four more years anyhow. His wife's no hand for managin', a city woman not knowin' buttermilk from clabber. A man with a smart wife, a good sensible girl—like Delph for example—why she could sell 'em enough milk an' butter an' eggs an' such to nearly keep her in pin money. An' when th' man that bought it was out a debt he could move to th' big house on th' hill if he wanted to. But, Lord, when th' corn's all in tassel, fourteen feet tall an' a blue black green, stalks big as your wrist like I've seen it there—I couldn't think of any place that a farmer'ud rather be."

He turned abruptly away. "Where's Delph? I've not seen her since dinner."

"Upstairs sewin' on her weddin' dress, I guess. Mebbe she'll get somethin' done with Katy off to school for a change, an' not drivin' her crazy with talk."

"She likes to hear Katy talk," he answered with the curiously gentle yet troubled smile that touched his mouth sometimes when he spoke of Delph.

Dorie looked troubled, too, and fingered the fence as she said, "She's awful young, Marsh."

"I know—hardly eighteen."

"I don't mean that. Katy's thirteen, but in some ways Delph's younger than Katy. It's her raisin', I reckin."

"She's been well brought up, I'd say," he answered somewhat sharply.

Dorie nodded. "That's what I mean—too careful raised—keep a new calf in a stable all winter, turn it out sudden like on a bright wild day in spring, it's like a addled thing."

He tried to catch Dorie's glance, and failing in that, asked in a low voice, "What are you drivin' at, Dorie?"

"Nothin'.—Only when you're makin' your plans for South America you ought to be thinkin'—on—well on Delph."

He turned on her in an outburst of his weary perplexity. "God, Dorie, what have I been thinkin' on but Delph—since—since last summer you might say?"

She looked over the river with her upper lip growing long and her eyes narrow. "Well, all I've got to say is, that your thinkin's brought you some mighty pretty plans. Aimin' to take her for a year an' a half or mebbe two to a place where you're none too happy to be goin' yourself, a place you know nothin about, but from th' price they're givin' you to come it must be hard to get men. Mebbe not a doctor within fifty miles, mebbe not a white woman for a neighbor, mebbe Delph's th' kind that can't stand th' climate, mebbe there'll be fever.—When you talked to that man in Lexington did you tell him you aimed to bring a wife?"

He shook his head guiltily and mumbled, "Other men take their wives—sometimes." Then burst out in a louder voice, "Dorie, you know damn well I've thought a all that—an' more—but it's th' best payin' job I've ever had—why in two years I could mebbe save more than I have in th' last five. An' Delph—she's got her heart set so on goin'."

Dorie snorted. "How could she have her heart set on somethin' she knows nothin' about? Now, don't be mad, Marsh, I was never one for givin' advice or meddlin', but you an' Delph seem like my own. Recollect when you come to this country that first time, a green little driller hardly twenty years old. That was th' spring I learned that Sam wouldn't be back—but as a visitor. 'Peared like you come in his place, somehow. An' all this week I've been thinkin'; if I had a son an' he was marryin' a young tight-raised back country girl like Delph, why I've been thinkin' what I would do."

"An' what would you do, Dorie?" he asked after a time of looking over the river.

Dorie gave him a sidling glance. "Well, in th' first place I'd set myself dead against his goin' away, but if he would go in spite a me—why—I'd never let him take his wife. I'd keep her by me," she went on after a moment's study of his face. "She'd be a sight of company. Ever' day she stays she seems more like Rachel to me."

"Rachel, I reckin, didn't care whether she stayed with her man or not."

"She run away to marry him, but this is different. Delph'ull want to go with you, most likely cry an' beg. But, Lord, Marsh, many a woman's cried. A man's got to be sensible."

Marsh's eyes darkened with remembering. "Dorie, you can't tell me anything about bein' sensible—at least not much. I've been that way most a my life—too damned sensible."

"Well, it's a bad time to stop bein' that way now. It's sensible," she went on cautiously, "not stingy for a man wantin' money like you, to think—an' remember—that a lone man in th' oil fields can save a lot more money than a man with a wife."

"I'd never leave her behind just for that," he answered with a sullen set to his chin.

Dorie caught his arm. "Listen, Marsh," she begged, and waited until he had looked at her, then said, "You think I'm stingy an' hard with not much heart."

He nodded. "You sound like it sometimes.—You don't know, Dorie. I mean you couldn't know how high land comes—to some. Workin' an' savin' then gettin' drunk an' gamblin an' spendin', or investin' an' losin' an' thinkin' ever' year—. Hell, you married yours. You're not a man—marryin' an'—."

She turned on him with bitter, understanding eyes. "Land? I can't know th' cost of land? I married my land? Listen, with this land I married a man—a good man but no farmer, brought up for the law an' county politics. For sixteen years I stayed mostly in this house tied down with babies an' watched him run with fox hunters an' th' courthouse crowd an' drink himself to death—an' mortgage an' waste th' land. I never quarreled. It would ha done no good. When Katy was a month old an' Sam was sixteen they brought him in one mornin'—November it was—I recollect th' river valley how blue it was in th' dawn. Drunk he was with his feet burned off. He'd dropped down dead drunk, an' th' fool with him was drunk enough to build a fire by his feet, an' then he laid down a little piece away an' went to sleep.

"I had seven children under seventeen, six hundred acres of land mortgaged up to th' hilt, needin' fence, fertilizer, an' ever'thing I couldn't give it. He laid five months a dyin'—mostly, I think, because he didn't want to live without his feet. An' while he was there dyin' do you think, do you think I could be there holdin' his hand? I was out seein' to things. I had it to do. It was in th' early twenties an' th' boom had got all th' farm hands north to Akron an' Detroit. Many's th' day I drove two mules in th' cultivator from daylight 'til dark, stoppin' just long enough to eat an' nurse Katy. Many's th' night that Sam an' Emma an' me would be up 'til midnight, rollin' out again at daylight, workin' to get butter or sausage meat or somethin' up to sell next day.—I've had a harder time than you'll ever have. You're not a woman."

Marsh draw a deep breath like a groan. "I know it won't be easy—but damned if I'm goin' to add Delph in on th' price."

"Well, always recollect, wherever you go or whatever you do, she'll have a price of her own to pay—ever' woman married to a man wantin' to get a start in th' world has. I hope you thought a such things when you was stealin' her away—eighteen years old."

He winced at that, and then he was angry, both with himself and with Dorie, talking of Delph as if she were a problem or a burden. "Come go with me an' look at Prissy—she's lookin' mighty big an' her time still more'n a month away," Dorie suggested in a kindlier tone, and started toward the barn.

"I want to see Delph," he said, and started hurriedly toward the house. He stopped on the back porch, cleaned the mud from his shoes, then went into the kitchen, calling loudly, "Oh, Delph."

He waited and heard soon her quick light feet overhead, and then down the back stairs; and when she came through the door, her coming made the world seem better than it was. He was brave and sure again, smiling at her, feeding on the warm bright life in her face. She was silent a moment, smiling at him with a shyness that seemed to increase instead of lessen as their wedding day came closer. "You want somethin', Marsh?" she asked, and waited, happy that he had left his work with the other men for even a little while.

He stood confused with his rain dripping hat in his hand. He couldn't for the life of him think of a thing he wanted except what he had—the simple pleasure of looking at Delph. He struggled to think of some need of the moment, but she, all unknowing, came to his rescue. She felt his leather jacket sleeves and shoulders, and said with a brisk housewifely air that made him think of a child playing house, "It's a good thing you got in. I'll bet you want dry clothes. You must be soaked to th' bone."

"Socks, dry socks, that's all I want," he said, and wondered if his feet were wet or dry.

She rushed away, and was back in a moment, and must scold him a bit because, though he sat with his boots steaming by the open oven door, he had forgotten to take them off. "You're already bossy as can be," he scolded, pleased that she took such concern for his feet. The business of changing his socks went slowly. He took advantage of their aloneness in the house, and pulled her down to his knees to learn how the wedding dress was coming on, and if she were still mad at the tobacco.

She smiled at that, and pulled his ear as she explained, "It was-n't th' tobacco an' waitin' I minded so much, just Dorie, I guess," she added in a whisper.

"Pshaw, don't say that. She's gettin' old an' a little childish maybe. She wanted you to have a proper weddin' like she'd give one of her own girls, an' never did."

Delph wrinkled her nose at the wedding dress. "All that time an' money spent for white goods when that new blue dress trimmed with red would ha' done just as well. I'm already feelin' scared some-how—Dorie's eyes water now when she looks at th' dress. She seems too sensible to be so silly; an' by my weddin' day I'm afraid she'll cry all over th' place an' with Brother Eli so solemn like an' old.—I wish we could ha' had a younger preacher."

"Who'd want to be married by just any young snip of a peacher? Brother Eli's a good man. Nobody can beat him for growin' garden truck," he said, and added haltingly, "I—I'd kind a like to see you lookin' like a bride myself."

She laughed and rumpled his hair. "You'll have a bride all right. I'll look so meek an' white an' good you'll never know me. You'll not even know my hand when you put on the ring."

"Delph?"

"Yes."

"Would you mind—I mean will it matter so much to you—if I don't give you a ring? Now, I mean. I'm a little—well, when a man's not certain how things—. I looked in Hawthorne Town but I couldn't find a thing I liked."

He felt her arm on his neck slip slowly away. "No,—that's all right, Marsh. It's—it's sort of funny. I planned on a ring—an' a bright weddin' dress, but—. Pshaw, what's a little thing like a ring?"

Her arms were around his neck again, and she was playing with his hair. "Don't look so sober like. I don't mind, not a bit. Some day you'll be able to buy me half a dozen. When you drill wells an' lease land on your own—or have a job high up for some big company, an' we'll live in a city, an'—you won't have it so hard."

· 9 ·

DORIE REFLECTIVELY scratched her head with a knitting needle, and stared at her stockinged feet propped on a stick of wood in the bake oven, while she considered the problem at hand. She turned and looked over her shoulder at Katy who sat by the kitchen table. "I don't think you'd better write up th' weddin'," she said. "Delph's Uncle John might get hold a th' paper. How'd he like it, me same as braggin' through th' paper I'd helped in Delph's runaway?"

Katy gave the answer she gave to all opinions of her mother with which she disagreed, a loud wailing of "A-w-w, Mama," and a tossing back of her hair. She turned to Delph sitting on the other side of the table with her back to Dorie.

"Wouldn't you like it, Delph?—Delph, you gone to sleep?"

Delph glanced away from the snow falling thickly past the window, and asked with a confused smile, "Wouldn't I like what? I guess I was wool gatherin'."

Katy laughed, and Dorie counted three purled stitches then said, "You mean you're thinkin' a Marsh. He'll be back, never you fear, tonight at th' latest. Just before Christmas like this there's maybe a rush on th' tobacco market, an' they couldn't sell right away."

"Last year Angus was gone better'n a week," Katy reminded her mother, and then catching the stricken look in Delph's eyes, turned back to her plea for news. "Aw, Mama, I'll need some news. Why, I've hardly got anything to write, an' I fixed th' weddin' up so pretty like an' all."

"It was a pretty weddin' to begin with," Dorie said with a softness uncommon in her voice, and looked at Delph until Delph

119

forgot her hunger and loneliness for Marsh in fearing that Dorie was going to burst into tears as she had done at the wedding.

"That's why I'm goin' to put it in th' paper," Katy said, and sprang up to read what she had written. "'On Saturday of last week the Fairchild home was the scene of what your correspondent hopes will be a long and fruitful union. Miss Delphine Costello, late of Costello, Kentucky, was united in wedlock with Mr. Marshal Gregory, known in this community. The bride was beautifully dressed in a flowing white gown, and carried a sheaf of late bloom- ing chrysanthemums.'—I'd like to say somethin' about how nice Marsh looked. I'd never seen him in a real suit before, but in city papers they never say a word about th' groom an' he didn't buy a new suit anyhow.'—They were married in the large front parlor'— Mama, couldn't I call it a drawing room?'—decorated with potted ferns and chrysanthemums. Brother Eli Fitzgerald who performed the ceremony remarked that in all his seventy-six years he had never seen a prettier bride.'—I'd like to say that he trimmed his beard an' had his suit pressed special, but I guess I'd better not—'Among those present were Mr. and Mrs. Higginbottom from Cedar Stump'—I ought to be truthful an' say a word about how Lizzie cried, an' how you did, too, for that matter."

Dorie smoothed her knitting and looked at it. "Katy, some day you'll live to cry at weddin's. I laughed, too, when I was young like you."

"Don't forget th' shower, an' say somethin' about how good ever'body was to ma," Delph suggested, anxious to get the conver- sation away from tears. "An' you might say, too," she went on after a moment's pondering, "that I'm awful sorry I can't take all their presents with me—to South America." She smiled a little secret smile. At last her name would maybe be in the *Fincastle Outlook* among the others who had gone away.

"Delph, maybe you'll be—," Katy began, but stopped when Dorie turned quickly about in her chair, and frowned and shook her head at Katy, and seemed to sigh with her eyes over Delph's back.

Katy looked at Delph in a troubled wondering way, the same speculative wonder in her glance that had haunted Delph all through her wedding day. Their eyes met; Katy smiled an embar- rassed, worried sort of smile and bent hastily to her writing. Her pen scratched busily for a time, but soon she must stop to ponder and twist a curl around her finger.

While she pondered, Angus came in; his wide shoulders were heavily powdered with snow, and there was more snow on his feet, but Angus, usually so slow and careful in all things, walked hastily toward Dorie with no pausing to clean his feet. He glanced uncertainly about the room, and seemed of half a mind to speak with Dorie, but Katy would not give him time. "I need a fresh audience," she said, and began to read rapidly, "'Salem news this week is mostly weather. We are having our first real fall of snow, unusually heavy for the time of year.

"'However, Mrs. Dorie Dodson Fairchild did not let the weather keep her tobacco from the market. Her son Robert Jonathon'— Mama, reckin they'll know that's Poke Easy?—'home from Lexington for Christmas vacation, left with Mr. Marshal Gregory and the tobacco on Monday of this week.'"

Angus opened his mouth, but Katy lifted her hand for silence and continued, "'Ray Higginbottom, fourteen year old son of Perce Higginbottom of Cedar Stump, reports that his 4-H Club Project white leghorn pullets broke th' county record for layers last week.'— I hope he was tellin' th' truth an' not just braggin'."

Angus shifted his feet and looked at Dorie. "Miz Dorie."

"'Brother Eli Fitzgerald conducted services at Salem Church on Sunday of this week. His text was: "But the fig tree said unto them, Should I forsake my sweetness, and my good fruit, and go to be promoted over the trees?" Judges 9:11.'"

"Miz Dorie—."

"'Mrs. Elliot, wife of Mr. Elliot who lives'—don't you think I ought to make it 'resides' for strange people like th' Elliots?—'in the old Weaver house on the Hawthorne Road—.'"

Angus turned abruptly toward Katy as if he had maybe lost heart to speak with Dorie. "Katy, if you keep on a readin'—why—why pretty soon you can say, 'Prissy she's had her calf,'" he finished all in a breath, and lowered his white lashed eyes and would not look at Dorie.

Dorie sat for a second with one needle sliding from her knitting, and her lower jaw dropped. She came to sudden violent life, threw her knitting to the floor, sprang up and rushed hatless and coatless out into the snow, crying, "Lord, Lord, it's a month before her time, an' Prissy my prize heifer."

Katy took her mother's hat and jumper from their nail behind the stove, and started with them to the barn. "Prissy'ull die or be ruined for life maybe, an' I guess th' little calf's already dead, an' Mama she'll have her stomach all upset," she said, and went away with a soundless sobbing, while Angus fidgeted by the stove and had the look of a man ready to be hanged.

Delph could think of nothing to do, but felt the situation demanded something. She built up the fire, filled the tea kettle and set it to boil. Katy was back in a moment, bursting into the kitchen, her hair white with snow, and Black Peter, Brown Bertha, and Caesar, cowed by a scolding from Dorie, racing at her heels. "Mama drove me away," she breathlessly explained. "An' Angus, she said for you to get down there quick. She said Prissy was a havin' it mighty bad."

"Prissy was a good way along, an' any cow has a hard time," Angus said in words even slower than common, and gave no indication of returning to the barn.

Katy flipped snow from her hair, and pulled on his arm. "I'm tellin' you, you'd better go. Mama's gettin' worse off than Prissy."

"To my mind she's goin' to be worser later on," Angus prophesied, and went slowly away. Katy's tears came as easily as her laughter. She sat now on the wood box and cried with Black Peter and Brown Bertha sitting with their heads on her knees and young Caesar chewing the laces in her shoes. "This'ull be th' death a Mama," she sobbed. "She's planned it all so long; how she'd breed an' raise some Jerseys subject to register, an' now she's waited all this while for a pure blooded calf of Solomon's breedin', an' now most likely it'll be dead." Dorie, too flustered to notice she had worn her comfort shoes out into the mud and snow, returned, scolded Katy for crying, and rolled a cigarette but was too excited to smoke it. She sat and waved the crooked cigarette and talked to the top of the stove. "I wish to th' Lord Marsh or Poke Easy was here. I never was any good at a time like this. Angus is what worries me so. He's handled many a calvin' an' foalin' but I never saw him worried like he is now.—I wish to God there was a vetinarian in this end a th' county. There ought to be a law havin' a county health for animals same as for humans. I wish I had Brother Eli or Az, but Brother's got no telephone, an' th' Cumberland's too high for Az."

Katy dried her easy tears, and studied her mother. "What about, Dr. Andy: he brought all of us. Maybe he'd bring Prissy's calf."

Dorie shook her head. "Dr. Andy 'ud never come out in this weather for a cow. Anyhow it would maybe insult him to ask him."

"You've insulted plenty a people in your day. One more wouldn't matter."

"He'd never come for a cow—not even Prissy."

"He wouldn't have to know."

Dorie got up and started to the barn. "I'm too much respected in this neighborhood to start tellin' lies at my age."

When her mother had gone, Katy smoothed the brown spots above Brown Bertha's eyes. "Nobody respects me—much. I'm young enough to live over it," she said to the dog, and got up and went to the telephone in the hall.

Delph and the dogs followed her, and watched as she took the receiver from the wall and began an immediate calling in a high excited voice, "Mattie—Oh, Mattie, give me Dr. Andy—make it quick—mighty quick.—Never mind what's th' matter with her, get me Dr. Andy's house."

A moment's silence with Katy rolling her eyes at Delph, then calling again in a voice shrill with terror, "Dr. Andy, oh, Dr. Andy, is that you, Dr. Andy. This is Katy—Dorie Dodson Fairchild's Katy. Please come quick. Mama's afraid she's dyin'. She's scared to death. Come mighty quick, or you'll be too late."

The telephone sounded with gruff excited questions, but Katy slammed the receiver and turned to Delph. "That'll bring him. He thinks th' world an' all a Mama, an' once he's here he'll do what he can for Prissy."

There was nothing to do but wait restlessly in the kitchen, and look toward the barnyard for signs of what might be happening there. Delph, to whom the pretty slender-legged Prissy was just another cow, thought mostly of Marsh. She would liked to have gone upstairs and hunted something of his she might have overlooked in the spell of mending his things she had taken while he was away, but since the rest of the household took the matter of Prissy in such tragic fashion, she feared she might be thought lacking in sympathy should she leave the kitchen.

Angus came again and stood cracking his knuckles by the stove. There were beads of sweat on his forehead, and his naturally pale eyes seemed paler yet. Katy, cheered by the prospect of Dr. Andy, began the business of comforting Angus. "Prissy's not dead an' there's still hope, mebbe th' calf will come all right. Do you reckin Solomon knows he's gettin' a son?"

Angus twisted his hat. "I ain't a sayin' what Solomon knows, but to my mind Prissy an' her calf'ull both live."

"Well, I wouldn't be scared to death. Th' way you act is one thing that's worryin' Mama so."

"I—I can't help it. Prissy—she seems uncommon quick with th' business so I come—I come away. I didn't want to be on hand."

The door was flung violently open as if by a whirlwind. Angus shivered and looked at his shoes. Delph looked at Dorie and retreated to a corner. The dogs sprang forward to greet their mistress, paused in mid-charge to study her with troubled eyes, then all, including the pup Caesar, walked with lowered tails behind the stove. Katy sat on the wood box and hugged her knees and bowed her head and looked at her mother from the tops of her eyes. Dorie, however, had thought for none but Angus who looked at Dorie and backed away. "I—couldn't help it, Ma'am. Th' fence in that back field next to Riley Sexton's scrub bull, it wasn't any good. He broke in one day—I saw him an' run like fightin' fire, but Prissy she was more than willin' an' beat me to him; an' it just a month before you'd told me to let her to Solomon."

Dorie found her tongue and poured out her anger and surprise and disgust in shrill breathless speech. "Th' calf comes, not dead but a kickin', an' I look an' I wait, an' I look again. Prissy starts lickin' it dry, an' it tries to teeter to its feet, an' I look an' I think th' lights all wrong, for I'm seein' spots where there's no spots to see. I look again. I go up close, an' what do I see, what do I see, but a knock kneed, pot-bellied, little scrub bull, spotted, an' no more kin a Solomon's than I am.—Oh, Angus—you, you—you could ha told me."

Angus retreated another step before her wrathful eyes and gesticulating hand. "I—I hadn't th' heart, Ma'am. Thought it was, well, kinder to let you keep a thinkin'.—Poke Easy—he—I told him last summer, an' he said you'd—you'd have more fun waitin' for a scrub bull an' thinkin' it was a pure bred than you'd ever have out a havin' a pure bred—so I thought it was kinder."

"Kinder? Poke Easy, he could ha—?" Dorie's comment on Poke Easy was never finished. The ringing of the telephone and a second later the sonorous clanking of the brass knocker on the front hall door followed almost immediately by the savage barking and leaping of the dogs from behind the stove, caused Dorie to think of the tobacco. "Go see who's wantin', Katy, an' I'll get th' telephone. It's most likely Poke Easy callin' from Hawthorne Town to say that th' bottom dropped out a th' market just as they put my tobacco up for sale."

Katy arose, smoothed her dress, ran her fingers through her hair by way of combing it and went to the door. Delph remained with Angus and with him exchanged a sigh of thankfulness at the interruption. Their relief, however, was almost immediately shattered by Dorie's heated conversation with the telephone. "Who's dyin'? Me sick? I never felt stronger in my life. You heard it in Burdine? Brother Eli told you? I've not seen Brother Eli since th' weddin'. He said Mattie Smiley told him? I tell you there's nothin' wrong."

The receiver banged, and there was a moment's quiet during which Katy could be heard in her best Sunday School manner. "Come right in, Dr. Andy, you an' Brother Eli. Th' side parlor's had a fire but it's about out now. I'll build it up." And Katy came flying kitchenwards, taking no time to answer the two men's single question of "How's your mother?"

Katy remained in the kitchen with Delph, leaving the explanations to Dorie who began and ended the matter with a few remarks of apology for Katy's scatterbrained ways, and then turned to with a spirited account of the weaknesses of Prissy and Angus. Between relief at finding no sickness at Fairchild Place and sympathy for Dorie, neither of the old men had any scolding word for Katy; Brother Eli even going so far as to praise her sympathetic, tenderhearted ways with animals. He went with Angus to look at the calf, and returned filled with comforting words. The calf showed that Prissy was a very fine cow indeed. The good Jersey blood showed stronger than Riley Sexton's scrub bull; and it was neither scrub nor bull, but a pretty little heifer that would grow into a fine all purpose type cow.

Dr. Andy, a dried up little man with a leathery wrinkled face, his cheeks grooved by the bedside smile he had worn for more than forty years, prescribed hot toddies all around, himself included, and not forgetting Angus at the barn.

Delph sipped her toddy, and felt sinful, taking whiskey in the middle of the afternoon when nothing ailed. She listened absent-mindedly to the attempts of the callers to comfort Dorie, but sat with her ears pricked for the telephone. Poke Easy might call about the tobacco, and she could get to speak a word with Marsh. Each time it rang she listened expectantly to Katy's answers, but always it was only some of the neighbors. Those who had not actually seen Dr. Andy and Brother Eli go rushing up to Fairchild Place, had heard from their neighbors that Dorie was dying, or Katy was in a bad way, or that that runaway bride was taken suddenly sick. Katy took the blame for everything, explaining in the polite ladylike fashion she wore at times as she wore a dress, that Prissy the cow had had such a time, that she, Katy, had lost her head from excitement and called Dr. Andy.

In spite of the strong hot drink and the comforting words from her callers, Dorie's hot anger gave place to nothing better than cold despair. She looked old and mournful and dejected as she sat and stared into the fire and vowed that she would sell or give Prissy away. However, her despair quickly changed to troubled eagerness when Katy, after a good bit of preamble with Mattie the telephone girl, called that Poke Easy, on his way home in Hawthorne Town, wanted to talk with her about the tobacco.

Delph hesitated a moment and followed her into the hall where she listened and watched Dorie as she received the tobacco news; the Fairchild tobacco had gone on a fast market at an average of thirty-two cents a pound, one of the highest averages for that day. Marsh and Poke Easy would be home soon, but first they must stop in Hawthorne for a bit of celebration. Dorie bade them drink no more than they could carry, warned them that Brother Eli would stay to supper, but said nothing of Prissy's bastard.

Delph had come gradually nearer, until when Dorie hung up the receiver, she was just by her elbow, her disappointed eyes still on the telephone. "Did—did he say anything about Marsh?"

"Marsh's fine. They're both fine. Everything's fine," Dorie

answered and started to tell the others, but stopped abruptly on seeing Delph's face.

"I—I just thought Marsh might ask to speak to me. That was why I waited."

Dorie patted her shoulder. "Now, Delph, don't start bein' like that. Why he's only been gone three days."

"But we've only been married five," she answered, and turned from Dorie's eyes, but not quickly enough.

"Why, Delph, you're cryin'.—Marsh had to go to see about his job."

"I'm not cryin'," she answered, and ran down the hall and up the stairs to Marsh's bedroom—her room now. Dorie's call of, "don't be foolish now," followed her, but she did not answer. She stood a moment by one of the windows, though she could see nothing of Burdine, only the old Weaver Place, a red brick house and a run down farm over the Cumberland.

Not long after Katy was calling up the stairs, didn't she think it would be nice to make a freezer of ice cream for supper? They could find plenty of ice left from the last hard freeze on the river hill. Delph dried her eyes, tied on an apron, and went hurrying down to help with the supper getting.

The preparation of food at Fairchild Place was never the prosaic, well-planned business it was in Fronie's kitchen. Dorie's method of getting a meal consisted in none at all; and Delph enjoyed it. Some things Dorie cooked because a member of her household had wished for or liked that particular thing; others she cooked because she just happened to remember, usually at the last minute, that she hadn't a mess of that certain food in a long while, and still other dishes she served because they were in season or going to waste.

Tonight, because of Katy's wish for ice cream and chocolate cake, Dr. Andy's love of a good sweet potato pie, Brother Eli's strictly vegetarian diet, Poke Easy's insistence that home cured ham be served each meal he was home, Marsh's love of beans and bean soup, and also due to the fact that in the morning a neighbor down the road had returned a leg of beef borrowed a month before, and since the smoke house was crowded with fresh pork from the last hog killing, Dorie's supper preparations took a more breathless turn than common.

Delph and Katy were kept busy running to the cellar, the smoke house, or up to the attic for herbs hung there to dry. Between times of running there was the stirring of this, the turning of that, keeping the stove stoked with wood, and ears strained, especially Delph's, for the coming of Poke Easy and Marsh.

Delph was rolling pie crust when Poke Easy's blonde head and wide shoulders came through the back door. She knew that Marsh was somewhere near. Heedless of Poke Easy's hearty greeting, the half rolled pie crust, and her floury hands, she dashed through the door and down the barnyard walk, never noticing that snow sifted into her low shoes. Marsh was fastening the barnyard gate, and did not hear her through the snow. She flung her arms about his neck and teasingly put her hands over his eyes. He straightened suddenly, struggling away and exclaiming, "Now, what th' Hell."

He saw her then, the heavy snowy twilight not deep enough to hide the eagerness in her eyes. "Why, I thought you'd be in th' kitchen with th' others," he apologized, and added as he kissed her, "You oughtn't to be out here, bare-headed and without a coat."

"I—never thought," she answered, and stood crimping her apron. She wished he hadn't noticed that she wore no coat, and that he had come dashing to the house like Poke Easy.

She felt better when he gently flicked snow from her hair and smiled and said, "Delph, you ought to ha been in Lexington."

She flipped her apron excitedly. "I guess you learned from that man all about how we're goin'. I just can't wait to hear it all. I wish I had a map right now. Will we start from New Orleans?"

"Delph?" he began, not looking at her face, but down at the snow on her shoes, "I—let's wait 'til after supper to talk a goin' away. Mostly, I stayed in th' tobacco warehouse, anyhow."

"Not three whole days."

He nodded. "I listened to th' farmers talk.—There was an, an old hill man from th' Rockcastle Country close to where Roan has his land—you know Roan's buyin' up land. He smoked a corn cob pipe an' didn't look to have a dime. He'd brought just a little crop a tobacco, maybe six hundred pounds, but on his bottom lands by th' river he'd raised he said better'n two thousand bushels a corn. —But there wasn't any way to haul out his corn, so he bought hogs—"

Delph pulled his sleeve. "I just recollected, I left Dorie's pie crust half rolled, an' I'm gettin' my feet wet out in this snow."

"I'll have to buy you boots like Katy's," he said, and with a, "We'll keep your feet dry now," he caught her up and ran to the back porch steps. She laughed and protested and tried to squirm free, and reminded him just as they reached the porch, "Marsh, recollect I can't wait much longer to hear about our plans."

They entered the kitchen, damp with snow, red lipped, warm eyed, and Dorie, finishing the pie crust that Delph had started, beamed on them and said, "Lord, such a pair of lovers."

What with the success of the tobacco crop and everybody's attempt to take Dorie's mind from Prissy, Fairchild Place was gay that night, warm and bright with lights from its windows brightening long reaches of the falling snow. Supper was a lengthy meal; the first part given mostly to food and drink, the last and longest to talk, talk that sometimes rose into heated discussions, or quieted again into brotherly agreement; solid talk of land and crops and cattle, the neighbors, the roads, markets, schools, Roan's troubles in trying to get a county stock law and a law making tuberculin tests of cows compulsory.

Delph listened for a time, hoping always that this conversation would take a different turn; that Poke Easy would talk a bit of his life at the university, Brother Eli tell of his experiences in China as a missionary, Dorie speak of Sam, but most of all she wished they would talk of Marsh's work and plans. Yet, no mention was made of his going away.

All through the dinner Marsh's eyes were continually straying into hers, gentle they were and kind, saying many things, but never of what she wanted to hear. He looked tired, she thought, and troubled, not gay and eager for their life away together as she had always hoped he would be; but worried as he had looked that day in the Little South Fork Country when he had asked her to marry him. But gradually when the business of eating was finished and the talk flew faster, he listened to the others and the troubled look left his face. Brother Eli was telling how his vineyard throve in the rocky limestone soil he had; Delph watched Marsh as he leaned across the table and looked at the old man with his eyes eager like a child's eyes, and seeing more than an old man's beard. She was suddenly lonesome, and wishing very much that she and Marsh could be alone together.

No one except Katy noticed when she slipped from the table and went to the kitchen; and Katy, tired from setting still so long, followed her, and marveled at her industrious ways when Delph said, "I thought I'd start washin' th' dishes."

The fire was out and the stove cold, but they threw in good dry sugar tree branches and sat on the wood box and waited for the dish water to warm. Delph hugged her knees and watched the maple flames flicker and snap with their yellow tongues at the stove grate bars. "Let's sit in th' dark an' see things in th' grate," Katy whispered and turned out the light.

Delph smiled and felt less lonesome. "I'm tryin' to imagine how it will be. I can't even think what I'd like to see first, so many things."

"I think I'd take th' sea for mine, Katy said. "It must be fine to see it in a storm."

"Oh, but th' hearin' of it," Delph whispered. "You know, I've wondered lots of times. I know it can't be peaceful like an' sleepy soundin' as th' singin' shells in th' parlor at home. More like th' wind in th' high back hills in winter or like th' wind in th' beech trees in th' spring." She felt free with the child Katy, more so even than with Marsh; and under cover of the darkness and the loud conversation in the dining room, talked on in soft hesitant whispers. "I'd like to see an island in th' sea, an' a mountain all white with snow, but more than that I think—I think I'd like to be—at least for a little while—with people different from me. Some that wouldn't look at me an' know—well ever'thing. Some that couldn't say, "There goes Delph. She must be pretty bad else she would ha joined th' church. She's one a th' Little South Fork Costellos, kin of—an' on an' on th' way they know. Oh, just once I'd like to be a stranger in a strange place."

Katy nodded, then glanced in a troubled way at Delph's eyes shining in the firelight. "It would be nice," she said. "I hope to do it some day, but still—it's like Mama always says, 'Never give all your heart to any one thing. Divide it out in pieces, an' then have back a piece in case—.'"

"In case of what?"

"I don't remember th' rest of it.—Lord we've set here talkin' away till th' dish water's hot enough to boil." And Katy sprang up, turned on the lights and began washing the dishes.

Laughter and talk continued in the dining room; Katy had almost finished the dishes brought to the kitchen, and was threatening to go clear the table, when Brother Eli was heard to suggest that they all go down and have another look at the new calf. They came trooping through the kitchen not long after, Dorie high-spirited now as she had been low not long before. "Maybe it is a nice calf, but all th' same I'll never keep it, or that Prissy either," she explained to the company, but with no touch of sorrow.

Delph watched Marsh, hoping he would not go with the others but stay behind with her. But he never saw her, and smiled with the others when Brother Eli paused to stroke his beard and study the ceiling as he did in his sermons, then suggest to Dorie with a crafty glint in his eye, "Tell you what, Dorie. I'll be glad to take her off your hands. I could maybe make you a better price than she'd bring on th' market."

"Now, Brother Eli, I appreciate your kindness," Dorie answered as if she meant it, "but I'll never sell Prissy like a common cow, no better'n so many pounds a beef. I mean to give her to Marsh."

Marsh looked more startled and incredulous than pleased. "But Dorie, I couldn't take a present like that. You've done—."

"None a that now. You've helped in th' tobacco all fall. Pshaw if I'd a paid you a grader's wages they a been more'n th' price a Prissy."

"But you'll have th' feedin' an' tendin' a her all th' while I'm gone."

"Law, Delph can do that. A pretty little thing like Prissy would be good company for her when you're gone."

"It would maybe help," Marsh said. He stopped abruptly, and stood hunting Delph with his eyes, hoping against a kind of certainty that she had not heard. He would tell her tonight when they were alone.

Something dropped to the floor with the splintering tinkle of breaking glass, and the room was still with everyone looking at Delph in the corner by the cupboard. She stood with a blue striped dish cloth in her hands, and looked, not at the broken glass by her feet, but at Marsh. He saw her eyes and looked away. They were wide with wonder and fright and disbelieving, unwilling to believe what she had heard. Young Caesar came nosing at the broken glass, and looked up at her and thumped his tail, while Dorie said in a strained embarrassed voice, not like Dorie's, "Pshaw, Delph, don't mind breakin' a little thing like a glass," and Katy ran for a broom and dust pan.

But Delph was still, like Lot's wife turned to salt, looking at Marsh with her great disbelieving eyes. Marsh glanced at her again, and it was easier to turn and follow Poke Easy through the door. He walked slowly with the damp snow slithering under his feet, but he had the sensation of running, of covering great reaches of space and of time, running away from Delph, putting an endless distance between them.

He walked with the others through the barn and listened to their talk, heard all the sounds he loved; horses breathing in contented regularity, hens craaking in the dark, and the rustle of fodder blades as some cow drowsily helped herself to a late snack.

He saw the mild eyed Prissy as she lay and chewed her cud, glancing now and then at her wobbly legged calf with as much love in her eyes as if it had been the expected blueblood, subject to register. He only nodded when Brother Eli said, "When you come back in a year an' a half or so you'll have a fine young heifer as well as a cow."

He slipped from the others and went outside and walked about in the snowy barnyard. It was too dark to see the snow, but he could feel the flakes cool on his face and his hands. He wished it were day and he could see over the Cumberland. Maybe when he came back he could look over there or at some piece of land, and plan, and know that he could meet his plan with no danger that he would lose his reason and go against his head for land as he had gone for Delph.

He heard the others leave the barn, the good-byes of Dr. Andy and Brother Eli on the front porch, then the sound of Dr. Andy's car chugging away toward Burdine. He waited, and saw lights leap out from the bedroom windows, Delph's window brightening with the others. He tried to shape sentences in his mind, have all the hard words of explanation ready patterned on his tongue, but Delph's hurt eyes kept scattering the words. Black Peter and Brown Bertha came from their quarters in the tool house and nosed his feet and smelled his hands as if to question his business there.

He went to the back porch then, and was careful and slow about cleaning the mud from his shoes. He opened the back door softly, tip-toed up the back stairs and down the dimly lighted hall. Dorie most likely thought he was with Delph, not hiding out in the barnyard like a coward ashamed of his plans. He listened a time by

Delph's closed door. She would be crying most likely, crying because he was going away; but he would comfort her, make her understand—maybe not now—but soon, some day she would see.

He opened the door, glanced first toward the bed, but it stood untouched and smooth. He saw her then, standing stiff and straight with her back to the fire. She was smiling a fixed hard smile that made her face a mask with two holes for eyes; the stricken eyes of some wounded animal, strange above the woman's smile. He wished he had found her crying. Her tears would hurt but not like this; cry with her eyes and lie with her mouth as if he were a stranger permitted to see the parts of her she would have him see.

She watched in silence as he closed the door and waited while he walked up to the hearth. She glanced at his feet, and he thought guiltily of his cowardly vigil in the snow. "I—went with th' others to see Prissy."

"Yes, I saw you go," she said in a quiet voice unlike her own.

He put his arm around her shoulder, but she took no notice of the gesture, and in a moment stepped away. He looked into the fire while words rolled clumsily through his brain, but shape themselves on his tongue they would not. He fingered a china hen on the mantle while he said, "Delph, I meant to tell you tonight. I—I'm sorry it came so sudden like before th' others. But you'll see it's th' best way, th' only sensible thing."

"For you to go away—an' me stay here?"

He nodded and set the china hen back on her nest. "I can't risk it, Delph."

She turned to him, Delph again, alive and eager, warm blood laying a stain on her cheeks and her eyes bright hot blue. "I'm not afraid, Marsh. I wouldn't mind anything. Dorie she's talked to you. Made you think I'd be no good for goin' with you to th' oil fields.—Marsh, I married you. I'm your wife. Please, can't you see?"

He looked at her, and then into the fire. He somehow couldn't tell her tonight, that it wasn't only a question of her safety, but money, something that could ensure their being together always.

· 10 ·

MARSH DID not cry as Katy cried, or turn to stone like Delph; he cursed sometimes; cursed Dorie's mules with clenched teeth in low toned oil man's curses. The mules flipped their ears and rolled their eyes, but never tried to run away from him as they sometimes did with Angus. One day not long after Poke Easy's return to the university, Angus watched Marsh as he brought the mules in from watering and said, half enviously, "You're a natural born hand with stock."

Marsh pushed his hat back and stared hard at nothing. "Looks like stock's about all I know how to handle, though."

Angus shifted his tobacco to the other cheek and observed, careful to keep his eyes on the ground, "Lucky with horses, unlucky with women—that's a old sayin'."

Marsh's eyes snapped. "Who in th' Hell says I'm unlucky with women. I've got th' best wife in th' world."

Angus smiled down at him. "But you're leavin' her," he said, and strode away whistling "Shady Grove."

Marsh stood still and looked after him until he had walked down the barn hall and disappeared behind a stable door. He started after him, remembering he had offered to help in the messy work of cleaning cow stalls; then wheeled abruptly about and hurried toward the house. He wanted to see Delph. There was always the hope that he would find her as he had expected she would be. Sad, or crying even, but reasonable, agreeing that his plan was a wise plan, the only sensible one. He couldn't leave her as she was; stony calm in speech and action, but under that calmness, fighting eternally, continually alert

134

for signs of his weakening. She was the one to weaken. Some day she would realize that her notions were those of a child.

The kitchen was empty, and he ran up the stairs and into her room. She sat in a low rocker by the fire and mended a pair of his oil man's corduroys. He hated the sight of the trousers, discolored by oil and salt water, frayed at the cuffs and pale at the knees. He must have mixed and shot and hauled a million gallons of nitroglycerin while he wore trousers like those—or at least it seemed that many. "I wouldn't mess with that junk, Delph," he said, and came and squatted on his heels by the hearth.

She smiled, the forced unnatural smile that touched her face so often now, then bit a thread and said, "It's only six more days. I want to do ever'thing I can."

"That's right. It's not long." He looked up into her sad rebellious eyes, and wondered wearily why it was that when he was most certain of her love, he was least certain of her mind. "Delph?"

"Yes."

"I wish you wouldn't take it so. A year an' a half or even two's not a life time."

"It'll seem like it."

He waited a time with the room so still he could hear his own breathing, then tried again, "Delph?"

"Yes."

"I wish—I mean it's hard to go away an' have you—well—not wantin' to do what we are doin'. Can't you—well—think it over an' see it's th' best thing.—You'll maybe see a lot of th' world—someday. An' if you don't you've not missed much."

She ran the needle through the cloth in careful even stitches, and looked at it with flushed face while she said, "It's not that—now. You know it's not. Marsh, I didn't marry you just because—well because you would go away. If seein' th' world was all I wanted I'd a run away or waited there 'til I was twenty-one. After—after I started goin' with you th' other things I wanted didn't come first anymore. I'd go any place," she went on slowly, her voice like the taut beating of a too-tight fiddle string, "I'd take anything—that oil shanty you batched in back at home—that is if you'd be there. Marsh, couldn't you get a job closer home—Texas or Oklahoma or Kansas—someplace where there's oil?"

He shook his head. "They'd never pay as well. An' this is only a year an' a half, Delph, an then we'll have money, enough to—."

"Money," she flared, then sorrow overcame her anger, and she bent meekly to her sewing. "All that time in this sad old house, Marsh, with its attic full of books an' such, all tellin' of Dorie's children that are gone. An' Dorie, she's old. I can't just stay here like a knot on a log—I can't—not without you—an' hear th' trains blow an' th' cars pass, an' wait an' wonder if you're all right." She was crying now, hard unwilling sobs.

He put his arm around her and struggled for comforting words, and felt the hopelessness of trying to give her what he needed most. After a time she wiped her eyes and sewed again, and smiled her stiff unnatural smile. "I'm sorry. I hate women that cry an' beg an' carry on.—I've been thinkin', Marsh." She hesitated and looked at him, then continued, "You know I've more than a hundred dollars of my own—Uncle John gave me money to save now an' then. Katy's told me that some business schools in Louisville or Cincinnati might take me—even if I've not finished high school."

"But Delph—."

"Now wait. I've planned it all. I had to think a somethin'—to, well, kind of take th' place of you. Katy knows a girl who graduated from Burdine High School an' went to Louisville an' worked for her board an' took a business course on hardly nothin' at all an' now she has a job. If she could do it I don't see why I couldn't. My teachers, of course they didn't know so much themselves, always said I could learn anything I wanted to learn."

Marsh was on his feet now. "Delph, you're married. You can't do that."

She smiled into the fire, and never noticed his face. "I know it would seem strange to live in a town, a real town, but other girls from th' sticks they go an' work an' live. I could, while you're gone."

"Delph, you can't go off an' hunt a job like—like you didn't have a man to look out for you."

She saw his startled angry eyes, and threw out her hands in a helpless, bewildered way. "But, Marsh, I've got to do somethin'. I can't just wait an' wait. An' pretty soon I'd be makin' money. That's sensible."

"I'll make th' money. Your uncle would say things had come to a pretty pass when—."

"What do you care what he says?"

"You—you workin' like a hired girl to get through a business course you'd use just a little while, when you could be here safe with Dorie. Of all th' damn foolishness." Delph was crying again, and his voice echoed in his ears like a great thundering, gruff and loud. He dropped to the floor beside her and caught her hands. "Please, Delph—I didn't mean to quarrel. But in your talk you're silly like a child. You're better here with Dorie. I'd feel better with you here."

"You don't love me or you wouldn't want to go away an' leave me like a prisoner," she burst out with a wild sob.

"Delph, don't talk like that. With you off someplace I'd always be worried. Can't you see, no matter where I am—I can be thinkin' sort of—seein' almost. Spring come, it won't be spring there, but I'll know it is here, I can—sort of see you—growin' flowers an' such in Dorie's garden—talkin' an' laughin' with Katy an' Poke Easy when he comes home—evenin' come I can see you, mebbe at th' barn lookin' after Prissy or in th' kitchen here. Can't you see, Delph, what I mean?" His voice had grown gradually slower and slower, more hesitant and indistinct, and then it was nothing; his face buried in her lap.

She stared at the bright shine of his hair in the firelight, and wondered through her tears how he with his foolish notions could call her silly. "But that would be so little, Marsh. Nothin' when you get right down to it. If—if I mean so much to you, you'd want me there."

"It's a lot, Delph. More than I've ever had—somethin' to think on, an' know it's there. Couldn't we be satisfied with that much for a little while—so later we could be certain, I mean—."

"Certain." She spat out the word with hatred, but added more gently, "You talk like an' old man, Marsh, like John, not like a young one lookin' ahead."

"To what?" he snapped. He got up suddenly, took his hat from the mantle, and without looking at her said in a hard choked voice, "I'm damned if I spend th' rest a my days quarrelin'," and walked stiff legged out of the room. He knew it was better to walk on, but at the door he must turn and look back to meet Delph's eyes, hungering after him, like arms that would fasten themselves about him.

He mastered an impulse to go back and say the things he had already tried to say; then walked heavily down the stairs, the iron cleats on his shoe heels ringing with such loudness, that Dorie, sitting in the side parlor, left off her reading, and came out to see if a stranger walked on her stairs. She glanced at him suspiciously, and when he did not speak she followed him to the back porch, and asked as he started down the steps, "Where you goin', Marsh?"

He stopped and tried to think what it was he had intended to do, but could think of nothing except Delph. Dorie looked out across the Cumberland and said, "Th' old Weaver Place looks mighty pretty on a sunny day like this."

He nodded and looked over the river, too. The day was clear and sunny with the wind more west than north, a warmish wind that would by sundown thaw the frozen ground and maybe bring rain or snow. "It's a good day for walkin'," Dorie said, and added with a quick glance at him, "Whyn't you take a walk over to Perce Higginbottom's. You could look over th' Weaver Place on th' way—Just see it, I mean. You've not much time left to look over th' country."

He was silent, staring at the gray slate roof of the brick house on the hill. In the sun the slates glittered like ice, and near them black limbs of apple and pear trees, indistinct in the distance, seemed like bits of black lace ruffled in the wind. Dorie sighed and smoothed her apron. "Poor Delph, it fairly tears my heart out to look at her. She's takin' it harder than I thought—but it's th' only sensible thing."

"How in th' hell do you suppose my heart feels—if I've got one?"

Her only answer to his outburst was a heavy sigh and a mournful glance over the river. "I'd never be one to say but what you're doin' th' sensible thing in more ways than one," she went on after a time. "Why, you'd be a fool to take a soft young thing like Delph to such a place, an' then there's th' cost.—But pore Delph, I'm beginnin' to think she'll never see it that way. If somethin' happened to you down there—a boiler blowed up or gas exploded, say—she'd never get over it. Woman like she'd be thinkin' if she'd a gone she'd a had you for a little while." She paused, cleared her throat loudly as if to free it of sobs, and continued, "On th' other hand if you did lose your head an' took her an' somethin' happened—well—a lot a things that could happen to a woman in a place like that, things men like you know nothin' about, you'd be to blame, criminally." She repeated the last word with loud emphasis, flapped her apron indignantly, and went into the house.

Marsh said, "Hell," and walked away, rapidly, as if he would like to run. Caesar the pup came running on short clumsy legs, but the barnyard gate was fastened. Caesar was forced to stop behind it and whine and beg with his greenflecked eyes for the privilege of chewing the raw hide laces in Marsh's shoes. Marsh opened the gate, scratched Caesar behind one ear, and uttered a long oath, expressing many of the things Delph put into her tears and Dorie into words.

Caesar put his paws on one shoe top, and smiled, and lifted the brown spots above his eyes with an air of knowing and of sympathy. "When I come back you'll never recollect me," Marsh said, and picked up the dog.

He looked hastily about in all directions, up to Delph's windows toward the back porch, and then at the barn, but saw no one. The barnyard was quiet; a dominecker rooster strutted in the sunshine, and a fat, full-breasted hen was still with admiration, then made as if to run away with a great to-do, squawking and cackling in pretended fright when the rooster followed. Somewhere Solomon bellowed with a low throat growling. Caesar squirmed and growled and lifted his ears, then was silent looking at Marsh as if he should be the one to decide whether he, Caesar, should go at once and put an end to Solomon or let him live a time.

Marsh cuffed him gently on the nose and said, "Shut up," then looked along the high wire fence. In Dorie's yard there was a back gate opening on a path over the river hill. He glanced at the gate, then walked to the fence, and still with Caesar in his arms climbed a square or so, then vaulted over. He hurried down the steep hill side, slipping and sliding at times, with his shoes plowing furrows in the frozen moss and leaves. He met the twisting, curving path and followed it, down and around a narrow strip of bottom land that farther down the river widened into the stretch where Dorie's renters lived. He scarcely glanced at the houses and barns, but went on and came soon to what he hunted; a thick-trunked sycamore tree, the lower part of it hidden by the river bank where the land fell abruptly away to the river.

The place was much as he remembered it from seven years before. A spring bubbled from under one twisted root of the tree, while chained to another root was a skiff, painted red, with oars locked and looped in a smaller chain. He set Caesar in the boat, and broke the locks with a round granite-like stone. He sprang in then, drew up the chain, and slipped under the trailing willow trees out into the open water. Caesar was still in the boat, his tongue lolling with excitement, but his eyes unafraid and bright, fixed on his master. A wind furrowed the water and rattled the sycamore limbs, and overhead the sky was high and blue with puffs of gray white clouds like spring.

It was sundown when Marsh and Caesar returned to Fairchild Place, not by way of the river and a stolen boat, but in great state in Mr. Elliot's car. The old dogs ran in a thunder of barks to greet the car, but on seeing their child, the first to climb out, they fell silent with wonder. Caesar did not run whimpering to Brown Bertha his mother as befitted a runaway child, but waited for his master and fat Mr. Elliot to climb out of the car, and escorted them through the gate and a distance up the walk. Then and then only did he take notice of his parents. He walked with new dignity, strutted, ears lifted proudly, and tail held high and straight like a brown plumed flag.

Caesar had that day taken part in the stealing of a boat, the inspection of a farm, helped flag a ride on a truck to Hawthorne Town, visited a bank and sat in on a conference, had visited a saloon and watched clinchers of good corn whiskey put on the bargain, had visited the stockyards, lingered a time by the windows of a farm machinery store, had been to Roan's office on the second floor of a rickety frame building, had gone to another saloon with Roan, this time for a congratulator. There, they had met Mr. Elliot and had been whisked home, past the Weaver Place, over the Cumberland Ferry, across the lower corner of Burdine, over the Big South Fork Ridge and up the Salem Hill, and home.

Dorie and Katy heard the opening of the front hall door, and came from the kitchen to find Mr. Elliot standing uncertainly in the hall while Marsh bounded up the stairs calling, "Delph," at the top of his lungs. Dorie stood gaping after him until his heels disappeared, then turned to the mill owner for explanation. "Drinkin'?" she asked.

Mr. Elliot nodded, making of his double chin a triple. "Some— mostly though it's th' fine investment he has just made. The old Weaver Place. It will be something good when the Cumberland Bridge is made and land goes sky high again."

It was Katy who at last remembered to invite Mr. Elliot to hang his coat on the hall tree and come into the side parlor and warm. Dorie stood speechless with her eyes after Marsh. Delph heard his call and sprang from the bed where she had lain and stared with dry hot eyes at the ceiling for half the day. He flung open the door, and she was in his arms, eager to ask questions of where he had been and what he had done, but feeling somehow that the answers didn't matter. Marsh was different, all of him was hers, with no air of guilt or of trouble. "It's all fixed, Delph," he gasped, when he could get his breath from running up the stairs. "I won't be leavin' you, an' we'll always be together."

She felt weak, soft with love and forgiveness. South America didn't matter. Nothing mattered except that Marsh was back, gay and sure as she had always hoped he would be. They sat in a fat leather rocker by the fire, and he talked in brief excited sentences. She understood that he had made a large down payment on a farm, the old Weaver place, over the Cumberland. She listened and smiled like a child in a half-dreaming, half-waking sleep. Marsh was no farmer. He was an oil man. Some day he would go away and do the great things she dreamed for him. His going into the world would be delayed, but that didn't matter. Nothing mattered except that they would be together, now: and he was world enough, a whole world to understand—and love.

"I wish it could be different, Delph," Marsh said. "I mean it would be fine to say, 'I've bought a farm an' own it,' but—."

She jiggled excitedly on his knee. "But that's what you've done, silly, taken over a farm."

He nodded soberly. "Took it over, maybe, but hell, Delph, why— I don't even know if I can farm.—I always wanted to have a try at it an' for a long while—." He looked down at her, saw the fearless gaiety quivering in her eyes, and the debt he had made seemed less burdensome than an hour ago—and if he failed, Delph need never know him for a failure, could think it only some small thing he had tried, could look at him always as she looked at him now, gay and certain that he could do what he wished to do. He tried to put a light not-caring in his voice as he said, "It may be that—well—if th' season's bad or we run low on money, I'd have to go away to work come fall—th' way th' back hill farmers have to do sometimes."

"Pshaw, runnin' out a money wouldn't kill us.—Maybe by fall th' oil business in this country will be better, an' you can get a good job in Texas or California."

"Maybe so," he said, and sat rocking her and staring into the fire.

The business of buying the farm shone in a still brighter light when Marsh remembered Mr. Elliot and asked Delph to go down and meet him. Delph was shy in the presence of the great man; a millionaire she had heard said who must dash continually about the country to ask after his mills; and his wife was a fine northern lady with a cook and a maid. He beamed on Delph, slapped Marsh on the shoulder and said, "That's a fine investment, my boy, a good safe place to put your money. When they build that bridge over the Cumberland that land will double in price."

"Yes, it's been a fine farm in its day," Marsh said, and Delph wished he would use the word investment. In Mr. Elliot's mouth it had a mysterious, magical ring, like a corner stone laid for important things.

Dorie sat in the battered armless rocker which she loved, and beamed and rocked with dizzy speed, too happy to notice the creaking of the chair. Mr. Elliot stated somewhat hesitantly that he had come not only to drive Marsh home, but also to see if he couldn't buy an old hickory smoke cured ham from the Fairchild smoke house. Dorie had never been known to sell one of her special hams, cured by a secret process known only to Dorie. She made presents of them to her children and closest friends, baked them in wine or with maple sugar for times of high festivity, and ordinarily the mere suggestion of selling one to a person like Mr. Elliot would have brought at best a polite sarcastic refusal. But today so great was her goodwill for the world, including Mr. Elliot whom she despised, that Katy was sent dashing to the smoke house with directions to get the oldest, best-smelling ham she could find.

Supper that night was later, longer, and more topsy-turvy than ever. The cornbread burned while Dorie rummaged in the attic for odds and ends of furniture she thought Delph might be able to use. Katy, instead of turning a skillet of sizzling pork shoulder, stood with the meat fork in her hands and stared at the meat until it burned while she composed the piece she would write for the *Westover Bugle* on Marsh's buying of the Weaver place. Delph wandered about in a dreamy way and was good for nothing. When Marsh was in the kitchen, she had eyes only for him. It was pure happiness to smile at him and receive his smile, closer than a kiss yesterday. She had no doubt of his love for her. He had changed his plans and was doing a thing he had doubtless not wanted to do, all because he could not leave her.

She felt a pleasant warmth of victory, of having through Marsh taken a step toward the wider world. It would be fun to be alone together, even in the renter's house in the bottoms. It wasn't as if they would be there always. Marsh would most likely buy a car, now that he knew he would be a time in the country. They would drive to Lexington, maybe buy the little furniture they would want there. She could see the university and the fine bluegrass country, or maybe they would even go to Louisville to the races; Marsh would like to see the horses. Her blood tingled pleasantly at thought of that. She had always wanted to see a race, a real one, not the kind at the County Fair. She would take some of her own money and make a bet, just a little one, so that when she lost she would not feel so wicked. She troubled a moment for her morals; she realized that she wouldn't feel wicked at all if she won.

· 11 ·

ONE AFTERNOON in mid January Katy slipped away from school at afternoon recess, and ran to the bottom of Depot Street in Burdine. There, she saw and flagged a strange truck, but one with a Fincastle County license that would most likely go by Fairchild Place. "It's Friday," she shrieked above the screeching brakes to the startled driver, "an' I want to hurry home an' read th' *Westover Bugle*."

When she was settled and the truck was groaning down and around the steep hairpin curve above the post office, she smiled at the driver, a lanky, black-haired Scotch-Irish hill man, and explained, "I'm hopin' ole Reuben Dick, he's th' editor, you know, will print my piece today, th' one I wrote about Marsh Gregory takin' over a farm just across from us on th' Cumberland."

"Whoever he is, I don't guess he was raised on a farm like I was," the driver said, and except for occasional interjections and speculative remarks with his eyes on the nature of Katy, said nothing more, and only nodded when his passenger thanked him at her own front gate. "You should cultivate a happier disposition," Katy told him, and ran between the wildly barking dogs to the kitchen door. The paper, still in its wrapper, lay on the kitchen table. She tore it open, glanced at the front page, and screamed at the top of her lungs, "Old Reuben put it on th' front page. Not just with th' common news."

Dorie and Delph, upstairs in the clutter room tacking a quilt for Delph, heard and came racing down the backstairs, while Angus and Marsh left off their corn husking in the barn to come and learn the

144

cause of the commotion. Katy bade them all be quiet while she stood with a hand on the kitchen table and read:

"'January the twenty-sixth will be a great day in this neighborhood, and a lucky one for Cedar Stump over the Cumberland. On that day Mr. and Mrs. Marshall Gregory will settle on the old Weaver Place. Mr. Elliot will continue to live in the brick house on the hill. Mr. Gregory feels that with just his wife the renter's house in the bottoms is large enough for him. He has been very busy for the past few days, going about the country selecting stock and tools and seed. One of the finest things he has bought is a five-gaited saddle mare, named Maude, once the property of William Copenhaver, Senior, in Fincastle County. Just before Mr. Copenhaver died of pneumonia, not long after Christmas time, he had his son write a letter to Mr. Gregory offering to sell Maude. He wanted his mare to be in good hands, the old man said.

"'Mr. Gregory plans to practice a form of diversified farming. He will grow mostly corn on his bottom lands with the upper fields for hay and pasture. This year he means to try a fair sized crop of melons as a quick cash crop.

"'Beginning with next week your Salem correspondent will write no more of the Cedar Stump news. She only did it because there was no one there who cared to write for the paper. Delphine Costello Gregory, talented young wife of Mr. Gregory, has kindly consented to take time from the many duties she will have as a farmer's wife, and write the Cedar Stump news. We feel certain that the Gregorys will make a true promised land of the old Weaver Place. We all wish them good seasons and abundant crops.'"

Katy finished the reading. There was a moment's silence in the kitchen, while all, including the dogs, looked at her in admiration. "I want to send a clippin' of that to Sam," Dorie said. "It 'ud do him good to read it."

Marsh fumbled with the broken arrow head he had carried in his pocket for years as a lucky piece, and looked at Katy with beaming, grateful eyes. "I'd sort a like to keep a clippin', too," he said.

Katy, however, was mournful and ready to cry as she flung the paper to the kitchen table. "It doesn't tell th' half of it. My pieces never do," she wailed.

Marsh smiled at her and shook his head. "Pshaw, Katy, you've done a good job. Nobody could put it in words in a paper—all of it—ever."

Delph praised Katy with the others. Still, while she had listened a moment's misgiving at Katy's words of the future had racked her, only to be blown away like a last year's leaf in an April wind. It was easier to enjoy the goodness of the moment, and leave the future to shift for itself. Marsh had a future; he would turn eagerly back to it when he learned what farming really was. Life now was one long adventure with each day bringing some new understanding of him, learning more of what he loved and what he hated, drawing him a bit closer. The days when she had thought that he would go away without her were remembered less as days than nightmarish dreams that made the awakening to reality, even though it was not what she had planned, sweeter than it might have been.

It was fun to use the bit of money she had and buy things for the house. Marsh was busy with his own buying, and she with help from Dorie was left to take full charge of the picking of this and choosing of that. Dorie was a rare one at getting the most from anything, be it an acre of red clay sheep skull land or a dollar. She and Delph, sometimes on foot, sometimes with Angus and the truck, hunted bargains over the country side.

Luck blew their way like a wind. There were two auctions within a week. The old Shearer couple down the Jefferson Pike sold out in preparation for a move to a city in the north in order to be near their children. Their furniture was old, solid stuff that sold for almost nothing. Delph, at Dorie's insistence, bought a good bit of it, for though she disliked it, she knew she wouldn't live with such furniture always. That night Marsh looked at it, smoothed the heavy doors of a massive walnut wardrobe and said with pleasure in his eyes, "No flim-flam about this." The wardrobe made Delph think of a double coffin stood on end, but still she smiled to see that Marsh was pleased.

It was fun to go to Mr. Cheely's store in the upper Burdine Bottoms and buy no end of things, especially dishes; nothing so stolid and expensive as a set all alike, but odds and ends of broken sets with no piece matching another. Mr. Cheely had inherited the store from his father who had in turn inherited from his father. The store was divided into three parts; a large front or main room where Mr. Cheely kept an assortment of newer things, ranging from fat bologna sausages hung over a counter where shoes and dress goods were displayed to the piles of shot gun and rifle ammunition stacked in the rear by the hoes and under the horse collars next to a counter of ladies' hats and men's underwear. The back room was reserved for feed and seed and fertilizer, while the side room, receptacle for more than sixty years of all that would not sell, might contain anything, and was unlocked only for such privileged persons as Dorie.

Dorie and Delph spent the most of several rainy afternoons rummaging in the side room where dishes, pots and pans, odds and ends of unmatched wall paper might be found among the dresses with leg-o-mutton sleeves, spittoons, bowl and pitcher sets, shaving mugs, Indian masks, painted shells, and lightning rods.

Upon finding an article that might be of use to Delph, Dorie would carry it to Mr. Cheely who in winter weather sat reading and rocking in the main room by the stove. On seeing whatever she happened to bring, he would feign great surprise, leave off his rocking, push up his hat, and say, "Why, I can't see how that got in th' back room. It would ha sold in no time out here." Dorie would point out numberless reasons why nobody but a foolish young bride like Delph would want such a thing, driving the price lower and lower until Mr. Cheely would suddenly commence rocking again with especial violence as he exclaimed, "Dorie, not one cent lower, an' that's disgraceful cheap," but when Dorie's eyes sparkled over the bargain she had made he would grunt and add with high satisfaction, "It's all clear profit to me, anyhow. If you hadn't a found it I'd never a knowed it was there, an' couldn't a sold it."

Dorie liked the bargaining, but Delph found the Sears Roebuck orders much more exciting. She, with Dorie's advice, ordered bundles of remnants, curtain goods, toweling, sheeting, gingham, and percale. There was no end of excitement in waiting for the bundle and wondering just exactly what assortment Sears Roebuck would send. The buying of cloth in remnant bundles was a trick Dorie had learned when her children were small and every penny counted, and a place could be found in her household for any scrap of cloth.

Though she bought remnants now mostly to satisfy her gambling instincts, so she said, Dorie remembered the days when she had had to think of cloth in terms of covering young bodies at the cheapest possible cost. As she and Delph sat sewing in the clutter room, now and again she would forget the curtains she hemmed or the dish towels she cut, and fall into long, minute descriptions of this or that thing she had made from remnant bundles. "Many's th' time Sam used to say to me when I'd made him a remnant shirt, th' tails pieced out like a crazy quilt, th' collar lined with one color and th' cuffs with another, 'Mama,' he used to say, 'it's a pity you couldn't a studied higher mathematics. With th' way you can figger things out you could ha learned it, I know.'"

And she would go on; tell of bonnets for the girls with a crown of one color, hooded by still another, and tails pieced from something else, "Ever'body in th' country said my girls had th' prettiest bonnets," she would add, and tell on of aprons and skirts and dresses put together from hand-me-downs and remnants. She sighed a bit sometimes for Ethel; she had rebelled continually against such clothing and vowed many times that when she grew up she would have money enough to buy all her dresses ready made. She praised Emma, the oldest girl, only eighteen months younger than Sam; the one who had with him suffered most from the burden of a mortgaged farm, but Emma, no more than Sam had ever complained at anything. They'd both been born with sand in their craws and strength to back it up. Rachel had laughed at everything and cared no more for clothes than Katy, but it was a good thing that by the time Joe was ready for college there was more money for clothes, for Joe took everything seriously including the color of his ties.

Dorie, like Juber at home, was a great teller of tales, some of her stories were old like his and began with a "back before th' War," or "This is one old Aunt Rachel Kidd used to tell." But the ones that Delph liked best were those of Dorie's children, accounts of their adventures in the wider world: Emma's fright on her first day as copy writer for a big Chicago department store, Rachel's adventures in hunting cheap food, clothing, and shelter in Cincinnati's west end, for Rachel had graduated from high school one day, and on the next ran away and was married in sun socks and a gingham dress to a college friend of Joe's, a member of the unemployed. There was Joe's winning of his first case; and Ethel's husband and home in Detroit which Dorie had never visited and doubted if she ever would. Ethel had married well, and lived in the suburbs with a cook and a maid, one over scrubbed little boy, and a house with landscaped grounds instead of just a yard planted with things, so Katy who had been there said. Katy much preferred to visit Rachel; she had two children, two dogs, a pleasant tempered husband, who though he made little money, was never "always lookin' hard run an' all in a fluster like Ethel's."

Delph for some unknown reason she had never stopped to puzzle out, had never asked of Sam, though in her eyes he was more important than the others. One afternoon when Marsh was with them in the clutter room, and Dorie as usual when with him was talking of crops and land, Delph heard her mention him, and stopped to listen. Dorie was by a window pointing out a rolling pasture field to Marsh. "We always called that knob 'Ole horny heel.' It was never any good 'til Sam took it in hand. Let me see." She paused and counted years or children's ages on the knuckles of one hand. "He couldn't ha been more than eleven years old when he took it into his head to try sweet clover there. Aye, I'll never forget how he looked. He was little for his age—then, an' th' clover was nigh as high as his head. I'd look up there; it was th' summer Poke Easy was a year old, an' see him a cuttin' away. Aimin' to cut some for hay, he said. There'd be just his black head a shinin', he had hair black as his father's, an' th' bees swarmin' 'round. They take awful after sweet clover. Lord, he was made for a farmer."

"But as long as he's gettin' along so well where he is I guess you don't mind it so that he's away," Delph suddenly said, somehow impelled to speak in defense of Sam.

Dorie turned from the window, and snatched up a sheet she had been hemming. Anger snapped through her eyes, and then it was gone, leaving her face old and empty and tired. "No, I don't mind," she said and looked at the stitches she had basted. "Sam he is a great success. He had too many brains to waste 'em workin' with th' land. He went to college interested in land and fertilizer an' nitrates. He had learned about 'em workin' with th' clovers." Her voice had grown level and toneless as if her mind had taken for itself all the shades of meaning her tongue could give. "In college he aimed to learn how to match land with fertilizer. He studied chemistry. He learned a lot—about nitrates. He learned their most important uses. He's high up in research in one of th' biggest munitions plants in th' country—spendin' all his days searchin' out th' cheapest ways to kill th' most men in th' least time. An' he could be workin' out ways to build up th' land."

Delph looked at her; and wished that she, Delph, had kept silent. Dorie seemed for the moment not to be Dorie, owner of a fine farm and mother of successful children, but only a disappointed, defeated woman growing old, with her back above the sheet she sewed bent more than a back should be.

Marsh looked at her with pity in his eyes, opened his mouth as if to speak, then closed it, and went downstairs. Delph followed him, and soon both forgot Dorie upstairs as they talked excitedly of this and that. For better than anything else, Delph liked the endings of the afternoons like this when Marsh came from work on the old Weaver place, or scouring the country for tools and stock. She must show him something of the work she had done during the day, and he would tell her of the bargains he had found; a hive of bees dirt cheap—he didn't need a hive of bees—but it was so cheap he couldn't resist it. There was the great brood sow that in her last litter had borne fourteen pigs with never a runt to the bunch, and the six shoats, practically pure Poland China, not too high, and all vaccinated for cholera; and a fine Jersey cow to go with Prissy.

Marsh was rapidly gaining the reputation of being "uncommon cautious when it comes to buyin'." Known as a man who knew enough to feel a hen's breast bone and look at her feet and her feathers as well as her comb; one who wouldn't buy a cow just because she was pretty and young and healthy looking; a lover of horses but with sense enough to know that with pure love and kindness only he would never get very far with a mule; and a man who wouldn't risk cheap fertilizer or cheap mixed grass seed.

The southern end of Westover County watched him and wondered how he would turn out. Some thought he'd make a go of it, some held him as nothing more than a flash in the pan—any fool, give him plenty of bulletins to read and some observation could, with advice from Dorie Dodson Fairchild, farm in his head. It was a well known fact that the finest crops of all were grown and harvested in winter by a good warm fire with seed catalogs for farms. Some said that unless he got a renter to take at least half the bottoms he could never manage the whole farm without a good bit of machinery. Others held that his wife would count for more than farm machinery. Most had heard of the old Fincastle County breed of Costellos, and all of Delph's father, so that they accepted Delph and knew what she would do. Some of her people might be a bit on the wild side maybe, but all in all she came of a good strong back country stock of women who knew how to work, and could live for a time without frippery or foolishness; not like a city woman.

Mr. Elliot on the rare times when he discussed anything with those he termed the natives, talked in a jovial way of his new landlord. He seemed like a sensible chap, but anybody must admit that it was pure foolishness for him to stay and try to finish paying for his land by farming it. He knew oil and could have rented the place and made a great deal more money in the oil fields. Still, if he worked a season or so on the place, it would probably bring a much better price when he sold it.

Brother Eli put the Gregory family into his regular Sunday prayers in Salem Church; was thankful for their presence in the county, prayed that they might be prosperous and fruitful, and asked God to give them strong backs and stout hearts to bear their troubles and their burdens.

He preached then, one of his usual gentle sermons, more eloquent than fiery, for Brother Eli since his return from China, a failure ousted by the Board of Missions, a man saddened by the death of his wife, and saddened, too, by the loss of something else, whispered by some to be the loss of his faith, had dwelled but little on hell fire and damnation. He married the young ones, visited the old and the sick, buried the dead, and grew flowers, and fruits and vegetables on a fertile but rocky hill farm above Burdine. Today, his sermon was little different from those he usually delivered to the farmers of Salem: "and the land shall yield her fruit, and ye shall eat your fill, and dwell therein in safety."

Marsh sat and watched his nodding beard, and listened to his talk of the struggles of those other men for peace and safety and security, and a bit of land and a way of life in which they had had some hand in the shaping. Brother Eli caught his steady, intent gaze and looked more often at him than others in the congregation, and the eyes of the listeners gradually followed the preacher's glance. Marsh grew unpleasantly conscious of them; the doubt in some and pity in others, but worst of all there were the eyes that called him a fool and those that looked upon him as a strange oil man and nothing more. He dreamed of the day when he could sit in Salem church and all the congregation could look at him in respect; a respect built on the knowing that he could farm and hold his own in their world with the best of them. It wished it were spring, time to begin the plowing. He hadn't plowed since boyhood; and he forgot the watching eyes in the cold fear of wondering if he could.

· 12 ·

I T WAS Sunday again, afternoon, and Marsh rowed Delph over the Cumberland to their new home, ready now. Delph had been gay and full of talk as they ran down the river hill, with her eyes laughing like the eyes of a woman going to a dance, but now in the boat she was silent with Caesar in her lap and her arms about her drawn up knees. Marsh looked at her, and wished as he had wished many times for a smooth quick tongue not given to halting and stumbling, to be able to tell her that this was maybe more than a boat ride over a river.

But she sat and watched the coiling yellow river water, and seemed to notice for the first time that blue hill shadow had touched the valley. "Sundown comes early here," she said.

But th' twilight's long," he answered, "an' th' cool of th' evenin' comes early, an' there's a high knoll in th' pasture where we can see th' sun go down."

She brightened at that, but was silent again as she listened to the oars creak in their locks and water lapping and whispering against the boat. "It'll be awful quiet down here," she said, and shivered a little and pulled her coat more closely about her.

Marsh smiled and looked at the sky as he lay back on the oars. "There'll never be anything to bother us. Not even storms—they can't strike full around this curve in th' river. Not many places so sheltered as this."

She nodded, and was silent while he fastened the boat, and while they walked up the river bank and across the stretch of bottom land, muddy and pulling at their feet under the snow. Though Delph had

153

visited the place and worked in the house several times with Dorie and Katy, it seemed strange now as she walked up to it. She swept her eyes over the land, and saw the house, gaunt and ugly in its mistreated yard. Past the house were gray sheds and outhouses, and a great barn set on the highest bit of bottom ground, so that the windows of the house seemed to stare up at the barn and the encircling arm of the river hill in a frightened beseeching way. She saw what had been the garden, rows of last year's bean stalks black and ugly against the snow, and farther away in the open fields lines of leafless cornstalks standing like skeletons of the summer. And worse than such things, the steep river hill towering above everything; its sheer limestone crags, red clay banks and stunted cedar trees striking against her eyes when she would look out and away as she had used to do at home.

She was glad when they came to the house, and could go into their own kitchen and shut the door against the dreary, snowy twilight. Marsh smiled at the kitchen and praised her for her clever ways. The windows were gay with red striped curtains and the furniture and dishes looked much at home in the large square room, almost as large as Fronie's kitchen. Marsh had never really looked at the house since Delph, with Katy and Dorie and Perce's wife helping her, had papered the downstairs rooms and arranged the furniture. They made a circuit of it now; the four rooms below and the two above, all plain and square and large, like boxes tacked together.

Though Marsh praised everything he saw, and declared she was a fine one to make such a showing for the little money spent, Delph was disappointed in her work. The house seemed bleak and lonesome, not gay and filled with life as she would have it be. Last week while she lived in the overflowing, overfurnished Fairchild house, her future home in the bottoms, because of its very difference, had seemed gay and exciting; the way a secret play house deep in the woods or on some hidden spot by the creek had used to seem—something all her own where she could do as she wished. Still, after a day spent in the play house she had always been glad to come home. Now, as she stood by the stove and listened absentmindedly to some talk of Marsh's about the work he would do tomorrow, she looked at the bright curtains and the little makeshift stove, and wondered how it would be to live with them day after day—at least for a while.

Then Marsh was bringing her coat, begging her to come outside and see the many things he had done. They made a brief circuit of the lower farm with Caesar scampering at their heels. In all the buildings there was the air of age coupled with solidity that made her think of Costello's Place in the Little South Fork Country. The main barn was a mighty thing, high with a great loft for hay, stout cobwebby rafters, and halls and stables separated by log walls. "Most a this barn was built before th' Civil War," Marsh said with pride. Signs of his rebuilding and mending were everywhere, strongly and securely fixed with good timber and new nails as other men built. He apologized for not having had time to mend the underpinning of the house, or fix the chimney of their living room, but Delph laughed away his apologies. She didn't mind not being able to have fire any place except in the kitchen; there was precious little furniture in their pretended living room anyhow, and mostly she thought she'd rather stay with him while he worked than in the house.

They returned to the yard, and Marsh pointed out what looked to be a leafless twig stuck in the snow by the gate. "Look, that's th' first thing I planted—pear trees by th' gate, an' more fruit trees by th' road across th' pasture hill." And he smiled down at the little twig as if he could see it as a great tree, holding boughs of yellow pears high above his head.

Delph smiled and praised everything she saw; the pussy willows planted by the spring house, and a box elder that was to grow at the corner of the yard where the spring branch trickled. She thought with him of the spring when the plum bushes by the window would bloom, and was the first to suggest that then the river hill would be less ugly when the dogwood and red bud and mock orange bush flowered.

She forgot the flowers in the excitement of cooking supper, the first meal she had ever prepared for Marsh. She was flustered and awkward with him watching her, strolling about the kitchen, and never knowing that he was in the way. She felt as she had used to feel at school when the county superintendent came and the teacher had her diagram a sentence on the blackboard or work a hard arithmetic problem.

She was almost glad when he took a milk bucket and went whistling away to do the barn work. Left alone, she discovered soon that, though she was held to be a good cook by all who knew her, the preparation of a whole meal seemed for the moment a hopeless task. Heretofore she had always had Nance at her beck and call or Fronie handy in case of trouble, but now when the potatoes threatened to burn and the coffee boil over at the same instant, there were only her two hands to stir the potatoes, shift the coffee pot, look at the bread, turn the bacon, mix flour and milk for gravy, and keep the stove stoked with wood. The stove in spite of its diminutive size gave proof of a large and stubborn disposition. It browned and threatened to burn the bread on top while it left it raw on the bottom, so that the baking of it must be finished on top of the stove. It was not without a sense of triumph that, when Marsh returned from the barn, she announced supper as ready and waiting.

She told him nothing of her cooking troubles, for he was gay and full of talk about the animals in the barn, especially Prissy and her calf, and Maude, already bred to Perce Higginbottom's big black stallion. He praised Caesar who had shown no fear of any animal, but little as he was, had driven Ivy, the new cow, the length of the barn hall. Now he insisted that Caesar instead of Piper, the gray cat they had found in the barn, should have the good warm foam when Delph strained the milk.

Delph laughed and teased, "Marsh, you're like a little boy with his first dog."

Then she was sorry she had spoken so. Marsh looked red and miserable as he mumbled with all the glibness gone from his tongue. "I guess I do carry on like a fool. But—well—Caesar is th' first dog I've ever had."

They sat down to supper then, and Delph could not eat for watching Marsh. She was anxious and a bit fearful of what he would think of the first whole meal she had ever cooked for him. He studied the blue checked tablecloth and the bright, though unmatched dishes, and said, "It all looks mighty nice, Delph."

But she thought some of the pleasure left his face when his glance happened upon the platter of fried eggs. "Don't you like eggs?" she asked.

"Y-e-e-s, but I thought we'd maybe sell a few. Mrs. Elliot up at th' brick house wants some, an'—." He stopped, angered by the apologetic note in his voice. It was foolish to begin so, apologizing for his plans to sell the things that other farms sold. The startled, puzzled look in Delph's eyes both hurt and worried him. But he ate heartily of the food, and praised everything, especially the cornbread. "This couldn't be beat, Delph," he said, and helped himself to another square.

She flushed with happiness and answered, "That's good yellow meal."

"I thought you wouldn't mind cookin' with yellow meal," he said, his eyes intent on his plate. "It's—it's a little cheaper than white."

"Oh, it's just as good when—when you know how to mix it," she faltered, and wondered that such a little lie could hurt so. It was so little it was hardly a lie at all. It was just that she had remembered in time that eggs maybe cost more than meal, and he might not like it if she should say that yellow meal was good when mixed with eggs.

"I bet you're thinkin' hard on Juber an' th' ones at home," Marsh said when she had remained some time silent, picking at her food instead of eating.

She smiled into his tender troubled eyes. "I'm thinkin'—that you've started out a farmer right. Th' boxes you've fixed in th' side room for cabbage an' tomato plants are ten times big enough for th' few we'd need."

Once again he thought of trying to explain, of telling her that in Burdine there might be a good sale for fresh vegetables, but he hated to see her puzzled or worried so he only said, "You're already more farmer than I am—thinkin' on th' farmin' when I was thinkin' on you."

She laughed at that, and was light hearted again, pleasantly flustered when supper was over, and Marsh insisted on helping her with the dishes. Men in the Little South Fork country never did the work of women, and she didn't want him to begin in any such fashion. It would scandalize the neighborhood.

In the end Marsh must content himself with letting her do the dishes alone. He stood uncertainly by the stove a time, and then went to one of the upstairs rooms where he had stowed his government bulletins. He came down soon with a good sized stack on his arm, which, after glancing hesitantly at Delph a time or so, he laid near the lamp on the kitchen table.

Delph turned about and asked, with a good bit of curiosity, "What is all that, Marsh, magazines?"

He shook his head. "Bulletins," he mumbled, and watched her face and hoped she wouldn't be as most others had been. His collecting and reading of bulletins on farming had, in his oil field days, caused him many a fight with those who ridiculed. But worse than the fights had been his embarrassment before the wise ones, usually settled farmers with land of their own, who had smiled knowingly and pitied the roving oil man reading up on how to farm.

But Delph, when she saw what he had, forgot the dishes and came on wiping her soap sudsy hands on her apron, eager to see first one and then the other. "I didn't know you ever read anything, Marsh—but papers now an' then," she said, and he could see that she was pleased—and surprised, too.

"There's one I'm tryin' to find. It's about graftin' fruit trees," he explained. "I'll not have any time this spring, an' it's too late to do much anyhow, but I thought tonight I'd kind of like to try my hand with a few plum switches."

Delph let her dishwater get cold while she hunted the bulletin he wanted, and then when she set the pans on the stove to heat she let the water get too hot while she leaned on the back of his chair and helped him by reading the directions and advising now and then. When she had finally finished the dishes, she sat with him by the table and watched the work closely with her head over his shoulder.

He worked slowly, his bowed head close under the lamp, and absorbed completely in the work, as if the little cuts he made on the twigs mattered more than anything else in the world. His square hands lost their blunt hard look, and became gentle things, careful not to bruise the bark he cut, skillful and quick with the small sharply pointed blade. Delph smiled at his patience, his pausing to examine each incision, then trying again, choosing a proper bud, cutting it and gently slipping it between the edges of the loosened bark, sighing with satisfaction when the work pleased him, swearing under his breath when the knife went too deeply.

Now and then one was so perfect that he must stop and have Delph take it in her hands. He would smile to hear her praise; and agree with her that the work was good, and say that if the shoot were properly finished with grafting wax and thread, it would grow when put into the ground. Even though the work seemed tedious and unimportant, more suited to an old womanish soul like Juber with his love of fiddle tunes and flowers, Delph was generous with her praise. Marsh's interest gave it importance, just as the mere being alone with him here made the barren kitchen and the ugly house fine and good—things she would remember always. There by the kitchen table with Caesar sleeping between their feet, and the fire in the kitchen stove crackling and whispering, there was no feeling of being shut away from the world as in John's quiet house. When Marsh smiled or their hands touched over the grafting, it seemed to Delph that she could never dream over or hunger after anything not found there in that one room.

With the practice grafting, the popping of a skillet of pop corn and Marsh's round with the lantern and Caesar to see that all in the barn was well, they were late in going to bed, and later still in falling asleep, especially Delph, haunted as she was with the fear that she would oversleep in the morning and Marsh would think her a lazy wife.

But next morning, though the winter dawn was yet a long while away, Marsh came to the kitchen with a sheepish air when he learned that Delph was up before him, and had not only built the fire but had a breakfast waiting to be eaten. It was a busy day for him, he said, and hurried through breakfast and the barn work and was gone with ax and saw to get firewood before the dawn had scarcely lost its look of blue. Delph did her morning chores, singing as she worked. She straightened the house, baked a cake, set a kettle of pintos to boil, and still the morning was not half gone. She could see the sun on Dorie's roof tops, but the river valley lay in cold blue shadow with a curious look of sleep or of waiting for something to come and bring it to life.

She heard the ringing of Cedar Stump school bell, whistles of the Burdine lumber mills, trains blowing lonesomely for the Cumberland bridge and tunnels, two miles or more up the river; but always the sounds were faint and muffled, never loud enough to smother the ticking of the blue tin clock she had bought from Mr. Cheely. She thought of Juber and the ones at home, and was lonesome with that restlessness that had used to seize her in the Little South Fork Country when she would ride and ride or go running down through the beech grove.

She started a letter to Mrs. Crouch in answer to the one she had received at Christmas Time, but the scratching of her pen on the paper sounded loud in the empty house, and when she had sat still a time in an attempt to collect her thoughts, the silence deepened until she could hear her breathing and her heart beating in her ears. She sprang up quickly, dressed for the outdoors, pushed the beans to the back of the stove where they could simmer with no danger of burning and went hunting Marsh in the woodlot.

She knew it was silly to go running after him in the middle of the morning, as if she were some spineless wife who must forever have her man at her apron strings. Still, when she had thought it over as she walked along, she decided it wasn't Marsh she came to see, but the brick house and the upper farm, since she had never seen them except from the road. When she had followed the wagon track that twisted up the hill, she went first to the high knoll in the pasture, and stood among the leafless walnut trees, and looked out over the country. She could not see so far as on the hill at home, but so much farther than in the valley that it was like getting a breath of outside air after a long stay indoors.

Behind her, east of the Cumberland were the last of the high back hills. West lay a farming country of gently rolling hills, much like some of the land on the other side of the river. She forgot Marsh for a moment in the excitement of looking at the new strange land. She knew that toward the west the hills flattened into the pennyrile, while north they crossed the knobs and became the famous blue-grass country where the homes were finer than castles, and even the negroes were richer than some of the poorer hill renters.

She saw Cedar Stump School, an ugly, mud-bespattered one room building in unfenced treeless grounds on the other side of the creek from Marsh's lands, bleak and cold somehow like the rest of the country. The few farm houses she could see looked almost dirty against the dazzling whiteness of the snow, while the road to Hawthorne Town was no more than a narrow gray thread, its edges lost in red clay banks or buried in the snow.

The red brick house, Marsh's house where the Elliots lived, was the only cheerful thing on the landscape. It was finer than she had imagined, larger, more gracefully built than the Fairchild Place; set in a great sweep of yard that in back dropped over the river hill and in front swept down to the Hawthorne Road. The eight white columns of the wide front porch were graceful, fluted things, hinting of some fineness and freedom in living foreign to any that she knew.

In order to see better, she walked nearer, first only to the orchard fence, but the trees kept hindering her vision, and so after a quick glance about to see that no one watched, she climbed the fence and walked up to a side gate in the yard. The place looked alive and warm with blue threads of smoke rising from its chimneys, and in a first floor window she could see bits of brightness that looked to be flowers. She stood in the snow and studied it all until a growing numbness in her feet reminded her that she had stood a long while in the cold gaping like a child. She was just turning away when she heard the notes of a piano, clear and gay, rising and falling in a laughing, tinkling tune, different from any she had ever heard.

She couldn't leave the music; something about it matched something inside her, and it was like the tunes she knew existed but had never heard. She hesitated a moment, then walked to the grilled iron side gate, and followed a brick walk that led to the front of the house. She walked slowly, anxious to be within the sound as long as possible. Now and then she paused and pretended to look at something, so that if the strange northern woman should see her and ask her what she was about, she could tell her she only wished to look over her husband's property.

The tune ended, but she walked on, hoping there would be another. She came to the window with the flowers, and stopped when she saw they were yellow roses, real ones in January. She had always known there were florist shops and hothouse flowers, but had never seen more than a carnation. She stood on tip-toe and was lost in the marvel of the roses in a silver bowl on the window sill. The flowers were too perfect, and for a moment she doubted their realness until she saw one yellow petal fall with a gentle deliberation as if the rose had felt her doubt and wished to show that it was real.

She smiled at the window and the roses, for the window seemed less a part of a house than an opening into that mysterious way of life of which she had read in the women's magazines. The looped drapes of a cloth different from any she had ever seen and the fine, unbelievably thin, curtains seemed grand enough for the governor's mansion.

She was suddenly ashamed and confused and felt like a thief found stealing when a slender young woman with yellow hair brighter than Katy's hair lifted the curtain and studied her curiously. Delph knew she was the stranger, the mistress of the house. She matched the thin curtains and hot house flowers, and no woman native to the country, not even the well-to-do housewives on Burdine High Street ever wore silk in the mornings, or had pinky-white fragile hands like the ones that lifted the curtain.

Delph smiled at the woman and was glad when she raised the window part way and she had an opportunity of explaining her childish gaping. "I was just passin' by—an' I heard th' music an' saw th' flowers, so I thought I'd come a little closer. I'm Mrs. Marshall Gregory. My husband owns this place, you know."

"Oh, yes," Mrs. Elliot said in a thin quick voice. "Your husband told me the other day that you knew a great deal about flowers."

Delph laughed. "I'm afraid he bragged too soon. At home—that is down in Fincastle County—I always had a lot of flowers, but just plain ones—nothin' fancy like th' roses here."

"Old fashioned ones?"

Delph hesitated, not exactly certain what was an old fashioned flower. "Do you mean things like bachelor's buttons an' lady fingers an' marigolds?" she cautiously asked after a moment.

Mrs. Elliot nodded and seemed delighted. "Those are the kind I want to grow. I've always thought a big old fashioned flower garden in the back here would go well with the place but somehow I've never been able to make them grow. I've studied several books on gardening, but last summer the garden was a failure."

Delph studied the woman's hands, and wondered what she meant by gardening. Hands like hers had most likely never known the feel of a hoe handle. "I have some seed, flower seed that Juber— he was my uncle's hired man—slipped into my things when I ran away. I'll give you some slips this spring—that is if you'd like 'em."

"Better than anything," the woman said, and invited her inside, but Delph remembering suddenly it was Marsh she had started out to see, shook her head. She was just turning away when Mrs. Elliot asked in her quick sharp voice, "Do you make nice firm yellow butter?"

She whirled about and stared at the woman in angry puzzlement, of half a mind to ask her whose business it was what kind of butter she made. "I wouldn't eat any but good butter," she answered after a moment's stony silence.

Mrs. Elliot flushed and appeared confused as Delph. "I didn't mean that—but some of the women about make scalded butter, and Mr. Elliot doesn't care for that. I'm sure yours is very nice, and I know I'll be able to use at least two pounds a week."

Delph's look of angry perplexity grew. "I don't know as I'll be sellin' any," she said, and started away again.

"But your husband said he wanted to sell me milk and butter and eggs," Mrs. Elliot called after her.

She stopped abruptly as if a hand had caught her shoulder, swallowed something like anger or shame in her throat, and turned slowly back to the woman, managing a stiff smile as she did so. "I—my husband was tellin' me last night he'd made arrangements to sell milk an' butter an' such, but he didn't say to who. So—so when you spoke I didn't know it was you."

The lie she knew was unconvincing. "That's all right," Mrs. Elliot said, and smiled on her kindly, pityingly it seemed to Delph as she said, "I know every one here is strange to you—and that's never much fun." She took a handful of the yellow roses and handed them to her, saying in her sharp, abrupt way, "They help wonderfully to brighten things up a bit," and closed the window quickly, before Delph had time to protest or even thank her.

She turned and almost ran to the pasture field; a dreary place where sage grass and blackberry briars gave the land a poor bleak look. She carried still the roses, held carefully from her as if they were a fire brand instead of flowers. When the brick house windows were hidden by trees and fields, she stopped and studied the roses. Then with a sudden gesture as if she threw a stone to kill a snake she flung them hard into the snow.

"I hate her," she whispered, "so full of airs an' wonderin' if I make good butter." She looked at the flowers, and the flowers looked back at her. She knew she was childish and foolish and silly, but she didn't want to go bowing and scraping, carrying milk and butter and eggs to a neighbor's back door like a peddler woman. She walked on, slowly, until she heard the sound of Marsh's saw, a pretty sound it was like a singing in the sharp frosty air. He would be kneeling in the snow, with his hat pushed back, and his eyes bright and soft, underlaid with smiles as they had been since he came that afternoon to tell her he would not go away.

She stood a moment, listening to the sound, then turned and walked slowly back, careful to step in her tracks. The flowers lay as she had left them. She picked them up, and gently brushed the snow from each, then arranged them carefully in one hand. Marsh would like to see the roses, and he would be pleased to hear of the milk and butter and eggs she was going to sell.

· 13 ·

DURING THE wildest days of February when snow whirled on sharp biting winds, Marsh's blue jumper could be seen moving over the barren upland fields, bowed many times under great burdens; stones or loads of cedar brush, or the grass sacks filled with earth that he carried and threw into the yawning red clay gulches to hold the land. Seasoned farmers marveled at the work he did; no man in the country had ever taken the time and trouble to build a great lime kiln such as he built in order to have quick-lime for white wash and sprays.

He worked like a man to whom all weathers were as a day in spring; feared snow and mud and cold for his animals but not for himself. Many nights he was silent by the table, eating the food Delph put before him, no longer praising this or that, just eating, then sitting a time by the kitchen stove. Soon, it was time to light the lantern and make the last rounds of the barn and chicken house with Caesar. After seeing that all was well he would return to the house and go to bed, and usually he fell asleep after a brief good night.

He never complained of the weather, though the spring that year was a wayward giddy thing. In early March Delph picked wild greens on the hill fields and by the river, and Marsh sowed his grass and clover seed. April came with frost and snow. Anemones and liverwort stood wide-bloomed and frozen in the woodlots and on the hill fields that he had sowed to grass, Marsh found grass and clover seed sprouted and frozen. Delph's young chickens, hatched in early March, yipped all day with the cold, and though it usually meant

165

scrubbing the kitchen floor, she brought them sometimes to warm in the house. The young growing chickens would many times bring a look of pleasure into Marsh's eyes, often tired now, and showing signs of trouble.

One Sunday morning Delph stood by him in the kitchen, and watched in silence while he cut a frozen peach flower carefully in half with his pocket knife. He showed her the tiny thing that was to have been a peach, dead now from the frost. She felt a foolish pity for the flower that only bloomed to die, but when she looked at Marsh's face she forgot the flower. "Pshaw, there wouldn't ha been much fruit, anyhow. Th' trees are old," she comforted, and watched his face. And when his eyes continued dark and filled with trouble, she patted his jumper sleeve and said, "Well, at least it didn't get th' little chickens, an' my cabbage an' tomato plants are growin' like weeds. You've not seen 'em in two or three days."

She led him to the dining room, unheated and empty of furniture except for a large homemade table and three hickory bark bottomed chairs that had been in the house when they came. The room was used mostly as a catch all for the overflow of the kitchen and barn, with a basket of eggs and a churn of cream in one corner, buckets of milk on the table, sacks of corn and clover seed, with watermelon and various other seeds stacked here and there. The boxes of plants were set by the windows, cunningly arranged so as to catch any rays of sun that might come through. Marsh stooped and gently touched the small fuzzy stem of a tomato plant, that though young had the good strong smell of a green tomato. He smiled on the shiny leafed cabbages, and said as he had often said in the first days of their marriage, "Aye, you're a wonder, Delph. There's nothin' you can't do from bakin' good corn bread to raisin' chickens."

"There's nothin' that'll grow like a dominecker if you give it a good start," she answered, proud that he had praised her for even a thing that Fronie's hired girl Nance could do as well.

He studied her face a moment with kind concerned eyes. "Delph—you don't mind, sellin' things—peddlin' sort of, just this once.—I know it's different from what you've been raised to—but—." His tongue fumbled and halted as it always did when he tried to talk to her of money matters and his plans which he could maybe never meet.

But she only laughed at his foolish concern. "Mind? You know I don't—now. I wouldn't mind to haul a load a watermelons to Hawthorne Town an' stand between th' cannon in th' fountain square an' scream 'watermelons' at th' top a my lungs."

"You'd scandalize your Aunt Fronie if she ever heard of it."

"Law, what do I care about scandalizin' Aunt Fronie, an' anyhow," she continued more soberly. "It's sort of fun sometimes—to get away I mean. It's so quiet down in this valley, an'—well, ever'body likes a change. At first, that is just th' first time, I didn't like to take Mrs. Elliot her things. Now, I'm always glad to go."

"You an' Mrs. Elliot get along right well together," he observed.

She nodded and her eyes brightened. "It's like she was sayin' th' other day, mostly we try to see which can ask th' other th' most questions. She's always wantin' to grow things an' goes at it so awkward like. She was raised in a city an' she's been to Europe, but I think from th' way she talks that when she married Mr. Elliot she was hard up."

Marsh grunted, "She must ha been, marryin' th' likes of him," and turned away to look at his seed corn.

"An' Marsh, she knows so much about music an' books an' such. I guess you've heard her play th' piano, an' she's always gettin' good music over th' radio, not a bit like what Hedricks get on theirs. It's fun to hear an orchestra, an' have her tell me what they're playin' an'—." She stopped for it was plain that she talked to herself alone. Marsh stood with his hands buried in a sack of heavy white-kerneled seed corn, and in a moment turned to her with his cupped hands heaped with the grain.

"You ever see prettier corn, Delph? I'll bet ever' grain of it sprouts. Dorie can certainly grow th' corn."

She nodded, and looked at him, his rough hard hands, the worn blue cotton jumper, his prickly chin, reddish gold with a week's growth of beard, and his mouth, thinner and tighter than in the winter. She wished it were fall, and he had finished his first crop and learned what he must learn. He took no notice of her searching glance, but continued to look at his corn. "I wish to th' Lord this damned weather would let up so I could get some ground turned," he said, and after a last caressing glance emptied the corn gently back into the sack.

"You need a shave, Marsh," she said, and added after an appraising glance at his hair, "An' a hair cut too."

He rubbed one bearded cheek as he stooped to look at the watermelon seed, and answered absentmindedly, "You go an' get ready for church. I can shave an' scrub all over while you're braidin' your hair.—Are you goin' to sing a solo today? They seemed to like that one last week might well."

She shook her head. "Marsh—if you don't mind I think I'll stay at home. It's a long muddy walk in this cold misty weather."

He turned abruptly away from the seed. "Aw, Delph. I don't want to go without you, an' I've got to go. Angus is goin' to take me someplace to see about gettin' a second hand disc. You'll be by yourself all day, an' Dorie's expectin' us for dinner."

She laced her fingers and studied them. "Just this once, I'll stay at home. You can have as good a time without me. We wouldn't be together anyhow. In church you'd be with Dorie an' I'd be in th' choir, an' when we're at Dorie's you'd be out in th' barn with her or Angus, an' I'd be listenin' to Katy—or readin'."

"Aw come on. Th' weather's worse to look at than be in. I'll take you for a little boat ride down th' river, an' maybe catch some fish for supper. There's a family of muskrats on our side you ought to see."

She smiled and shook her head, and he came and caught her hands, teased her, said she was lazy, and was Marsh again, smiling his dark bright smile. His rare mood of playfulness was hard to resist, but in the end he went alone. Delph stood in the door and waved, and he turned and waved until the brush near the river swallowed him. She closed the door quickly, and hurried to the fire, shivering a little, less from the sharp spring cold, than the dreary stretch of the sodden corn fields.

She felt half guilty in having sent him away alone. Still, he wouldn't miss her, not with Dorie; and it was a treat to stay at home just once and read. Brother Eli's sermons, though less harsh and more learned than those of Big Cane Brake Church, were always dull. She cared little for the after service talk of Salem Church when farmers' wives lingered by the stove or in the aisles and talked of sickness and birth and death, work and food, children and young things growing on their farms.

She built up the fire in the cook stove, popped a skillet of popcorn, then arranged herself with her feet on the stove hearth, a book on her knees, and a pan of popcorn within easy reach. Soon it was as it had used to be at home in her own room when her own world dropped away, and she built a land of her own from printed words. The book was one that Katy had loaned her—*The Count of Monte Cristo*. She read greedily, swallowing whole sentences at a gulp, never pausing at the end of a chapter, but rushing right on, reaching blindly now and then for a handful of popcorn, nibbling it grain by grain, chewing sometimes slowly, but most often very rapidly as the story became more and more involved.

A loud insistent knocking at the back door caused her to spring up, then stagger and clutch the chair when her feet and legs, numb from sitting still so long, refused to support her. She was unpleasantly conscious that it was long past dinner time, that she had intended to slop the hogs and had not, and that her youngest chickens had not had their noon meal. She rubbed her numb knees and tired eyes, pulled off her apron, and hurried to the door, hoping that since she had to be bothered with somebody it could be Katy or Lizzie Higginbottom, wife of Perce.

Instead she found Sadie Huffacre, wife of a farmer living on the other side of the school house. Delph had heard Katy speak of the woman, say that she was a mighty one for talking, and that she wasn't overly particular of what she said. She stood stooping now with her broad back to the door, scraping mud from her overshoes, but straightened slowly and turned about when Delph had stood a moment on the step. "I was beginnin' to think nobody was home, an' I'd had all my walk in this mud an' wet for nothin'," she said in a loud, nasal voice, meanwhile looking closely at Delph with her pale blue, marble-shaped eyes. She was an uncommonly big woman, both fat and tall with a wide loose mouth and a large fat face that looked larger than it might have, surrounded as it was by masses of stiff, straw-colored hair. "I'm Liz Huffacre," she explained, and held out one fat, sweaty hand, then asked before Delph could answer her greeting, "Sleepin'? I'll bet I waked you from a nap. You look like it."

"I've been readin'," Delph said, and shook hands as heartily as she was able. She invited her in, sat her to warm by the stove, and after picking a few grains of popcorn from the floor and building up the fire, sat down and began the not very promising task of entertaining the woman. Mrs. Huffacre at first talked but briefly, while her eyes fingered first this thing and that, and her head busily twisted on her shoulders in order to get as wide a range of vision as possible. Delph watched her with a growing anger; she would not apologize for the bareness of her kitchen with its three kinds of wallpaper, bargain lengths from Mr. Cheely's store, nor would she explain that since she could not safely have fire in the living room fireplace, she must on a cold day receive all company in the kitchen.

The visitor's hunting eyes found her book on the kitchen table, and when she had craned her head and read the title, asked, "You like to read?"

Delph nodded. "More than almost anything."

Mrs. Huffacre's answer was a heavy sigh and a drooping forward of her shoulders. "Aye, child, you'll not be findin' much time for readin' with a big place like this on your hands." She seemed to find a greater cause for sorrow, and sighed again, more heavily than before. "But then it's like I was tellin' Tobe th' other night, 'they'll no more'n get fairly settled till he'll find out what farmin' is—no pay check at th' end of ever' week in farmin'—an' he'll be off an' gone. He'll sicken a mud an' weather too wet for plantin', then maybe a summer too dry for growin'. He'll find out just you wait an' see." She stared fixedly at Delph, then nodded knowingly. "An' you with him to my mind."

Delph's shoulders stiffened with anger at the woman's hint that Marsh couldn't, if he wanted to, do what any fool could do—farm. But she tried to keep her tongue civil as she answered, "Oh, he could stay if he wanted to. But mostly he just plans to get th' place in shape. When business in this country picks up he means to go back to th' oil fields. He'll make lots more money there."

"Lord, but you'd be th' lucky one to get away, now, go before th' spring a th' year. I always dread th' spring, work from mornin' 'til night, an' seems like th' youngens are punier then, an' all th' meat an' canned goods run low, an' a body hates to run up a bill at th' store, never knowin' whether they'll raise enough by fall to pay it off or not."

Delph fidgeted uneasily in her chair, and tried not to look out the windows. The black twigged plum bushes with their frozen flowers and past them the ugly corn fields made the woman's words seem drearier still, yet true somehow. She glanced longingly at her half finished book, twisted about sometimes and looked at the clock on the cupboard, and even hinted that the sky promised rain, but Mrs. Huffacre noticed nothing.

Mostly, she discussed the neighbors. Perce Higginbottom wasn't tight enough on his boys, and Lizzie, his wife, was dumb and easy minded, not tight enough on Perce. She mourned a time for the school. She had wanted her children to get good educations and learn to be something better in the world than one horse farmers like their father, but they would never learn anything in Cedar Stump School. Perce Higginbottom was trustee; the teacher he hired was always partial to his children and neglected the others.

Delph ceased to look at the clock, gave the afternoon up as lost and sat and listened with what poor grace she could summon. Mrs. Huffacre warmed to her subject, and after a time of discussing the general weaknesses of various of the neighbors, hitched her chair nearer, put her face so close that Delph could smell her breath, and launched into a long series of specific examples of the shortcomings of each, dropping her voice so low that the ticking of the clock sounded above it.

There were some who said—she was never one to call names and carry tales—that Big Jim Burnett beat his wife, or at least tried it, and she was practically certain from all signs that Mrs. Cowan was going to have another baby. The last time she saw her, her eyes were red like she'd been crying. She claimed to have a cold, but it was an uncommon funny cold; that would make four in less than five years, and the last one not paid for—so she had heard.

Of course Delph mustn't misunderstand her; she was only trying to he helpful because Delph was young and new in the community and didn't know her way around—but, well, she oughtn't to be overly friendly with that hired girl of Mrs. Elliot's; Vinie, the one that did the house work, not the cooking. Oh, yes, she was mighty friendly and harmless as a dove, but, Lord, she'd hate to have to tell what she saw going on one day between her and a certain neighbor-man. Vinie had never been much, but after going away and working a time in Cincinnati then living with high steppers like the Elliots she—but then she, Mrs. Huffacre, was never the one to talk about defenseless young girls.

Delph in order to get the conversation away from Vinie, a buxom, laughing black-eyed girl whom she liked, inquired after the health of Big Jim Burnett's new baby. She regretted the question in a moment. Mrs. Huffacre went off on the subject of its birth in particular—she had been there. Finished with that she entered upon a perfect orgy of childbirth stories. Told fearful and gruesome tales in whispers of the terrible times this one or that one had gone through. So-and-so had chewed her tongue till it was black and blue, another had had to have her child—a great overgrown monster—taken from her in pieces. So-and-so had nearly died from a miscarriage at four and a half months, and some said she had done it on purpose, but Lord, she was never the one to handle such talk. Still, it looked mighty funny the way she acted and all. Delph sat with her hands clenched in her lap and her toes gripped in her shoes, and wished Lizzie or Katy or Vinie or somebody would come. She had always shunned and hated the morbid tales of childbirth, stories filled with pain and smelling of blood, making the mere business of being a woman ugly and beastly.

When she could stand it no longer she sprang from her chair and dashed to the stove for a square of cornbread in the warming oven. "I just happened to think," she hastily explained to the surprised Mrs. Huffacre, "that I have to go feed my little chickens. They'll be yipping their heads off." And without giving her caller time to follow, she hurried out the door.

In the chicken run she crumbled the cornbread slowly down, squeezing it hard between her fingers. She tried to count the fluffy black balls of chickens, but could not. The mother hen clucked peacefully, secure in her coop from the other chickens, and Delph thought of Juber with his, "Easy now easy," clucking somehow like the hen. He would laugh at that fool woman and go away and play a fiddle tune.

She gave a great "Shoo," flapped her skirt at the gathered hens, and ran back to the house, ashamed that she had been such a poor hostess. She felt a flood of guilt and contrition when she saw Mrs. Huffacre at the door, looking inexpressibly mournful as she balanced on one foot and drew an overshoe on the other. "Not goin' so soon?" Delph asked cheerfully.

Mrs. Huffacre gave her a long sorrowful, forbearing glance, accompanied by a slow shake of her head. "Pore child," she sighed.

"I didn't know or I wouldn't a talked so—about babies I mean. But then you're married. You'll get used to such in time. More's th' pity." And she sighed and drew on the other shoe.

Delph's small store of patience drained away like water spilling from a bursted paper bag. She turned on the woman with blazing eyes. "I guess, puttin' it in straight words, you're sayin' I'm goin' to have a baby. It's kind of strange for you to know it before I do. But— but I can't see that it's anything to be ashamed of—or cry over either. I'm not afraid. I can do what others can."

Mrs. Huffacre straightened and drew her coat about her hips with short vicious jerks. "I must say some people in this world are mighty knowin' to be so young. But then when they're old an' wore out an' broke down with baby tendin' like me—they'll know. They'll know," she repeated and marched stiffly toward the gate.

Delph stood uncertainly and watched her go. She ought to run after her, beg her pardon and say that she was sorry; insulting a visitor in her own yard was going back on her raising she knew. But in the end, she turned away, comforting herself with the thought that she wouldn't have to live always near such a woman.

She walked slowly to the barnyard, and was slopping the neglected hogs when Marsh came, whistling as he walked across the muddy corn fields. He looked rested and happy, she thought, not troubled and constrained as when he went away. She threw down the slop bucket and ran to him, threw her arms around his neck and whispered, "Oh, Marsh, I wish I'd gone with you."

"Lonesome?" he asked, while visions of the second hand disc he planned to buy fled, and concern for Delph took its place.

She frowned and kicked at a soggy clod. "I wish I could ha been.—That Sadie Huffacre came—th' awfulest woman."

He laughed. "She's harmless. Nobody believes her anyhow. She's your neighbor. Tobe's a good man. We'll have to treat 'em halfway right." He glanced at her flushed face and unhappy eyes, and asked cautiously, "I hope you didn't say anything to make her mad. It's better to keep on her good side."

She tossed her head impatiently. "What's she to us that I must waste a whole afternoon listenin' to her gossip?"

"She's a neighbor," he repeated in such a way that Delph asked a question she had never taken courage to ask, but of late had wondered more and more about the answer.

She tried to keep her voice light and unconcerned as she said, "Tell me, Marsh, how long do you expect to stay here?"

He looked past her to the wide flat fields, wet but waiting for his plow and seed. "I don t know," he said, and they walked together to the barn, but Marsh was not whistling now.

Days later Delph remembered his cheerful whistling as he had walked across the fields that Sunday afternoon, and wished for the sound again. Though continuing cold, the weather turned dry enough for the turning of corn ground, and the most she had of Marsh was his brief presence noon and night and morning. Even then she had nothing more than the sight of his body; impatient he was to be at the plowing of mornings, tired at night, hunched over his food, the lamplight brightening his sweat soaked hair, his eyes intent on his plate, his thoughts on the land he had that day plowed and the land he would plow tomorrow.

About ten o'clock of mornings and again in the afternoons she went to him in the fields with a jar of hot coffee and a bite of food, usually cornbread and bacon, for that he liked better than pie or cake or cookies. He would hunker on his heels by the furrow and eat hastily, taking great mouthfuls of the bread and meat, gulping the hot coffee, saying sometimes a word of this or that, and always looking with pride to the strip of ground he had plowed since sunrise, great clods and ridges of the rich brown earth, fresh turned and glistening. Usually Delph smiled and praised him, but one day late in April when he had worked especially hard because he had to knock off early and go up to Lewis's store, she tried a bit of gentle remonstration. "Marsh, you're workin' too hard. Why th' mules they're beginnin' to show it."

He laughed and his white teeth glistened in his wind tanned face. "Aye, Delph, it takes a good man to sober down a big young team like Ruthie Ann an' Charlie. You'll see I can plow with th' best of 'em."

She pulled her coat more closely against the cold dry wind. "But what's th' good, Marsh? Sober Creekmore, that big nigger down by your lower land, they say he can outwork any man in th' county—but what of it? You're not that strong."

He sprang up, impatiently wiping cornbread crumbs from his mouth with the back of one hand. "There's a hell of a lot to it. He's a nigger—but he's gettin' himself a farm," he answered as he heaved the plow into the furrow then slapped Charlie with the reins.

"You'll kill yourself," she said, and hesitated, unwilling to go away. "It's not like you didn't know how to do somethin' else, an' had to take it so serious like. Some a these plain dirt farmers about would give their hearts to know as much about oil as you do," she pointed out, and followed him a step or so down the furrow.

"Oh Hell, Delph, forget once that I worked in th' oil fields won't you? —You got your list made out for th' store?" he called over his shoulder without looking at her.

"Couldn't I go on Maude, an' save you th' trip?" she asked hesitantly. "You'll be so tired," she went on when he continued with the plowing and gave her no answer.

"Delph, I wish to God you'd quit worryin' after me. To hear you talk a body would think I'd never done a day'a work in my life. I'll go to th' store; there's some business I have to see to.—You'd better be lookin' after your chickens 'stead a worryin' after me. They're yippin' their heads off."

She stood a time and looked after him; followed him a step or so, then turned abruptly about and went to her chickens, crying from the untimely cold. But at the barnyard gate, she stopped and looked after him again. He and the mules looked small, lost in the wide dark fields. And he seemed so far away; no closer somehow than if he had gone to South America.

Marsh continued with the plowing until the lengthening hill shadow told him the afternoon was almost gone. He stabled Charlie, threw an old army saddle on Ruthie Ann, stopped for Delph's grocery list, and rode on to Lewis's store. He had hoped the place would be empty, but as he dismounted at the porch it seemed that half the neighbormen were there. They had, through Uncle Jackson Lewis, ordered some tons of fertilizer together in order to get it cheaper; it had come during the morning and all had knocked off early to haul it home. Perce Higginbottom called to him in hearty greeting as he entered. He answered readily enough, but he wished the man had kept silent. The others noticed him now. One of Quarrelsome Sexton's tall black-eyed boys measured him in speculative silence, while old Jackson Lewis, keeper of the store, lay down his paper, pushed up his spectacles and smiled at him from his seat by the amber-stained stove. Tobe Huffacre was there, a big man, strong, a successful farmer, but with something cowed and timid in his eyes. He looked at Marsh and said, "Still stickin', I see. I kind a thought you'd turn that place over to some renter come spring, but your wife was tellin' mine you thought you'd stay till fall."

"I thought I'd have a try with it myself first," Marsh answered, and studied Uncle Jackson from the corners of his eyes. He had traded with him on several other occasions, but never until now had he bothered to think what manner of man he was. He looked to be a good hearted old soul with wisps of white hair smooth and neat on his pink shining skull that gave his head somewhat the look of one bland smile. He didn't seem to be the sort of man who would force a farmer into selling his cows to pay a debt, as long as he thought he would have a crop in the fall.

Marsh dropped to a nail keg in a corner by the counter and leaned his shoulders against the fly specked candy case, and thought he would wait a bit and maybe the others would go home. But Perce, after his usual talkative fashion, came and asked how much ground he had ready for planting, and remarked that Ruthie Ann didn't look so skittish as in the late winter. "You'd ought to be careful," he said. "I've seen more good teams than one worked to death on that piece a ground you've got."

"An' men' too," Big Jim Burnett said, and searched him a moment with his slow quiet eyes.

"I've felt no sign a dyin' as yet," he answered shortly.

Quarrelsome Sexton's boy studied him speculatively. "Th' hard time's not come," he said. "Pap an' me an' my brothers we rented that piece a bottom ground one year. God, it was awful layin' corn by in July, with th' sun strikin' back frum that limestone hill above ye." He spat contemptuously into the stove heat. "I'd sooner lay a sweet potato ridge in hell than plow high corn in bottom lands."

"There's nothin' like tryin'," Marsh answered, and was angrily conscious of being the center of attention. He had known it before, this being measured and appraised by men with whom he was to work and live. A long time ago before he was out of his teens, drillers had looked at him in silence, studied his legs and the set of his shoulders and said, "Well, boy, you look like you might be able to swing a sledge long enough to sharpen a twelve inch bit, but can you?" And he could answer, "Yes," and speak the truth. Later, when lease bosses asked him if he could drill, work twelve hours a day through weeks in which there were no Sundays, he could answer yes to that, and he could answer yes to hauling and mixing nitroglycerin, or holding his own in an oil fire or a free for all fight. Now, when men looked at him with questions in their eyes and the questions mattered more than the others, he couldn't answer. He didn't know.

He had a sudden uneasy feeling that every man of them knew how he felt; could look through his shirt and see the tiredness in his back and shoulders that came from the unaccustomed work he did. They maybe knew that sometimes at night after his first few days of plowing it would have been pleasant to drop by a furrow and just lie there and rest—and rest; and they maybe knew—. He got up abruptly and walked to the stretch of counter where men stood when they wanted to trade. Uncle Jackson laid down his paper and asked, "Want somethin', Mr. Gregory?"

"Fifteen pounds a mixed ten an' twelve penny nails," he began, and while Uncle weighed up the nails, his eye traveled down the list; coffee, he'd drink more buttermilk and less coffee; sugar, Delph was always baking cakes; flour, meal was forty cents cheaper on the sack than flour; vanilla, what in the hell did he need with vanilla? He'd batched months on end and never smelled the stuff.

He bought meal and nails and sugar and coffee. Uncle Jackson looked at him over his spectacles and asked, "Will that be all?" and when Marsh nodded, he figured the total on the edge of a newspaper. Marsh and the other men were silent while Uncle figured so that his solemn statement of the total sounded loud in the quiet room. "Three dollars an' seventy-six cents," he said, and extended his hand a little way, palm upward.

Marsh stood staring at the empty hand, conscious of the waiting and the watching of his neighbors. He'd be damned if he would admit to the whole neighborhood that before he even had his crop in the ground he was so hard up he must ask for credit. The words of asking he had planned to use wouldn't come past his tongue. It was easier to pull his worn black leather wallet from a hip pocket and take out the five dollar bill—his last one.

He watched the dirty, sweat stained piece of paper fall limp and loose on Uncle's, and the hand close and the paper go into the till.

Then Uncle was counting change into his hand—four quarters, two dimes, and four pennies. He dropped it into his jumper pocket, heard the faint jingle, and wondered when he would have another five dollar bill—for groceries. The monthly rent from the brick house was needed for feed and work bills, and what with the poor pasture the spring had so far brought, his feed bills were high. His harness wouldn't last the season, and any money made from early produce would have to go for harness.

The sense of uncertainty and fear of defeat which beset him as he left the store disappeared when he came to the wide new white-washed gate that opened on his road. As always he must pause a moment and study the gate; a fine gate, a proper gate, made like those of the bluegrass country, cunningly contrived so that a man might ride through with no dismounting. Some day he would have a grilled iron gate with the name Gregory worked in an iron scroll across the top like some of those in Fayette County; the gate would lead to a finely graveled road, and on each side the apple and pear trees would grow.

He followed the wagon track through a corner of the pasture, down past the brick house orchard where the dead flowered fruit trees were showing green. He rode up to a spot by the orchard fence and rose in the stirrups, and after much craning of his head he saw what he wanted to see, high on a forked limb of an apple tree. The limb swayed and jumped in the wind, and the robin's nest built on it rose and fell like a small ship riding out a storm, while the bird sat, helpless to do more than stay on the nest.

Marsh looked at the bird in a worried way, and the bird twisted its head about and studied him a moment, then only settled more firmly on the eggs. He lingered, and scolded his foolishness in wasting time, but there must be some way to feed the bird when it could not and would not leave its eggs for a moment to the cold. The bird looked at him, as it rose and stood above the eggs, then began a gentle conversational calling, half summons, half explanation.

He waited and the bird waited. Soon there was an answer from a pear tree a few rows away. He saw soon another robin, an enormous fat gentleman of a bird with a great expanse of bright red breast. He explained and apologized but took his time, coming along with short flights and masterful hops. He reached the limb, hopped up on the edge of the nest, while the other bird, after a bit more conversation which sounded much like advice or discussion of the weather, hopped out of the nest and flew away. The other settled himself on the eggs, careful to keep his head toward Marsh, for he seemed more wary than his mate.

Marsh smiled with his eyes on the bird, and said, "Well, I'll be damned. Is that th' way you manage?" and rode on, light hearted for no reason at all. He hurried, ashamed of having wasted time in such fashion, but when he came to the top of the hill, though it was near sundown, he must linger again to look at the lower fields. He saw Delph driving the cows down the barn lane for milking, and thought of the meal he had bought when she ordered flour; and he wished that she hadn't told that gossiping Sadie Huffacre he would go away in the fall.

· 14 ·

THE ROBIN'S eggs hatched and grew into birds that lived and learned to fly. Marsh saw them at their lessons a time or so, and then forgot them as he forgot many things in the hard press of work that came with summer.

Delph did the milking and barnwork now, went about in the foggy, dewy mornings with her dress tucked above her knees, slopping the hogs, feeding and counting her chickens, milking and driving the cows up to the hill pasture for the day. Finished with the morning outside chores, she did her housework, washed dishes, churned, carried buckets of milk and crocks of butter to the spring house under the hill, scoured milk vessels and set them to sweeten in the sun, boiled her clothes clean in the iron boiler set in a corner of the yard, and ironed them with irons heated on the kitchen range.

There were days when her mind raced ahead of her hands, and her body never seemed big enough or strong enough to do the chores and housework, peddle with Maude in the cart and keep the garden free of weeds. Her garden was a large one, and more and more Marsh left the tending of it as well as hoeing in the melon fields to her. Now that the weather was settled and dry, his mind and his heart and his body were only for the young corn, planted late but thriving—and he never seemed to know that most nights found her cruelly tired and that on some mornings when she awakened her hands and arms and back felt stiff and slow as if they belonged to some old woman and not to Delph.

Still, she knew that for all her tiredness Marsh worked harder than she. Mornings she would look across the dewy fields and see him and the mules moving through an ugly world of black earth and white fog. Evenings when the dew was falling in the valley he would still be there, moving more slowly than at noon. She would hear sometimes his long drawn "gees" and "haws," and other times his curses, black oil man's oaths, that gave her a feeling of guilt and of sorrow. She, with her stubborn ways, had been the cause of his trying to farm.

He never cursed the sandy soil that was continually getting into his shoes, nor the corn, nor the blistering sun, and seldom the mules, but often the harness which was old and given to breaking; and his furrows with the double shovel. They were not always straight as he would have them be, and now that the corn stood knee high, he broke it sometimes, plowed it up or covered it over; and he cursed his unskillful ways. Mostly, though, he was silent, especially through the hot close afternoons.

Delph would hear his silence, and know that he was tired. No matter what she might be doing, she would stop her work and take him a cornbread sandwich and buttermilk, cold from the spring house. Sometimes she could persuade him to walk down to the river and sit a time in the shade of the willows, and souse his head and his hands in the cool water, but most often he drank his milk with one hand on a plow handle and the reins about his shoulders. She would look at him as he tilted his head and drank the milk; his eyes lifted, a farmer's eyes hunting in the sky, his face beginning to be a farmer's face with the mark of his hat a pale band across his sun burned forehead, and fine sun wrinkles forming at the corners of his eyes. He was thinner than in the spring; the muscles of his arms and shoulders played under the skin like twisting ropes, and even his face was drained of fat, flat cheeked with cord laced temples, and a chin that seemed always set like a fighter's chin. Sometimes in the field or at night when he seemed more like some dumb overworked beast of burden than a man, Delph would open her mouth to speak; to say all the things she knew that sooner or later he would learn without her telling. Still, the days passed with her eyes alone speaking her troubled thoughts. Something about his face when he looked at the young growing corn or called to Caesar that it was time to go to the field, held her silent.

She appealed to Dorie one hot day in early July when the older woman came down to bring them a mess of fresh killed mutton and learn how things were faring. They were in the chicken run, admiring Delph's lot of Plymouth Rock fryers, fat and ready to sell, when Delph abruptly changed the conversation, and said in a choked embarrassed voice, "I know it's a funny thing for a wife to ask another woman, but—Dorie, I wish you'd talk to Marsh. I—he wouldn't listen to me. Think maybe I was complainin', but—I can't just go on an' on an' see him kill himself with work when there's no need."

But Dorie only sighed, and pushed back her bonnet. She looked a moment past the chicken run where Marsh plowed in the knee high corn. "Aye, Delph don't start out like I did, worryin' over your man. You can live with him for sixty years an' he'll still be one person an' you another." She studied Delph a moment, her brown face and sun burned arms, and her hands that were beginning to show the work they did. "You'd better worry after yourself. If anybody says anything to him, it ought to be about you—workin' from daylight to dark."

Delph caught her sleeve. "Don't say anything to him—about me I mean. I'm strong. I don't mind. An' in a way this fool notion he took for farmin', it's all my fault—th' way I carried on when he planned to go away. Work makes th' time pass—an' I know it won't be for always."

Dorie looked abruptly away from her up into the sky. "I'd never be any hand at readin' weather signs down in a valley like this," she said. "But valley or no valley long as them mare's tails keep a shinin' we'll have no rain. Garden stuff's needin' it now."

Delph studied the sky, too. Last night Marsh had mentioned the need of rain; and so she wished it would rain. One of the young fat fryers came pecking by her feet, and she smiled a little secret smile as she said to Dorie, "Don't you think these chickens are big enough to sell? I want th' money—for a special reason."

She hoped that Dorie would ask her why she wanted the money, but Dorie only studied the chicken and said, "I'd keep th' pullets though, but feedin' th' roosters any longer is pure waste."

Delph nodded and said nothing. Dorie like Marsh seemed to have mind only for crops and land and weather signs, with no gaps in her conversation that could be led to babies. There never seemed to be a proper time to say, "Marsh, one a these days next winter we'll maybe have a baby." It would be easier to buy cloth and baby's things and let him see. That was the way women in stories managed, and it seemed a very nice way.

Still, a few days later when she had sold the chickens and bought fine white cloth and other things she thought a baby might need, she wondered as she waited on Burdine Hill for the ferry boat, if she should have spent the money. They needed so many things, and Marsh was always speaking of the cost of this or that.

She looked out over the Cumberland, blue and sparkling in the sun, heard the lumber mills behind her droning with a sleepy, lazy sound, and gradually as she thought of Marsh, shame that she should make of him such a stranger in her heart took the place of fear. She saw the child, a little, helpless, ever-demanding thing with eyes gray like Marsh's eyes; and they would brighten when it smiled like quiet gray water turned suddenly to the sun, the way Marsh's eyes brightened.

The ferry boat came at last, and as always she and Maude waited until all the cars were on. She liked the short ride over the river. The little waves rippled and whispered against the flat-bottomed boat, and if she shut her eyes and the people in the cars were quiet she could imagine for a moment that she was on the ocean or some great wide river like the Mississippi. But today when she closed her eyes, she saw Marsh, red-eyed and haggard faced, studying the sky for rain.

She drove slowly up the hill, remembering Marsh's advice to be careful of Maude. She paused once and watched men working high up on the white limestone cliff where they blasted a tunnel for the road that would lead to the bridge. The strange working men with their sharp northern brogue were, except for the Elliots and the unfamiliar cars she met on the road, the only things new or different in the neighborhood of Burdine.

Mostly the town, more a memory of boom days than a town, seemed a place from which people went away. She saw them many times; the ones waiting to go away, up by the yellow depot watching for northbound number twelve, or at the bus station in the lower town waiting for a northbound Greyhound. Usually they were long-limbed hill men with suitcases gripped awkwardly in great-knuckled, sunburned hands, come up from the back hill counties to take the train to some one of the short-houred, easy-jobbed, New Jerusalems of the north; Indianapolis, Cincinnati, Akron, and Detroit. Sometimes they looked eager, and sometimes afraid, but usually she envied them. They were young and they were going away, and to all of them the world out there offered less than to Marsh. He was no ignorant unskilled hill man. He could get a job for the asking in any oil field, so she had heard Mr. Elliot say—and the pity of it hurt.

Her impatience to be home and take Marsh his afternoon snack increased as she drove around the shaded lower road. She hurried Maude more than her custom, and the mare's shoulders dripped with sweat when she drove down the barn lane and into the barn hall. She heard Marsh's short quick-tempered oaths from the tool house, and knew that the harness had broken again, and he had had to stop and mend it. She glanced furtively at the bundles below her in the wagon bed, and spread her dress a bit on the seat, but when Marsh came from the tool house he had eyes only for Maude. "You've let her get too hot," he said, and stood a moment frowning and studying the mare.

"I'm sorry," she answered, and felt a moment's jealousy for Maude. Marsh was hot and tired; but not too tired to think of the mare. "Had anything to eat?" she asked, and hoped he would smile and seem more like Marsh than this stone faced stranger she scarcely knew. Maybe he would come over to the wagon and ask her how was Burdine, or say that the sun was hot and he knew she was tired, the way he had used to do; and she could tell him now and not have to go thinking of it all through the afternoon.

"I'm not hungry," he answered shortly when he had studied Maude a time. "How much did th' chickens bring?"

"I—I've not counted th' money yet."

"You ought to always count your money, Delph," he said, "else you could lose some an' never know."

"I will next time," she answered, and waited until he was a good piece away in the corn before she stabled Maude and carried the bundles into the house.

She thought about the telling all through the hot close afternoon while she worked in the garden. Sometimes she paused, leaning on her hoe handle, and looked toward Marsh plowing down near the river; or up to Fairchild Place, the bits of it that could be seen between the trees. She thought of the brick house where the Elliots lived, high on a hill where there was a breeze, with a yard filled with flowers, by a road where she could see the cars go by, and windows from which she could see out over the country. Someday her child must live in a place like that. He must have the world and all it had to give, and never know the feel of being shut away in a valley low down by a river. Marsh would change when he knew there was a young one on the way; for no matter how sharp and tired he was sometimes he was always tender with young growing things.

She worked later than common in the garden, so that heavy twilight had come before she finished the barn work. Marsh came from the fields just as she stripped the last cow. Though she feared the bread might be burning she waited for him, hoping that he would be different from the afternoon. But he hardly glanced at her, only said in a low voice that seemed low because there was no breath back of it to make it loud, "I'll need a light."

She reached for a lantern kept hanging by the corn crib door, found matches in their usual chink in the logs, and when the light was strong and steady hung it in the hall. She turned then and watched him and the mules come into the barn. They came so quietly, so steadily, more like one than three, as if through the sixteen hours of the summer daylight they had lost their identity somewhere back there under the hot sun, given it to the sultry air and the long furrows of heavy soil. The mules stood still, heads drooping, tails hanging straight and heavy, ears motionless, shoulders and flanks shining dark with sweat. The day had done that to them, and for every step they had taken, Marsh had taken a step, too. She looked at him while he took collar and harness from Ruthie Ann. His blue shirt lay in clinging folds of sweat soaked cloth across his back and shoulders, and the dark earth of the corn lands clung to his shoes and the frayed legs of his faded overalls. "Got all th' feedin' done?" he asked without looking at her.

"Yes."

She turned away to carry the milk to the house, but stopped when he asked, "Cow's failin'? You didn't get so much milk as common."

"I—let Bud have too much an' Prissy kicked again."

"You ought to chain her legs like I said."

She said nothing to that; she felt heavy and tired and old. Why must he care so over a bit of spilled milk? He could in the oil fields make in one day enough money to buy all the milk the cows gave in a week. She smelled the burning bread before she reached the yard gate, but forced herself to walk slowly so as not to spill more milk.

In the kitchen she hated herself for her clumsy ways; the bread black as the stove, and the gravy and coffee not made, the milk to be strained and the table set, and onions and cucumbers to be peeled and sliced. She hurried, but Marsh came before she was finished. She heard him at the water bench by the back door, washing slowly and heavily, not quickly with a slapping and blowing and sousing as he had done in the morning. "Supper not ready yet?" He stood in the doorway, and looked at her with tired vexed eyes.

She flushed as she tried to explain. "I got a late start on th' supper, but I'll have it on pretty soon."

He reached behind him for a piece of frayed harness he had brought to mend with a leather thong. He stood there, looking at it, frowning, turning it over and over in his hand. She glanced at him across the pan of cucumbers she was peeling. He needed harnesses so. She wished she had waited to spend the money—and that the baby had waited, too. That was maybe what made her so tired. She wasn't through yet; the dishes to wash and a churning that ought to be done after supper, and tomorrow—he would know by then and maybe things would be different.

She hurried. The coffee had boiled and everything was done but the gravy. It was going to be lumpy again. She stirred it hard. Maybe he wouldn't ask about the money, or—"Delph, it'll be midnight 'fore you get that gravy stirred."

"I—I'll soon have it ready." She wished he would sit down, and not stand there, so big and towering somehow. But he sat down only when the food was on the table, and brought the frayed leather and laid it by his chair. She sat and watched him break a piece from the pone of bread, and saw his frown at the thick black crust. "I—let th' bread burn while I was milkin'."

He said nothing, hardly thought of the bread. He was tired, and his eyeballs ached, and his body felt heavy and filthy with sweat caked soil. The day had been long and hard, crueler than it might have been because of the harness that was always breaking and coming apart, vexing him into a weary anger at the waste of time. The plowing must be finished before the next rain, and the rain should come any time now. The watermelons fared well, but the young corn needed rain, and tonight the sunset had been red. He thought of the poor pasture and of buying hay and feed, and tried to reckon in his head how much this would cost and that, and wondered if he could manage hay and feed and harness all within the next week.

"Did you ever count th' money, Delph?" he asked, and pushed his plate away.

She looked at him with timid, troubled eyes. "Marsh—you're not eatin' much. Don't you want some custard?"

He glanced at the custard and frowned. He had never cared much for sweet things, not since his days in the oil fields when the boarding house flies settled first on the sticky, frosted cakes. "I wish you'd said somethin' sooner. I'm full, an' what's th' use of takin' eggs an' time to cook foolishness we don't need? You've got too much to do as it is."

She hastily swallowed a sip of coffee to make her food go down. "I—I just used two eggs, an' th' little time I took wasn't enough to keep me from th' gardenin'."

"You know I wasn't thinkin' a that," he said, stung by her seeming hint that he cared nothing for her, but only the work in the garden. "Where'd you put th' money, Delph?" He got up, took the broken harness, studied it as he said, "With what I've got an' that I'll mebbe be able to get some harness." He waited and when she continued to sit silent by the table, staring at the lamp, he asked again with a rising impatience, "Where'd you put th' money? I want to see if there's enough."

"I'll get it." She got up, took the lamp, then set it down.

"Your hands are shakin', Delph."

"It's—it's just workin' in th' garden—or milkin's made em tired," she answered in a low breathless voice, and walked slowly away to their bed room. She saw the bed dim in one corner, and the bundles in a dark little mound by the foot board. Her hands were damp with sweat, and she wiped them carefully on her apron, then reached under the feather bolster and took out the sticky wad of one dollar bills and the few pieces of silver. She walked back and laid it on the table. Her hands were wet again, and a worn dime clung a moment to her palm before she shook it away, and it lay on the oil cloth with the rest, shining a little in the lamplight.

She took the bowl of butter and started to put it away, but turned instead and watched Marsh as he stuck the harness leather under one arm and bent over the money. He counted it, and it was such a long while. He counted it a second time and that was longer still. He raised his head and looked at her. Worry and vexation tightened his mouth and changed the color of his eyes. "But, Delph, that's not all."

She nodded.

"Why you must a lost—somethin' over twenty dollars."

"I didn't lose it. I spent it."

"Spent it?"

"Marsh—I—we're goin' to have a baby."

"A baby? Now?"

"It'll be late February—I guess."

He stood there with his mouth open, the money half in his hand, half spread on the table. The piece of harness slid from under his arm, and he reached impatiently and caught it in his hand. He looked at her with anger and surprise hardening his eyes and his chin. "You—you goin' to have a baby—an' me with melons to peddle an'—. What in th' hell has a baby in February got to do with money now?"

She stood a moment staring at him with wide disbelieving eyes, her head thrust forward, and her black brows drawn with the effort to understand all in the instant something for which there seemed no understanding. She looked at his angry eyes and stubborn chin and saw him as a stranger—a Marsh she had never met until now. She swallowed a choking nothing in her throat, and nodded once and slowly. "You—you mean, Marsh, that all you can think of is that—that my baby—our baby'll be in th' way? That—th' melons an' th' work they come first an'—." She heard her voice trail away and die, smothered by a wildness that rose and rose like a storm not to be checked by right or reason.

He fumbled with the harness and looked at it while he said in a lower, quieter voice, "But, Delph, how could I want a child now? Can't you see—always I used to hear my father say that too many of us put him in a—renter's shack. You could ha waited, to spend th' money I mean. We ought to ha been careful when there's so many things, an' my land—."

Delph flung up her head at the one word land. All the half formed doubts and fears, the small rebellions, the never mentioned hatreds she had hoarded through the spring, the dreams cast aside like outgrown clothing, the bewildering conviction that Marsh didn't want a child, the spilled milk, the burned bread, her tiredness and the ache in her back; all seemed sprung from the land. And greater than all of it was the loss of Marsh; his foolish wish to farm had changed him for the moment into a beast no better than his mules. She gripped the back of a chair until her knuckles gleamed like white bits of fleshless bone, but she never felt the chair. She choked once, and her breath came in wild quivering words. "Your land—always your land. I don't mind workin' on it from mornin' till night. I'd peddle, I'll do anything. I'd a stood by an' watched you work yourself to death an' spend money you'll never get back, but this baby it comes first. I'll never have another one to tie you down, an' have you begrudgin' its food an' its clothes. Be careful you say— who was thinkin' a babies an' such th' nights in th' spring when you were beggin' me? Now, all you can think of is your land. Land—you don't even own it, killin' yourself with work an' gettin' nothin' for it. You're no farmer. There's been many a one raised to th' business that can't see its way through, an' you—you can't farm."

"Th' hell I can't," Marsh began, but while he stood struggling for words, Delph flung the chair from her, came nearer and stood with her hands on the table, and looked at him with fearless blazing eyes, that seemed more wild blue flames leaping above her red flushed face than a woman's eyes. "You could ha told me you had nothin' in your head but farmin' when you married me—that you wanted a farm hand 'stead of a wife—an' children, that once you started you'd sooner live on dry bread an' beans than go back to—."

"Delph, for God's sake—you know there's no truth in what you're sayin. I didn't mean—." But Delph was speaking again, smothering him in a torrent of words, the same doubt, the same ridicule, the same determination to shape him against his will that he had found—and fought—in the rest of the world. He retreated a step from her wrathful eyes, and tried again. "Delph—th' land it's for you an' th' children we'll have—someplace to hold to an'—."

Delph never heard him for the hot wild words she said. He felt her words like blows, directed at something that gave his body excuse for being; all the plans and hopes and dreams of his life, the years of dangerous hateful work, and the years of waiting. Always when something hit him he hit back; he stood now with his hands useless, powerless against Delph's tongue. He felt the uselessness of his hands; and it was a maddening thing, like being trapped in a crude oil fire he could not fight.

She was looking at him now, her head tossed back above her proud high shoulders, her eyes flashing, secure in the certainty that she was right, not fighting for her self, but for some future for the child—and for the Marsh she had wanted him to be—flinging his foolhardy ways in his face. "You'd be a fool, Marsh, to throw your life away—here down in this lonesome valley by a half dead lumber town—workin all your days an' maybe endin' up with nothin', gettin' old, maybe never payin' for your land."

He clenched and twisted the leather in his hands. "Listen, Delph," he said in a low voice between set teeth, "get this right once an' for always. I'm stickin' here—see. Always."

She heard his words, but they were weak, loud talk like that of a child frightened in the dark. She saw the terror in his eyes and understood it; she had felt the same a moment ago when it had seemed that all the brightness of their life together must die for the sake of a mortgaged farm. She tossed back the damp curls from her forehead, stood with arms akimbo and looked at him with neither love nor fear nor hatred in her eyes, only anger and the determination he should not stay. "You fool—you'll never make a go of it. Any fool can farm—if he works his wife to death an' lives on nothin' an'—no matter what you do you'll never pay that mortgage." She saw his eyes, wide and gray with terror for the future he saw the same as she did. He stood there knowing that she was right; his hands doubled into fists over the leather, fighting to hold out against reason a moment longer, but knowing he would lose in the end. "Think how it'll be ten years from now, still goin' on so—."

"Shut up," he cried in a choked hard voice, and she knew with a gladness like a weakness that she had won.

It was only for him that she had talked so, turned on him like a wild woman. "You'll see, Marsh," she began, and looked down at his hands clenched over the piece of leather. "It's foolish to—."

"Shut up," he said, and she felt the black leather hard against her cheek and forehead. Her head jerked backward and then forward. Then she was still, looking down at the hickory splints in the chair. There were no words—nothing. She heard Marsh. "Oh—Delph—Delph," with the words like drunken things staggering out of his throat.

She heard the leather fall to the floor but she did not raise her head. Marsh never beat his mules. She heard him again. "Delph—I—."

She bent her head over her hands on the chair back and looked at them. Something dripped on one, and she watched a red stain spread—slowly until it touched the chair. Marsh was by her now, his hands on her shoulders. "Delph—for God's sake.—I went crazy—I." She crouched lower over the chair and would not look at him. He had no right to look at her. No one had ever seen her so. "Go away, please," she said.

He stood a moment and looked at her. He could not see her face. Her back was bent and quivering. He thought of a mortally wounded dog he had once watched; it had crawled away and looked at nothing and made no sound. He called her again, and when she did not answer, he backed slowly through the door. He stared a time at her quivering shoulders, then turned and walked rapidly away. Outside the dew was falling. He smelled it on the fresh plowed ground and on the growing corn; and the smell sharpened his sense of failure and of foes and of sin. He thought of Delph, the way she had been, nothing in her heart for him but love and laughter when she thought him no more than a roving oil man. His head ached with a dull wonder of how he could have done what he had done; and the only answer he had was an ugly sickening one; he might come away from the oil fields but maybe the life he had learned there would follow him always; they were the place where he had learned to use the only weapon that he had—his hands.

He stumbled against a ledge of stone, and found that he was going up the pasture hill. He stopped, and wondered why he went up the hill, but remembered when he glanced overhead and studied the stars. Many nights when they were not too tired, he and Delph would walk to the high knoll in the pasture and look for signs of rain and watch lightning play low in the west.

He did not go on but sat a time on the stone with Caesar by his feet and looked down into the valley, where in the darkness he could see nothing but the squares of yellow light from the windows of his own house. It would be so good to go walking back and find Delph there, just as she had been yesterday—or as he had thought she was; one thing in life of which he could be certain, more than a woman to live with all his days, but something to feed his life and hold it as the soil fed the corn.

Down in the house Delph roused herself and washed the dishes, moving slowly with aimless, fumbling gestures like a woman old or blind. Finished with the dishes, she churned, drawing the heavy dasher up and down in the stone churn. Sweat trickled down her breasts and across her thighs, and sometimes pain in her face pricked through her numbed consciousness. But she was not tired. Sometimes she glanced through the open door into the early heavy darkness, thickening now with rising river fog. A train blew over the Cumberland bridge, its whistle coming with a lonesome cry down over the dark flat lands, calling her like a live thing to some splendid world she had wished for and now would most likely never see.

A moth came and fluttered about the lamp globe, and she watched it a moment, then bowed her head and stared at the blue and yellow bands on the churn. She watched the bands a long while, saw them grow dim and faint and thought it strange that they should change so. She lifted her head and saw the lamp flame flickering pale blue. The oil was burned away and she had filled the lamp that morning. She put more oil into the lamp, and lifted the butter from the churn, but felt still the same numb wonder that this could be Delph who worked alone in the night in a strange house while a strange man walked somewhere near.

She thought of him, and the loss of her dreams seemed nothing. She had loved a man who didn't exist. She sat for a time in the kitchen door, and felt the cool damp night air on her bare arms. Sometimes she looked for long moments over head and tried to search out the fog-hidden stars, but always her glance was lost in a nothingness of mist and darkness.

She never knew how long she sat, not trying to think or feel or wonder, just sitting. It might have been midnight when she heard feet walking with heavy hesitant steps across the dry hard ground in the yard. That would be Marsh, she knew, and got up and went into the kitchen. She glanced wildly about the room. He might maybe say that it was time they went to sleep. She saw the two steps leading to the stair door. Somewhere in the mostly unfinished upstairs there was a bed with one broken slat and a half filled tick, but it would do. Anything would be better than being near him.

She left the lamp on the kitchen table and went upstairs. She heard soon his feet go clumping about the house, and then he was by the stairs and calling in a low hesitant voice, "Delph—Delph."

She dropped her shoe to let him know that she was there. He called again, and when she did not answer she heard, after a time of waiting, his feet go slowly away.

· 15 ·

MARSH AWOKE to the misty in-between-time of neither night nor day. He lay a moment and heard fog drip from the eaves, and felt the morning air, cool through the window, and heavy with the smell of plowed earth. He remembered, and lifted suddenly on one elbow and looked at Delph's pillow. It was smooth and neat with a curiously empty look in the gray light.

He got up and dressed quickly, and carrying his shoes in his hand went to the kitchen. The clock ticked loudly there, and the house seemed dead and empty, like the shanties he had batched in during his oil field days. He tip-toed to the stair door, and listened on the bottom step until he thought he heard a bed spring creak.

He turned away, put on his shoes, and went hunting in the wood box for cedar wood and hickory bark. When the bark snapped and crackled in the flames, he washed, filled the tea kettle and set it to boil, put on the coffee, sliced bacon for frying, and stood then looking about the room, hoping to find a bit of work or some excuse for staying until Delph came.

He went to stand by the screen door, and now and then glanced up through the fog, trying but absentmindedly to learn if the day were cloudy or clear. The sky mattered less than yesterday. Mostly he listened for Delph.

His heart quickened when he at last heard her feet on the sttirs. He started across the room, but stopped abruptly when the door opened and he saw her face. Last night she had not cried out or spoken of pain, yet half her face was swollen and discolored, with the skin on her nose and forehead broken.

194

He watched in silence while she came slowly down the last two steps, as if since yesterday she had grown slow and old. She paused to fasten the stair door with particular care, turned again and said with her eyes careful to look at nothing except the stove, "I must have overslept, but I'll have breakfast ready by th' time you feed."

She spoke so carefully, like a child saying a poorly memorized and greatly detested bit of scripture before a strange and hated audience. He knew she lied. Most likely she had awakened when he came into the kitchen, and had lain, hoping that he would go away. She walked on to the stove with her shoulders straight and high above her proud breasts, and her head tilted a little as if her braids had been a crown. He tried to find the old Delph in her eyes, and for a moment something hurt and broken fluttered in their even stony blueness, and then they were like her shoulders, hard and proud and still.

Wordless he went from the kitchen. A growing realization of what he had done took away all the pleasure of that first trip to the barn. He liked the walking about on his own land with Caesar at his heels in the gray shifting fog of a summer's morning when the smells of growing corn and dew dampened earth and of cattle and hay and harness leather lay close and clear like things he could touch. Other mornings, before the full heat and the hard work of the day, he had felt strong and unhampered, able to live the life he wanted, forever here on his own land.

But today nothing was right or good. Breakfast was a long struggle to swallow food that kept sticking in his throat. The early morning's plowing was less the work in which he took much pride than a continual reminder of what he had done to Delph. He had taken time to mend the harness, patch it and brace it in a multitude of places, putting into the work the realization that it would be a good while before he could buy new. And so the harness had not broken like yesterday, and Delph's spending of the money, the thing that had started the quarrel, seemed a mere nothing, a little childlike thing at which a sensible man would have smiled.

When he saw her come out to hoe in the melon rows, he stopped his work and went to her. He tried to tell her that now she must not work so hard, but she hoed on and answered stonily from the recesses of her sunbonnet, "It would be a pretty time to quit work now—knowin' that ever'thing—maybe our winter's bread depends on what we make this summer."

"But, Delph—th' baby—," he began hesitantly.

She whirled about at that. "You're a fine one to be thinkin' of th' baby. Hatin' me because—because I'm havin' it. I never fussed an' quarreled for myself only—but—but for it an'—you."

She choked and turned abruptly back to the hoeing. He stood and watched her, angered by the never-to-be-untangled mingling of truth and lie in her talk. He hadn't struck her because she was going to have a child. He didn't know exactly what of her hard words had flung him beyond the borders of sanity and reason; but he did know past any doubt that all the hateful things she had said had been mostly for the child, and for that foolishly brilliant future she saw for him.

He stood a time shifting hesitantly from one foot to the other; the hot sun on his back reminding him that it maybe felt hotter still to Delph. He at last touched her on the shoulder, but when she lifted her head and looked at him, he saw a barrier in her eyes which his words, never free and easy like those of other men, could not pierce. He went back to his work, and his hope for rain was dwarfed and small by the greater hope that somehow, sometime Delph would at least let him reason with her.

Days passed and mostly things remained the same. A few thunder showers fell on the withering crops, and Delph's healing face sometimes had the look of a woman's face, but mostly it seemed a thing cut from stone. Marsh plowed his corn six times, watered his stock in the river, worked harder than he had ever worked, and found little time to think and wonder— and fear. When thoughts of Delph goaded him into the misery of bafflement, he turned more fiercely to the land. There he was sometimes able to find the old goodness again; and because of that his wide fields seemed more than a road to security, but filled with a strength and kindness greater than that to be found in men. There were times especially at twilight after a hard day's work when some of the patience and the strength of the land seemed entered into him, and he could think of Delph, not as she was now, but she had been and would be again.

August came and Delph drove the mules and peddled melons in Burdine and the surrounding country. Marsh had suggested that he peddle and hire Sober Creekmore, the negro down the river, to do the hot back breaking work of gathering, but Delph had stubbornly insisted that she peddle. Now, for her the peddling days were like bright holidays when the fierce struggle not to cry or think or let her mind wander past the birth of her child was easier than when she stayed at home. The mules were not gentle as Maude, but young and hard to manage.

Everywhere people shook their heads over the drought and the heat, and sighed for the burning crops. Dorie and Marsh seemed the only ones that never complained. Dorie came often to comfort and advise the Gregorys. She would look at the sky and then at the land and say, half in pity, half in scorn, "Aye, it's maybe not half as bad as it'll be. A wet spring, dry summer, an' then maybe a hard winter ended by a flood. It's weather like this weeds out th' farmers."

"Only th' no good ones," Marsh would say, and Delph said nothing. Only now and then when she drove by the Burdine depot, she would go slowly by and study the crowd of waiting men. The group was larger now, not only the young ones, but older, family men with sober timid eyes and great gnarled hands who, while they waited for the north bound train, showed in their faces that their thoughts were less for the factories that maybe lay ahead, than for the things they left behind. Delph pitied them, old as they were, the best of their lives and their bodies already gone to years of farming thin hill lands; the cities of the north could hold little future for them. She would think of Marsh, see him in them, old, with his strength gone for nothing. She would drive on, blind to the road.

One afternoon when a second load of melons kept her late in the town and the depot seemed deserted, she drove to the back where the mail trucks waited, and without climbing down from the wagon, called in a low voice to a man weighing sacks of dried mayapple root by the express office, "How much is a ticket to Cincinnati?"

The man stared at her a moment before asking, "One way or round trip?"

"One way," she said.

"Three-sixty-five," he answered, and after studying her a moment longer, smiled and asked, "I believe you're Marsh Gregory's wife, th' man that took over th' old Weaver Place?"

She nodded, and fumbled with the reins as she explained in a hesitant voice with her eyes on the ticket window showing through the door, "One a my cousins in th' back hills—she wrote to find out. She was thinkin' a goin' up there for work."

The man came and put his foot on the wheel, and smiled up at her as he talked. "Work's mighty slack," he said. "Two people fer ever' job in them big towns. You'd better write an' tell her she's better where she's at. Them that have got a roof to their heads an' somethin' to eat's lucky these days."

She gathered up the reins, and looked at them while she said, "I guess this woman—my cousin—would be kind a foolish to take a baby—an awful little baby—to a place like that—not even knowin' she could get a job."

The man spat then gave his head a short hard nod. "She wouldn't just be foolish—criminal I'd call it to take a baby to a place like that.—Well, from what I've been hearin' your man'll have them that was sayin' back in th' spring he couldn't farm, a talkin' out a th' other side a their mouths by fall. Some are sayin' he must ha knowed a dry spell was on th' way, an' a planted his corn late an' a good sized melon field on purpose. From all th' loads I've seen you haul, he'll more than pay for his summer work if it don't rain another drop," he said, and there was admiration in his eyes.

"Mostly I guess it's beginner's luck," she said and tried to smile. When he had taken his foot from the wheel, she turned her team about and drove rapidly away.

Though she had not intended to, that night at supper Delph told Marsh of the stranger's comment on his luck; and in spite of the little lie she made by saying he was a truck driver instead of a man who knew the price of tickets, she felt rewarded in the look of gratitude that came to Marsh's eyes. There were days when his eyes were like pages written full of troubled words, and some hope would come to her that the weather might do what she and his reason had failed to make him do. Yet even while she hated him for his stubbornness, pity tightened her throat when she watched him as he watched the sky. If it happened that they were in the melon field, she would pause and say, "Maybe there'll come a good soakin' rain."

"Maybe so," he would say, and continue to search the southwest where day after day he saw the same stretch of cloudless sky, no longer blue, but a glittering white like a quilt of milk weed down.

Then Delph would work again, waiting to hear the things he never said. She saw his face when at noon he looked at the withered corn, and in his gray eyes she could see no despair, pity rather for the corn that seemed certain to die, maybe a hard stony anger when he looked at the sky, but never despair.

She marveled sometimes at the happiness he found in trivial things such as the melons. Them he seemed to prize not only because they were bearing a crop in spite of the drought, but because they fought so to live when other plants died. When he looked at them it was as if he saw people and not plants, and his eyes never yearned over them as over the corn. Though there was still plenty of hope for the corn, so Dorie said. It was from her seed, large and slow growing and white, a type that with good soil and the careful tending Marsh gave it could take most anything the weather had to give and return a fair yield.

Delph wished sometimes that Dorie would stay away. She accepted the drought as Marsh accepted it; not as a monster that came and blasted hopes and made as nothing months of work and money spent for seed, but only as one of the many misfortunes liable to overtake any farmer. "This is th' worst part of a drought," she said one day while she visited with them in the melon field. "Th' heat won't kill us, an' things are not all dead, but now it's th' waitin' an' watchin' 'em die that hurts a body so."

"Th' corn's puttin' up a hard fight," Marsh said, and looked down the pale rows where the plants held their withered, tightly curled leaves like spear points raised against the sky.

Dorie nodded. "It's a curlin' its leaves tight to keep in ever' bit a water." She shook her head slowly, and some strange delight kindled in her eyes. "Aye, you know a plant is a wonderful thing. It's hard to understand how they live in all this sun—a hundred an' four yesterday in th' shade."

"An' look at that pile a melons there," Marsh said, and something of the old woman's pleasure glowed in his own eyes. "I can't see for th' life a me where they get their water." He took a handful of soil, looked at it a moment, then blew it slowly from his palm, and in the air it made a little cloud.

"It's wonderful what hot weather a melon can take an' still thrive," Dorie answered. "They'll be your salvation this season."

Delph looked down the rows of withered, limp-leafed vines. They looked dead. Their frail stems were black in spots, but everywhere the great cool looking melons lay. They were mostly water;

yet the leaves died for lack of it and still the melons grew and made their seed. It was a marvel—maybe, just as there was a wonder in the way the corn leaves curled to keep the plant alive, and the cunning of the lower leaves that died so that the upper ones might live and bring the plant to seed. She stared at the two before her; Marsh, gaunt with red unshaven beard and his blue shirt, a darker blue with sweat, and the old woman standing motionless above the hot soil; they were like the melons and the corn and the garden beans that bloomed and bloomed. They accepted the land and the sky as the melons accepted, fought as they fought with all the cunning in their power, and whether they won or lost they accepted still. She studied them a moment longer, then hastily dumped the muskmelons in her apron into the wagon, and hurried to the house. Though her own room upstairs was like an oven when the sun struck full on the tin roof, she went there. After drawing the blinds to shut out the sight of the fields, she flung herself face downward on the bed. She thought of Marsh as he had been, and as he was now—no better than a plant of wilting corn. She could have cried for him, but he didn't want her tears. He didn't want her; he wanted the land, and always his farm would be the master and he the slave.

She thought of her child, and her hands clutching and twisting over the feather bolster grew still, and the ache that seemed so many times too big for her throat went away. Soon, she got up and went back to the melon field. Marsh looked at her and smiled to see that she seemed happier than she had been for days. She never saw his smile, and hardly noticed that her bonnet was limp with sweat or that her dress was wet on her back as if she had stood in a rain. She saw her child; a part of her it would be, like a piece of herself to go on and on, higher than any dream she had ever had for Delph.

August dragged through dog days, and the drought ceased to be a simple thing like lack of rain, but was a presence that entered their house and lived with them, sat at their table, and haunted their sleep on the dewless nights. They no longer listened to the rain crow's mournful cry on the river hill. The rain crows lied that year so Dorie said, and all other rain signs as well. The earth worms burrowed deep to find a coolness in the earth, and now when Delph carried buckets of cool water from the spring house, the bucket showed but little sign of sweat in the hot dry air.

Great cracks appeared in the hard ground of the yard where the few flowers had long since been uprooted by hogs bursting through the makeshift fence. Hot winds from the north raised streamers and eddies of the dust-like soil of the corn rows until the limp ragweeds by the road stood more brown than green. The spring ran thin and quiet, and the mint by the spring house door gradually paled, lost its green crispness for one of brown, and died.

There was dust and silence and murky yellow light, and worse than those, there was the waiting, and the watching of plants, and searching of the sky. Marsh worked and gathered melons and tended stock and never seemed to know he had a body. Hope gradually drained from his face, just as the bit of fat in his body melted away in sweat. Still, he said nothing of going away.

More than the sight of the dusty corn fields, or the dying melon vines, it was Marsh's face Delph wanted to forget when she peddled. Often she drove as far as Patty George's store, a barn like building set a good distance back from the main road and well hidden in a clump of scrub oak trees where unlicensed liquor was sold. There, it was no uncommon thing to see drunken, sunburned men, gaunt under sweat clinging overalls, lying in a stupor by some tree, or loping a mule helter-skelter through the trees to the tune of a hill-billy song.

Sometimes, a deputy sheriff who was usually by or some one of the men, more sober than the others, would tell her it was no place for a woman. But her melons sold well there, and she would laugh at advice, and stay until they were sold. Marsh didn't know that she came there, and he would maybe not like it. Still, the occasional fights, drunken brawls with now and then a bit of gun play helped take her mind from its tortured ways. She didn't care what others thought about her going. It didn't matter. Nothing seemed to matter.

She was sick of being Delph, a farmer's wife, forced to talk and smile and never let anyone know that the healing wound on her face—one night she'd been running after Prissy's sassy calf, and hadn't watched where she was going, and banged her face hard against a set of harness Marsh, fool like, had left hanging in the barn hall—was a little thing compared to the great wound that made her whole life ugly . . . and Marsh's with it.

He stayed about the house no more than necessary, and dreaded the Sundays when there was no work to keep him in the fields, and he could not go to church. He would not go without Delph, and Delph would not go. She could not wear a deep brimmed bonnet to church, and since he had made the mark on her face she had never been among people without her bonnet. Usually he spent the day puttering at first this and that, but feeling always guilty and lazy because on Sundays Delph did the house work she had neglected through the week. He would go sometimes to sit by the river, but was miserable there, thinking always of Delph hard at work in the hot kitchen.

One Sunday morning, sick of staying always away from her, he begged for the privilege of doing her churning, but Delph no more than in the first days of her marriage could stomach the idea of a man doing woman's work. In the end he did what he usually did, went for a scrub in the river, finished with that he washed Caesar, then sat a time in the shade and watched the water.

He thought of his dying corn, and the debts, and the dead pasture, his stock beginning to show the sparseness of their fare, and the long months of buying all the feed he needed; and he knew that he was beginning to be afraid. He thought of Delph, working too hard, eating her heart away, maybe doing some mysterious damage to the child—if she were going to have a child. There was little change in her that he could see; her body thinner if anything, with her eyes big and a wild bright blue against her sun burned skin.

He got up and walked quickly toward the house, but stopped when he came to the edge of the field. It had happened before, and it would happen again, and always he would master it in time—that wild wanting of Delph; not just her body, or her willing, patient hands, but all of her, the part he wondered if he had ever had. If he could go to her and talk, tell her that he was afraid, that maybe the cows must be sold, that maybe in the fall he would have to go hunt a job and work until spring. If he could say all that the things he feared would matter less. She would smile and toss back her hair and say, "Pshaw, a little hard work won't kill us." He would feel better then, and know that things would right themselves in time. She could do all that, and it was hard to remember that she was the one he must fear most. It would be so easy—and so good—to make her his again, complain of the hard times, and let her persuade him to go away—and always after he would hate himself, and her, too, maybe.

He went back to the house not long after, and after some search-ing found Delph in a freshly ironed dress and apron sitting in the spring house door with a book on her knees. He brushed past her with the excuse that he wanted one of the melons they kept cooling there. "What you readin', Delph?" he asked.

She looked up quickly in a dazed sort of way as if he had roused her from a sleep. It was plain she preferred the book to him. "A book about India Dorie loaned me, It's all about jewels, an snakes, an' tigers, an' droughts, an' child marriages," she answered. Her face lost its look of happy absorption while something like hunger and anger shadowed her eyes. He wished he had not spoken. Still, he had to speak.

He had to content himself with what little bits of herself she gave him, and when after supper she walked away, though with never a word, he was glad, and followed her. He knew she was going to watch the sun go down; that was almost the only thing they did together now. He walked in silence a few steps behind, with Caesar trotting before him. They went up the hill and then into the pasture where the sound of their feet over the brown grass and stubble sounded loud like thorns crackling in a fire.

They came to the high knoll with its crown of little walnut saplings that let yellow leaves fall on their hair as if the time had been October. Down in the bottom dark had come, but here on the high ground the red-washed twilight stained the world like the hot glow from a melting sky. The color touched their faces and their hands, and the hair along Caesar's back seemed more red than brown.

The sunset was a high mysterious land of castles and islands and mountains formed of red and gold and purple cloud. Bands of red rose higher, and they watched their rising until their heads were tipped far back and their eyes ached with the red light. "We might as well go," Marsh said. "We could look all night an' see no sign a rain."

"That's right," Delph answered, and turned and looked toward the north where Hawthorne Town lay. There, when it was dark enough and clear, she could see rows of lights from streets and rail-road shops. She looked a time, but tonight the lights were no more than a pale glow, smudged by dust and dimmed in the sunset.

They went away then, silently as they had come. Once Marsh plucked a weed by the path, felt it in the darkness and said, "There's no dew fallin'."

"No fog either th' last few nights," Delph answered, and added, "That helped a little."

"Don't forget," Marsh said when they had reached the house, "this is th' night you write up your news."

"I know," Delph answered wearily. She hated this writing of little petty news from Cedar Stump in order to get the paper free.

Tonight the writing went slowly. The moths swarming about the lamp were a torment to her heat strained nerves, and her sweating fingers were awkward and stiff over the pen. She watched the black letters curl over the page, and saw again the heartless beauty in the sky, the blade-curled rows of corn, and the melons that ripened fruit and died. In the face of the drought the births and deaths and sicknesses of which she wrote grew small and unimportant, more like the doings of ants who lived in the shadow of some stone that any day might fall and hide all sign that they had lived.

· 16 ·

MARSH WIPED his face and neck with a soggy blue bandanna, and once more turned from his work of gathering melons to look at the southwest where the sky no longer lay white and shimmering, but was gray and cool to the eyes. He thought it had darkened a little in the last hour, but still it was nothing against all that dry white blue.

He heaved a watermelon to his shoulder, cradled another in his other arm and started to the wagon, sinking ankle deep in the dry sandy soil. He watched his sinking feet, felt the hot dry soil in his shoes, and was glad that his plowed lands were flat. Hill fields loosened with a plow and stripped by the drought of every plant that might have held a bit of soil would wash to the bone this winter. The winter would most likely be wet, or cold with a good bit of snow. He'd sow the melon fields and maybe some of the pasture to alfalfa—if he could buy the seed. Alfalfa would be good for early pasture next spring—if he could hold on till spring.

He put the melons in the wagon, and wished there were a patch of shade for Maude. She was heavy with foal and it was not good for her to stand in the hot sun. He wondered if the foal would be colt or filly, and hoped it would be a good piece of horse flesh, something like what he had always wanted, though he knew he ought to have been sensible and let her raise a mule colt. He looked at a dead melon vine by his feet, and knew that Maude and her foal didn't matter. He'd most likely have to sell them both to pull him through the winter.

He glanced at the sky again, and thought that somewhere Delph was maybe looking at it, too. She had been peddling since

205

full sunrise—sold one wagon load and was back for another before he had enough gathered to fill the wagon. He had asked her how she sold the melons in such a hurry. Her eyes had flashed up at him from her sunbonnet, and she had laughed and answered, "Some fool man thought th' mules were runnin' away, an' yelled, an' all th' mill men came on th' run. They bought th' melons."

"You be careful. They could hurt you bad," he had warned, and wished he had paid Sober Creekmore to do the hot back-breaking work of gathering, so that he could have peddled. He thought of her selling to the mill hands, and the thought sickened him. He was her husband, and the mill men were strangers, yet they had as much of her as he had; her presence and her smile—sometimes.

He was almost ready to drive to the barn with his load when Perce Higginbottom and Roan Sandusky hailed him from the lane. "I brought Roan here down to look at your melons," Perce explained, and came and leaned his elbows on the wagon side and cleared the melons with a neat stream of tobacco juice, then added, "I picked him up celebratin' in Hawthorne Town."

"What over in this God awful weather?" Marsh wanted to know.

It was Roan's turn to spit. "High Pockets Armstrong over on th' Little Yellow Branch had joined hands with progress an' built a cow barn, an' nailed cross pieces in his apple trees for chicken roosts," Roan answered a little sadly, for High Pockets had been promising to build a chicken house for the last ten years.

Perce slapped him on the shoulder. "Cheer up, my son, we can't all be Samuel Dodson Fairchilds, like that new school teacher said to one a my boys when he couldn't get his interest problems straight— like he had more brains than my youngen."

"He was brainy all right," Roan said, and something in his eyes or voice caused Perce to change the conversation.

"How's your farm?" he asked. "You ought to live on it one a these days an' raise a little somethin' just to show people you can farm."

Roan's face brightened at mention of his land, and the talk then turned to the hundreds of acres of cheap cutover land he owned in the Rockcastle Country; a rough wild place forty miles from a railroad where there were more wildcats than people so Perce said.

Marsh liked to hear of the hill country, a place where pine and poplar grew tall, and full of little fertile coves and narrow river banks where a man so minded could have a crop and garden, with orchards and vineyards on the limestone slopes of the hills. There was scrub oak and hickory in the valleys, so that hogs could fatten on the mast. There, so Roan said, he meant to spend his old days and prove to all men that where trees had once grown they would grow again, and that Kentucky's hill lands, if properly farmed, could be made to support a family.

"It's a good country," he said, turning to Marsh. "This winter when it's so cold you can't work you ought to let me take you huntin' there. Last winter I made a good bit—foxes and skunk."

"I couldn't get away," Marsh answered somewhat regretfully. If he didn't have to leave for the oil fields, he would have liked to make a little extra money by hunting in the back hills where there were no people, only trees, and rocks and a river.

Perce was talking again, telling of how he had licked the drought with tobacco. It was funny, the drought, of course he'd be lucky if he made fodder and nubbins from his corn, but his tobacco was a different story. It was so funny that he must now and again pause for laughter. This summer because the boys were a good bit bigger than last year, all able to spray and sucker and worm and such, he had put in an uncommonly large tobacco crop, so large that he had laid off to build a tobacco barn, though he had wondered at times where the money was coming from.

Well, Sir, the drought came along and changed his plans. The flyin's, trash, and lug leaves had cured on the stalk, and the boys and Lizzie had leaf strung them. With so little left to the tobacco and it stunted anyhow, it hadn't taken up very much room, and he didn't have to build a new barn. He figured from reading the papers and listening to the radio, that he would make more money this season on half a crop than on a full crop in a good growing summer, since the dry weather in the blue grass had cut the crop by more than half.

Marsh listened, and wished the same could be true of corn. He was glad his visitors did not offer to look over his fields. During the last two or three days he had looked at the corn no more than necessary. It hurt to walk down the rows of high stalks, no longer alive and rustling, but with soft limp blades that sighed thinly in a breeze, or stood pale and silent with yellow pollen sifting down into dead hot air that would in a few days longer dry the silks at the end of each coming ear. When that happened his corn would be finished the way Perce's and most other crops, planted earlier, were finished.

He drove Maude into the hot dusty twilight of the long barn hall, and promising his callers a feast of cold melon, he started to the spring house. Outside again, he noticed first his shadow, pale and thin, and looked to find that a creeping blackness touched the sun. For the first time in weeks his wish for a good steady rain was touched with hope. He walked to the spring house with his eyes on the sky, hurried in for the melons, came out with one under each arm, and when he walked against the pig sty instead of into the barn, he stopped rather than take his eyes from the sky.

Long bands and streamers of black cloud torn from some great mass he could not see came leaping over the southwest rim of the horizon, flew up to the zenith and wreathed the sun until it darkened and the shadows of all things merged slowly into the pale yellow twilight enveloping the land. A strong breeze came singing up the river, bringing dust and a smell of rain that made Marsh think of spring and a harvest of corn, of water dripping from a roof, cattle knee-deep in rich dark clover, and Delph's eyes brightening over the rain. He pushed his hat back and it fell to the ground, but he did not bother to pick it up. He never knew how long he watched the sky. He heard men's voices, and remembered his neighbors. It was always twilight in the barn hall, and they, deep in talk, would maybe not have noticed the good sign of rain.

He stepped to the door and heard the words they said, and stopped and listened and forgot the rain. Their backs were to him and they did not know he was near. Their talk held him and he hardly knew he listened. They were talking of Delph. They had taken no care to lower their voices; the things they said were true, and mostly praise. Both men liked Delph, respected her skillful hands and her way of never complaining. Perce had praised her many times, teased her, and said that she with her garden and cows and peddling was making more money than Marsh.

He talked of her peddling now, was describing her, the skittish mules, the drunken crowd at Patty George's blind pig where she had gone to peddle on the first Saturday in August—primary election day. It was no place for a woman, so he, Perce, had told her, but she had laughed and said she thought she'd sell her melons. Perce paused for laughter and laughed so hard that the chunk of muskmelon to which he had helped himself, trembled in his hand. "'Uncle John,' she says, 'was always an' election officer, an' ever' election day he kissed us all good-bye. Why, we've killed more men in Fincastle over politics than you all up here have sent to jail.'"

Perce took a bite of melon and shook his head. "I didn't argue. What she said was th' truth. Her paw was a good man, but ever' time he killed a man there wasn't a sheriff in three counties would try to arrest him. They'd send him a postcard tellin' him he was under arrest, an' pretty soon he'd drop into th' court house civil as you please with fifteen or twenty of his cousins all armed to th' eyebrows, bent on seein' that justice was done."

Marsh watched Perce, and wondered that he did not go on, say it all, and be done with it; say that Delph was one of a wild, headstrong race, that she was like her father, that a man might keep her by him for a little time, but he could never have her to know that she was his. But Perce made no observations. He only ate melon and finished the story. One of Quarrelsome Sexton's boys had fired at Rufus Nunn in the store, something over a card game he thought. Sexton had missed. Rufus had run out of the building and around Delph's wagon with Sexton after him.

Perce laughed again, and selected another piece of melon. "There was Andy Sexton, his gun out, aimin' anti-godlin at Delph's head, tryin' to get a bead on Rufus Nunn runnin' off through th' trees on th' other side a th' wagon. I'll never forget how that girl looked. Her bonnet was danglin' on her shoulders, an' her head was throwed back, an' her eyes throwin' off sparks while she was curlin' back with a long black snake whip. Then ever'thing happened at once. Delph's whip sizzled an' cracked, an' Andy swore an' a bullet whined, right through my hair seemed like, then Delph's mules were tryin' to run away, an' all th' men half sober, a swingin' on to them. An' that Sexton stood quiet a slingin' blood from his hand an' a lookin' at his pistol on th' ground."

Marsh didn't want to learn any more. He had in a way forced Delph to go into such a crowd, though he had supposed she peddled only in Burdine and by the Hawthorne road. It came to him that maybe all he knew of Delph was supposing, that maybe she belonged in the oil fields instead of a farmer's world.

Roan said something about Marsh's mules, and he remembered he was listening when men didn't know he was near. He kicked a swinging stable door, for he didn't seem able to find his tongue. They heard, and Perce called, "Marsh, we've been talkin' about your wife. You ought to let her run for high sheriff. She'd clean up th' county in no time."

Marsh said nothing. He remembered that a while back something had pleased him. He had wanted to tell the men. Now, his thoughts shaped themselves no better than his words. He thought of Delph and wished she were home. He found himself sitting in the crib door, eating a watermelon he did not taste while he listened to some talk he did not hear. He roused himself when Perce said for the third time, "Speak up, Marsh. It's th' only way I see. I'm sick a th' job anyhow, an' th' school's by your land where you can keep an' eye on it."

"Anything for peace," he said, and listened until he learned that he had promised to run in the school trustee's election in the fall. Perce said that more than one had suggested it. Lately there had been much hard feeling about the trustee business. Every man had some relative asking for a teaching job, or children hard to manage. Now, they wanted a sober, sensible man who would get a strange teacher for next year, good to all and partial to none. Hence, Marsh was just the man. He had no children and no teaching kin of whom anyone had heard.

The thing was settled. Marsh, with the backing of Perce and the good will of Roan, a little electioneering from Dorie, and some good talk from Brother Eli—neither of whom lived in the district—would be elected. Marsh tried to feel the pleasure he knew he should feel. Last winter he had been no more to these men than a roving oil man—now he belonged in their community, was one they trusted. For an instant he savored the triumph of one victory toward his dreams—and then he thought of Delph.

Perce was telling some tale to illustrate the hard, thankless life of a school trustee when the blue fire of lightning trembled and danced through the barn hall. Each man sprang to his feet as if the fire had singed his hair. The tongues of flame had hardly died when the air seemed changed to sound, thunder crashed in one wave of noise and motion that clanked the trace chains on the wall and rolled and tumbled over the roof like wagon loads of rock dumped there, then growled and muttered in the high secret places of the sky. Then there came another sound that made the thunder and the wind seem as nothing, a great roar that hummed in the ears and caused the men to look at each other with unbelieving eyes. Perce thumped Marsh on the shoulder and yelled, "It's rainin'," and Marsh staggered under the blow and knew that he would maybe have a crop of corn.

They stood in the barn door and watched the walls of water ride over the fields silent, lost in the wonder of the rain. The young pigs in the barn yard stood with heads lifted enquiringly toward the sky, blinking their long-lashed eyes in puzzlement, and seemed to know that the rain was good, though it was mostly strange to them. Young chickens who had not followed their mothers in days went hunting them now, alarmed by the strange new noise of thunder. Caesar was little better. Marsh laughed at the way he cocked one ear and growled when the thunder growled, but when lightning spun and thunder boomed and roared Caesar grew still and wrinkled the brown spots above his eyes and looked first overhead and then at the rain as if he would decide the beast that made the noise. He looked at Marsh to see what he thought of the strange business, and after one glance at him, Caesar grew happy and bold and went trotting out into the wet after Prissy's calf, too full of scrub to come in out of the rain.

Marsh breathed deep and heavily, filling his nose with the hot earthy smell of the rain. Perce and Roan were talking, but the noise on the roof drowned the most of what they said. They talked of the rain and what it meant. Marsh knew that so many things; pasture, a fair-sized yield of corn, a payment on the mortgage, and—. Caesar barked and ran down the lane, and Roan said, "I'll bet Delph has been caught in this rain."

"She wouldn't ha had time to be on her way home," Marsh answered, but a moment later a pair of mules and then a wagon cleared the high spot in the river road, and Perce bellowed, "Good God, it's your team a runnin' away."

Marsh started to run, looked, stopped, and continued to look while Roan swore behind him, and Perce groaned, "God, she'll never make it over th' hill."

But Delph continued to stand in the swaying wagon and watch the sky. Her bonnet dangled from her shoulders and the wind and rain blew through her hair. One long braid and then the other uncoiled and streamed behind her, but she didn't care. She liked storms and wind and thunder. She liked the coolness of the rain and the lightning flashing blue over the rocks and the waves of rain dancing over the bottom fields like women whirling in silver. It was fun to be behind the mules; they knew it was raining and they were going home, else they would not have run so. She laughed for no reason at all, and felt young and free and like Delph again. She hardly knew she held the reins, but let the mules go at their will.

Marsh stood in the barn lane and held his breath as he saw the rear off wheel spin for a second on nothing when the wagon lurched too near the edge of the road. He silently cursed the mules when, as they rounded the sharp down hill curve, they gave every sign of galloping over the embankment and plunging into a ditch. He heard Perce's great sigh of relief when the wagon was safely turned into the lane, and then his admonishing advice, "You oughtn't to let her out with them mules. Lizzie was sayin' th' other day that bad harm might come to her—young an' newly married—with no more thought for some things than a chicken."

Marsh flushed and said nothing, only watched her as she stood in the wagon and laughed and wrinkled her nose at the rain. She never noticed him or the others as the wagon came rattling down the lane, careened around a corner of the barn and plunged into the hall, and stopped with the mules standing quiet, and sedately flipping their ears as if they had known all the time they would not run away.

Delph was smiling as she sprang to the ground, and Marsh, remembering Perce's words, frowned in thinking of the child and her safety. Delph saw first his frown, and the laughter left her face as she said, "I didn't hurt that new harness comin' on so fast, an' th' wagon's good an' strong."

"I wasn't thinkin' a that," he answered shortly, and might have tried to explain, but could not with Perce and Roan about and both talking to Delph.

Perce told her she was liable to break her neck, and Roan advised that when she drove mules to remember always that she drove mules, while Delph laughed and called them her Aunt Fronies. The rain seemed to have given the men and Delph the same unthinking gaiety it gave the farm animals and Caesar. Marsh listened, and

though he said nothing, gradually something of their light hearted-
ness entered into him.

He invited them all to stay to dinner, promised fried chicken and
hot biscuit, and the half of a custard pie for Roan. Perce rubbed his
beard and considered, decided to stay, though maybe it was not the
thing to do. Lizzie had been promising him and the boys a mountain
of fried chicken if it rained in time to save any of the late garden and
corn, and she could be certain she could spare a chicken from market to fry. "We'll all have chicken now. At least once," Marsh said,
and glanced at Delph.

She was not looking at him but outside at the rain, studying it as
if slowly realizing for the first time all that it meant. She turned
when Perce called her Mrs. Trustee, and told her that Marsh was to
start hiring the teachers soon, and would most likely fall in love with
a pretty one and run away with her and Maude and Caesar. She
looked at Marsh in a questioning way, and he answered, careful to
betray nothing of what he knew was petty childish pride, "Yes,
they're goin' to have me run for school trustee."

"He'll be elected, too," Roan said.

"An' I hope he picks a teacher that won't always be tellin' my
boys to be smart an' go away from home like that Samuel Dodson
Fairchild," Perce said.

"Well, he was smart," Delph answered, and turned away and
watched the rain.

Marsh looked at her shoulders. They were straight and still, but
once he thought they shivered slightly. He took a jumper from a nail
on the wall, and walked up to her and said, "Here, Delph, hadn't you
better put this on? Th' air's gettin' chilly."

She shook her head. "I'm not cold," she said, and continued to
look at the rain.

He stood a moment with the jumper in his outstretched hands,
looked past her to the fields of reviving corn. He wondered with a
weariness like an ache which was the worse—to be pitied in the face
of defeat or scorned in the promise of victory; and always alone.

He was glad of his visitors. All during the good dinner and into
the rainy afternoon their laughter and talk stood like a wall between
him and Delph's somber eyes. Roan talked again of hunting in the
Big Rockcastle Country, and continued to beg Marsh to go with him

there in the winter. "You'd like it fine," he said. "An' you'd maybe pick up a good bit of extra money—more than pay you to go."

Marsh sat with his elbows on his knees and watched the rain. "I couldn't leave my stock an' such," he said, and glanced up to find Delph's head lifted from the overalls she mended.

"Sober Creekmore would be more than glad to take care of your stock," Roan insisted, "an' Delph there, she wouldn't mind to live two weeks without you. Would you, Delph?"

"Law, no, I wouldn't mind. I won't have th' neighbors sayin' I keep my man tied to my apron strings," she answered with a quick toss of her head.

"But I'd mebbe be gone mor'n two weeks," Marsh reminded her, nettled that she seemed to have such a little need of him.

"That's no life time—if you want to go. Mrs. Elliot, she'll most likely be gone to Florida then, she'll let Vinie come an' stay with me nights, or pshaw, I wouldn't be afraid to stay by myself."

Perce laughed. "Why, she's sickened a you already, Marsh. Same as sayin' she'd like to see you gone for a spell."

"It looks like it," Marsh answered, and hoped his tongue hinted at nothing of what he felt.

"We'll go in a cold snowy time—no need to try to hunt when it's open an' rainy—when you'd have nothin' much to do at home but feed an' stick by your fire. An' if you did have, a little rest wouldn't kill you anyhow," Roan went on, all eagerness to show someone his land.

Marsh waited, glancing hopefully at Delph's bent head. He knew he couldn't go. He couldn't leave her in winter—when the baby was to come in February. Still, she was the one to say he couldn't go. Lizzie wouldn't let Perce stay away that long, even with all her children for company. "Delph," he haltingly began when she had shown no sign of speaking, "might get lonesome an'—."

Delph flung up her head, and impatiently pushed raincurls from her forehead with the back of one hand. "Lord, don't use me for an excuse like—like I was Maude to tend or somethin'. Go on. I'll be all right. Th' money you'd make would maybe come in handy."

Marsh got up and strode to the door. He wished he could read Delph's mind. She couldn't have changed so—in spite of the quarrel. Last winter when he was gone three days with Dorie's tobacco she had come rushing to meet him as if he had been gone a month. Now, she practically sent him away for two weeks—when she ought to want him most. He glanced cautiously in her direction, but she sat as if she had eyes and thoughts for nothing but the overalls she mended.

"Come on," Roan urged. "Your farm won't run away in two weeks time. Delph will be all right."

He gave her a last beseeching glance, then turned abruptly back to Roan. "All right. I'll go."

Delph continued with her sewing as if she had not heard, though now and then, while the three men talked enthusiastically of hunting and fishing and the tall timber in the Rockcastle Country, she paused to listen. She stopped suddenly with her needle half through a fold of cloth when she heard the word, "January." She listened and understood soon that they planned to go the first or second week in January if the weather were right. She tried to count weeks and months on her fingers, but gave it up soon, and sat a moment and watched the rain with dark troubled eyes. She had never been one to watch calendars and clocks—but the baby might come in late January, not late February as she had told Marsh. She didn't know.

She sprang up, scattering thread and scissors from her lap, and walked across the room to the busily talking men, all hunkered now by the empty hearth over a map Roan was making with cedar splinters and his fingers. "Right here," he was saying, "is a pure stand a yellow poplar, virgin growth—about th' last left in Kentucky. I want you to see it, Marsh."

Marsh nodded, and then he wasn't interested in the poplar. He felt Delph's fingers pulling gently at his hair, the way she had used to tease him before their quarrel. He twisted his head about and looked up at her. "What a you wantin' now, Delph?" he asked gently, unmindful of the company.

She studied him a moment with soft, kind eyes, then Perce was booming, "Now, Delph, don't be beggin' him off. You can live without him for a couple of weeks. You've not had time to get so set in your ways as my Lizzie."

She turned short about and walked away. "I don't want anything, an' I was never much on beggin' anyhow," she answered over her shoulder.

Marsh got up and started after her, but stopped when she went to the kitchen and up the stairs. Since the quarrel he had never followed her there. He remembered his guests and went back to the map on the hearth, but the talk was less interesting than it had been.

It was late afternoon before the men went away, and at their insistence Marsh rode with them to the top of the hill. Though there had come no slackening in the rain, he and Caesar began at the gate on the hawthorne and made a leisurely solemn circuit of the farm, stopping sometimes for whole minutes together to stand stock still in the steadily falling rain, just standing and looking and sniffing. Caesar was a fool for water, splashing with his big feet through the deepest puddles, then when his thick black coat was properly soaked, running to Marsh and shaking himself by his knees. Marsh only laughed at the muddy water, and smiled to see the mud on his shoes. He wished Delph were with him, splashing about in the mud, laughing at the rain the way she had used to do, loving it as he loved it. But he and Caesar continued to walk about alone, stopping often in the pasture to marvel on the grass and clover, which in the morning had stood brown and seeming dead, now showed past any doubt that its roots were alive.

They even grew bold enough to go near the school and lean a time on the fence and frown over the poorly kept building, and decide that one of the first things a good trustee should do would be to plant a few black locusts and maples in the yard, or maybe it ought to be fenced first. Stray cows or hogs were always wandering into the schoolyard.

The school house was forgotten in the wonder of the bottom corn fields; it seemed that he and the dog could never get their fill of looking. The corn leaves stood unrolled, and though the lower blades hung limp and gray and dead, the silks showed green and tender, and over the whole of the bottom lands the warm earthy smell of the rain was sweet with the odor of green reviving corn. What with a stop in the garden, followed by a round-up of the youngest chickens, to learn if the now strange weather had caused them to run yipping witless in the rain until they drowned themselves, it was near barnwork time when he and Caesar returned to the house.

Delph, wrapped in one of his old jumpers, was just coming from the kitchen with milk buckets in her hands. "God, Delph, it's a wonder to see th' change th' rain's already brought," he cried and hurried up to her.

"I guess things will grow—now," she answered and walked on.

He said no more of the goodness of the rain, but reached for the milk buckets, and said with something like contrition in his eyes, "From now on, Delph, I'll do th' barn work. There's no need for you to help with th' milkin' anymore—or peddle. Th' melons are mostly done, anyhow."

"I'm plenty able to do th' milkin' while you feed," she answered stonily, and did not give over the milk buckets.

He tugged gently at the pails. "There's no need," he answered, and added with the embarrassed haltings that always overtook his tongue when he spoke of the child he had not wanted, "Delph, I don't think—you ought to do such work any more. A cow might kick you or—or."

"I'm plenty well an' strong an' I won't be lettin' this baby make a puny sickly thing out a me for that Sadie Huffacre to sob an' sigh over."

"Aw, Delph, please—can't you kind a feel better because it's rainin'?" he begged, and when he had waited a time in her cold silence, he turned wordless away and went to his cows.

Delph watched him a moment, triumphed over a wild hot wish to run after him, cry on his shoulder and tell him they were both fools, then turned into the house with a great slamming of the screen door. The room smelled of damp earth and was filled with the gray light of the rain. She went to stand by a window and stare at the wet fields of corn. She felt the mark on her forehead, almost healed now, and wished she could lay it away in her mind as a part of the price she had paid for the corn, and forget it. Marsh with his melons through the dry spell and his corn planted late was the victor now—more so than on that night they had quarreled.

She thought of the fall and the winter, and shivered and turned from the window, and started a fire in the stove; and when the flames whispered and fluttered like wings and the red light showed through the stove grate bars, she stood with her hands outspread by the oven door and smiled and forgot the dreary fields; this time next year her baby would be big enough to notice the firelight and the rain and, oh a lot of things. No matter what Marsh did or the weather did, there was one thing they could not do—take her child. She was young and strong and not afraid; and her child would be like herself, strong and unafraid—but it would never know the taste of being bound to the land and governed by the sky.

Through the fall and into a hard cold winter with snow piling on snow, she knew many times the taste of loneliness, and strange wonderings of how it might have been had she never known Marsh. She learned to hate the long blue winter twilights, and the silence, and the cold, and the house that was heated by nothing but a kitchen stove. More and more she felt the burden of the child; there were days when her back ached as she churned or ironed or did her housework, and she felt clumsy and ugly and dull. Sometimes she hated Marsh, his continual concern for her body as if she would harm her child, and his eternal old womanly patience when, weary of her close silent world, she turned on him with sharp words and sudden flurries of temper over little things. Then she would hate herself and pity the child to be born from such an ill dispositioned mother, and something inside her would start crying for her to make it up with Marsh. While he was gone from the house she would spend long minutes in thinking of all the good kind words she would say to him. And when he came she was silent, mending some of his clothing or cooking a thing he liked especially well—she could forget the past as long as she thought only of herself, but not when she thought of her child.

Through the winter many of the neighbor women visited her, now and then bringing something they had made for the baby, or some food they thought she might like, for it was hard for a woman in Delph's shape to eat always of her own cooking, they said. Dorie came now and then to advise her, Sadie Huffacre to sigh over her and cast mournful glances at her distended stomach. Mrs. Elliot came with envy in her eyes, and Katy with pity that she should change so, and Delph was sometimes thankful for their presence. Marsh left her scarcely any work to do, and she sickened at times of always reading about the world, and so was glad when a neighbor came to help her pass the time.

There was one she learned to like better than the others; Lizzie Higginbottom who had cried so at her wedding. Lizzie alone of all the others saw the baby after it was born; and she and Delph would spend whole afternoons in happy conversation, wonder if it would behave like Lizzie's oldest did on his first day of school, decided that it would be a child wild, and hard to manage, never afraid of anything for it would of course take after the old Costello breed, though it would most likely have a chin like Marsh's. There was the question of where it should be sent to high school—Hawthorne Town or Burdine. Lizzie was in favor of Hawthorne because her two oldest boys went there, and when her Little Lizzie was a senior Delph's child would just be starting and Little Lizzie could keep an eye on it and show it around for the first few days; the Hawthorne High School was a big place, and a young country child like Delph's was liable to get lost going all alone.

· 17 ·

I T WAS four o'clock on a black January morning, intensely cold and still. Marsh crunched over the frozen path to the barnyard, and wished as he had wished many times through the winter that he had not told Roan he would trap with him on the Big Rockcastle. The barn door latch stuck to his fingers, tighter than on other mornings. He looked overhead and the stars were bright as midnight, for dawn was yet a long while away. He heard ice creak in the river, and was still a moment with listening. There was something foreboding in such hard cold and hard silence, as if somewhere behind it all something waited.

He shrugged his shoulders and called himself a fool and went into the barn where the animals slept their heavy last sleep, and only Ebony, the young colt, stamped and trembled in his stall. The fierce cold was going hard with Ebony, though he had the warmest stable of all with a good bed of clean fresh hay. Marsh flung another blanket over him, and then after looking stealthily about to see that no one watched in all the darkness, he set the lantern by the crib door, felt about in the crib until he found a barrel of oats, plunged his arm deep into the barrel, and searched for something hidden there. He drew up a cardboard box, and with quick thief-like motions removed the lid part way, took something out, closed the box and quickly hid it again.

He took the lantern and returned to Ebony's stall, and, leaning on the low stable door, fed the colt a lump of brown sugar, while he stroked its neck and told him the cold would pass, that spring would come and Ebony could frisk in knee high clover under a hot June sun. He talked softly, stopping at times to listen. If a man were going to be a fool, it were best that no one know.

Caesar came and watched the feeding of the colt. Marsh gave the dog a bite, too, and they both looked at him, and the lantern light glowed in their eyes and showed love and unquestioned adoration. About him there was the breathing of cows, and mules' feet shifting on a stable floor, and one of the brood sows grunted softly in her sleep. He stroked the colt's neck a long while. He wished Delph would look at him that way. He fed and curried the mules and returned to the house, half hoping that she was still in bed, and not up working in the cold, getting him off for the early start he said he had wanted. The smell of coffee and frying bacon reached him at the gate, and he knew she was up, dashing about, getting him ready to go away. He opened the door, blew out the lantern, set it under the water shelf, and hoped she would raise her head from the biscuit board and look at him, but she worked on until he said, "It was so cold I thought I wouldn't call you."

And she answered with no lifting of her head, "I didn't mind. I was awake anyhow."

He watched her, and a fresh trouble smote him when he thought that Vinie might maybe not rise as early as Delph, who would from pure impatience get up and build the fire and catch cold. She noticed he was watching her and said, "I know it's not Sunday, but since— since you won't be here for a while I thought I'd bake biscuit this mornin' 'stead of cornbread."

"'Why don't you have 'em ever mornin'," he suggested, and was nettled by the startled look she gave him. She ought to know that now things were not so bad with him but that he could have biscuits three meals a day if he wanted them. Last spring when he said that cornbread was cheaper than biscuits, and he would just as soon eat it, he had not known from one week to the next how the mules were to be fed.

The biscuits were good, but the third one stuck in his throat. He watched Delph. She sat so still, seemed hardly to know he was there, and as always in the lamplight, her eyes were deeper, more filled with what had grown to be for him the shadows of some secret wall she put between them.

"You ought to eat more," he said. "Lots a times you eat hardly nothin'."

"I'm all right," she answered, and as always the toneless, commonplace words silenced him.

He finished his coffee, the second cup which he had sipped slowly to hold him there, but stayed yet a time longer and said again all the things he had said last night at supper. Delph listened and looked most often at her empty plate, and promised to do all that he said; not go about the barn or any of the stock; she might get hurt, and Sober Creekmore would take good care of things. She was not to spend a single night alone. If something happened and Vinie hadn't come by the time Sober came to do the night work he was to go after a couple of Perce's boys or take Delph up to the brick house.

At last he had said all he could think to say, and there was nothing to do but go. He got up and dressed for the outdoors, and Delph was silent watching him. She got up and handed him the package of lunch and basket of uncooked food she had packed, hesitated a moment with her hands smoothing her apron, then said, "Wait a minute, Marsh. There's somethin'—I made for you a while back. They might be handy on a huntin' trip."

He waited while she took the lamp and went to her room upstairs, and returned soon with a small bundle which she shoved hastily into his hands. "It's socks," she explained with an embarrassed smile. "Some a my knittin'. I meant it for a Christmas present—but—but my knittin' was so bad I was ashamed of it—th' first I've ever done."

"I know they'll be fine," he said, and held her hand along with the blue knitted socks. It was small and cold against his own, as if maybe it was ashamed of the lie she told. They had had a quarrel on Christmas Eve. Delph had wanted to skate with Katy on the frozen Cumberland, and he, fearing harm both for herself and the child, had refused, first with the patient reasoning, but when she turned on him with sharp angry words, accusing him of tending her as if she were a brood mare, he had lost patience and thundered at her until she cried. Christmas night had seemed a young eternity with his sitting on the stairs and listening to her smothered sobs. Now, he had the sudden wrenching fear that when he had gone she might cry and cry—and there would be no one by to hear.

He held her hand as he walked to the door. She opened it, and he felt the bitter cold, and knew he was a fool to go away. Caesar came wagging his tail by his knees, and Delph said, "I'll keep him by me 'til you're gone," and turned to the table for a bit of bread. Then he was outside, still seeing her back, straight now as always in spite of the child. He turned about to see her again, but there was the door closing in his face. He heard, first the outraged barking, and then the puzzled whining of the dog. Caesar would rather follow him than eat. He stopped and listened and wished for a sound from Delph. He watched the door and hoped that it would open. She wouldn't just shut it like that and let him walk away.

Last spring when he was riding away in the dawn to attend to some business in Hawthorne, Delph had flung open the door and called to him as he rode down the barn lane. He had dismounted, thinking something was forgotten, but she had only come, laughing and tossing back her hair, crying, "I just wanted to see you again, Marsh." And he had kissed her once and lightly, half grudgingly, for Hawthorne was a good piece away, and already the dawn was changing from gray to red. He had seen the red fire of it flaming up in her eyes.

Now, the door did not open. There was nothing to do but harness the team and drive away, but he knew as he went down the lane that no matter how long he stayed or what he saw, the most of him was left with Delph. He continued to know that, during the drive to Hawthorne, and the two days ride into the Rockcastle Country.

He was not disappointed in the place; the ridges were high, crowned with tall pines, and below their steep dark shoulders there were tall growing poplars in the narrow twisting valleys. He and the mules and Roan lodged in a great cathedral of a rock house above Left Long Branch, at a spot a few miles back from its mouth on Rockcastle. He thought he would have liked the country and the life there, had not the thought of Delph taken most of the pleasure away.

Trapping and hunting were good. The long grip of the hard cold had brought hunger to the wild things and made even the foxes less wary than usual. Some days Marsh would tramp for hours alone, turn sometimes and look back down the long ridge he had come, and see his tracks winding through the pine trees. It pleased him that his tracks should he the only sign of life about. Most always he had been with people, and he had been lonesome, not because he wanted the company of others and could not have it, but because the more he learned of most men the emptier did the world about him seem. But the trees and the rocks and the snow were not like men, they were what they were and left him to be the same.

Sometimes he went hunting for sights to describe to Delph. He explored forgotten rock houses where wildcat tracks were faint in the old dust and chips from Indian arrowheads had lain undisturbed for the last hundred and fifty years about great fire blackened stones. Other times he found walls and mounds of stone which he knew were Indian graves, or the graves of men older than the Indians.

He learned the boundaries of Roan's land, saw sometimes fine tall timber, but most often other things and ugliness which the snow could not hide; trunks of great trees felled in unhandy places and left to rot, young saplings that would never grow straight because logs had been rolled over them, or because they had been left to struggle with the loped off limbs of larger trees. There were whole valleys, usually near some deserted moonshiner's cabin, where the blackened trunks of dying trees stood everywhere, and all but the smallest of the undergrowth was dead. Some hill man had wanted easy fuel and so had fired the woods.

It was then in such a waste that Roan came alive. Anger would replace the pessimism habitual in his dark brown eyes, and he would berate men and governments, call them blind and crazy and wasteful; and his anger was like Dorie's sighs; not meant for one or a thousand acres of land and trees, but for the whole of Kentucky, or the nation, or maybe the world. One day Roan showed him a line of dying chestnut trees, a few holding frozen sick brown leaves that had died with their twigs during the summer. "Chestnut blight," Roan said, and cursed Sam Fairchild.

"You hate that man as bad as his own mother does. He can't help th' chestnut blight," Marsh observed.

Roan nodded. "I know.—But used to be I thought—that maybe Sam would try to do somethin' about such things." He sat on a snow-covered log, and dug with his heel under the snow for partridge berries he thought might be growing there. He looked but absent-mindedly for the berries, for he talked of Sam Fairchild, and under his talk Marsh saw many things that Roan did not put into words, or maybe there were no words. Roan seldom spoke of himself, but now when he talked of Sam he talked of himself also. There was no helping it.

He and Sam had been young together, almost alone in a whole country of preachers, teachers, and speakers from the outlands who told stories of poor boys who became famous, and held always before the minds of the young that hope for their future lay in thrift and education—and in going out into the world. Any, even to the poorest, might, if he practiced all the virtues, go away and be a success; be a rich and famous banker, doctor, lawyer, another Abraham Lincoln or John D. Rockefeller. The world was out there, full of rich plums for any boy who had the grit and determination to go after them. And all the boys—that is the good ones, the bright ones—were going.

"It's hard to think what it was like fifteen years ago," Roan said, getting up and walking away. "A boy with any brains was a fool to talk a farmin'. Teachers looked troubled like they thought he was throwin' his life away, an' other boys thought when a boy planned to stay at home he was afraid he'd fail in a city."

"It's still like that," Marsh said.

Roan shook his head. "Th' hard times an' men comin' back from th' cities without jobs have changed things—a little. I know of maybe a dozen men in this county that want their boys to be farmers an' are not ashamed to say so. Look how Perce Higginbottom hopes an' plans for his Ray to go to agricultural college an' then come back. In mine an' Sam's day I guess that Dorie was about th' only person in southern Westover that thought a man never got too well educated or too smart to farm. Ever'body laughed when a boy said he was goin' to study agriculture, an' then come back home an' do nothin' but farm."

"I guess it was different in college, though," Marsh said a little enviously. There seemed such a lot of things about his land and crops and stock he didn't know and couldn't always get from government bulletins, that he thought he might have learned in college.

"Not much," Roan answered. "Th' few that studied agriculture were aimin' to do ever'thing in th' world but farm; teach, work for th' government, or sell farm machinery. But Sam wasn't crazy after money—altogether."

"I reckin," Marsh said. "Sam—he had to give up his notion a havin' a farm—to get some girl to have him—maybe?"

Roan laughed at that. "You don't know Sam—he could always get a girl. They flocked to him like bees after clover.—You never saw Dorie's man—Sam's father, I reckin?"

Marsh shook his head. "I've heard things though about him an' women, but all gossip I guess."

"He was th' one human on earth that could hold Dorie, doin' it mostly, I reckin, by his winnin' ways an' handsome looks. He was made like Sam, tall as I am, but slimmer an' straight as a stick, an' a proud high head.—Delph, somethin' about th' way she holds her head, puts me in mind of Sam, but his hair's darker than hers, coal black, an' his eyes bluer than Katy's.—He had all the brains that either side a th' family ever had, on top of that he had his father's pleasant ways, but at bottom he was Dorie through an' through. When he found out what he wanted he went after it hell bent for leather—like Dorie payin' for that farm."

Roan got up and strode slowly on, stopping at times to look at this or that, talking still of Sam, with easy fluency as if his life were a story Roan had long since memorized and turned over in his mind until any meaning it might have once had was gone. In college—for the first year or so—their plans grew and became exciting, tangible things that they could touch. There had never been in the hills, a model all-purpose farm such as he Roan would have, and no man would ever experiment as Sam would experiment. But Roan's thoughts turned more and more to trees and wasted soil and wasted people until a farm of his own seemed too small a thing to hold his dreams. Sam's interest in the chemistry of plant life and growth, and the chemical content of soils had driven him deeper and deeper into the ever-narrowing world of chemistry.

At first the dreams of his boyhood had remained more or less unchanged; he would farm only enough to live and give the most of his time to research; there were so many things—chestnut blight, peach tree borer, corn smut, the need for types of grass and clover that would grow in leached soil and build it up, and the learning more about the types of soil and fertilizer—and chemistry had seemed the answer for it all.

"It was slow like that," Roan explained. "I hardly noticed. I had too good a time, I reckin. Sometimes I was fool enough to feel proud.

There were all th' others, worryin about jobs when they got out, an' talkin' a what they'd do, wonderin' if they'd make any money. I knew what I'd do. They were gettin' ready for somethin'. I was beginnin' to do mine right then. I'd already started buyin' land—fifty cents an acre—with any money I could get my hands on.

"I thought Sam was th' same way. But more an' more I noticed he spent his time in th' laboratory. By our third year I began to get worried. He went home that summer an' worked on th' farm like he always did, but nights he studied—chemistry. That fall he talked nitrates, always nitrates—but hardly ever' a word about th' clovers an' such that store nitrates from th' air.

"I noticed somethin' else, too. When we first went there, many was th' fight Sam an' I had with th' ones fool enough to call us hill billies. There was a bunch of us—Combs boys from Harlan an' th' Hargis boys from Wolf—we'd talk sometimes, brag that we'd some-day show th' world that life in th' hills could be good as any an' better than most. 'We've got brains,' Sam used to say, 'but th' brains like th' coal an' timber an' money all leave th' country,' an' he'd talk on, aimin' to live down here an' have a farm on th' Cumberland that would show what could be done in this country.

"But by th' end of his third year he hardly ever talked of livin' in th' hills. That fall when we came back together, somethin' about th' way he looked when th' train went over th' river made me know then an' there that he was tellin' th' country good-bye. He'd learned by then that he had more brains—at least for chemistry—than most. Nights sometimes that fall he'd wonder, say things like, 'Do you reckin I could do graduate work in an eastern university?' or 'I wonder how our brains would match up with th' ones in th' north?' He never told me he'd gone out for a scholarship in chemistry at an eastern university 'til he'd won it. He was pleased that night. Almost th' only time in my life I ever saw him proud. 'I'll show 'em,' he said, 'that hill billy brains can be as good as they come.'

"I tried to congratulate him, but I couldn't somehow. There he was thinkin' of nothin' but brains an' chemistry—never a thought for plants an' th' land or Dorie still expectin' him home. It seemed to me he was a fool—like a child dazzled by a Christmas tree. I tried to talk with him—a little.

"He just laughed and looked at me. I'll always recollect it. 'You're a mess, Roan,' he said. 'Think about your future, man. Where'll you be twenty years from now—livin' in Westover County, wonderin' if you're fit for anything?'"

Roan stopped and studied the bark of a half dead beech tree. "He said a lot, I don't remember all he said. He laughed, too, at me an' my kiddish plans. I'd never be satisfied, he said, to come back here an' live—always. Other people had laughed at me all my life, but it never mattered. With him it was different. I reckin that's why I knocked him down, knocked out two of his teeth, smashed his lip, an' cut my knuckles. He lay there an' looked at me, an' I stood there an' looked at him. I thought he'd get up an' take his Colt off th' wall an' kill me. He was too slim built for fightin' with his fists. But he got up an' went off an' didn't say a word. Next day while I was out he moved.—I've never seen him since. He went east soon as school was out—didn't even bother to wear his cap an' gown, for he'd never cared much about such things."

That evening while they sat in the rock house eating supper, Roan spoke of Sam again and wondered what the world had done to him, and if Dorie would ever give in and invite him home, or if he would come should she invite him. "Th' whole country would like to see him, that is if he's like he used to be. Take Delph now," he went on, "why she gets mad at me, I can see it in her eyes, when she asks about my travels in Europe an' I can't tell her anything she wants to hear, but Sam, Lord, he could have her seein' New York or th' inside of a munitions plant."

"Yes. I guess Delph would like him," Marsh said and got up. He went to the mouth of the rock house and studied the stars, sharp and bright above the cold. Roan came, too, and looked at them and said, "Looks like this cold snap will hang on."

"I wish it would turn warm," Marsh answered, and wished it were spring, time to begin the plowing. Things with Delph would maybe be different then. He thought of her, and as he had done countless other times since coming away, he went over all the things which he had told her to do or not to do, checked the provisions; tried to think of some bit of work he had left undone that she might try to do, but as usual everything at home seemed in order. Caesar was with her, Vinie would come at night, the neighbors would drop in, and she would be all right. Still, he was glad it was night. That was what he liked best about the stars just now. They reminded him that another day had gone, and the time for his returning to Delph was that much shorter.

His impatience to be home grew with the passing of the days, and each night he looked at the stars with a greater pleasure. It was Roan, however, who called his attention to the sky one evening when twilight had scarcely fallen, pointed out the blurred road of the Milky Way, and said he thought the other stars looked larger, and faintly filmed as if a cloud might be gathering high overhead. "Maybe it'll turn warm," Marsh said. "This heavy cold's goin' hard with stock, but Dorie said it would hang on till th' new a th' moon."

"Dorie could be wrong," Roan said, as if he hoped she were right. "It's a good thing it's January, an' not March—all this snow piled up an' maybe a warm spell on th' way."

"It can't turn warm too soon to suit me," Marsh said, suddenly tired and eager to roll into his blankets and think of Delph.

But sleep was slow in coming. He was almost there when Roan raised on one elbow and called, "Marsh, when is Delph's baby comin'?"

"Sometime in late February, I reckin."

"You reckin. From her looks last time I saw her I didn't think it was that soon, else I wouldn't a begged you off this way." He made sounds as of counting on his fingers. "Why, it's maybe no more'n a month away."

"I'll be home in another week," Marsh answered, and wondered if Roan's thoughts were not a great deal like his own.

"Babies don't always come by th' clock, no more'n sheep," Roan observed, and rolled over and appeared to fall asleep. Presently he snored, and Marsh lay and listened and wished he would hush. The snores stopped, but he had scarcely time to be thankful before Roan was calling, "Marsh?"

"What?"

"It's gettin' lots warmer."

"Yeah. I noticed an' took off a blanket."

"Warmin' up awful fast for January."

"It's time."

Roan got up and looked at the stars. They were dimming rapidly now. He lay down and after a time of silence said, "We'd better start out in th' mornin'."

Marsh spent a second in controlling his pleasure enough to say with reasonable conviction, "I thought you planned to stay two weeks."

"Weather's likely to turn bad, now in th' full a th' moon, an' this place is one God awful bad one to get out of if th' creeks get up," Roan said, and lapsed into silence but not sleep. Some time later he called again, "Marsh?"

"Now, what th' hell?" Marsh answered, and turned and saw in the red glow of the low fire, Roan sitting in his blankets, his head turned sideways toward the cave mouth in an attitude of troubled listening. Marsh listened, too, and heard, not the brittle howl of the north wind or the dead silence of a frozen sleeping world, the sound and lack of sound that had filled the rock house for days, but the long drawn, gently said s-w-i-s-s-s-sh of a south wind in the pine trees.

"Th' wind's swung clean around since dark," Roan said, and got up and walked to the cave mouth and looked at the sky, bright mother-of-pearl and silver gray toward the east where the moon rose.

"It's warmin' up fast," Marsh said, and threw off another blanket.

"God, I hope them clouds mean snow," Roan said, and lay down again.

Marsh slept at last, but awakened to the radiance of cloud filtered moonlight and a feel of rain in the air and the earthy smell of thawing snow. It was not such things that awakened him, but the sound of Roan throwing snow on the fire. He sprang up, folding his blankets as he did so, though by the look of the moon he knew it was far from morning. Roan ground out a coal with his shoe heel and did not look at him as he said, "Moon's light enough for travelin'. We'd better be goin'."

"Might as well," Marsh said, and stopped to listen to the south wind.

"For Christ's sake get a move on. There's a rain blowin' up—fast," Roan said, as if that were excuse enough for his crazy notion of beginning a hard ride over rough ground at midnight. Marsh asked no questions. He wanted to be home, and Roan's haste gave him little time for questions. The mules were saddled and loaded and they were riding away before the fog of sleep had lifted from his brain. Roan led the way and set the pace, and Marsh was glad his mules were big and young.

The fourteen mile ridge trail was well broken with the three trips he had made to High Pockets Armstrong's cabin with a load of pelts as his excuse, but Delph the real reason. If trouble came she was to send word there. High Pockets lived less then ten miles from a telephone. Once out of Left Long Branch Holler the road ran flat and fairly smooth along the twisted back of Kittle Pot Ridge. Roan rose in his stirrups, tickled Charlie's left ear, dug hard into his flanks with a ten penny nail, held fast while he bucked, then eased his grip when Charlie broke into a long swinging lope that made Marsh call from the now loping Ruthie Ann, "Roan, we'll kill these mules."

And Roan answered with no looking back, "Listen to that roar."

Marsh heard it then, a curious, muted thunder rising above the thud of the mules' feet; the sound of heavy, big-dropped walls of rain driving hard into thick layers of melting snow. A moment after they were in the rain, a lashing downpour that drove through their cloth-ing, and made the snow under the mules' feet grow first gray and sodden, then form into pools and rivulets that flooded the way, as if the world had turned to water that could not race fast enough into the creeks and rivers.

Marsh could see nothing except Roan's hunched shoulders and Charlie's streaming sides. He called again, but Roan continued to ride like one who could not hear, and seemed not to care that the hard pace would in time wear down the best of mules. They came to a low spot in the ridge where white snow water rose knee deep on the mules, and Roan took advantage of the slackening in the pace to turn to Marsh and explain, "We've got to go while th' goin's good, 'fore ice starts comin' down the creeks." He fingered the bridle a moment and looked down at the rising snow water and asked, "Know anything about floods, Marsh?"

Marsh nodded and called above the thunder of the rain for Roan was galloping again, "Yes, once on th' Ohio. It was awful, ever'body had to start movin' out soon as they were warned, had to be out in three days."

Roan only seemed to ride the harder, and as Marsh followed he slowly understood that the Cumberland was not the Ohio, and that there would be no three days warning. Once he heard a man call as if from a long way, "Marsh, Marsh, you'll kill that mule," then angry cursing and "God, God, he's lost his head.—Th' neighbors will get her out."

• • •

The sound of the rain awakened Delph. She arose early, glad that the cold did not hurt as she went down to build a fire. She aroused Vinie, and sent her early away, for the spring branch was rapidly flooding the road, and told her if the rain continued not to walk through all the mud and wet to come again in the evening. She'd been laying off to visit Lizzie Higginbottom, stay the night and have a bit of cookery not her own. Now that the snow was going and it wouldn't be so slippery, she'd like to walk out and get a breath of air—that is if the rain slacked; a good warm rain like this wouldn't hurt anybody, and she was sick of staying so close inside.

Vinie didn't know what about it and urged her for a time not to do such a thing in her shape, then remembered that she'd been want-ing to visit a girl friend in Hawthorne Town, and thought that she would go with Mr. Elliot if he drove in that day. However, as she went away she warned Delph whatever she did not to stay alone. "Marsh would kill us both," she said, "if he ever heared a you bein' by yourself a single night."

"Pshaw, if I decide not to go up to Lizzie's I'll tell Sober an' he'll get somebody to stay with me," Delph answered, and directed Vinie to buy her some peanut brittle in town. Lately she'd been craving it, and Uncle never kept it in his store.

Sober came late to milk the cows and feed. He hurried with his work, stopping only long enough in the kitchen to say to Delph, "Ah don't know how general this rain is, but if'n it keeps up you'd better have that Vinie to tell Mr. Elliot or somebody they'd ought to bring a car or somethin' for you about tomorrow, an' git you up on th' hill."

Delph laughed at the worried look in his eyes. She would not bother to move. On the kitchen wall there was a mark above the door near the ceiling for the highest flood that had ever been, and that was twenty years ago. If the river came up, she would with Vinie's help move her bed clothing and such to the upstairs, and go up to the brick house. Mrs. Elliot had already suggested many times that she stay there while Marsh was gone.

Sober went away and she was left with Caesar and the sound of the rain, hours and hours of it, lashing the roof and the bottom lands, long sheets of water under descending walls of rain, the river bluff giving voice with a thousand tongues of gushing, foaming water. She liked it—for a little while. In the rain there was a life and a noise that made her feel less dead and drugged with loneliness and hurt that Marsh should go away, leave her with scarcely a word of good-bye, only solemn old-man talk, advising her to take care of herself as if she had no more sense than the addle-headed Prissy. She even sang a little under cover of the tumultuous sound, and the sadness that crept now into all her songs was smothered in the rain.

She sat all day in the kitchen with the lamp lighted against the heavy twilight the swiftly falling water brought to the valley. The clock stopped—Marsh had always tended to its winding and she had forgotten it—and though she listened all during the day, she could hear no mill whistles or any other sound she knew. She read a good bit, mended a suit of overalls, and cooked some food which she fed mostly to Caesar. And the day was very long. So long that many times she went to stand in the door and see if Sober had come to do the barn work. He was a black man, but he was a human being, something that lived like herself in a gray world of threshing beating rain. When he came she would have him go for Vinie or if she were not home, one of Lizzie's children, or any one to spend the night with her.

She never knew when twilight fell. She raised her head, and the windows had changed from gray to black, and the sound on the roof seemed less a voice of the rain than a roaring tongue of darkness and loneliness and misery.

She took milk buckets, lighted the lantern and started to the barn; and when she at last reached it she seemed to have come a long way. The path to the barn had seemed less a path than a creek bed where muddy, ice-cold water swirled sometimes over the tops of her galoshes.

She milked and fed, and it seemed to her that the cows and even the smallest calf and the lazy sows were kind, gazing at her with tender, troubled eyes. She half thought of climbing above them in the hay, rather than try the cold wet walk to the house. But she remembered the baby. It might not be good for it if she slept in the hay with her damp clothing and wet feet.

She knew it was foolish to try to reach the brick house. The rain and the darkness made it seem miles away for her feet, slower and less light than they had ever been. The rain slackened as she went to bed, though as she fell asleep the cascades on the other side of the river and the rivulets in the bluff above the road, roared and trickled and cried.

Sometimes in the night a troubled whimpering, broken by short excited barks awakened her. Caesar was at the kitchen door crying to be let in. He sounded frightened, terrified by something that was neither beast nor man. She pitied him. There was in his cry the same quality of blind, unreasoning terror she had struggled against at times through the week of her loneliness.

She went down and opened the door. He sprang into the kitchen, circling about her and whimpering still. Whatever had frightened him was just beyond the door. The night was light with a full moon thinly veiled with cloud. She glanced outside, took her eyes away, looked again, and then without moving her eyes walked into the yard, but stopped when she had gone a little way. Water, black under the white light of the moon, reached beyond her, one strange twining sheet, animated by a hidden snake-like motion, stretched as far as the river, farther; there was no river, only the creeping, crawling blackness. She watched what looked to be a shed go riding down, clutched a little by the tips of the willows that had marked the course of the river.

Her feet felt cold and strange. She looked at them, and saw that now she stood in the gulping blackness. She watched a moment, held by the life in the water that rose about her shoe and swallowed a pebble by her heel and made no sound. Caesar snapped at her ankles and backed away. She wondered with a cold numbness like the water on her feet how it was she could be so calm, and think of nothing except the drama of the water that was so silent and so ugly, and yet more powerful in its way than all the men in the world.

She thought of Marsh, and came to sudden life and tried to think what he would do if he were here. She stood a moment then went to the barn, wading in spots, and with Caesar helping her, herded all the animals into the lane and opened the gate into the big road. She opened the doors and windows of the chicken house so that the hens, if they were sensible enough, might fly into the sycamore tree. Caesar returned from driving the cows, and started with her to the house, and she remembered that by the time she had carried her bed clothing upstairs, and was ready to go to the brick house, the water might be too deep for the dog. It seemed to be rising rapidly.

She bade him go after the cows, but he only looked at her, the brown spots above his eyes dark, like the heavy eyebrows of some wise old man, filled with a wisdom that made him stubborn. His foolish wish not to leave her alone wrung her heart, but in spite of that she caught up a bit of rope and struck him across the back and sides, and he stood dignified and patient under the blows. She struck more fiercely and cried to him until he lay on his back with his paws in the air, baring his tender chest and belly to any blow she might give. She threw the rope away, and tried a last, "Please, please, you fool, go away." He arose and shook himself and laughed in her face and called her the fool.

After that his nose was ever by her heels. She packed the dishes in the wash tubs so that they would not float about and be broken, carried the bedding upstairs, and could do no more, for now she worked in water to her knees, and the walk across the yard to the hill would be long and slow and cold. She blew out the light and stepped through the door, remembering as she stepped that the floor of the house was higher than the ground. The water reached her waist. She took a few steps, and stopped to look at the river hill. It seemed strangely far away, and all the walk that lay between held treacherous low spots, hidden and secret under the dark water. Still, she thought she could follow the fence, and did so for a little space but stopped again to look at Caesar. He swam awkwardly behind her, and his fur was soggy now. She told him to go back and go upstairs, but even as she said it she knew it was no good. The dog was an out-and-out fool, or maybe she was the fool in trying to get away. The water could go no higher than the mark on the kitchen wall.

She returned to the house. There, it was strange to feel a floating chair bump against her knees as she groped in the darkness for the stair door. Upstairs the moonlight made the place bright with a ghostly shadowless light that seemed to rise from the water and hold its silence and its darkness. She noticed for the first time that she was numb and cold, drenched with muddy, icy water that had lodged twigs and blobs of mud and flakes of ice on her skirt. She changed clothing, but shivered still, even when she lay in bed with blankets wrapped about her She felt the child move in her body, and for the first time was afraid. She could maybe harm her baby with all this carrying of things upstairs and being wet and cold. She called Caesar and bade him lie by her feet, and rubbed her arms and legs, but the cold seemed more in her blood than her skin.

Sometimes she looked out the window. There, it was always the same; the long stretch of black water, writhing and coiling, sprinkled with foam and chunks of white ice and dark shapeless nothings riding away in the night. She lay she did not know how long and heard a noise as of someone knocking softly on the floor. She listened and heard it again—repeated with soft uncertain taps all through the rooms of the house like the ghosts of those dead in the flood asking for shelter. The coldness in her body seemed to reach her hair. She looked at Caesar, watched him as he listened, and understood, and sat bolt upright clutching the bed covering. She heard a sheet tear under her twisting hands, and felt them then, the fingers of one twisting the fingers of the other, and it hurt but she could not stop her hands. The sound she heard couldn't hurt her; the chairs and other furniture, floating higher now, tapped against the ceiling.

She listened, and the tapping grew fainter, and not long after the dark stain of the water appeared on the floor. She watched the stain darken; then thicken, first in dusty pools, and then the thin quiet sheet. She thought of the attic and looked toward the trap door. The opening was small, and there was no ladder, and the child had made her body clumsy and big—it was no good to think of the attic. When the water was ankle deep she took Marsh's papers and government bulletins she had brought upstairs, and tied them in sheets and hung them on the highest nails she could reach by standing on a chair.

Then there was nothing else to do, but sit and watch the water. She called Caesar, and they walked to the window that faced toward Burdine. Near it there was another bed, never used, but higher than the other. She took the two chairs and put them on the bed, and coaxed Caesar to stay on one. He was quiet now and obeyed her in all things. She looked at him and wondered if she would watch him drown. She thought she'd sit and make her head no higher than his own. Either way it didn't seem to matter. Whether she lived or died the flood would most likely destroy her child. Her feet were wet again, and her hands too cold to feel each other now. She got out of bed, and brought the lamp and lighted it and set it on the window sill. She could see the water now, watch it on the wall. She'd papered the room with odds and ends of this and that. Under the window there was a strip of pink and yellow flowers with buds and narrow leaves, and it was strange to see the water swallow a leaf, slowly, so that it was only by taking her eyes away that she could tell what happened to the leaf. She looked once and there was the whole of the leaf, again and there was no more than half, and then it was but a thread. She tried to look at the leaves and flowers and not think of herself—first her toes and then her ankles.

She glanced sometimes at Caesar, and pitied him. He was such a fool. He looked steadfastly through the window, his forehead wrinkled a little, his ears pricked with listening. Once she said, "It's no good listenin', Caesar," but he only looked at her a moment and turned back to the window.

She watched a small barn go floating down, and wondered if the house would float. Sometimes it shuddered slightly, but most often it was very still, as if it held its breath so that the river might not know it was there. Sometimes she listened to her own breathing and that of the dog, and wished for a great wind or a mighty roaring wall of water—anything to break the silence of the creeping water. Once across the stillness there came the sound of screaming as from Burdine. The screams came again, and again, grew fainter then and died. She wondered at the foolishness of those who screamed. In her there was nothing left for screams; no strength for either hope or terror.

Sometimes she had a thought for little things; Piper would be safe in the barn, but Ebony, the young colt might catch cold as he wandered about in the weather. Marsh would not like that. She spent long moments in staring at her hands. She frowned a little sometimes in trying to decide if they were her own. Her other hands had been brown and warm, quick to do her bidding in all things, whether it be lying still in her lap or moulding butter. These hands were cold with the palms yellow white and the finger nails blue, and they were slow in doing the things she wished, and it was troublesome the way they would not be still, but quivered even when she held them tightly clasped above her quivering knees.

Sometimes she petted Caesar, buried her hands in his thick black fur, but he would only glance at her briefly, then turn to the window again and sit on the chair, still listening like a dog cut in stone. The whole of a cluster of leaves and flowers was gone, when he sprang and flung his paws against the window pane, and sent a wild barking roar crashing out through the stillness. He barked again, and whimpered and howled and pushed with his paws on the glass.

She sat and watched him, and once said, "It's no good barkin', Caesar." No one would come this time of night. All the boats would be chained under the flood before any one knew there was a flood. Mrs. Elliot and Perce and the others most likely slept and did not know. Sober and his whole family were maybe caught sleeping in their beds.

So great was the dog's uproar that Sober was breaking through the window with an oar before she heard. She watched him. He seemed like a figure in a dream. "You'll never make it with me an' Caesar," she said, and Sober answered in his usual sullen tone, "Ah made it once on th' Mississippi."

She got up and stood by the window, but could only stare at the swaying boat. Sober steadied it with an oar, and called to Caesar, but the dog stood with his paws in the window and whimpered and looked at Delph. "You might at least think a him, if'n you care nothin' about bein' saved," Sober said, and sat waiting, unable to leave the boat and come to her.

Then somehow her stiff cold body had climbed through the window and into the boat, and Caesar was sitting quietly by her feet. She watched Sober's face as he flung it forward low on his chest as if he prayed and then back with set teeth as if he cursed the sky, while his great shoulders and long black hands heaved and pulled against the flood. She pitied him. Sober seemed not to know that she belonged not with the living, but with the dead, but the river knew and would take her. When an ice cake or a log struck the skiff he would be with her, a dark shapeless nothing swallowed and forgotten. But Sober acted as if he could lift the river from its bed and set it on a mountain.

They rode over Marsh's corn fields. Sometimes Sober fought to reach the river hill, but when the swift water threatened to swamp the boat, he eased his strokes and floated with the flood that would, if he were strong enough and skillful, be made to take them to the lower arm of river bluff that circled Marsh's lands.

Delph watched the bluff, a mountain of blackness in the moon shadow, grow gradually nearer, and felt no victory but a foretaste of sorrow and a loss greater than that of all her bright dreams for Marsh. While Sober rested on his oars again she asked, "Sober—all this—it'll, well—it won't be so good for my baby, will it?"

He looked over his shoulder at the nearing river hill and said, "It's comin' now, Ah reckin."

She nodded and gripped the seat of the boat. "It's too soon," she said when she could speak again, "an' I don't guess it will ever—."

But her voice trailed away, and Sober answered nothing, only bent again to the oars.

She heard men calling on the river bank, and saw rocks and trees outlined in lantern light. After that she was sometimes in an upstairs room with Caesar and the muddy water coiling to her chin, and other times she ran singing through the beech groves of the Little South Fork Country, but always there was pain. Hours of it that saw the lamplight change to daylight and the daylight fade and the light grow: yellow again.

Then it was hard to believe that it was she who lay with closed eyes and wished for nothing except that all the people would go away. Someone was always in the room—a large room with pale green paper that made her think of spring and dark wood paneling that shone sometimes brown and sometimes red in the flickering light of an open coal fire. She recognized the room, and knew that her child had been born in the brick house.

Mrs. Elliot came in and laid her hand on her head and said, "How are you, Delph?" And she answered, "I'm all right."

Dr. Andy came with his quick cat like steps and said, "Quit worryin', Delph. He'll be fine an' healthy as his daddy, even if he did get a bad start."

"I know," she answered, and wished they would go away. She wanted to think about something—something she could not get out of her mind—and it was not of Marsh somewhere in the back country hemmed in by roaring creeks and flooded roads. She closed her eyes again, and thought for a moment she was back in her own house, in the upstairs with water rising over her feet; they were so cold, and her hands were cold, but her head and chest were hot like fire, and in her shoulders there were knives of pain.

The pain startled her into wakefulness, and she wondered if the baby had come. She remembered that that was what she had wanted to think about—it wasn't enough that her child must come too soon, but she must, even before it was finished being born, be a sickly, puny one who couldn't nurse and tend it as a mother ought.

She heard talk in the next room, and held her mind like a kite tugging on a string, and listened. She heard Sadie Huffacre's loud shrill whispers, some talk about her baby; it wouldn't pull through, so Sadie said, and whispered on until some one silenced her with a low, "She'll hear."

Somewhere a baby cried, a hoarse weak cry that drifted away soon with the women's voices. Then there was the sound of Katy's talking and chattering with Mr. Elliot. Katy had come by the same route as Dr. Andy over the railroad bridge and through the tunnel. But Katy had had excitement. Dorie had been so out of her head with worry for Delph and Sober Creekmore's family and not being able to rouse Mrs. Elliot by telephone, that she had given little thought to Katy and Katy's worries. So Katy had run away sometime about midnight and was scarcely over the Little South Fork when the pounding ice sheet sent the South Fork Bridge down the river.

Delph heard and tried to make sense of the words, but she was cold again and shivering. Dr. Andy came and looked at her and smiled and she saw the trouble in his eyes. He had left those drowned in the Burdine bottoms and others sick with pneumonia from exposure to come to her, and now he didn't know but what his time was wasted, his eyes seemed to say.

Sometime later, it might have been near sundown, had there been a sun, she heard Katy's cry of, "Here he is," and she wondered who it could be, but was too weary to bother. She closed her eyes and wished for sleep that would make her warm and take the river away.

Some voice, hoarse and faltering, like that of an old man called, "Delph," and she opened her eyes. She saw a big strange man with red rimmed eyes and matted hair, and face and beard and clothing wet and splashed with mud. She pitied him. He seemed so cold, cold as her self. He twisted a black felt hat in his hands, but crush the hat as he would he could not still the trembling in his hands.

He looked at her, and she at him, and her pity died. He was broken at last. He stood there knowing now that all the things she had tried to tell him through the summer were true. She knew she ought to feel something, be gay as she had been when he asked her to marry him. She heard her baby's weak cry, and could feel nothing for herself—or for the man. The cost of his learning, if he had learned, had come too high.

· 18 ·

NEXT MORNING it was raining again, a slow cold drizzle that sheathed the fence wires in ice, and beaded the twigs of the trees. Marsh as he walked across his upland pastures from Higginbottom's where he had spent the bit of night that was left after coming away from Delph, felt rather than saw the icy rain. Though it was long past his usual breakfast time, the murky dawn seemed more the ending of night than a beginning of day.

He walked slowly with his legs feeling curiously light, and his head, too; and his eyes felt strange as if propped open with sticks and sprinkled with sand. Still he wasn't sleepy. He wasn't tired or hungry. He felt nothing as he plodded through the rain. He reached the brow of the pasture hill and stopped and studied the brick house, but found only the upper windows yellow in the heavy gloom. Caesar came whimpering by his feet and laid his nose against his knees. Since the flood Caesar had somehow changed from an overgrown playful pup to a dog, given sometimes to wrinkling the brown spots on his forehead and talking with his eyes. When his master stood so long in the rain he cuffed a leg of his overalls and looked up at him, but Marsh continued to study the brick house windows with no glance for Caesar.

When he had waited a time and the kitchen windows did not brighten, he swore a long bitter oil man's oath and went on over the hill toward his lower farm, stopping every step or so to turn and look back at the brick house until it was lost to his sight. None of them would be up till noon, he guessed, worn as they must be from caring for Delph and the baby. Dr. Andy had not started for Burdine and his other patients until the small hours of the morning. But Delph would be all right he had said. Pneumonia side by side with child birth was bad, but what would have killed another, Delph would throw off in a few weeks' time—already her fever was not so high as it had been. She would get along fine—if she didn't fret herself to death over the baby. And Dr. Andy had spoken but briefly of the child. True, it had come only a bit too soon, but it was thin, not fat as he had expected the baby of a healthy young couple to be, and a child born from a woman with pneumonia must be bottle fed from its birth, and that was not a promising start for a delicate baby.

Marsh thought of Dr. Andy's words and wished for some hard heavy work for his hands. At the spot where the road turned over the bluff, he stopped and tried to see what was left of his lower farm. Through the night the river had drawn almost to the willow trees, though pools of water in the fields shone dimly like black islands in the seas of yellow mud.

He saw the toilet that had stood at the back of the garden face-downward on the other side of the barn. The chicken house lay in what had been the melon field. Rails and limbs of trees and paling slats were strewn about with the half of what must have the roof of a barn up the river, lying by an upper corner of the house. He saw wire fence broken and sagging under walls of dripping debris, and long stretches of paling flat on the ground or carried away.

He looked a time in silence, then whistled to Caesar who had circled away, and walked on, and did not stop until he reached the house. He studied it a time; already the water-soaked weather boarding had loosened in spots, here and there were broken window panes gaping like torn eyes, stones in the foundation had slipped to the ground, and heavy layers of mud reached half way up the second story windows; but such things seemed no more than scratches on some battle scarred warrior. The house stood firm and true and straight, moved no whit from its foundations, with roof and walls and floor that showed no signs of sagging.

He circled the tool house, the smoke house, spring house, and barn and found them in more or less the same condition; wounded but not mortally, showing the manner of men who made them and the good stout timbers that had gone into their making. The barn, standing as it did on the highest bit of ground had suffered least of all. The hay and fodder stored in the loft were dry, though the hall and stables and pens were gutted of many of the things they had once had. He saw the new harness which he had bought with melon money and had somehow always hated, half buried in the mud. He saw his tools, and the bit of farm machinery he had, scattered about, covered with mud, or beginning to rust.

He returned to the house and walked slowly through the rooms where water-soaked, mud-covered furniture lay fallen to pieces, wall paper weighted with mud dropped from the walls and ceiling with soft thuds, and the mud-covered floor was strewn with mud soaked clothing, broken dishes, pots and pans, and all the little articles of Delph's housekeeping.

He hesitated a time, then opened the stair door, and after removing a chair and piles of wet bed clothing caught in the stairs he went up to Delph's room. He stood a long while and looked at the bed with Delph's chair and Caesar's chair fallen against the headboard. He studied the broken window, measured his height against the rim of mud on the walls and found it to his shoulders. He saw his papers and government bulletins safe and dry on the nails where Delph had hung them in towels and pillow slips.

He went to the kitchen, and, after staring a time at the mud-covered stove and the pipe, its battered joints scattered on the floor, turned sharp about and walked away. He was just walking through the place where the front yard gate had been, when a woman called, "Oh, please, Mr. Gregory, I am afraid I need some help."

He glanced up and saw Mrs. Elliot on the river hill, and she seemed to be burdened with a strange load for Mrs. Elliot. He wondered angrily what business she had walking down to see him in his misery; she had always looked to be such a useless, artificial sort of woman, always chattering about flowers or manicuring her finger nails or having her hair "done," that he had little use for her. However, he remembered that she would at least have some word of Delph and hurried up to her.

She handed him the most of her load, a can of kerosene, a bundle of cedar kindling, cloths, reserving nothing more than some newspapers for herself. She chattered amiably as they walked down the hill. Delph had only three degrees of fever, and was much better than yesterday, asking about him and the baby and everything. Mrs.

Elliot had telephoned Higginbottom's to tell him how Delph was, but Lizzie had told her that he had gone off someplace with never a word of where he was going. She, Mrs. Elliot, of course knew that he had come by their place and finding them still all in bed, had come on down to his farm. She of course didn't know, but she bet he had come away without a bit of kindling, and that was of course the first thing he would have to do, start a fire—wasn't it?

Marsh hesitated and stood staring at the wreck of all he had. "Sure, sure," he suddenly said, and went striding away so fast that Mrs. Elliot was hard put to keep up with him.

It was a slow business, the scraping of mud from the stove, and was scarcely finished and the pipe up before Lizzie Higginbottom came. She was a plump, brown haired brown-eyed woman who reminded Marsh of a placid tempered brown leghorn hen. She had been a frequent visitor all through the winter, and usually came with a bit of her mending and a bag of the fat, clumsy sugar cookies she kept always baked for her boys. And through the whole of the community she was never known as Mrs. Higginbottom, but always as Perce's Lizzie, and not even Sadie Huffacre could quote a bit of gossip from Perce's Lizzie. Mostly, she quoted Perce, the Bible, and Brother Eli, and occasionally some bright remark of one of the boys or Little Lizzie, and she had never been known to give an opinion all her own on anything.

Today she stood in the door, and quoted Perce, who had 'lowed that Marsh had gone down to his farm; it would be wet and muddy down there, and Marsh had eaten so little breakfast and slept not at all that he'd better look out or he'd be sick next, and he must eat and keep up his strength, so she had brought him some cookies and coffee and sandwiches. Perce said tell him he'd be down pretty soon. He and the boys wore still hunting two of his shoats; in case Marsh came to his senses and remembered he was a farmer with hogs and cattle—and here Lizzie stopped for lack of breath. The stove pipe was not as straight as she liked, and she came and fixed it; that was Lizzie's way, so Perce always said. She never spoke her mind on anything, but if a thing were not done to suit her she did it herself.

Perce and his boys, all walking behind like a flight of stairs, came soon with word of the shoats. They had been out scouring the country, and their eyes were big with wonder at the things they had seen by the river, and the fearsome flood tales they had heard. A man up the Cumberland had had six cows drowned right in his barn; and less than eight miles away there was a woman and her two children drowned, and nobody yet knew how many were dead in the lower Burdine bottoms. Marsh, they said, was lucky, and so was Sober Creekmore. He had not come to do the milking that night because he had been too busy moving his corn and fodder up from his bottom fields. Still, he had not expected such a flood. His house was on a hillside, supposedly out of danger. It just happened that sometime in the night when Emma was sitting up in bed nursing her month old baby, she had looked out the window and thought she was seeing things in the moonlight. There looked to be a little barn or something right by their yard fence. She had wakened Sober and sent him to see.

After that Sober had been too busy making shift for his family to think much of Delph until Emma remarked that the excitement she would maybe go through might be bad for the baby. And Sober remembered he had not seen her since morning. He had sent his children—they were all out up in the hill under a cliff anyway—rousing the Higginbottoms and the Elliots to learn if Delph were safe. When he learned what had to be learned, he had kissed Emma goodbye, told her to pray, then taken his skiff, and with first his children and then the neighbors helping him, had carried it four miles up the river in order to get it to the right spot above Marsh's land; for no man alive could have rowed up the Cumberland on that wild black night.

Lizzie listened to the talk for a time, then reminded her boys that they would either have to get to work or go to school. They could all get hoes and start scraping mud from the floor, or they could start husking out the water soaked corn in the crib, or they could start washing Marsh's plows and other tools and machinery and get them in shape for oiling, but whatever they did they must get to work, or they would have to go to school. She, Lizzie, had to be getting back pretty soon for there was dinner to get, but first she thought she'd gather up some of Delph's clothing and bed clothing and see if it couldn't be washed and saved. It was too bad that Perce was so big that Marsh couldn't wear his clothing, but maybe she could find enough of his things about the house that could be washed and ironed and made fit to wear. He and Delph had been mighty lucky; it didn't look as if the flood had washed much of their stuff away, just wetted and muddied it, and that of course could be remedied. If he didn't want to leave off to come eat his dinner she'd send one of the boys with it; her cooking wasn't maybe so good as Delph's, for she had heard that Delph came of a breed of good cooks, but maybe he could put up with it for a few weeks until he had the house fixed to live in and Delph was up and about.

And Marsh turned short about and walked away; he wanted to go down and look at the river, he said. He was glad he wasn't a woman; he thought he might have cried. However, he would have had no opportunity. Mrs. Elliot came calling and chattering behind him. She had just remembered that in the brick house attic there were some odds and ends of furniture that had been in the house when they moved there. There would maybe be something he could use.

He continued to live with Perce during the weeks that his house remained wet and furniturelsss while Delph lay in the brick house and seemed to wander in a shadowy land that was neither life nor death. He went to her noon and night and morning, and always the time it took on the back porch to clean the mud from his shoes seemed long. He wanted to race up the stairs and into her room and see if maybe this once, she would be Delph again, at least in her eyes. Dr. Andy had cured her of her sickness, but it seemed that no one could bring her back to life. Her eyes from bright blue seemed changed to gray, a dull gray with no light and no shadow.

When Marsh called she never asked but the one question, and of late asked that in a low hopeless voice with no lifting of her eyes, "Don't you think th' baby's lookin' better?"

And Marsh would answer in loud tones that always rang with an empty sound, no matter how hard he tried to lie, "Sure, he's lookin' fine. He's a layin' a suckin' his thumb now."

"If I could a had milk for him like I ought—he—well he wouldn't a started off so slow," she would say, and fall into a lifeless silence that seemed less that of a woman keeping still than of a woman gone.

Sometimes he tried to comfort her, would pat her hand or smooth her hair and say, "It's not your fault, Delph. Mine for goin' away. You can't help it if we can't find anything that'll suit him. God knows you've done your part."

"Havin' him an' then lettin' him starve to death," she would answer, and lie staring at the wall.

Now and then Marsh tried to pierce the blankness in her eyes with slow worded accounts of this or that. "Delph, you ought to see Ebony—shines like a piece a new mined coal. An' th' way he can throw up his heels," or, "Delph, I found a pussy willow in bloom by th' river.—Th' buds are swellin' on th' apple trees.—Delph, you'll hardly know th' house. We're mendin' th' chimney an' fixin' a new under pinnin'."

But Delph never answered him, and only shivered and turned to the wall when he spoke of the house. Many nights he tip-toed away, and never knew if she lay awake or asleep. He always stopped in Mrs. Elliot's room and looked at the child, bedded in a low basket on a couch. But the child, no more than Delph, gave any sign that it knew or cared for him.

"It's going to be such a pretty baby," Mrs. Elliot would say, and smile at him. At first there had been a hunger like an envy in her eyes when she smiled, but now there was nothing but pity and sorrow. More and more it seemed to Marsh that she hesitated when he asked to see his son. Such a little thing it was to hurt a man so, to make his heart and his hands and all his strength useless and of no account because they could not make it eat or grow.

At first he had taken the pillow in his arms, had hefted it, proud to feel the weight of his son, but lately he left it in the basket. The pillow grew lighter instead of heavier, and the face that twisted sometimes into a grimace of crying grew smaller, and made Marsh think of some little toothless old man. The baby cried a lot, a thin hungry cry, too weak to carry past the house, but all the same Marsh heard it, especially at night when he sat a time after supper with Perce and Lizzie and their children. Perce had six strong healthy children, and he couldn't have one.

One day late in February about the time of sundown when he was finishing his barnwork, for his stock was home now, he heard the rattle and creak of a heavily loaded wagon on the river hill. He went down the lane to see who it could be and what load they brought this time of day. The big clay colored mules and the heavy jolt wagon were familiar, and when a little man pulled off his hat and waved it, he knew that Juber had come with John's wagon and team from the Little South Fork Country.

Marsh forgot that Ivy's calf would strip her dry, and hurried to open the barn lane gate, then rushed up the hill to meet the wagon. "Delph'ull be tickled to death you've come," he called while still a few feet away.

Juber kept his eyes on the wagon tongue while he answered, "I've already seen her."

"I'll bet she was glad."

"She give no sign."

Marsh walked on by the wagon with all the gladness gone from his eyes. He wanted to ask Juber if he had seen the baby, but somehow could not. He saw the old man's fiddle case, carefully wrapped in a saddle blanket and packed on the wagon seat. "I know she'll be glad to hear a fiddle tune. Last winter now an' agin she'd speak a you an'—." He glanced hopefully at Juber, then stopped. There were tears in the old man's eyes.

Juber continued down the hill and after a time cleared his throat and talked of the ones in the Little South Fork Country. Mrs. Crouch, the Hedricks, and Fronie had sent letters by him to Delph, while John had sent this wagonload of Delph's rightful belongings. John had acted up a sight when Delph ran away, got down the family Bible and threatened to blot out her name, but Fronie wouldn't let him. God worked in strange ways, she said, and maybe God had sent the oil man to tame and keep Delph straight. Juber was silent for a moment with his eyes wandering out over the fields, up past Dorie's river hill and then into the sky. "I reckin he did," he said, but whether he spoke to the sky or to Marsh it was hard to say.

All along he'd hardly ever heard them mention Delph, he went on to say when he had driven into the barn and stopped his team. John would sometimes grunt and say that no wandering oil man could ever settle down and farm, and Fronie would sigh and declare Delph would never let a man of hers spend his days in a river valley. But now and then word had come of how Marsh was making out; Fronie and John would listen and look pleased, he thought, but never say a word.

The Hedricks were the first to hear of the flood; news came over their radio of how bad it was on the Cumberland, and Sil Hedrick had come knocking in the night to bring the news. Fronie had divided her time between praying and crying while John had walked about like a wooden soldier. Juber had gone to the barn to comfort himself with a fiddle tune, and in the crib he had stumbled over John on his knees in the dark. He'd had to laugh at John. He had jumped to his feet all in a fluster at being disturbed, then turned on Juber with an oath and said, "Blood's blood, by God, if she did run away."

Next day word came from Dorie by telephone and messenger, and later on she had written them of Delph's sickness, the baby, and the wreck the flood had brought to the lower farm. All had been certain then that Marsh would never stick. But tales had come, the way tales travel in the hills—swiftly and easily as smoke on the wind—of Marsh's work of rebuilding. It was John then who suggested one night at supper that they get together a load of Delph's rightful things and send them down.

Marsh looked at the heaped wagon, and his jaw tightened as he thought of John and the hard words he had given him. "I've got neighbors—an' my credit's good. I'm wantin' no help from th' Little South Fork Country,"

"You needn't be bull headed.—Delph, mebbe might like to have her things. You might think a her once in a while," Juber advised with a surliness unusual with him, and started the wagon toward the house.

Marsh followed in silence, ashamed of his unneighborly ways. Juber looked tired and old with all the heart gone out of his eyes. "You rest an' I'll do th' unloadin'," he insisted, but Juber shook his head, and shouldered one of the two feather beds stuffed in the back of the wagon.

Marsh marveled at the wagon load. There seemed no end to the quilts and pillows and linens that he and Juber carried and stacked in the empty dining room. Many times Juber paused over this or that and explained its history. That blue and white checked thing like a quilt was a coverlid Delph's great-great granma had woven nigh onto a hundred years ago, and that silk crazy quilt she'd got when she was a little girl from a great-aunt in Texas, but the red cedar, copper bound water bucket had been made in the Little South Fork Country, and the long heavy muzzle loader with the hand hewn, silver mounted black walnut stock had come from Virginia and was a "keep sake" from her mother's side of the family.

But Juber fell abruptly silent when he uncovered a small, low rockered trundle bed, made of wild black cherry, its diminutive head and foot boards carved with finely traced pine cones and sheaves of pine. Marsh picked up the small old thing, and smoothed the plump feather tick it contained, but did not touch the baby's things some one had put under the tick. "Take it on in. You'll be needin' it one of these days—mebbe," Juber said in a rough loud voice, and began tugging at Delph's old dresser, the only other piece of furniture he had brought.

Full dark came before they had emptied the wagon, for Juber talked long and lovingly over the last of the load—two bushel baskets of roots and shoots of herbs and blooming things taken from the yards and gardens of the Little South Fork Country. "I wish Delph could see all this," Marsh said more times than one, and even Juber smiled and seemed less forsaken when he took packets of flower seed tied in mail order catalogue leaves from his overall pockets, and talked of Delph's love of flowers.

Still, he showed no eagerness to see her again that night. When his mules were stabled and fed, and they were going into Elliot's yard, Juber hung back at the kitchen porch. "I'll see her agin in th' mornin'," he said, and, too timid to go into the kitchen, rested on the porch while Marsh went up to Delph alone.

He heard the baby's cry, weaker it seemed than at noon. He thought of the seed he would plant and the roots of living things he would put into the ground. They would grow while his child shriveled and died like some small water-loving plant on a dry hill side. Delph lay propped on pillows and watched a low fire flicker in the grate. In the uncertain light her forehead and cheek bones and chin glimmered sharp and white, but her mouth and eyes were dark shadows where nothing seemed to live. Marsh closed the door, careful to make no noise, and called softly, "Delph."

The face moved a little, and her voice came, tired, but with a touch of her old anger through the tiredness. "That you, Marsh?—What—how did Juber like th' looks of th' baby?"

"Fine," he said, and came and sat on the edge of the bed. He tried to tell her of all that Juber had brought, and of the flowers that would grow in their yard next year. But it was hard to talk when Delph gave no sign she heard. He had a moment's terror that maybe he would lose her, too, when the baby—didn't cry any more. And then he felt that unreasoning certainty that she couldn't die. The quick-blooded, bright-eyed Delph he had married wouldn't simply lie down in a room and die.

"Any of the neighbors come today?" he asked, unable to go away until she had talked a bit, said something he could remember and think over until he saw her again.

"You know they're always comin'," she answered, and added with something of her usual spirit, "I wish they'd all stay at home."

"Pshaw, Delph, they mean no harm, always tryin' to think of somethin' nice for you to eat or askin' about th' baby."

"It's my baby, not theirs' an' to hear that Sadie Huffacre talk you'd think I didn't care if—if—." Her voice trembled and hesitated then went on in a cautious whisper. "She kept a sayin' she'd raised six of her own an' never lost one—but they'd all been dead if she'd fussed an' fretted an' bothered like Mrs. Elliot does—an', Marsh, Mrs. Elliot loves him so. She's tryin'."

"Don't pay that old gossip no mind, Delph."

She moved her head impatiently. "An' Dorie, she's no better. She was here today sayin'—sayin' I'd got to get some backbone—an' face things—an' get—. She told me how she lost one—it was puny—like mine—an'—it just couldn't live."

Marsh put his hand on her thin soft shoulder. "Delph, listen, you've got plenty backbone—don't let anybody tell you different.— An' anyhow mebbe—you can't ever tell. Recollect my corn last summer, how it nearly died an' then when it rained."

But Delph was crying, weak, heart-broken sobs. She raised suddenly on one elbow with hatred and accusation and rebellion fighting through her eyes. "It's not right, Marsh, an' fair. Nothin' can make me say like some, 'It's th' way it had to be,' an' fifty years from now I can't sit back like Dorie an' call it, 'Th' one I lost.' To go through all that—an' think on it so before it was born—see it somehow. An' then have it—die. An' all th' time you lay a thinkin' you'd go through that much an' more all over if it would help. Somethin', somebody could save it."

Her voice had grown gradually louder and wilder until it rang through the house and brought Vinie and Mrs. Elliot. They soothed and smiled and hoped, declared the baby was looking better, while

Marsh sat feeling helpless and clumsy, and Delph looked at them all with hot angry eyes, more rebellious than sorrowful. Though Delph said nothing more, Marsh went down to Juber with her hard, angry sobs ringing in his head.

When Delph was left alone at last and after failing to eat as much of her supper as she should, she lay and listened to the baby's crying in the next room, a hungry cry that goaded her into a wild anger at her useless, spineless ways. She could never hope to have milk for her child, Dr. Andy had said, unless she ate, and she couldn't eat. Too weak to do more than let tears trickle down the corners of her eyes, she lay and listened until Mrs. Elliot carried it to another part of the house.

She saw the bundle of letters and such that Juber had brought, but letters mattered little now. They wouldn't do the baby any good. For lack of anything better to do, she opened the package and saw first her old scrap book, and there was Sam smiling his strange mocking smile. She flung the book away; her baby might one day have gone as far as Sam. There were odds and ends of other things; old letters, a bank book, and other documents she had never seen. She saw Fronie's slanting school-teacherish script, and felt an unexpected rush of eagerness to hear from Fronie; no woman in the Little South Fork Country had ever had better luck with babies.

She tore the letter open, glanced briefly through the long beginning, talk of weather, and church, and hope for Delph's soul. She raced to the bottom of the third or fourth page, found the word "baby" glanced back and read. ". . . I have thought it over. There can't be anything bad wrong with your baby. It must have good blood on both sides or it would be dead after what you and it went through. I am not blaming you. But I guess before it was born you didn't take care of yourself like a woman ought. But what is done is done. And now I will have my say. Delph, it is going against God and reason to try to raise a baby on store bought stuff.

"I would not say all this now but because it is my duty and for the sake of John. The baby is his own blood kin like a grandchild you might say. If I had a baby nursing now he would bring me down after it in a minute. But I don't have. Now what you want to do is find a good strong healthy woman, willing to take and nurse it and tend it like her own till it's big enough to wean. If there's a negro woman in the neighborhood, half way clean, and willing to take it, she would be more pleasing in the sight of God than all this store bought stuff. Recollect one of your grandmothers and several of your great-aunts were all raised on black women's milk. And on your mother's side in the old days all the babies—."

Delph only glanced through the remainder of the long letter. She saw some mention of timber lands from her father and a bank account from her mother, both to be given her when she was twenty-one, or at John's discretion if she married before that age. John had thought it over, and from all the talk he'd heard of Marsh, decided he was at least an honest man, maybe a bit on the stingy side. Delph must keep her property in her own name, but John advised her to have Marsh see to the timber. A good bit of it was right for cutting, and could be sold for a pretty penny.

Delph flung the letters aside, seized the bell by her bed, and rang it so violently that Mrs. Elliot, Vinie, and Myrtle, the cook, all came on the run. "I want somebody to telephone Perce's for Marsh," she said. When she had convinced them that she had not had a forewarning of death, that she was not out of her head, that the evening was early and the Higginbottoms would not have gone to bed, Mrs. Elliot went to call Marsh. She came back and listened with surprised, horror-stricken eyes when Delph told her what she meant to do.

"Emma Creekmoore might be a good healthy, well-meaning black woman, but she knew nothing of sanitation. She might—why she might even let her children touch the baby or—maybe he would even have to sleep in the same bed with the last Creekmore—or with Emma. She might even give him a meat skin to suck as she gave her own babies—." Mrs. Elliot's voice failed her, her eyes filled with tears, and when Delph's only answer to her objections was set lips and defiant eyes, she left the room.

Marsh came not long after. When Delph told him what she meant to do, surprise and consternation so held him by the tongue that he could do little but stand, clasping and unclasping the footboard of her bed. He struggled against her with his eyes, seeing nothing more than certain death for his son if Delph's dictates were obeyed. He tried a last argumentative, "Delph—I don't know much about babies—but from all I've read, why—."

"An' what have you read?"

"Nothin' much but government bulletins.—I sent for all I could get last fall before—."

Delph dropped back to her pillows with a shrieking, sobbing wail. "You—you mean you'd try to raise our baby on a bulletin like a—like your pigs. It's not a baby to you, but just somethin' you'd like to see grow—like corn."

Marsh swore an oath he'd picked up in Mexico addressed to the Virgin Mary, belatedly remembered that it was a black one even for the oil fields, and after one glance at Delph's outraged eyes he fled from the room. He rushed for comfort to Mrs. Elliot and the baby, but things were little better there. Mrs. Elliot cried into a lace handkerchief and wished Mr. Elliot were home. Delph seemed to have much respect for him. He could maybe talk some sense into her head.

The baby lay and cried its troubled, tremulous cry. Vinie came coated and hatted with a traveling bag in her hand. "Miz Elliot, I gathered up its things. Delph'ull have her way or die—takin' it to a place like Creekmore's," and Vinie looked beaten and woebegone with her black eyes dull and robbed of their usual laughter.

Mrs. Elliot nodded and sobbed over the baby. "You'd better go with Marsh. You carry its things and a light so he won't fall."

Marsh shifted uneasily from one foot to the other and fingered the broken arrow he carried in his pocket. "Th' weather's mighty cold an' misty to take a baby out in," he said after a time.

Mrs. Elliot sighed and wiped her eyes, and he continued, "Couldn't we wait a day or so—I mean—till I talked to Dorie or a doctor or—somethin'?"

No one answered him, and he tried again with a brightening of his eyes. "Maybe Sober an' Emma won't want th' baby. They've got six a their own."

"And only four rooms," Mrs. Elliot sobbed and looked ready to collapse.

He waited, and when no one offered encouragement he understood what they were thinking. It was Delph's baby and she was to have her say. He picked up the basket, waited while Mrs. Elliot pulled a blanket over the baby's face, and then went out the back way. On the porch steps he heard Vinie walking behind him, and saw the shine of her flashlight on the brick walk. "I'd rather go by myself," he said. "You wait an' bring his things out later—if he needs 'em."

He walked on with Vinie's tongue like a senseless clatter in his head. He'd better let her go with him. He'd need a light, and he ought to take the upper road across the pastures. It would not be so muddy as the one across the bottoms. But he went on and left Vinie calling by the gate.

The child gradually hushed its crying, and they walked on together down the hill and by the house and into the barn hall. He stopped there and set his load on the ground. The silence of the basket troubled him. He lighted the lantern he kept in the barn, and hunkered on his heels and pulled the blanket back a little way, and looked at his child. Caesar came sniffing at the basket, and the child opened his gray eyes, wider than Marsh had ever seen them, and lay looking at the dog and the man and the shadowy spaces of the barn with a faint curiosity, untouched by fear. Maude whinnied in her stall, and somewhere pigs grunted and squealed softly in their sleep. And the child listened to the sounds, and was quiet with his eyes wide with wonder. "You like a barn, you little devil," Marsh whispered, and waited a moment or so before covering the basket. He blew out the lantern then and they walked on across the muddy corn fields.

Marsh walked more and more slowly as he neared the Creekmore place. When he came to the foot bridge that crossed the creek to Sober's steep farm with its narrow strip of bottom land, he stopped and uncovered the basket a bit, but it was too dark to see.

He stopped again at the front yard gate and looked at the small poor house on the hill side, looming dimly out of the heavy gloom. The flood had gone three feet above the floor. He had the sudden fear that the place was maybe not yet dried—not a fit house for a weakly baby. Caesar began a cursing and a calling of Sober's three hounds vile sounding names, and they were answering in kind. While Marsh stood, trying to think up a way of calling that he, Marsh Gregory, had brought him his baby on Delph's orders without so much as a by-your-leave, and he hoped Emma would refuse it so that he could take it back to where it belonged, Sober asked Caesar what did he, Mr. Gregory's dog mean, coming to bother his hounds.

"I'm with him," Marsh called, and a moment later Sober came running in his shoes and a voluminous night shirt that made Caesar bark the harder.

"Miz Gregory, is she worse?" Sober began, but when the baby cried he, after a moment of listening, began a loud calling of Emma.

Marsh went with him to the kitchen door, for someone slept in every room but the kitchen. Sober lighted the lamp, and told Marsh to put the basket on the table. Emma came soon with unlaced shoes and a dress pulled hastily over her nightgown. She looked angry and sullen, throwing black accusative glances at Sober who stood laying a stick of wood on the half dead coal in the stove. "Since th' day that youngen come I've asked that man ever' day to go tell 'em to let me nuss an' raise it till it's weaned—an' what does he do but do nothin'.—Law, honey don't you cry. Yo starvin' days are over." The last remark was addressed to the basket, not to Sober.

Marsh stood with his hat in his hand, feeling still that some talk or explanation was necessary. He watched Emma, cautiously from the corners of his eyes—the way she went pawing into the basket and pulled the baby out with what seemed to him precious little concern for its delicacy. She cradled it carelessly on one big black arm and went prodding its belly, its back, its head and its toes, and seemed in no wise alarmed by the outraged howls. "It's plenty strong or it would ah died 'fore now—starved like it is," she said with a pleasant smile that made her fat black cheeks seem fatter still.

She studied Marsh critically as she seated herself in a straight backed chair and began a mighty thumping back and forth that made her fat body dance and quiver. "Mistah Gregory," she said after a thump or so, "you might as well go along. He an'—what's his name?"

"It's—it's—."

The front legs of the chair came down with a violent bang—"Mistah Gregory, yo'awl don't mean you've not named yo youngen—a month old. Lawd God but that's what ails it."

Marsh swallowed, and looked to Sober for comfort, but Sober's eyes were troubled. "Yo ought to allus name a baby, Mistah Gregory—'fore it's three days old. Didn't you know that?"

Marsh shook his head.

"Yo'll have to name him now," Emma said in tones that invited no contradiction. She smiled down at the red-brown curly head on the pillow, "He's got a funny little burry head," she said.

Marsh glanced wildly about the room, as if he might possibly pick a name from the air. "Yo name's Marshall, ah reckin, Mistah Gregory. That's fine soundin'," Emma suggested.

"He ought to have Miz Gregory's name—Costello—that's th' way white folks used to do in th' old days," Sober said.

"Delph's been right sick, an' we've never thought much on namin' him," Marsh said, "but well—." He stopped and stood twisting his hat. Thanking Sober for saving Delph's life when there was not another man in the neighborhood who could have done it was a thing he had never tried. It seemed foolish to smear a great thing like that up with words. "But—well—you saved Delph an' it—."

"Him, not it," Emma interrupted with an especially violent thump of the chair.

"You saved him from th' flood—so—so I thought I'd kind a like to call him after you—Sober."

Sober fell against the wall in a fit of embarrassed laughter. "Lawdy, here Ah've been namin' youngens after white men but this is th' first 'un Ah've ever had named after me."

Emma shifted the baby to her right arm, looked at him while she said in a loud solemn voice, "Well, Sober Marshall Costello Gregory, you've got a name. But me, Ah think Ah'll call you Burr-Head." She glanced at Marsh. "You might as well go, Mistah Gregory, you look tired," she suggested as if to be rid of him.

He walked slowly toward the door, but stopped with his hand on the knob. "Vinie or me—we'll bring its—his things down tomorrow an'." He cleared his throat and tried to give his words proper emphasis and some tone of authority which he did not feel. "Mrs. Elliot has some books on babies you maybe ought to read."

Emma's yowling, derisive laughter cut short his little speech. He heard a chorus of soft giggles from the back of the room and looked up to see some four or five of the younger Creekmores peeping at him around the door. He looked at them and the black heads above the white night gowns disappeared, but he felt that they were laughing at him still. He tried a stern glance on Emma, and though she lowered her eyes her shoulders continued to shake with laughter. He wondered that a thing as little as his baby could change a family so. Last fall and winter when Emma came to wash for Delph it was always, "Yas suh, Mistah Gregory," or "What evah you say, Miz Gregory." Now she sat and laughed at him.

She stopped suddenly and smiled down at the baby and then at him. "Mistah Gregory, would you go givin' Sober there a book on how to raise watahmelons?"

"Well seein' as how I learned most a what I know from him, it wouldn't be exactly sensible," Marsh said.

"Well it's all th' same with me an' youngens," Emma said, and he left her slapping her knee in another fit of laughter.

He had no heart to return to Elliot's or to Perce's. The evening was early yet. Perce and Lizzie most likely sat in wait for him to learn how Delph and the baby fared. He wished he could see Dorie and learn what she thought of the business, but outside of her he didn't think he could face another woman that evening. He stopped at the barn and made the rounds with the lantern, and when Caesar, instead of going down the land and up the hill, trotted toward the house, Marsh followed him, and spent the night on one of the feather beds that Juber had brought.

· 19 ·

MARCH CAME with mighty trumpeting winds, a great blowsy, strong-armed woman who scoured the earth with rain and wind and sun. The sycamore limbs grew gray again, and on the hill pasture the grass and unfolding clover leaves were green and lush and tender. Clouds raced all day long in a high blue windy sky, and at night the wind sang and whistled through the little cedar trees on the river hill.

Marsh, batching now at home, would listen to the wind and smile, think of Delph, able to be up and about, and of Burr-Head, getting bigger and so mean his hide wouldn't hold him, so Emma said with pride. That child was always up to something; one day he hit her own Sammy right in the nose, and another day he grabbed Louvinie's crackled meat skin and sucked it a bit before Louvinie had the heart to take it away from him. Though it happened regularly twice a week, it was always a great occasion when Emma brought Burr-Head to see Delph, and after the first visit Delph was more like herself than she had been for weeks.

That afternoon when Marsh walked down the hill, he stopped a time in the road above the yard, and looked at his place. He liked to look at his house, especially the great chimney that he and Sober had built from gray, unpolished limestone quarried from his land. He liked to build in stone, and now when he looked at the chimney and thought of Delph and Burr-Head, an old dream stirred and filled his head. He could not remember the beginnings of the dream, no more than he could recall the sights and things heard about that had shaped it through the years. Sometimes, if the dream came while he

260

was alone, not too busy and with a bit of pencil handy, he would draw lines and squares; study them, erasing here, adding a mark there, lost in the figure until he remembered that it was all a foolishness that tricked a man into wasting his time. But whenever down the river hill he saw the good, strong, granite-like limestone and then the chimney he had made, thoughts of a whole house built of gray stone would come into his mind.

He would have it on a hill, up in the pasture, say, near the grove of little walnut trees where he and Delph had used to watch the sun go down. Sometimes he thought he would like to talk to Delph of such things, but somehow he never did. Through the spring she was too taken up with thought for Burr-Head to give more than half an ear to anything he told her of the farm.

Many times when he came away from her he felt a loneliness and a troubled wordless foreboding of something worse than loneliness; he wished she would seem more eager to come home, would go against Mrs. Elliot's determination that she stay until the weather was warm and settled. Still, he had little time for tortured probings into Delph's mind. Nights found him tired and ready for sleep; the days were filled with work and plans and something else that he had scarcely ever had—the interest and good will of a neighborhood.

He found less speculation in the eyes that watched him now. More men greeted him in Hawthorne Town and by the road, and the county seat merchants offered him credit, while High Pockets Armstrong and other hill men whom he scarcely knew would stop him in the street to ask after his family, for the whole country had heard of Sober Marshall Costello Gregory. The piece that Katy wrote for the *Westover Bugle* on Sober's rescue of Delph not only made the front page in the county paper, but was mentioned in a Lexington paper as well, and so great was Katy's delight that she played hookey from school for a week, and spent the time in helping the neighbor women straighten the Gregory house.

While Marsh lived alone on the lower farm many a farmer from both sides of the river came down to see how he was making out, and give a hand or lend advice on this or that. He planned a tobacco crop—nothing large, no more than a couple of acres at most—and seasoned tobacco farmers from all over the county offered advice on the buying and setting of plants, fertilizer, the cheapest and best tobacco sticks, and what sprays to use. He listened to long arguments over high late topping and one suckering versus low early topping and suckering three or four times, and learned from Wiley Davis, a hill farmer from east of Town, that the best way to make tobacco seed sprout in a hurry—in case a man got behind in his planting—was to leave it for a few days under a setting hen.

However, the prospect of his first try at tobacco was tame compared to another venture into which he was led, more by community opinion and suggestion, than his own efforts, though he was by no means backwards in the business. Dorie's bull Solomon had long been a source of worry to Dorie's children, the neighbors, and Angus. Solomon's disposition had grown worse with age until even Angus scarcely dared approach him without a pitch fork, and though he wore a ring in his nose, getting a lead rope through it was no easy matter. Poke Easy, almost every time he was home, had hinted to Marsh that he wished a good neighboring farmer would buy Solomon. One of these days somebody would come in and find Dorie gored to death for she wouldn't listen to reason—no more than would Katy. If Angus were not about, and somebody came with a cow to be bred, either Dorie or Katy would grab up a pitch fork and go after Solomon.

One day in late February, Solomon had been so restless all day that Dorie decided he needed a bit of an airing. Angus was working a good piece away from the house, and so rather than bother him, Dorie took it upon herself to drive Solomon down the lane and into a small pasture reserved for him. She was doing fine, as she had explained from her bed a few hours later, when Solomon decided to go in the other direction and had turned on her. She had struck at him with the pitch fork, and somehow he had knocked it from her hands. Dorie could remember little of what happened next; for once in her life she had been thoroughly frightened; there was no time to climb the fence, so that all there remained to do was run, and she didn't think she could outrun Solomon.

She might have been dead, had not Angus heard Solomon and guessed what Dorie was about. He had come on a run, and with Black Peter and Brown Bertha helping him had just managed to save Dorie, though Brown Bertha had suffered a gash in her side from one of Solomon's horns, and Angus had had his arms near jerked off from trying to hold on to a horn.

Roan had heard and telephoned Poke Easy that if he loved his mother he'd better come down and force her to part with Solomon. Much to everybody's surprise, Dorie had scarcely objected—so long as he was kept in the neighborhood for breeding. Though Dorie had offered him a ridiculously low figure, no man had wanted the job; a Jersey bull was an uncommon bad thing to have around, and unless a man were strong as Sober Creekmore—who had no use for bulls and no fit fence—he'd better leave such alone. Still, Marsh Gregory seemed an unusually good hand with stock; he had plenty of pasture, no children big enough to go climbing into a bull pen, and he certainly wouldn't let Delph be out and trying to mess around where she had no business the way Dorie did.

After some discussion with Delph, who didn't seem to care one way or the other, Marsh drove Solomon in one day, and though Solomon growled and muttered and swore, he tried no wild pawing and bellowing for he seemed to know that he had met his match. Caesar, however, had little use for him, and barked and growled each time he passed his stall or saw him in the pasture.

Marsh told Delph that night of the bull's behavior, and Delph nodded and smiled, and when he came away he knew she had scarcely heard. His eagerness to have her home had grown from a calm contentment when she began to get well to a wild racking hunger that tore him on the windy nights when he could smell the bursting plum tree buds by the windows and the rich sweet smell of growing grass.

It seemed to him that she was prettier now than she had ever been; gay with lights and shadows racing through her eyes, her hair curly from the damp spring air, the skin of her face and hands fair and soft and fine, and her breasts and body plumper, more like a woman's than the slender girl he had married. He wished she were out of the brick house; he, in spite of Mrs. Elliot's friendliness, felt ill at ease and out of place there in his faded overalls and heavy shoes, which, though he wiped them carefully on the iron scraper at the back porch steps, were a danger to the thick soft rugs. He never stayed long in the house; there seemed painfully little for him and Delph to talk about. Usually he found her listening to the radio, playing the piano, or reading; and there were times when he felt that his coming was an interruption. It was almost pleasanter to be at home and think of Delph, imagine her there with him and plan how it would be next fall when Burr-Head was weaned and they could all be together.

And Delph also watched the spring and thought of Burr-Head. Some nights she lay and listened to the winds beat through the orchard trees and dreamed long bright dreams. Many times when the night was too filled with wind and moonlight for sleep and the smell of the lilacs in the yard made her restless, she would crouch on her knees by a window. There, she could see the ribbon of Hawthorne Road, black in the moonlight, unrolling over the hills. Sometimes cars passed, and she would watch their lights until they disappeared. Other times she would take the bank book and the timber land deed, kept hidden in a dressing table, and study them for long moments, hardly seeing statements of dollars and cents or acres of land and timber, but Burr-Head—the future she would make for him. There was slightly less than twelve hundred dollars in the bank book, and she had no idea of how much the timber would bring; at least enough to maybe tide her and Burr-Head over in some city until Marsh came to his senses—or until she learned to make her living in the world. The money was a blessing sent from God; a promise that Burr-Head would be something better than a hill farmer's child, measuring his years by county fairs.

But there were other nights when the south wind brought the smell of the pear blossoms heavy and sweet—Marsh loved a pear blossom better than any other flower, she thought—and it was hard to see Burr-Head's future through her hunger for Marsh.

She would see him as the man she had married, a man with a young man's blood in his veins and a hunger in his eyes that seemed to match her own—and want to go to him with no waiting for Dr. Andy to say that she was strong enough to do her own work. She wished sometimes her mind would stop there, stay with him as he had seemed to be; but always it went on to the ugliness and the work and the pain of that year she had spent with him in the valley; and no matter how many times she remembered there was always a sudden sharp pain in remembering that the man waiting for her down in the valley was one thing, and the man the smell of the pear flowers brought to mind, another. She never knew on that night before she returned to him on a Sunday in late April whether all her tears were for him or for her.

Marsh came up to Elliots, intending to walk with her over the hill, for he wanted to see her surprise and pleasure when she saw the many improvements he had made about the place, but while he stopped in the orchard to cut a sheaf of pear and apple blossoms, Delph came down alone. He hurried back again, but when he was half down he must stop a moment to admire the house, freshly painted, white with a trim of green, and there was the bit of stone terrace he had laid before the door; a good place that would be to sit in the evenings when the trumpet vine and honeysuckle that he and Katy had planted grew higher, and some day when he had the time and money he would roof it and have a front porch.

He called as he had used to call when entering the house, "Oh, Delph," and when she did not answer, the house seemed less fine than when he had looked at it from the hill. He laid the flowers on the walnut mantel, shaped and carved by a Burdine carpenter. He walked away, but turned again, and looked at the mantel and the flowers. Caesar wanted to be off and hunting Delph, and leaped at him in impatience with his slow ways, but seeing that his master was stubborn, he, too, looked at the flowers and smiled when Marsh said, "Not bad, eh, Caesar," and followed his glance to the cedar chest and cedar chairs. They were strong heavy things, bound with copper, fashioned of bright red cedar from Marsh's pasture hill, and made by the Fitzgerald man in Burdine who worked by hand and made things solidly, for a life time of use. Most of the furniture he had collected was like that; strong stuff of solid wood, not so pretty as some maybe, but sensible and suited to a farmer.

He called Delph again, and when she did not answer went outside hunting her. Solomon bellowed from the barn with a mighty roar. He raced down to see what the trouble was and found Delph laughing as she peeped at him through his stable door. "At least he's one thing on th' place that's lively," she said when he went up to her.

"You'd better be careful of him," he warned. "Katy ruined him with teasin', an' now he hates a woman worse than anything."

"I wouldn't be afraid of him," Delph said, and laughed again, and then went flying away, running as if she had never known what it was to be sick, when Caesar barked that guests were coming.

Perce and Lizzie with their children had come to congratulate Delph on her recovery. They were the first of many, including Sadie

Huffacre and Tobe, who dropped down for a Sunday afternoon's visit. Delph was kept busy talking with first one and then the other, thanking them for their help and kindness, and praising Katy who was there with Dorie and Brother Eli, for her skill in interior decoration. Katy had scoured the country for maps, and pasted them here and there about the house; Katy loved maps almost as much as Delph, and kept a large one of the world handy in her room.

It was near supper getting and barn work time before the Fairchilds were gone, and Marsh and Delph were left alone down by the river where they had walked with their departing guests. Late as it was, Marsh must stop as they walked back to the house, to show Delph this and that; point out the land he intended to set to tobacco, and show her a strip of alfalfa that, planted in the fall, had survived the flood. And when they came to the house he had to call her attention to the screened in back porch he had made with a stone and cement floor so that mud or a bit of barnyard muck wouldn't hurt it.

"It's fine," Delph said, and went on with some glib talk of how pretty the place was, and how nice he was to do so much. He glanced at the vines he had planted by the porch and windows and the holly hocks he had set by the paling fence. Of course they were not yet up, but she could see that something was planted there, but she never mentioned it, no more than the lilac and snow ball bushes he had planted in the front yard. He started to call her attention to what he had done for the yard, but began and ended with a hesitant, "Our yard's—" which Delph never heard.

She was talking again of Burr-Head, saying that she was certain Burr-Head knew she was his mother, even if another woman nursed and cared for him. Marsh went on the back porch, feeling dull and empty with no heart to demonstrate the marvels of the cream separator he had bought to put an end to all her hours of churning. Delph wasn't like herself. Last fall when he sold his first batch of hogs he'd brought her nothing more than a bolt of good strong blue cloth for work dresses for herself and shirts for him. Even cross and moody as she had been sometimes before the child was born, she had been pleased, had kissed him shyly on the nose in gratitude for the first thing he had bought her since their marriage. Now, when he had spent money on the house that ought to have gone on the land and farm machinery, Delph never seemed to care.

He took milk buckets and started toward the barn, then turned abruptly back. Delph was busily moving about the kitchen, straightening this and that, hanging a pot or a pan on a different nail and arranging the window curtains. He walked up behind her, hoping to catch her unawares, but his heavy shoes were never any good for tiptoeing. The kiss intended for the back of her neck below her beaucatcher curls fell as a mere brush on her cheek.

She whirled about and stood blushing and confused as a school girl. He caught her hand. "Don't run away, Delph.—You've—you've not said yet that you're glad to be home."

She didn't run, but her hand touching his, held nothing more nor less in its touch than there might have been for a stranger. "Of course I'm glad to be home," she said after a moment, and with a bright empty smile. Then she was gone, dashing up the stairs, and in a second was calling, "Marsh, where'd you put my things when you brought 'em down yesterday?"

He opened his mouth but only stood staring overhead and listening until she called again, "Marsh, where'd you put my things?"

"Downstairs in—in our bedroom of course," he called in a stiff dry voice, and waited, watching by the door.

She came running down, and would have brushed past him had he not caught her shoulder. "Listen, Delph," he began, and waited, afraid of her answer but hoping against his fear that she would reassure him with her eyes. But when his eyes remained empty as her hands had been, he went on, struggling against a rising anger at this need for saying anything. "Delph— will things be between us—like they were last summer?"

She flushed and pulled her arm away with careful gentleness as if he were little better than an acquaintance she did not wish to offend. "If you mean—will I keep on—sleepin' to myself upstairs— yes," she answered in a low voice and with one slow nod of her head.

His eyes searched her face while he hoped with a kind of blind desperation that maybe her tongue said one thing and Delph another. When he understood that she meant what she said, he tried again to speak for himself, say all the things he had dreamed of saying through the summer and fall. But after a stumbling word or so he knew it was no good.

She was suddenly gentle, patting him on the shoulder. "Marsh—don't take it that way. I—I'll be here an' I'll help you all I can.—You know what Dr. Andy said that with Burr-Head comin' a little too soon like he did I ought to—to wait a good while before havin' another one."

"But, Delph, I talked to him, too.—My God, not all men an' women have babies like accidents."

Anger leaped through the wall of her calm reserve. "Burr-Head I know's nothin' but an' accident to you, an' a—."

He swore a black heathen oath that made her eyes blaze like blue flames. Then he was ashamed and sorry that the oil man part of him must always be stepping over the farmer. He shook his head with a heavy weariness. "Delph, can't you understand—ever? It wasn't because a him. I've done what I've done, an' God knows I've tried to tell you I'm sorry. Can't you forget—ever, Delph, that one time—?" but his throat hurt and he was tired, more tired than he had ever been last summer after sixteen hours of plowing.

Delph stood a moment and looked at him, then whirled about and ran sobbing up the stairs. She flung herself on the bed, and never noticed that her tears stained a bright red patch of silk in the crazy quilt. After a time she heard Marsh's feet across the kitchen floor, go with a heavy dragging sound as if he were tired or old. She got up then and drew the bank book and the deed from under a corner of the feather bed. She sat for a long time with drawn up knees and puckered brow, just staring at the papers.

After a time she was able to think of Burr-Head as she knew he ought to be—first in her mind. She ran to the back window and stood on tiptoe and tried to see the Creekmore Place.

She saw Marsh instead. He drove the cows down the barn lane for milking, walking slowly behind them with his eyes on the ground. The cows came on, but he stopped to stand by the fence and look at the strip of land by the barnyard where he would set his tobacco in May.

She walked restlessly away from the window, put the papers away, and after hesitating a time at the top of the stairs, went back to the window. Marsh had not moved. He stood like a stone man with his eyes riveted on the field, and never seemed to know that his cows begged for milking. She gripped the window sill and wished he would not look so—so—he gave her a guilty feeling, and she knew she did what was right. It would be weak and sinful to go hungering after him when maybe all Burr-Head's future could be lost through such foolishness. Still, it would do no harm to go to the barnyard and talk to him about the tobacco. His eyes would brighten as they had used to do last spring when she had grown such fine tomato and cabbage plants.

Weeks later it seemed to her that her conversation with Marsh that Sunday evening in the barnyard about the tobacco and Burr-Head had been the beginning of a half-sad, half-pleasant way of life in which they came and went as polite tenants of the same house—most of the time. There were days when the excitement of having a child like Burr-Head and raising a tobacco crop all in the same summer made life seem full and good, even for Marsh, who sickened at times of always thinking of Delph as she would be because he could not accept her as she was. And the hurt of it was that she was a kinder, more completely satisfying Delph than she had ever been.

Now, when she came morning and afternoon to bring him a snack, she hurried on to Creekmore's and visited a time with Burr-Head. Never as long as she wished. Emma was a busy woman, but too polite to go on working while Delph was there. There was another reason why Delph hurried back across the fields. Marsh was always eager to hear a bit of talk about Burr-Head. Even though he asked the same sober questions he might have asked about a pig or a calf he asked them in a different way. She had to laugh at the way he took every least thing about Burr-Head so solemnly. He knew nothing of babies. If Burr-Head only bubbled over as little well-fed babies were apt to do, he looked alarmed. And if Burr-Head noticed any small thing, or pulled Caesar's ears or waved his hands at a butterfly, Marsh marveled mightily and was certain that no other child had done just that thing.

"We'll have him with us at least by October in time for th' tobacco strippin'," Marsh would say, and Delph would go quickly away when he talked so, and be glad that there was some work to which she could put her hands. She couldn't sit still in the house and feel her thoughts like two people fighting in her head and tangling in her heart.

In May when time for setting the tobacco came she watched Marsh a time at the tedious bending work, the sort of thing he hated.

Then almost before she knew it, was at it herself. He quarreled a bit, said the work in the hot sun would maybe not be good for her, but she only laughed and went on setting the tobacco. She could see he was pleased to have her there with him.

Late in the afternoon as she was cooking supper she heard his angry troubled call from the field as he passed it on his way to get the cows. "For God's sake look at th' damned stuff," he mourned when she ran up to him. "It's dead." And he nodded sorrowfully toward the rows of tobacco, each freshly set plant fallen with its head on the ground.

Delph smiled at his foolish worries. "Pshaw, Marsh, recollect Juber an' me we raised chewin' tobacco for him in th' garden all th' time. It always fools a body like that. It'll be up straight as you please in th' mornin'. Just you wait an' see."

"I hope to th' Lord you're right," he said with more hope than certainty.

Next morning before she was scarcely dressed she heard him below her window calling in the blue misty dawn, "Delph, oh, Delph. Th' tobacco's lookin' fine. You ought to come an' see it."

Then it seemed that scarcely a week had passed before full summer and hay making time had come. What with the tobacco, a larger field of corn, a good hay crop to be gathered in and more stock to tend, Marsh was busy as it was possible for any man to be, and must often get Sober and others to help in the press of work. Still, for all his tiredness at times, he was not the harassed angry Marsh of the previous summer, uncertain that he could farm, uncertain of everything. He seemed happiest in the fields, and the only time that trouble touched his eyes was when he looked at Delph sometimes. She would smile at him, praise the promise of crops he had, cook and fetch and work for him, be everything to him except his wife.

The summer was a season of good growing weather, hot still days when the moist air lay close and silent over the land; a time for men to sweat and corn to grow. Marsh, though his first and best loves would always be clover and corn, never tired of looking at the tobacco, of walking through it day after day on his way to and from the corn fields. More than one farmer came down to see it; a prettier patch they'd never seen they said. It stood even and straight in the field, and by late July the lug leaves touched each other across the rows. Delph loved the tobacco as she would have a crop of flowers, for it was curious stuff with dainty, womanish ways. It was she who showed Marsh the cunning of tobacco leaves when it rained; come a shower and the broad leaves stiffened and lifted themselves until they were like gutters, sending all water down the stalk to the roots of the plant.

It was Delph who found the first pale green, half formed cluster of flower buds in the top of a plant. She went hunting, and found others until it looked as if the whole patch were ready to bloom. That meant that topping time was near, for Marsh had decided on late high topping when the plant was ready to flower so that there might be as little suckering as possible.

It seemed no more than a day or so before Delph awoke one morning to look and find half the field dotted with wide clusters of opening bloom. She and Marsh were out long before the sun had touched the valley, breaking and cutting out the pink flowers. And it seemed a sin to throw them on the ground, such pretty things they were. Delph worked at cutting out the flowers until it was time to carry Marsh his snack and visit Burr-Head.

Marsh had had to leave the tobacco to go lay by a small piece of late field corn in a swaggy bit of bottom that could not be planted as early as the rest. He worked with an impatient haste unusual with him; it was pleasanter to be in the tobacco field with Delph, hear her call across the rows, "Look, Marsh, here's th' widest tobacco leaf I ever saw," and he would turn and look around, or maybe hold up an especially pretty cluster of flowers for her to see.

When she came with his food he smiled to see that the crown of her bonnet was decorated with tobacco bloom. Burr-Head, seeing the flowers, would snatch and reach for her bonnet, she said, for now he was getting to be a mighty one to grab for things. Marsh wished he could leave off the plowing and go with her as he often did, but thought of all that tobacco crying to be topped, held him back.

He had scarcely finished the last of his meat and cornbread, before he saw with some surprise Delph coming hurriedly back across the fields. The most of the upper half of her was hidden under an enormous black cotton umbrella which she carried slightly forward as if afraid of the least bit of sun. He wondered if she had had a touch of the heat to be going about in such fashion, and stopped the mules and called to know what ailed her.

She lifted the umbrella a bit and he saw Burr-Head riding on her hip, his red bonnet, borrowed from Emma's little Lurie, nodding and bouncing as Delph strode down among the corn. "It's Burr-Head," she called, all out of breath from hurrying with such a load.

"God almighty if he's sick this hot sun'ull do him no good," Marsh cried and dropped the plow lines and started toward her.

Delph laughed and tried to show a proper unconcern. "Law, Emma made me bonnet an' umbrella him like he was an ice cream cone. Nothin' ails him. It's just that he's cut a tooth, silly.—I just thought you'd kind a like to see it—maybe."

"Tooth? You mean he's cuttin' teeth little as he is?"

Delph nodded and Burr-Head nodded, and Caesar trotting behind looked aloof and wise. Delph held the umbrella while Marsh took Burr-Head and saw the marvel for himself. Burr-Head clearly showed that he knew what it was all about; he did not cry or offer resistance—much, to the probing finger, but laughed and wrinkled his nose and grabbed for the copper buttons on Marsh's overalls. When both had examined the tooth to their satisfaction, Delph took Burr-Head, but after remaining a time silent, suggested somewhat hesitantly and with a guilty glance in the direction of Creekmore's place, that she take him to the house and let him see the pink tobacco flowers, He had liked the ones on her bonnet, but she had given them to little Lurie in exchange for the loan of her bonnet for Burr-Head.

Marsh looked out across the wide stretch of corn where heat waves trembled in the hot still air, then squinted at the sun from under his hat brim, and reckoned that it was no more than an hour until dinner time anyhow. He thought he'd knock off early and take the mules in, and he could ride and carry Burr-Head. Delph agreed, and then she was sorry. It was a fearsome business to sit on Ruthie Ann, watch Marsh on Charlie with Burr-Head on one arm, the umbrella and the bridle in his hands as he rode bareback down the rows of tasseling corn. Now and then she glanced over her shoulder half expecting to see all Emma's children running after her with maybe Emma too. It had taken a deal of persuasion to get Burr-Head for just a little while; the sun was hot and the corn pollen might make him sneeze, and there were a lot of reasons why he should stay with Emma.

Still, the dangers of the trip were well repaid. It was a wonder to see Burr-Head wave and reach for the tobacco flowers, and when they sat him under a great wide leafed plant he took a bit of the yellowed flyings in his hand and studied it with bright admiring eyes, then bubbled and crowed and waved it around. It was clear he knew his father could grow fine tobacco. "Aye, he'll be home in time to help with th' strippin'," Marsh said.

Delph was suddenly silent, no longer bragging about her child. Marsh bent and searched out her face shadowed under the deep hood of her sunbonnet. "Why, Delph, there's tears in your eyes. What's th' matter?"

She wiped her eyes on her apron. "Nothin'—Just thinkin'," she said.

"About th' flood—an' all that time we thought we'd mebbe never keep him. Well, that's over now," he reminded her gently.

She only nodded to that, but soon she was laughing again at Burr-Head who scooted to his father's feet and was searching out any treasures of dirt or weed leaves he knew were sometimes found in the turned up cuffs of his father's overalls. Both forgot Emma and treated Burr-Head as if he were their own, and were caught red handed by Emma's oldest girl who slipped to the back porch door and peeped through the screen to see Burr-Head with cow's milk on his chin.

And that afternoon, Marsh must quit work early again. He just happened to recollect that yesterday morning at breakfast Delph had wondered if she had coffee enough to last until Saturday. It was only Tuesday; still there was no use in taking a chance on running out of coffee. Delph, he knew, would insist on going on Maude to save him the time and trouble. So as not to bother her he left Charlie in the shade of a sycamore by the river, and rode Ruthie Ann bareback.

He crossed the creek and went by a roundabout way that did not lead directly to the store, but passed Huffacre's place. Much to his delight, Sadie sat on her front porch, mending a suit of Tobe's overalls, and in between times directing the work of her two middle sized girls as they hoed some late beans in the garden. She hailed Marsh and invited him in for a drink of fresh water, cold from the well. He declined her invitation, but stopped to agree with her that it was a mighty hot day, and that such weather was hard on everything and everybody except green growing stuff. He nodded again when she added with a heavy sigh that it was especially terrible on young babies—especially ones that were not over strong. Sexton's youngest had the summer complaint, and she'd heard that over in Salem some little baby had died of thrush or hives.

She studied him a moment in silence, and when he seemed loath to give any word on the condition of Burr-Head, she sighed again and hoped that he would pull through, but if he lost a good bit of weight and was sick and fretful it was no more than could be expected from a baby born too soon and not overly strong at that. She ended by thanking God that all her young ones had been born well and strong, while she looked at Marsh with pity in her eyes.

Marsh mopped his face again and fiddled a time with the bridle. "Aye, it is a pitiful thing to see a youngen sick an' weakly like," he said.

Sadie nodded in sympathy. "An' I reckin you know how that is, Mr. Gregory."

Marsh pushed his hat back and pondered until Sadie sat on the edge of her chair in her eagerness to learn just exactly what ailed the Gregory baby. "Aye, Burr-Head's mebbe a bit cross now an' then," he said when he could no longer be silent, "but then fat as he is—fatter than when you saw him last—an' teethin', an'—."

"Teethin'," Sadie cried, and then smiled in pity at the ignorant ways of men. "Pshaw, Emma's just told you that in case he gets sick or somethin'. He couldn't be teethin', hardly six months old, an' born too soon."

"Emma told me nothin'. I saw an' felt for myself—a jaw tooth about here.—But th' little devil crawled away before—."

"Crawlin'," Sadie exclaimed, but Marsh gave her no more time for questions. He left her sucking a pricked finger and looking after him while he dug his heels into Ruthie Ann's sides and galloped toward the store. He knew he had lied a little. Burr-Head was toothing, not teething, and he scooted instead of crawled. Late last fall, when Marsh had made a payment on the mortgage, the surprise of Andy Rankin at the bank when he learned the bushels of corn he had raised had sweetened his life for weeks, but Burr-Head's tooth was better yet. Plenty of men could, with good seed, grow corn on river bottom land, but not many had sons as fine as his own.

· 20 ·

THE DAYS passed and the lug leaves of the tobacco showed signs of ripening and the flyings gleamed yellow white above the field. Marsh's corn was laid by, the hay crop in, and except for the tobacco the hardest part of his summer's work was done; and from the look of things his work would not be wasted.

He felt free and light hearted in spite of having a wife who seemed more housekeeper than wife. He wished as he had wished many times that he had someone to share his gaiety. Dorie loved him like a son, Lizzie Higginbottom was always telling Perce what a fine man he was—so Perce said—, Vinie, the hired girl, sometimes said things to him with her eyes that almost made him forget he was a father and a respectable farmer instead of a roving oil man, and Mrs. Elliot praised him always; but none of them were Delph. He came upon her late one afternoon as she leaned on the barnyard fence and stared at the tobacco, and when he had looked at her closely, he saw there were tears in her eyes. Now, when he had the finest tobacco in the country, even if it didn't bring as much as a poor crop last year, all she could do was stand and cry.

That afternoon she gave the falling tobacco prices as an excuse for her tears. "I did so want you to have a good fine crop an' make lots of money this fall," she said with more sadness than she had shown all last summer when the drought threatened to kill every green thing on his land.

"Hell, if I don't come out clear it's nothin' to bawl about," he said. "One time—three years back—Perce didn't make enough out of his tobacco, a bigger patch than this, to pay his expenses, an' so far as I know neither him nor Lizzie cried."

"But it'll be different with you—this fall," she said, and as if afraid she might weaken and let him so much as kiss her she fled to the house.

The tobacco market opened in South Carolina, and the prices from being low fell lower. Men who visited the bluegrass country predicted a bumper crop; Roan who was good at forecasting prices, offered scant encouragement. And the tobacco, as if in defiance of all laws of supply and demand, continued to grow. It was contrary stuff. The long red and the short red refused to ripen for cutting, suckers would leap out two inches long over night, and in the meanwhile the lower leaves, the most valuable part of the plant, were dead ripe and would soon in the hot rainy weather show signs of rot.

Marsh cursed the stuff and cursed the good growing weather that would rot instead of ripen cut tobacco in his barn. He went one morning to have a consultation with Perce, who had grown tobacco for twenty years and was on to all its trickeries. He found Perce in the barn hunkered on his heels and busied with darning needle, coarse thread, and tobacco flyings. In similar positions and so occupied in different corners of the barn were all Perce's children including Little Lizzie, six years old, a beautiful child with great brown eyes and yellow curls, and so petted she could not tie her own shoes. But today Little Lizzie sat by her mother and strung tobacco leaves. Marsh watched a time, and envied Perce with such a family.

However, he did the best he could. He bought carpet warp and darning needles at Lewis's store, borrowed all Sober's family including Emma and the babies, and returned across the fields with his army, wondering what Delph would say to such a funny business. He found Delph with Katy in the tobacco patch, stripping off the trash and flyings and the yellowest of the lug leaves. None of the Fairchilds had had time to get down for a week or so, and Dorie had worried for Marsh's tobacco. The price at best would be low this year, so he had better make the highest priced leaves as good as possible, else he wouldn't make any money at all. Such was the advice she had sent by Katy, and further deputized her to demonstrate. Katy had had plenty of experience; the Fairchilds had leaf strung a good bit of their own.

During that day and for several of the next, Marsh's barn took on the appearance of a factory, though Delph who had read of such things said it was more like a sweat shop. Dorie came down to help and Emma's five year old, though he could not string for sticking his fingers, learned to measure string on the nails of a board.

Marsh cursed the day he had ever heard of tobacco and counted the days until corn cutting time; some work at least half worthy of a man and not this constant fiddling with leaves and strings that the women could do better than he. His one comfort was Burr-Head. He could crawl like a beetle now, and must forever be watched. He feared nothing, and would as soon have crawled between the mules' hind legs as on his proper pallet. Once Delph was thrown into a panic of terror when she found him attempting to chew a bit of especially bright tobacco, but Emma only laughed and said that Burr-Head was too sensible to start chewing tobacco at his age; he only wanted to get the taste of it.

Katy came one morning, flying across the fields before Delph had finished the breakfast dishes. She had great news to tell. Her sister had come home last night and surprised them. She had a new job; a better one in New York with the head store of the chain for which she wrote advertising copy. She was most likely coming down with Dorie sometime during the day.

Delph was more excited than Katy. She flew about and set the house, neglected a bit during the tobacco stringing, to rights, put fresh flowers here and there, and felt a twinge of sorrow that her home was so plain and bare. It would most likely seem poorer still to Emma, fresh from a large city where she had made lots of money and could have most anything she wanted.

Finished with her house work, Delph went to the others in the barn. It was not likely that Emma and Dorie would come before the afternoon. She would make some lemonade, put herself and Burr-Head, who was always grubby like a farmer, into fresh clean clothes, and receive her guests in proper style.

She had scarcely had time to play a bit with Burr-Head before commencing work, then Katy, outside helping Marsh strip leaves, was heard to scream, "Here comes Mom an' Emma now."

Delph jumped up, all in a fluster at having to receive any stranger in a faded cotton dress, thick with tobacco smell, but when she saw Emma some of her dismay left her. Emma wore one of Dorie's bonnets, and a plain gingham work dress. As she walked across the barnyard she, like her mother, must stop to look at everything, admire a cement watering trough Marsh had made, and exclaim over some of Delph's zinnias showing through the garden fence.

Delph went out to meet her, and marveled that any woman from Chicago could look so like a farmer's wife. Emma was brown as a fodder blade, and her hands looked as if she might have a garden. She was a tall, wide-shouldered woman, larger than Dorie, but with her mother's blue-gray eyes and hearty way of shaking hands. She smiled at Delph, and wanted to know if Burr-Head had cut any more teeth. Oh, yes, she knew all about Burr-Head. She took the county paper, and always read Delph's news.

Delph suggested that it would be pleasanter in the house, but both Emma and Dorie said they might just as well string tobacco while they talked, Delph was pleased by her friendliness and her air of being always at home, but during that day and the numerous other times she was with Emma through the month of her vacation, the pleasure of knowing her was weakened at times by disappointment. Emma could seldom be led to talk of the things she, Delph, wanted to hear.

Now and then Delph, with Katy helping her, could lead her to talk of Chicago and life in a big department store, but they would be scarcely started before Emma would maybe insist on asking questions about some one with whom she had gone to high school, or talk of her garden. She worked in town but lived a distance out and had a large flower and vegetable garden. She was proud of her new job and a bit thrilled at the idea of living in New York, still she was worried for fear that she could never afford a place for a garden about New York. She never felt at home without a garden. That was how she got such a good tan; all the people in the office envied her her tan.

One day when the tobacco was strung and Marsh was cutting in the field, Emma came alone. Delph was breaking late green beans for foddering. She and Emma sat in the shade of the house corner and talked through the whole of the afternoon. They talked at first as any country women might have talked; crops and weather, canning, and apple drying, the neighbors, and the way Ezrie Cutler, the teacher Marsh had hired, was straightening things out up at school.

But when there came a lull in the conversation, Delph asked, without lifting her eyes from the beans in her lap, "Tell me, Emma, would it be—well, hard for a girl that didn't know how to do much of anything—to get a start in a city?"

Emma snapped a bean with vigor. "It's never been easy—I mean for all the young girls that go out from this country." She hesitated and pondered with her eyes on the fields of corn that led from the back yard to the river, then went on, breaking the beans more slowly as she talked. "But well, I guess that every one of us that ever went away were disappointed in a lot of ways, and think sometimes we'd been better off at home."

"But th' others?" Delph asked impatiently. "Th' ones, not like you, them that have got nothin' but their two hands?"

"I guess it's worse for them," Emma said, and nodded over the beans. "Jobs are scarce—now. They all go off thinkin' they'll come back some day and show people what th' city's done for them. But mostly they never do. I guess most end up as factory workers, or waitresses, or at most stenographers. Then they marry. Their men don't usually make much more money than they did. Maybe they'll have one child; maybe none. Then pretty soon after they're married they'll go back to work.—And keep at it till they're too old to get a job."

Delph broke another bean. "It's not always like that. Is it?"

"Oh, no. Some get better jobs and better men. They don't all get in a rut."

"That's what I thought, some's bound to succeed," Delph said, and straightened her shoulders, but continued to look fixedly at the beans as she talked. "I know a girl back in th' Little South Fork country. Her people wouldn't let her go away to learn anything. She married, an' now she has a baby—a little girl—an' some money, enough to keep her in some city till she learned to make her own livin', I guess. Her man, he's a funny one—givin' up a good job in—th' timber business to farm. He's so smart an' young an' strong. He could make his way in any world. An' she hated to see him molder an' rot an' kill himself with work on a—." Her eagerness carried her away and she forgot and lifted her head to find Emma's eyes searching over her face. She flushed and bent hastily back to her work, but after a time went on in a slower, more careful voice, "She's always botherin' me with letters—wonderin' what she ought to do. Don't—don't you think it's better for her to at least make a try—for her baby? An' when she went away her man would come, too—I think.—An' that way in th' end her baby an' her man, they'd both be better off."

Emma seemed uncertain of what the girl in the Little South Fork country should do, but sat and stirred the beans in her lap, and looked up at a flock of feathery mares' tails, silvery white in the high calm sky. "Off hand, I'd say," she explained after a time, "that any girl with a good man like that ought to stick by him, but then—since I don't know this girl, I couldn't say what was right for her."

"I—I never did know what to tell her either," Delph said, and she, too, studied the feathery clouds. "Always she wanted to go away.—She used to think on it a lot—you see I knew her right well. She read books an' magazines, an' studied maps like mine—an' listened to radios. —An' sometimes it seemed to her. I think—recollect I knew her right well—that maybe out there she'd feel more at home, somehow, than with her own people in th' back hills. An' all that tryin' to find out how it would be, made her want to go more than ever—I guess.—An' she knows, I think, that when her baby gets older he—she'll be that way, too."

When Delph's voice had trailed away in slow uncertain words, Emma leaned her chair against the house wall and sat with her head resting on the back of one arm. "I guess nobody would ever know what to tell that girl in the Little South Fork country," she said after a time of looking over the river. "It's like a fever in a body's bones, I guess. Still, if she went away she'd maybe think sometimes that it was nice back home. She could get old and die and never know, just go always wondering."

Delph smiled. "At least, when she goes away, she'll never have to wonder how it feels bakin' cornbread twice a day, always mixin' it th' same, one egg, plenty of buttermilk an' a dash of clabbered cream. Her man likes it that way. An' then washin' th' same dishes in th' same pan ever' day an'—Pshaw, I sound like Sadie Huffacre."

Emma laughed at mention of Sadie Huffacre. "Don't let that gossip worry you," she said. "I'll always remember the year I graduated from high school, twelve years ago it was. She told all over the country that

Mom was too hard up to buy me a white graduation dress, and took down the lace curtains in the parlor to make me one."

"An' it ever word a lie of course," Delph said.

Emma smiled. "Mom always said it was a great injustice both to her and th' dress—one of the prettiest I ever had. She had two old lace bedspreads, thin lace and pretty, but meant to be spread over silk. They'd belonged to our father's mother or grandmother. Mom said she'd never have silk to put under 'em, and that they'd never go for a better cause. She made them up, patched the holes with scraps of lace, and I've never had a prettier dress since.—The shade's all the way up the hill, and I promised Mom I'd be home and cook supper." And Emma jumped up, put on her bonnet and started home.

Delph walked with her to the river. There, Emma as she unlocked the skiff seemed strangely embarrassed and confused while she said with her eyes held carefully on the boat, "Delph, I've thought it over, an' I think if I were you I'd tell that girl in the Little South Fork country to stay at home—at least till she's certain—well, that her man would come too."

Delph smoothed her apron and kicked at a clam shell with the toe of her shoe. "She couldn't ever' be certain 'til she's tried it," she said.

Emma sprang into the skiff, but lingered a moment leaning on an oar. "Delph, I've just thought of something I know you'd like to have for Burr-Head—a map of Fairyland I bought once, a long time ago, but, pshaw, I'll never be using it, and it's too pretty to go to waste. It shows Jack-in-th'-Beanstalk's country, and the gingerbread house, and—oh, a lot of things you'll be telling him about one of these days."

Delph thanked her and kicked at another clam shell as she said, "I wonder, Emma, would it be too much trouble, I'd pay you whatever it cost, for you to get me when you go there a map of New York City? I've always wanted one—just—just a foolish notion, I guess."

"I'll send you one," Emma promised.

And Delph as she walked back from the river wished she hadn't asked. Emma had not seemed half so eager to give her the map of New York City as the one of Fairyland. She went upstairs and took the deed and the bank book from under her feather bed. She looked at them a long while, then went to stand by a window and watch

Marsh as he cut tobacco. He went at the work viciously, she thought, fighting it as he had fought the plowing last summer. She thought of jovial Mr. Elliot, never fighting, never knowing the taste of his sweat or the feel of dirt in his shoes. Tonight he would be pleasant and talkative; Marsh would drop by the table, silent, too tired to do anything but eat.

He was that night much as she had expected, wordless and preoccupied, thinking mostly of the tobacco. The work of tobacco cutting was new to him. The hard work of splitting, sticking, loading, and hanging the plants used every muscle in his body. And though he had to make speed, for all the tobacco was ripe, he must continually treat the stuff as if it were some delicate mixture of eggs and tender young animals; something that would both break and bruise, blister if left too long in the sun, and rot if taken too wet to the barn. The work was further embittered by the growing realization that all his work and Delph's work would most likely amount to very little; tobacco prices continued to fall.

So great was his relief when he had finished the cutting late on a Friday afternoon that he decided to do a thing he had not done all summer; give himself the treat of a whole Saturday in Hawthorne Town. He would go to the stock markets, spend a time in Roan's office, for there he usually learned some new and interesting thing, and maybe hear a brighter prediction for the winter's tobacco market. Delph would like the little trip. She had been scarcely off the place, except to church, since coming home.

However, his plan for a holiday, seemed only half a plan when that night at supper, Delph, after listening to his suggestion, grew remote and secretive as she was at times, and said she thought she'd better stay at home. He argued in vain. Caesar would see to it that no one came meddling. Solomon wouldn't break out of his pasture. Burr-Head wouldn't fall sick or die if she missed seeing him before sundown, and the apple drying could wait a day. She had enough dried to feed Cox's Army with Sober's family thrown in. But Delph only primped her lips and said flatly that she wouldn't go; it would be a long hot drive in the wagon, and if she wanted to do any trading later on, she could go with Elliots in their car. They were always inviting her to go.

Marsh made a few remarks concerning Mr. Elliot that did not help the situation, and under his scorn and anger hid the hurt that Delph should not want to go to Hawthorne Town with him. He had planned to take her to a picture show; she had seen scarcely half a dozen in her life.

Next morning he drove away immediately after breakfast, too angry to ask her if there were any supplies she wanted. And the pettiness of his doings goaded him all through the drive. But once in Town his troubles with Delph were gradually dwarfed by a multitude of others. He first saw Poke Easy, who had come out with his mother's truck to visit the stock yards and pick up a few thin cows or young steers for grazing in the fall.

School at Lexington was only three days away, and Poke Easy, smelling of liquor and looking sad as his sister Katy when she cried, though he could not tell exactly where he had left his truck, was filled with remembering. Marsh saw him on the courthouse steps, standing alone, just looking over the court house lawn. "Do you realize, Marsh, that this time next year Robert Jonathan Fairchild will be a lawyer in Chicago with his brother Joseph Ezekiel? Always after that he can come home an' look at this, just look. He won't ever be a part of it any more." And he waved his arms toward the court house lawn where little groups of miners and farmers stood, talking and eating watermelon under the beech and maple trees, and hill men fiddled their tunes or whittled in the shade.

"You ought to a thought a that a long time ago," Marsh said, and followed him as he teetered down the steps and across the lawn.

Poke Easy went to sit on a bronze and granite marker of Casimir Pulaski under a silver maple tree. "Aye, it'll be fine," he said, and swayed gently on the stone. "Twenty years from now I'll be old an' fat an' bald. I may even look important. I've got a damned good tongue. Both my father and my mother had good tongues. My great-great-great grandfather Peter Alexander Fairchild, Esquire, he was the first judge of this county. He had a good tongue, too. He had this marker put here. He'd fought with th' man, so I've heard. Nobody recollects him any more—nor Pulaski. Peter Alexander never went away—and so he couldn't amount to anything."

He got up, looked uncertainly about him, then climbed on top of the stone, and stood swaying and waving his arms. "When I visit home old Reuben Dick will make it front page stuff on th' *Westover Bugle*. Teachers will hold me up to the school children. 'He went off an' made good,' they'll say. 'Go thou an' do likewise,' they'll say. Fellow citizens as I have told you I have a damned good tongue. I've got brains too. I could win cases. I could make connections. I might even go into politics. Sirs, am I not a Kentuckian? Every Kentuckian is a politician else he could not remain a Kentuckian. But every man from our eleventh Congressional District—God Bless it, Sirs—is twice a politician. If he were not he would not long remain alive. Some day I will be important, I shall interview country boys studying law. I shall slap them on the back and shake their hands, like this." And Poke Easy swayed toward a grinning hill man and shook hands before continuing, "Your record is good I shall say. We like good sensible, steady goin' country boys.—Aye, my friends, th' purpose of these hills is to give not only oil an' coal an' timber, cattle, corn, and tobacco, but children. I shall offer him a cigar, a twenty-five cent one—hell, no, I'll make it fifty, an' I shall say—."

Marsh would listen to no more. Poke Easy was rapidly drawing a crowd, and it seemed a sin that the marker given by one brave man in memory of another should be so desecrated. He pulled the protesting Poke Easy through the crowd, and since there seemed no other suitable place, he took him to the small saloon and restaurant at the end of Maple Street around the corner from the Baptist church.

He had scarcely got settled with a drink for himself and buttermilk for Poke Easy when he heard Perce's loud bellow from a corner of the room. Perce was drinking heavily, and explaining what he intended to do with his tobacco. Of course his corn wouldn't bring much either. There was a bumper crop of corn but he could feed it out to his wife and children and hogs and cows. The tobacco was what worried him. He had never yet been able to train a single thing about his place to eat tobacco leaves, but he'd be damned if the market went to the bottom as was now predicted if'd he sell his crop. He would buy a pipe for his wife Lizzie, teach all the boys to chew and Little Lizzie to smoke cigarettes, and they would use it up before they'd give it away.

Marsh listened a time to others talk of bumper crops and falling prices. He ordered another drink and felt a deepening sadness that nobody wanted his corn or his tobacco, such pretty stuff that he had raised. He thought of Roan and went hunting him, leaving Poke Easy to weep over the price of corn. He found Roan in his office, but Roan had little time for him. Harlan Shadoan, County Superintendent of schools was there, and with him the new head of the County Board of Health, a thin young man in a white linen suit, perspiring heavily, but not entirely from the heat.

An outraged hill man in the eastern section had threatened him with death because he had, when going over a school, vaccinated three of the man's children for typhoid. The hill man was opposed to such because it went against nature and God. The young doctor had made the mistake of carrying a gun when he returned to give the second shots; and now it was extremely doubtful if he could even get into the neighborhood for third shots. The sight of the poorly concealed weapon had aroused the anger and suspicion of all the parents.

Superintendent Shadoan had brought him to Roan with the hope that the county agent might be able to talk some sense into his head. Few men in the county had the respect and the confidence of the hill men that Roan had. He was talking now in an attempt to make the stranger see the foolishness of carrying a weapon. If it came to a show down he could not outshoot a hill man; and he would be better without a gun. But the young doctor, his head filled with tales of the doings in Harlan, a short distance east, insisted that he be permitted to go armed.

Roan begged him to go on about his duties with no attention to what anybody did or said. With typhoid raging in three communities in the Rockcastle country, seven dead within the month, four cases of infantile paralysis reported south of the Cumberland, rabies, tularemia, and young children's diseases rising to their usual late summer highs, it was important that the head of the county board of health be a man of some backbone.

When he had gone his perspiring way, Roan fell into one of his bitter pessimistic moods, and wished that one, just one, of the many men out of Westover County now practicing medicine in various parts of the world, including two foreign missionaries, would make his home county his life's work. They would at least understand the people.

Marsh could suggest no comfort except a drink. They returned to the saloon and found both Perce and Poke Easy drinking buttermilk and exchanging grievances. Roan's presence added little sprightliness to the conversation. Marsh listened to their talk, and wondered how two weeks ago he had dared be proud of his own little community. The county doctor and his nurse had come to Cedar Stump School. Marsh had been too busy in his tobacco to go, but he had deputized Delph to go and set a good example by getting herself vaccinated for typhoid. He had the day before told Ezrie in the presence of the school that if any of the bigger boys ran away or acted up to send for him, and he would round them up while Ezrie managed the others. Nothing had happened; all the children needing shots were given them, including Sober's four bigger ones whom he had sent with Delph.

He had, following directions in a government bulletin, treated the cistern water, and it on being tested was found to be clean and pure as was the water of his spring. But now the water of one school seemed nothing when Roan pointed out that so far less than half in the county had been tested within the year, and less than half of those tested were fit for drinking.

Marsh listened and drank again, and felt the drink, and the bitterness in Roan's eyes, the disgust and sorrow in Poke Easy's, the sticky heat, the troubled talk of farmers about him, his memories of the drought, the flood, Delph's unfathomable ways, the long years of saving, the longer years ahead of paying. He felt it all and didn't want to feel it, and drank and sank deeper and deeper into the wild not-caring that had used to seize him at times in the oil fields when he would drink and spend and gamble and fight, usually just before he went into new territory where he would drill wells given to gushing or haul nitroglycerin.

This anger seemed blacker, more bitter, and more bottomless than any he had ever had. He tried to walk away and leave it there in the hot saloon. Then he was drinking again and the anger dissolved like snow in a south wind.

Instead there were visions through the drunken clouds that wrapped his brain. He saw his dream of paying for a bit of land, his dream of a day when for him there would be no wonder and no doubt nor fear nor change, only peace and security and Delph's love, grow feeble and pale like the flame of a candle at sunrise. In its place there was a greater something; he had seen it sometimes, the memories of it in Dorie's eyes when she talked of what she had hoped her children would do. Last winter when he tramped over Roan's lands in the Rockcastle country, he had glimpsed it dimly through Roan's talk, had heard it again today when Poke Easy made his drunken speech on the marker of the Polish soldier; never a dream of land alone but of the people who would some day live on it, and be weak or strong as it was weak or strong.

He saw the mountains and the rolling hilly lands like some great garden out of paradise. The time would come when men like Roan and Poke Easy—and Burr-Head—would shape this land into what it was meant to be, a place for people to live. Hill men would some day plant trees as they planted corn, and raise fruits and cattle and sheep and quit trying to live only from cane and tobacco and corn. Their children would quit having rickets; the land wouldn't wash away, and all the cows in the country would be fine as his own. It took no more to feed a good cow than a scrub; the whole world ought to know that. He ought to go up and down the streets telling all the farmers that it took no more to feed a good cow than a scrub.

Then somehow, it might have been minutes or it might have been hours, he was only a drunken farmer, remembering his wife and his child and ashamed to go home or even face his mules. He was fighting somebody, and somebody else was holding him, and someone else was laughing, and somebody else was driving away with his mules. He saw things now and then, but they made little sense. He was on his back, staring through green leaves at the sky, but he wasn't in the woods, but in a wagon, with a red trim like his own. Only he guessed the wagon belonged to Roan and Poke Easy. They sat in front and drove. He questioned them once, and Roan explained that they had swapped Dorie's truck and his car for it and the team.

But mostly there was little in his head but trouble. He thought of Delph. She would look at him and her eyes would turn stony cold like her Uncle John's or else they would be like fires covering him with angry sparks. He grew easier in his mind when Roan told him not to worry. They were taking him to Lexington to see the fine horses and buy a registered Jersey cow.

He roused again when he heard Poke Easy calling loudly, "Sure, Mrs. Huffacre, this is Marsh's wagon an' team. Business is keepin' him late in Town, but he'll hail a ride on a truck or come home on th' bus. These green tree branches in th' wagon? Oh, that's just stuff Marsh had us put on to keep his groceries cool; he bought a big mess of fresh killed beef."

The wagon went at a faster pace, and he heard their laughter, and then he heard nothing. He awakened slowly to the sound of heavy grunts and groans, and after a moment's listening he knew they were his own. His head felt as if someone had used it for breaking rock, and his mouth and his throat and his stomach seemed lined with fire. Then he forgot his body in the fear and trouble that racked his soul. Poke Easy and Roan had lied to him. They had brought him home. He knew Caesar's whine by the window, and he could see the outline of the morning-glory leaves.

He raised on one elbow and a damp cloth smelling of camphor slid down his nose. He listened, but could hear nothing more than heavy snores from Delph's room above his own. The other bedroom was filled with tobacco. Delph never snored like that. She was not in the house. She had when he came back taken Burr-Head and run away, maybe to the South Fork country, or maybe to Cincinnati. All summer long he'd made her save the milk and butter money for clothes for herself and Burr-Head. That would have more than bought a ticket.

He sprang up and dashed across the room in the direction of the kitchen, banging his shin against a chair as he did so. He jerked open the door, and heard Delph's startled scream from the back porch. He saw her then as she stood in one of her full-skirted, white cotton night gowns, with one long braid of hair over her shoulder, the other half braided in her hand.

"You—you all right, Marsh?" she asked. and picked up the lamp and came to him as he stood, floundering in a sea of misery, by the kitchen table.

He nodded, but could think of nothing to say. She came on with the lamp, and before putting it on the table held it a moment and studied his face. "You do look better," she said, "but kind a peaked still.—Could—could you drink some coffee or some buttermilk? I saved some back from th' spring house."

"Buttermilk would taste mighty good," he said, and watched her as she went rushing about, to the cupboard for a glass, out to the porch for the buttermilk, spilling a bit in her haste, then dashing for a dish towel to wipe the glass clean before she gave it to him. He continued to look at her as he took the milk, and drank it in a few long swallows, his eyes studying her above the rim of the glass. "You've been cryin', Delph," he said, and set the glass on the table. "I—I'm sorry I made you cry," he went on when she gave him no answer, only stood flushing and staring at the floor, looking all ready to cry again.

"You'd ha cried, too," she burst out in a quavering voice. "Here, them two come bringin' you in. Why—I thought—just for a minute—that you might be bad hurt, or—worse."

"Would that make you cry, Delph—thinkin' all that?" he asked, and took the half finished braid of hair and started to braid it, the way he had sometimes used to do, and when she did not answer him he said, teasingly as he had used to say, "Now, Delph, don't think I can't braid your hair smooth as can be. I learned from braidin' horse's tails."

And she smiled as she had used to smile, gently somehow when he touched her, with the Delph in her eyes and the Delph on her mouth the same and mostly just for him. "Pshaw," she suddenly said with a little breathless laugh, "don't think I wasted any time cryin' when I learned what ailed you. I knew in a second from th' way Roan was laughin'—takin' you out an' havin' you drink a lot a poisoned moonshine, an' Poke Easy had been in a fight. He's got a black eye big as my fist."

"Did—did he say who hit him?" he asked with careful unconcern.

"Some fool farmer that was drunk an' wanted him to go to Lexington for a Jersey cow, but law, maybe it was a mule kicked him. He wouldn't know.—Whatever he got he deserved it. I certainly gave him a piece a my mind, gettin' you out like that—an' you so troubled an' all."

"Troubled?"

"Yes—about th' low prices—an' th' money you've spent this summer," she said, and he was certain she was going to cry.

"Lord, Delph don't ever pay attention to a man's talk when he's drunk. I reckin you heard me, just talkin'. We'll pull through."

She dropped suddenly into a chair by the table, buried her face on her folded arms and fell into a fit of easy weeping. He dropped down beside her, put his arm around her shoulder, and begged her to hush; he was not dead, they were not going to starve, and he would never get drunk—well, at least dead drunk again, but Delph persisted in crying. While he sat feeling helpless and ashamed, his eye happened upon a worn bank book and some paper that looked to be a deed laying on the table. "What are these things, Delph?" he asked, less from curiosity than from the hope that she would maybe talk a bit and leave off her crying. "Just read 'em an' see," she sobbed, and cried the harder.

His head was not exactly clear, and what with the surprise of all that timber land and some money belonging to Delph and her crying over it like a crazy woman, it took him some little while to get everything straight in his head. Delph's explanations, though they were sweet to have, were not exactly helpful. She was crying because she had got all that some time back but hadn't told him of it sooner. John had wanted her to keep it for her own, she said, but now when he was not going to make any money this fall, she felt he ought to take at least some of the money from the sale of the timber. That sounded fairly sensible, but when she changed her mind and said she was crying because he loved Burr-Head so, he gave up and just sat patting her shoulder and staring at the back of her head.

He wished she would laugh instead of cry. In spite of his splitting head and Poke Easy's black eye, he felt like laughing, more like good long laughter than he had ever felt in his life. The money was a nice thing to have—but money could never make any man feel as he felt now, but he did wish she would hush crying. "Pshaw, Delph, don't take it to heart so. Mebbe I don't love Burr-Head. Why, th' little devil pulled my nose th' other day. That's no way for a son to act, pullin' his father's nose."

Delph giggled unexpectedly and lifted her head and studied him, with the tears on her lashes shining like rain in the lamplight. "Marsh, you must love him an awful lot, not even to forget him when you were so drunk an' all—or me either. Th' first money I ever knew you to spend foolish."

Marsh sat uneasily forward in his chair and made a desperate effort to think what he might have bought, maybe gone in debt and bought a car, or a pony for Burr-Head. He dropped back in his chair and smiled when Delph said, "They are so cute. If I wasn't afraid Sober would shoot us for chicken thieves, I'd go get him now. I can just see him blubberin' an' carryin' on over that toy horse an' cow, but, Marsh, honey, you ought to ha known he's lots too little for overalls—but he'll like th' red aprons you bought for me. He takes awful after bright colors."

"Aye, he'll grow into overalls before anytime at all." Marsh smiled and didn't feel like laughing anymore. He did wish that so long as he was drunk and didn't know what he was doing, he had bought her something better than an apron.

Delph never noticed his tender, remorseful eyes, but leaned her chin on her hands and was lost for a moment in thought and plan. "Don't you think, Marsh, that next fall we ought to take him to th' fair to th' baby show? I'll put him in a little blue suit—or green— he'd look mighty pretty in green—but I don't guess that would be so well for a baby, especially a boy. I'll make it with buttons here an' here, an' a little pocket on this side." And she was Delph again, talking with her mouth and her eyes and her hands.

· 21 ·

THE WINTER that year was cold and snowy with a skim of ice on the river and frost on the window panes, a time of long gray twilights and slow dawns. Marsh was busy as always, cutting firewood, mending fence, getting out stone and building an enormous cellar for Delph, and tending his mules and hogs and cattle. Prices had continued low; it was cheaper to keep a hog and feed it corn than try to sell either the hog or the corn. When men asked him how he was making out, his answer was apt to be the same as that of other farmers about, "Well, I reckin I'm hangin' on." But there was no complaint in his answer, or fear, nor even the grimness that had colored his speech when during his first hard summer men asked him how he fared.

Then, he had never known the taste of walking into his house, tired and cold from a good day's work in the winter air, have Burr-Head, first crawling and then staggering tipsily toward him in short exciting sallies from chair to chair, have Delph come running up to him to kiss him on the chin or pull his nose or tweak an ear the way she always did—now. He always went first to the kitchen, but from there he would go into the living room, stand a moment with Burr-Head in his arms and warm his back to the fire, maybe say nothing at all, for there seemed little need of saying anything. He would take the milk buckets then and go to do the barn work and the milking, maybe snatching up the half of a fried dried apple pie or a sliver of souse meat or ham on the way. Before meal time he was always hungry just as at night time he was always pleasantly sleepy.

It was good to finish the barn work and return to find the lamp lighted in the kitchen and the firelight in the next room flickering and flaming over the wall. Supper was always good, a bountiful meal like breakfast and dinner. He and Delph, since they could sell little, were sometimes hard put to take care of their food. Marsh complained at times that both he and Caesar were getting fat, Burr-Head was like a butter ball, and even Delph had curves to her elbows.

That winter, partly because she must always have some plan or scheme or dream, to which to put her busy mind, Delph gave much time and thought to her cookery, and Marsh learned what it was to be well fed. The days when Lizzie Higginbottom or Dorie could sit and brag of well-fed families and low grocery bills were gone. Some said that Marsh and Delph either ordered their groceries from Sears Roebuck or else just didn't buy any, for all they ever seemed to buy at Lewis's store was a bit of salt and coffee with maybe a few pounds of sugar now and then. Delph made her own soap, and they didn't even buy dried beans. Last summer Marsh had sowed cow peas in his corn. Delph had picked and hulled better than ten bushel, and Marsh had taken nine of them to a produce house in Hawthorne and swapped them for three bushels of good pinto beans. He never bought meal or even flour; he'd swapped some corn for wheat and had that ground in the Burdine mill as he had his corn ground.

He had, after much urging from Delph, sold a good bit of her timber, but every penny that came from it had gone as a payment on the land. It seemed unfair to use her money for food and clothes; the land and its mortgage were in her name as well as his; and if her money must be spent it should go only for that. Money the Elliots paid as rent had to buy fence—it seemed he could never be done buying fence-tools, a bit of mending here and there, a roof for this or that; and many times it hurt to see a thing going month after month in need of paint or roof he could not buy.

He went for weeks that winter, and hardly knew the feel of a dollar in his pockets, and all of January was a scurry to meet the taxes. He would not touch Delph's cash for taxes. There were times when he was conscious of the mortgage, smaller than it had been, but still standing like a threat to his land. But though he went in thrice patched overalls and shirts solid with patches across the shoulders and down the sleeves, the patches, and the mortgage, and his empty pockets troubled him but little. He had Delph and he had Burr-Head and he knew he could farm.

Many winter evenings when he was walking home from some work on the upper farm, he would stop at the top of the hill and stand a time, looking sometimes down into the valley, sometimes at his rolling pasture fields. In the valley the twilight would stretch quiet and blue and cold, but the snow on the higher land lay streaked with bloody crimson in the red sunset light, while the western windows of the brick house seemed set with jewels and gold.

He would stand in the sharpening cold, feel the frozen snow crunch under his feet, and wait sometimes until the upper fields were quiet and blue as the valley. There were moments while he stood so that he felt the roots of his life, and the flower, and saw the fruit, clearly as he could see the apples on the sprouts he had grafted in the fall. It was good to look into the valley, see his house and barn and smokehouse, see with his mind and feel in his hands the things there that he and Delph had made and grown together; the great barn bursting with corn and hay and cattle, the makeshift crib he had made to hold his overflowing corn, the mountain of fodder stacked in the garden, the smoke house filled with ham and bacon and sausage and lard, the mounds in the garden that covered potatoes and turnips and cabbage because he had no cellar to hold it all, the attic with popcorn, strings of red pepper, sage, catnip, and dill hung from the rafters, an upstairs room weighted down with sweet potatoes cured to keep through the winter, the apples and the pumpkins and the pears buried away in the hay, the barrels of cider vinegar, crocks of honey and pickles, stacks of homemade soap, the spring house where canned goods and such were stored waiting for the cellar, the sacks of dried apples and peaches and fodder beans that Delph had made stored here and there because he had not room enough to put them. There were his hogs and cattle and mules, worthless now in dollars and cents maybe, but all the same they were hogs and cattle and mules and he had corn and fodder and hay to bring them through the winter. How with all that and with Delph could a man mind patched overalls and empty pockets?

But finer than such were the things he could not see and could not feel with his hands, but a something he and Delph had made together as they had made the corn. There was the look in men's eyes when he met them in church or at some store in Hawthorne, eyes that held little doubt, or suspicion, or wonder of what he could do. There was the eagerness of merchants to offer him credit when credit was hard to get, and the respect and the admiration of men like Ezrie the school teacher who asked his advice on the growing of corn or clover, or asked for the loan of a government bulletin.

He knew triumphs of which he could never speak; not even to Delph; they were at once too little and too big. But it was sweet to think of the trip he had taken in the fall to Delph's timber lands a few miles east of the Little South Fork Country. He had spent two weeks there. Roan had come and shown him how to mark out trees for cutting and then gone home, but Marsh had stayed a time and worked in the timber.

He'd been hard at work one day, bent over the end of a cross cut saw, when John came riding up on his big white stallion. John was never the man to beat about the bush or mince his words. He said what he had to say when he had dismounted and shook hands as befitted an uncle-in-law. He made no apologies for what he had said that day more than two years ago. Marsh was a stranger then; he, John, didn't know what he might or might not do. It took a while to know a man; and now seeing as how he knew him and being as Marsh would be in the country a week or so, he must come and spend at least a night at Costello's Place. Fronie would be mighty bad put out if he didn't come; she wanted to hear all about Delph and the baby. It would be a long cold trip just to ride over there and back, so why not come around on his way home, bring the wagon; Fronie had a deal of stuff she wanted to send Delph.

He had gone with some misgivings but, though he was anxious to be home with Delph, he was sorry that the next day came so soon and he must drive away. He had never known such hospitality as Fronie's, forcing him always to eat more than he wanted, zealous for his comfort every moment of his stay, and because the night was especially cold Fronie directed Nance to slip and spread a feather bed over Marsh sometime while he lay sleeping so that he awoke all in a lather of sweat and fear, thinking the weather had suddenly changed and there would be another flood.

Still, he had heard it said that hill people always gave their company the best they had, but he knew they did not always give such floods of praise and admiration that spoke more clearly through their eyes than on their tongues. He was hardly through the door on the evening of his arrival and warming by the fire, before Fronie commented on his patches; and looked ready to faint with surprise when he only nodded in an off hand way as she asked if Delph had done the work. Nance was called in to see the marvel, and came drying her hands on her apron and declaring that she'd always said that if the right man got to Delph she would get over her flighty ways. Still, it was a wonder to think that hardly more than two years back she wouldn't so much as sit still and embroider, let alone patch. And all, including John, beamed on him as if he were the one to take the praise instead of Delph. And Marsh looked into the fire and tried not to show how much their talk of patches meant to him. He had always been proud of Delph's way of taking care of him. It was good to wear a neatly mended and carefully ironed suit of overalls to Town, different from his oil field days when many times a person had only to look at him to know he was a lone man in the world.

He liked Fronie; she seemed such a good sensible, substantial sort of soul. He was half sorry that John insisted that he spend most of his time with him. But when he had tramped over his fields and listened to John's slow talk of farming and Juber's proud comments on a pretty bit of meadow land or a good looking heifer, he was glad he had gone. A man could learn much from John Costello. He had never read so many bulletins nor studied the business like some, but he did know how to raise corn and cattle and make hill side pastures almost as good as flat land.

John made most of his money from the great droves of hogs he turned loose in the woods each fall and left to fatten on the mast, and then finished off on corn before he sold them. He, like Marsh, had a good bit of hogs and cattle he didn't care to sell because of the low prices, so he thought he would just hang on to them; it cost a man nothing to let his hogs wander in the woods. Marsh asked him what he thought a man like himself with no great reaches of timber land but with plenty of pasture ought to do in such times. John advised him to hang on, buy no more grown cattle to fatten but keep the ones he had and buy calves, all the calves he could get. They would cost him little or nothing to raise; cattle were good for the land—not like sheep—and there was always the chance that prices might go higher. He also suggested that he might, if he could get up the cash, get up a fair sized drove of hogs with plenty of old brood sows and late next summer drive them up into Delph's timber land. He, John, could send one of his boys over to toll them together now and then, or some of the back hill farmers living near the land might be glad to look after them now and then for a hog or so to kill for meat.

Marsh listened to the slow-worded advice and felt much at home with John. He was a straight thinking man, and no wishy-washy fool. He hesitated a time, then asked him how he had managed certain things such as the three-year high school John had forced the county board of education to put back in the hills, so that all country children might not have to stay away from home to go to high school.

John smiled. "Partly politics, partly hangin' on," he said, and went on to tell of how he had started talking up such a school the year he was married and became Delph's legal guardian. He had seen then that she was a smart child, better in her books than most. He had planned that she should go to high school—he had always thought he would have liked some schooling past the eighth grade— but he had seen, too, that it would never do to turn Delph loose in even a little county seat town. He'd always been afraid, he went on to say after a time, that Delph would go like the rest of his family and her mother and her people; go away for the pure love of the going. It was all right for some, but—well—he had never thought it would do for Delph; she was different. And he smiled a gentle, half-sad smile. "It's nice to think of her as a peaceful settled married woman with a child, 'stead of a hot headed girl liable to do anything," he said.

And Marsh knew that he had found a friend, a man who might be backward in his ways, hidebound in his politics and religion, but a man who understood better than anyone else in the world, maybe, that Delph had not changed from the old Delph into the new without a bit of struggle—and that she was worth all the hurt, and fear, and patience, and anger any man would have to wade through before he found the Delph she was meant to be.

He never told Delph of his talk with John or mentioned Fronie's praise of the patches. There was so much else to talk about when he got home. They sat half the night by the fire talking of this and that:

Delph asking another question before he had had time to finish the last one. When Juber came the previous winter she had felt too sick and troubled for Burr-Head to talk much with him, but now she could not learn enough of the doings of the ones in the Little South Fork country. Did Juber still court Mrs. Crouch and had Lucas Crabtree ever got saved, and how were the Hedrick girls? And did he recollect to get Fronie's recipes for spiced peaches and corn relish?

When he produced the recipes, Delph studied them and smiled and looked into the fire and nodded her head as she did when wrapped in some pleasant thought or plan. Sadie Huffacre most generally, she had heard it said, took off most of the pickle prizes at the Fair. Well, she, Delph, was going to see what she could do. This would be their first year at the Fair, and they must show Westover County what the Gregorys could do. Solomon and Burr-Head could of course be counted on to take first prize in their respective shows, but they must show some other things as well.

Marsh wondered if he dared exhibit corn in the face of Dorie and some of the other great corn growers in the county, and thought that maybe, for at least the next few years, he would content himself with showing hogs and stock. It was pretty well agreed that Solomon and Prissy were among the finest cattle in the county, and his hogs, though not purebloods, were among the best. But he had no sooner got into a good way of thinking on the Fair than Delph's mind as always went racing past him to more distant things. It pleased him to hear her talk of their future together on the farm—a thing she had never used to do. When she talked of the brick house, wondered how it would seem to live on the hill, near the road and close to school for Burr-Head in a house with electric lights and a real bathroom, he smiled and agreed with her that it would be a very fine thing.

It seemed sometimes that the night when they had sat and planned for the Fair was no more than a week gone before Burr-Head was learning to talk, Prissy was having another calf, Maude was being bred again to Perce's stallion, spring was coming on; then summer with Poke Easy home for his last vacation, with his state bar examinations behind him and work with Joe in Chicago ahead.

Dorie came often to see them that summer. Though she never spoke of Poke Easy or of Katy, going next fall into her last year of high school, she had a lonesome look sometimes when she played with Burr-Head. Delph, too, would think sometimes of the last of the Fairchild children going away, and have a moment's loneliness and a lost feeling of being shut away from the brightest bit of the world she had ever known. Katy now talked less of the life about her with its possibilities for pieces in the paper than of what she would study in college, and the still more exciting topic of just where she would go to college. Poke Easy said he would like to have her with him in Chicago for he didn't want to live with Joe; and Emma, making more money than she had ever made, invited her to New York. She and Delph would sometimes study college catalogues together, and always Delph thought she should go to New York. Katy could come home then and tell her how it was.

But Delph forgot everything and everybody, including Katy, in the excitement of getting ready for the Fair. There was so much to do. The season was a busy one; gardening and canning and pickling and drying, and Burr-Head always tempting her to forget her work and play with him. He was never a clumsy, whining, everdemanding baby. By the time he was eighteen months old he could run about and amuse himself—with no help from his mother. Caesar had never approved of his bold, unbabylike ways, and more and more as he grew older, more given to wandering the far corners of the yard and even into the garden if the gate were open, Caesar neglected Marsh at work in the fields to keep an eye on Burr-Head.

Nor was Caesar the only one. It seemed to Delph sometimes that the whole neighborhood would have liked Burr-Head for their own. Emma's youngest ones were always running away from home to bring Burr-Head crackled meat skins; a food of which Delph did not quite approve and Burr-Head was very fond. He always received a royal welcome at the school or store, in church and at the neighboring houses, especially at the brick house where Mrs. Elliot kept a bunch of toys for his pleasure.

But Burr-Head with his red-brown curls and freckled nose that wrinkled when he laughed, was a strangely self sufficient baby with little need of toys. Sometimes Delph wished, and she knew it was a wicked wish, that he would beg to be carried or cry sometimes to sit in her lap, or cut a great shine when she had to leave him at Elliots while she rode to the store, or in church when he sat back with Marsh and she sang in the choir. He seemed almost as contented with Marsh or Caesar or Mrs. Elliot as with her—and he would stand for minutes together, peeping through the fence into the barnyard, smiling on and talking over many matters with the hogs and cows and chickens.

Still, she knew she ought to be proud to have such a good baby; she could never turn out the work she did if he always hung about her legs and cried like some. And when the day of the Fair came at last, there he was standing good as gold on the hot crowded platform, not a bit put out by the judges and all the press of people. His eyes a bit bigger and grayer than common, and his hair curly as a sheep's wool from the heat. She didn't stand up on the platform with him and hold his hand or keep him on her knees, the way most of the mothers did their one and two year olds. She thought he'd manage better by himself, and though she was neat and clean as always, that morning she'd been so worried for fear Burr-Head would get himself dirty, and hurrying, too, that she had put on the first clean dress she came to, and hardly noticed until Marsh said as they were driving up the hill, "Delph, you ought to have dressed up a little, too, wore that pretty red linen or somethin', 'stead a that old brown cotton."

But she only laughed. It didn't seem to matter what she wore. The dress was three-year-old voile, one she'd had when she married; faded a bit across the shoulders, and tight, too, tighter than a voile ought to be. Then she forgot the dress in the excitement of the day. Her pickles won, and so did her spiced peaches, and so did her plymouth rock pullets, and then it was Burr-Head's turn.

She waited down below in the press of people and kept squeezing and rolling her handkerchief in her brown sweaty hands. It seemed the judges would never decide. Burr-Head's eyes were getting bigger and bigger; pretty soon his lower lip would quiver and the tears come splashing down, and he would stand there crying soundlessly the way he did at home sometimes. Then suddenly Burr-Head smiled and waved to some one in back of her. She looked and there was Marsh with eyes for no one but his son; he had not been certain he could come to the baby show, he had so many of his animals to attend to, but there he was laughing and winking at Burr-Head. Burr-Head tried to return the wink, but couldn't quite make it. He only squinched both eyes tight together then opened quickly with a blinking, and the crowd laughed so that Dr. Hobson, head of the baby judges, had to rap twice for order.

Delph listened, looking at the judge and tying hard knots in her damp handkerchief. Katherine Rebecca Weaver, six months old daughter of Mr. and Mrs. Archie Weaver of Clay Hill, had won in the class for one year olds and under. Sober Marshall Costello Gregory, nineteen months old son of Mr. and Mrs. Marshall Gregory of Cedar Stump, had won it for those between one and two.

Delph pushed her way through the crowd, rushed to the platform, caught up Burr-Head, blue ribbon and all. She wished that on the instant she could take him and just play with him for the rest of the day; take him down by the river and build castles in the sand the way they did sometimes on Sunday afternoons. But Marsh was there behind her and saying, "Here, let me have him, Delph. You'll never get him outside." And there was Katy with her sister-in-law, Joe's wife home with Joe on his vacation. Mrs. Elliot was there, pleased as if she were his mother, telling some nicely dressed woman, strange to Delph, of how she had fed and cared for him until he was a month old.

Outside, they all clustered around Marsh and his son, Marsh looking more as if he had won the blue ribbon than Burr-Head who only smiled at them all and seemed in no wise excited by the business. Delph wiped beads of sweat from his nose and upper lip, then moved away a step or so from the fluttering talking women in their dainty dresses and with their white gloved hands. She grew more and more conscious of the too-tight coffee-colored voile, her brown bare hands with their nails short and straight, kept that way from all the work she did. She wished she could hide the damp knotted and twisted handkerchief, and she wished the strange woman's voice were not so beautifully clear and quick with all the proper i-n-g's and d's and t's; it made her own seem slow and slovenly, like the Kentucky hill woman's voice that it was.

Mrs. Elliot suggested that Burr-Head ought to have his picture taken in his new blue suit and the blue ribbon on his chest. She'd always wanted a picture of him, a large one, not just the little snap shot she took from time to time. She could take him if Marsh and Delph didn't have the time. Burr-Head would go with her; he and she were great friends.

Marsh hesitated. He couldn't go. He had to see to several things. He glanced at Delph, and wondered at the tightness in her voice as she said, smiling a bit at Burr-Head, "Let Mrs. Elliot take him, Marsh. He wouldn't be a bit afraid. I—I have to go see to my pickles an' such—but that's no reason to keep him from havin' his picture taken.—You be good, Burr-Head," she said, and turned abruptly away.

She hurried back to the food show and found Lizzie Higginbottom and others of the Cedar Stump women. Lizzie smiled when she told of Burr-Head's triumph, and went on to describe how she had mixed and baked her red devil's food cake that had won a prize. Delph listened but absentmindedly. She kept thinking of Burr-Head, wishing she had gone with the others in spite of feeling out of place and ill at ease. She knew she wasn't timid or ashamed; she'd never be ashamed of being Marsh's wife. It was just the knowing that she didn't belong. She was a farmer's wife with a pretty child. They were something else; more like the people Burr-Head would know when he grew older and went out into the world.

She looked at Lizzie, smiling, talking, showing with her hands just how carefully she had folded the beaten eggs in; Lizzie never thinking of anything but her house and her cookery and her garden and family. Delph listened until Lizzie paused for breath, then said, "I'm sorry, but I'll have to be goin'.—I want to—buy some things in th' ten cents store," and she turned and hurried from Lizzie as she had from the other.

It was hot in the ten cents store; crowded with farmers' wives like herself come out to see the Fair, and women from the back hills who maybe got into Town no more than once a year. Some had babies in their arms and children at their heels, most were brown with work shaped hands, and shoulders not so straight as they might have been. But most smiled as they looked at this or that, bought their children ice cream cones and cheap candy, and were kept busy wiping sticky chins and noses.

Delph pushed through the crowd to the back of the store where records and sheet music were sold. Though she never bought music of any kind, the red headed girl who played the piano knew her and smiled. Sometimes when the girl was not too busy they talked a bit, or mostly it was the girl. Once, she had had a job in Detroit where she played and sang songs in a ten cents store twenty times larger than this; and one winter she had sung in a night club there—but that was a long time ago.

Delph wished that today she could tell her of Burr-Head and the baby show. She with her red nailed hands and her permanent wave didn't look as if she would be interested in spiced peaches or pickles. But there was no chance to talk to her of anything. The crowd kept asking for this and that, mostly hill billy and cow boy songs, and the girl was busy over the keys. The girl had a wilted look, she thought. There was a smudge of sweat across the shoulders of her dress and when a song was finished her head would droop a little wearily. Still, she smiled a fixed painted smile that made the music sad for Delph, no matter what she played. She knew the smile; and felt it passing over her mouth when an acquaintance from Salem spoke to her.

She turned away into the crowd, but the music kept drifting through the noise and following her. A lonesome, long drawn hill billy love song the girl sang now. Delph put her hands over her ears, but took them away when a passing hill man smiled, and she remembered where she was. She had had a memory like a looking back of how it had used to be when she listened to Juber's fiddle tunes—and the music of the dance that night. The songs had cried to her of many things, and now they cried still—but of different things.

She wished she were home. Maybe all this wouldn't hurt her so. The white-gloved women away with Burr-Head, talking of many things, clothes and books and places visited, music and furniture, magazines and shows, or flowers, or maybe nothing at all. They were there; here were the others, the farmers' wives, and she, Delph, felt lost and alone with either. It was all so little, this business of the Fair. To plan on making pickles for months ahead, and feed chickens in a coop after first carefully selecting the eggs and setting them under hens, and talk about it with the neighbors, and plan it thus and so—and all for a blue ribbon to lay away in the scrap book along with that picture of Sam and the clippings from the paper. It would hurt to write the news of Poke Easy's having gone with Joe, and there was Perce's oldest boy going away to college in the fall, and next fall there would be Katy—and none of them would ever be back except as visitors.

She wandered a time through the crowded streets, stopped a time and watched the fountain, then strolled through the court house hall, but always it was the same; women and children and men much like those in the ten cents store.

Usually when they came to Hawthorne she waited for Marsh in the office of the *Westover Bugle*. She liked it there; Reuben Kidd the editor had books and magazines and sometimes papers from large cities to read. She saw him as she went through the door, sitting as he usually sat, his back to her, his eyes on the street, and his feet on the massive table like affair he called his editor's desk. "Sleepin'?" she asked in a low voice, hoping not to wake him if he were.

"Now, Delph, you know I never sleep in th' day time," the old man said as he tilted farther back in the chair and shifted his feet a bit on the desk and continued to watch the street. "I was watchin' that boy there—th' one walkin' past that old hitchin' block. I can't make up my mind whose youngen he can be. He walks like a Fitzgerald, but no Fitzgerald ever had hair as red as that."

Delph said nothing, and picked up a copy of the Westover Bugle with a little rustling. She hoped the old man would hush and she could read. Reuben Kidd was like the old people as she remembered them at home. He could tell a man's voting precinct by the kind of mud on his shoes, and see a man dead forty years in a child's eyes or the tilt of a boy's head, and like the other old ones he would go wandering back into the days when the man he saw in the child had lived.

She threw down the paper after reading the news she had written—talk of little things, a new barn, and words on cider making time. She found a book that looked newer than the others, and settled herself by a window but did not read. Reuben's voice kept forcing itself between the words, asking questions about this and that in Cedar Stump, until in despair she closed the book and sat and studied him. He was an old man, older than Dorie, longer than Roan Sandusky, with a rough untrimmed beard and wavy untrimmed hair, whiter behind than in front so that when he raised his head from a session of resting the back of it on his clasped hands, he made her think of some pictured saint or prophet crowned with a halo of silver.

He roused himself, spat neatly between his outspread feet and the plunking clink on the other side of the desk not only proclaimed that Reuben had thus spat from the same spot for more than forty years but destroyed Delph's vision of a saint as well. She studied him and wondered as she had wondered many times since meeting him more than two years ago, how it would be to know a real editor, an exciting man who dealt with important things in important places. She wondered, too, how it was that a man with the sense Reuben seemed to have could spend all his days in one county seat town and find the procession of petty political scandals, gun battles between the law and the moonshiners in the eastern section, the trials and fights and elections, the births and deaths and weddings, the floods and droughts and failures still full of interest after forty years.

She looked at him again. He appeared to have fallen asleep, the back of his head resting on his laced fingers so that his beard stood pointing at the ceiling. She turned away. The old sleeping man seemed somehow an image of failure and wasted life—a picture of what she heard in the music crying out of the ten cents store. She wondered that if in his sleep he did not dream sometimes of the many who had gone from Hawthorne Town and Westover County and of whose success he had written in the paper.

She sat in the quiet room and heard the sounds that came from the street; the whispering of the fountain in the square, mule shoes clop-clopping over paving stones, the rattle of iron shod wagon wheels, slither of cars, and somewhere sheep, doubtless being driven homeward from the Fair, made a thin plaintive bleating. Nothing was of the city, or of anything except her own sky governed world, and that was built on fields and men in overalls. They came and choked the life from the town—if it had a life apart from them and their land.

She went to stand by the window and look for Marsh. It was long past his usual time for coming; with ten miles to drive in the wagon they would be dark getting home. She saw him at last, driving down the street in his heavy wagon, with a loose easy rein on the mules. Though there was no look of middle age or weariness about him, it seemed to her that the stamp of the hours he had spent with plow handles in his hands was strong upon him. Still, it was his face, she thought, that marked him as a farmer with no mistaking; brown as the side of one of his Jersey cows, with sun and wind wrinkles etching about the corners of his eyes. And the eyes themselves, wandering continually over earth and sky, searching out sign of rain or wind or sun or cold, glancing after stock and plants and soil, seeing only hardware and harness displays in store windows.

She watched him as he glanced a moment at the sky, and felt with a weary irritation mixed with wisdom loving foolishness, that if he were dropped into the middle of New York City he would go searching immediately for a bit of earth and a bit of sky. He looked tired, dejected she thought, and that old wish to make him laugh or smile came, and as always was stronger than any other thing. "Oh, Marsh, wasn't it fine about Burr-Head," she called before he noticed her by the window.

He glanced at her, and a smile flickered across the lost look in his eyes. "You'll have to give him castor oil tonight, though," he said. "Recollect it's your turn. He's had a lot of foolish stuff to eat like an ice cream cone, an' Mrs. Elliot has maybe give him more."

"She took him home, I guess," Delph said, and knew the question was a foolish one; there was nothing in the wagon but the hay she had brought packed about her canning exhibits.

Marsh stopped the wagon when he was just by the window. "Hell, no. Burr-Head would have none of that. He's sleepin' here behind me in some hay.—Aw you can't see him. I heaped it over him to keep th' sun out of his eyes."

Delph studied the mound of hay, then let her eyes wander to the back of the wagon where there was a great heap of hay, more it looked than they had brought. She wasn't certain but it looked as if there might be a big box or crate or something under the hay. "Marsh what is—?" There came the plunking clink, and in a moment Reuben came to stand by the window. "Marsh, if what I heard about an hour ago is th' truth I'm goin' to put a piece about you on th' front page next week. Why, that's th' biggest price any piece a horse flesh—an' it a colt not two years old at that—has ever brought in this county.—Go around to Coomer's Studio an' have your picture taken. Charge it to th' Chamber of Commerce or Slip Yorrow's campaign fund an' I'll put it in th' paper."

"Marsh, you—you didn't sell Ebony, th' prettiest thing we had?" Delph begged and didn't know which was worse, the lonesome look in Marsh's eyes or the loss of Ebony.

Marsh twisted the reins in his hands and looked at the knees of his overalls. "If you'd put his picture now. Aye, he looked so fine when they went leadin' him away. I went an' watched 'em load him into th' truck, an' it was a sight th' spirit he showed, rearin'—." He paused and spat at the foot of a maple tree by the street.

Delph glanced at him with troubled eyes. "Marsh—since when—since when did you start chewin' tobacco?"

"I've not started," he answered, too full of Ebony's loss to feel guilt in doing what he had always held to be a dirty, wasteful thing. "Roan gave me a chew when we went to see Ebony loaded."

"You ought to a kept him," Reuben said.

Marsh shook his head. "I did think about it, but I reckin it's like that man from th' bluegrass that bought him said. He'd make a good hunter' an' it would be foolish to keep a colt like Ebony. I had no need to ride him, an' all that time to be wasted breakin' him in an' trainin' him an' him eatin' his head off, an'—." He stopped, and would have spat again had not Delph's beseeching eyes restrained him—for a moment. Soon, he could not help himself.

He wished he would quit thinking foolish thoughts; the empty stable in the barn, and the wonder if they who bought him would change his name. He glanced at Delph standing quiet and unsuspecting by the window, and felt a sharp pleasure is spite of the loss of Ebony. He wondered yet if he'd done right or wrong to spend a good bit of the Ebony money on foolishness for Delph. He hadn't planned the business. He had gone hunting Delph to tell her of the good price he got for Ebony, but at the food show had only found Lizzie, gathering up the spiced peaches and pickles that Delph had forgotten. "She's gone to th' ten cents store," Lizzie had said, and added with a hint of question in her voice, "She seemed mighty down in th' mouth for a woman that's carried off so many blue ribbons."

He had gone to the ten cents store and had seen her there, staring at the red headed girl who pounded the piano keys. She looked lonesome, he thought, the way she had used to look when she stood on the hill and watched the sun go down. So he had gone and spent a lot of money foolishly, exactly why he didn't know.

Now, the problem was to get her home without her knowing. She came out and climbed into the wagon; in vain did he tell her that he couldn't waste the time for her to uncover Burr-Head and look at him. She pulled the hay away from his face and sat a moment on her heels and smiled at him. Marsh kept watching her over his shoulder, ready to call that she must come sit down, if she so much as went near the mound of hay in the back of the wagon. But just at the wrong moment High Pockets Armstrong called to him from across the street, and wanted to know if that Jersey bull had won first place again this year, and if he'd really sold that colt of his.

While Marsh was answering, Delph crawled on her knees to the end of the wagon, and when Marsh looked again it was too late. She had brushed the hay away and made a small hole in a burlap covering, and the next instant she was setting on her heels, just staring with her mouth open and her eyes wide. She turned to him and her voice was weak with surprise. "Marsh—why, Marsh, it's a radio."

"Aw, hell, Delph, I meant it as a surprise an' now you've gone an' found out," Marsh groaned, and was wrenchingly aware of the loss of Ebony and the scattering of all his plans. He had meant to have Delph's surprised delight in the radio to think upon all through the drive home and until tomorrow—a Saturday when she would be gone in the afternoon training the children at school for the pie supper program they were having in a week or so.

Delph had no eyes for his disappointment. "Marsh—you, you sold Ebony an' bought me a radio," she said in a choked smothered voice, and he had the terror that she might be going to cry there on her heels in the wagon with Reuben Kidd looking on. He would maybe write a piece about it in the paper.

She made the hole a trifle larger and peeped again while Marsh begged, "Please Delph, don't look at it anymore."

She felt the disappointment in his voice, and after one last lingering peep turned away. Marsh was such a silly fool; he liked to think on a thing so, turn it over and taste it in his mind. He'd maybe meant to keep it hidden in the barn a week or so, and then surprise her with it one day; and he was no good for thinking up little white lies. He'd started the wagon without waiting for her to get on the seat, disgusted with her poking, prying ways. She crawled under the high seat, and surprised him again by almost falling in his lap when she sat down.

"I always wanted a radio," she said, and sat well away from him and spread her skirts a bit on the seat, "somethin' like that, only not half so fine. Who you takin' it down to, Sadie Huffacre or th' Sextons?"

"Aye, I think Tobe bought it for Sadie," he said, and smiled at her from the corners of his eyes, "to kind a make her feel better for not takin' th' prize in pickles this year."

They both laughed, and Burr-Head awakened and rubbed the hay out of his eyes. Many waved and called to them as they drove through the town, but mostly their eyes were for each other, so much so that Dorie waiting for them on the steps of the Hotel Hatcher had to call twice before they heard. "I want to drive home with you all," she said, as Marsh stopped the wagon.

He leaned over the side to help her up the wheel, but Dorie continued to stand and clutch one of the pillars that supported the hotel porch. She glanced apprehensively up and down the street, then called in a loud shrill whisper, "I'm afraid one a you'll have to get out an' help me."

They both sprang down and rushed up to her, and then exchanged troubled glances between themselves. Dorie's eyes were awful bright like a person with the fever, but her nose and her long upper lip were covered with beads of sweat. "You're sick, Dorie," Delph said, and took her arm. "You're in no fit shape to drive home in a wagon."

"Come on, help me in th' wagon 'fore Joe or that wife a his comes along. There's not a thing ails me.—I—I just can't walk so well, an' this terrible heat has got me down."

Marsh looked at her uneasily. "You're sick, Dorie," he said.

Dorie wiped sweat from her nose with a hard angry gesture. "I tell you, I'm not sick. If you don't help me into th' wagon I'll fall tryin' to walk."

There was nothing to do but put her on the wagon seat, and then it took all Delph's strength to hold her, for Dorie sat swaying and nodding like a saw dust woman. However, when they had gone a mile or so she appeared to recover somewhat, and sat fanning herself with her hat and smiling at the road. "Marsh," she burst out suddenly, "from a few little things I've heard of you, you know how it feels to feel like you need a drink—bad."

And when he nodded she went on with a shame-faced smile, strange for Dorie, "Well, I took a spell like that this afternoon. At home I have my wine ever' day an' a little toddy now an' then—when I need it—but here in Town I couldn't go walkin' into a saloon. Sadie Huffacre would ha talked about it th' rest of her days." She hesitated, then went on after another sleepy, easy sort of smile, "There's been a good while I've been wantin' to see th' inside a this Hotel Hatcher, th' finest south of Lexington so I've heard. An' too—well, you know how a body is. Lot's a times I've heard Emma an' Joe an' th' others talk a cocktails an' I've read of 'em, too. —So-o-o—when I felt I was needin' a drink I went to th' Hotel Hatcher—in th' bar. Nobody from Salem would ever see me there. I had one—a Manhattan they called it—an' it tasted like no strength at all—then I had a Pink Lady—an' then a somethin' they called a Martini—but none of them tasted like much of anything.—But when I got up an' tried to walk I learned different."

Delph laughed, but Marsh looked at Dorie and asked in a low troubled voice, "It's none a my business, Dorie, but—well—when I need a drink so much—most generally there's somethin' wrong—or about to be wrong. If there's anything th' matter an' me or Delph can help why—."

Dorie waved her hand in a loose easy gesture, then wiped her eyes and blew her nose. "I won't be needin' help so much—anymore. Or a man comin' around in th' winter to see to this or that like you did last when Angus went to visit his sister.—You see—see, he never told me—I heard him givin' Joe a piece of his mind—after he'd made it up—Poke Easy, I mean, not Angus. He's goin' to stay an' practice law in this county—like some of his grandfathers before him did—an' he'll manage th' farm." And Dorie cried with her head on Delph's shoulder. Marsh looked straight ahead and said after a time, "Dorie, you're worse than Delph. What in th' hell is there to cry about?"

"When you've waited thirty years—for one—just one," she said, and might have continued with her tears had not Burr-Head, unable to walk in the swaying wagon come crawling on his hands and knees under the wagon seat and up between Dorie's feet. And she was thrown into a fit of bewailing that she had missed his judging at the Fair. She thought she'd go to the State Fair at Louisville in the fall. She'd always wanted to go; and this would be the first fall since her marriage thirty-four years ago that she could get away from home.

They said little after that. Delph was silent, thinking of Marsh and Burr-Head and the radio. Her mind was a welter of plans. She wished she didn't like Lizzie so well; she'd try to beat her next year on red devil's food cake, but she thought she'd at least try angel food, practice up on Marsh this winter if eggs continued cheap, but he would most likely grunt and say as he said of her lemon chiffon pie, "Delph, there's nothin' to this damned stuff but wind; if you want a worry with fancy sweetenin', fix somethin' that'll stick to a man's ribs." He liked good solid things like sweet potato pie; tomorrow she'd bake him a fine one—that is if he weakened and let her see all of the radio before she went to bed.

Burr-Head stood between his father's knees and waved to passersby or twisted about sometimes and studied his father's face or Delph's face. Once he waved toward a truck load of stock and said, "Pretty cow." He said nothing more until they had driven across the upper pasture and were turning over the hill toward home and then he said, "Pretty house, pretty, corn, pretty, Caesar," in his slow careful way, nodding his head with satisfaction when a word was finished to his liking.

Marsh nodded, too. Better than any other thing he liked going home like this, especially on an evening in late summer like this when he could look down and see his house and fields and gardens waiting there in the valley when early dusk lay thin and blue on the bottom lands, and the last red rays of the setting sun tipped the brick house chimneys. A few fireflies, earlier than their brothers, glimmered through the dark forest of the high ripening corn, and from the willows by the river the croaking of frogs came faintly, while overhead a bull bat made a buzzlike twanging.

· 22 ·

SOMETIMES AT Lewis's store or on the courthouse steps or in the little saloon at the end of Maple Street just around the corner from the Baptist Church, men would pay Marsh Gregory the highest compliment they ever paid to a stranger; one they never gave to Mr. Elliot or the strange preachers and teachers and doctors they now and then had. In addition to agreeing that he was tough as a hickory switch in the spring, they also said sometimes that somewhere behind him there was good blood, and that some of his generations must have been a fine breed of people.

As proof they would speak not only of himself, his farm, the remarkable child that was Burr-Head, but of the good wife he had picked for himself, since it was a well known fact that a man could not be judged by himself alone, but through his wife as well. There were others, the older, more skeptical ones, who said that Delph had made him what he was. Most any man with red blood in his body and sense in his head would go the limit for a woman like Delphine Costello Gregory.

Pretty she was, not young girl pretty as she had used to be, but a fine full figure of a woman with a straight strong back and a proud high head, and hands and shoulders that could turn off a sight of work if need be. She could run the cultivator through the corn or sit quiet and lady-like mending his overalls; it was all one to her. And everybody remembered how she had peddled and helped him through that first hard summer.

And her mind was strong as her body. It was from her most likely that the child got its bright quick ways. Look what she had done and was doing for the little Creekmores. She had decided one day that they ought to learn to read and write and figure. So through the winter months the five oldest came to her for a few hours almost every day, and Emma said they learned a lot, especially geography and singing. The maps on Delph's walls and her gift for song made her school ideal for such subjects. And if anyone asked her why she took so much time over five little negroes, she was apt to laugh and say that she liked to be busy at something, especially through the winter when there was nothing much to do.

Even Dorie wondered how Delph did all the things she did. If the school or Salem church planned a program or ice cream or pie supper, Delph could always be counted on to do her share, not only in baking a cake or pie but in helping the children learn their pieces and their songs. "I feel better bein' full-handed all th' time," she always said if someone marveled at the help she gave.

She sang at many churches as well as Salem Sunday School, and people never tired to hear her sing. There was a wonder in her voice. To look at her strong straight body she seemed more made for earth and rocks and growing corn than song. Still, her eyes never burned so blue in her weather browned face as when she sang, and the strength of her body grew dwarfed in the strength of her song. During the great revival meetings, hardened sinners, whom words of preachers had failed to frighten or beseech into grace and the life everlasting, would listen to her sing and go begging forgiveness for their sins. Her voice was filled with a something that none could name or explain. One of Quarrelsome Sexton's boys who had joined the church and quit his drinking, gun-carrying ways, described it one night to the early crowd gathered about the stove in Salem Church as they waited for the services to begin. "I heared her sing an' I felt th' eternal damnation of doin' without th' grace of God. I could feel th' wantin' an' th' wishin' an' th' beggin' after in her singin'."

Brother Eli had listened and smiled secretly in his beard, then said with his eyes on the ceiling, "There is no greater strength nor beauty than that of the soul that can dream on of seeing God—after he had learned and knows that he never shall see God."

The Sexton boy frowned in a troubled way. "Brother, you're— not meanin' Delph can't ever get th' spirit. She's a good woman if there ever was. Knocked a gun out a my hand once with a black snake whip, mebbe kept me from killin' a man an' bein' sent up."

Brother Eli studied the ceiling and smiled. "I speak figuratively," he said, "that is in regard to the word, God." He turned and went up to the pulpit, and that night preached his sermon on the parable of the fig tree, the olive, and the bramble.

Delph would only smile when after church many stopped her in the aisles and by the door to praise her song. Mostly she sang in church because it was a pleasant thing to do. She didn't especially care for the admiration of the congregation. They knew nothing of music, and had never heard great song—the kind she heard once in a while over the radio. Mrs. Elliot helped her pick the music from the air, would tell her or maybe come down when there was to be a good program. And they would listen in silence together while the music poured into the room. Sometimes Delph heard voices wonderfully clear and wonderfully strong, and with the hearing there would sometimes come the wonder of what her voice might have done could it have been trained so.

There were programs on Sunday afternoons that both women loved, and it was a grief of their lives that they so seldom could listen to music on Sunday afternoons. Up in the brick house Mr. Elliot either wished to go driving, take a nap, or listen to baseball scores. Mrs. Elliot bought a second radio which she had thought would solve the problem. But after one try at hearing her own radio and Mr. Elliot's below shrieking out baseball scores, she had clapped her hands over her ears and hurried down to Delph.

There, Sadie Huffacre was describing a fight she had seen on the court house lawn in Town, and Delph, rather than desecrate the music by teaming it with a voice like Sadie's, had turned off the radio. When neighbors did not come, Marsh wanted Delph for Sunday afternoons. He liked the Sundays in winter when they went to church and spent the remainder of the day with Dorie, who felt that Sunday was a failure if she had not fed from fifteen to twenty people. But he liked best the Sundays in spring and summer, when he and Delph with Burr-Head could do the things he liked to do, take a long leisurely boat ride on the river, or sit and fish in the shade of the sycamores, or swim and play with Burr-Head, walk up to hill pastures and look at his cattle, wander through the orchard, and in late summer come walking back through the corn fields.

He liked to look at tobacco and clover or see an orchard filled with fruit or bloom, but he thought that none of them could compare with a cornfield in July, when the air was bright with the golden dust of the pollen, and the great plants, twice as tall as he, whispered and rustled and said the things for which he knew no words. The air would be thick with the strong sweet smell of the corn, and on his shoulders and his hands he would see the yellow grains of pollen and the little husks from which they came.

He never liked to take such walks alone; half the pleasure was in having Delph to marvel with him over the corn. Usually she walked with a bundle of red strings in her apron pocket; when they came to a plant that seemed even finer than the others, she or he would tie the bright red string high up as they could reach. Then again in mid September if the stalks they had tied with red had ripened two good ears, long and heavy with their ends pointing toward the earth instead of at the sky, Delph tied on still another string as a reminder to Marsh when he was cutting the corn that such stalks with their ears were to be saved for seed.

Tired from their walks, they would rest a time in the yard or by the river, sometimes all three sprawled side by side with Caesar's nose at Burr-Head's feet, but usually at such times Delph would sit cross legged on the ground, and take the book she had brought and begin to read. Now and then she read to Marsh, when it seemed to her that she had found a bit too good to keep for just herself alone. Marsh would lie with his head in her lap and listen until he would interrupt with questions, eager to know what had happened before and how it would end—or else he fell asleep. And Delph would sigh a bit, not because he fell asleep, but because the exciting stories were the ones on which he fell asleep. She once read him the beginning of a book called *Silas Marner*, one Sunday night during Burr-Head's second winter, and for the next few evenings her mending was neglected and so were his government bulletins while she read aloud to him; and he never seemed to tire of the lanes of Raveloe or the slow talk of the English farmers concerning weather and cows. On Sundays when the weather was unusually bad or the Cumberland high and they could not go to church, Delph did what Fronie and John had done at home, and what many farming families in Westover did on churchless Sundays—read a chapter or so from the

Bible. She liked Revelations or Psalms or the Song of Solomon, but she seldom read those. Marsh liked best to hear of the lives of such men as Jacob, Moses, and Elijah, but his favorite was Job, especially the brief account of his old age—"for he had fourteen thousand sheep, and six thousand camels, and a thousand yoke of oxen, and a thousand she asses. . . . And in all the land were no women found so fair as the daughters of Job . . . . and saw . . . his sons' sons, *even* four generations. So Job died, *being* old and full of days."

She tried him once with poetry, one Sunday afternoon when Burr-Head was between two and three. They were setting by the river, resting in the shade. Delph had a collection of poems, a book that Emma had sent her; for Emma sent or brought her many things, as well as the map of fairyland and that of New York City. She found a poem she had long wanted to have in a book of her own, and because she liked it so, she begged Marsh to listen. He lay with his head in her lap, his hat pulled over his eyes, but not too much but that he could see his fields of corn. Delph read:

> The blessed damozel leaned out
>   From the gold bar of heaven;
> Her eyes were deeper than the depth
>   Of waters stilled at even;
> She had three lilies in her hand,
>   And the stars in her hair were seven.
> Her robe, ungirt from clasp to hem,
>   No wrought flowers did adorn,
> But a white rose of Mary's gift,
>   For service meetly worn;
> Her hair that lay along her back
>   Was yellow like ripe corn.

Marsh shook his head impatiently. "That don't make sense, Delph—a pretty woman's hair th' color of corn."

"But, it says yellow, silly—you know, like gold."

"Oh," he said, and felt uncomfortable, and restless at mention of yellow corn. He would have no yellow corn on his land, not even in the garden for fear that it might mix with and spoil his white.

Delph read a few words more, but stopped when Marsh, his head filled now with thought for nothing but corn, lifted on one elbow and looked out across the fields. "I thought I saw somethin' like smut on that stalk over yonder," he explained and threw a pebble to indicate the direction, then settled back to listen, but he was restless, twisting his head about to get all possible views of the corn.

Delph stopped and studied him. "You don't like it very well—do you?"

He looked up at her and smiled, teasingly from the corners of his eyes. "I can't say that I do," he said, and then was troubled by the disappointment in her eyes and a loneliness that came sometimes when she listened to the radio. "Pshaw, Delph," he comforted, "I'd like it if there was any use, but what in th' hell do I need with poetry anyhow?" and he lay with his head in her lap and looked out at his fields of corn and listened to their whispering.

Delph read again, but silently now, and after a time she let the book slip down on Marsh's head. He never noticed. He was sound asleep like Burr-Head. Caesar alone kept her company, lying with his nose on his paws, and studying her with his great brown eyes.

She sat a time and watched the sleeping ones, then began the tedious business of getting Marsh's head from her lap to the ground without waking him, but he gave a violent snore and then a long drawn "G-e-e-e," that threatened to wake Burr-Head, and caused Caesar to spring up and stand above him wagging his tail. Delph left him as he was, and sat and watched the evening shadow creep over the corn fields.

She had never grown accustomed to the shadows creeping over the bottomlands and plunging her house into a twilight when the afternoon was little more than half gone, and there were times yet when she lifted her head from some work she did and felt the stillness of the valley like some heavy air that choked her as she breathed it. But more and more when the twilight seemed too long and blue and the silence like a ringing in her ears, she would think of the brick house. It would be good to have a kitchen window from which she could see the sun go down, and other windows that looked out over the country.

She smiled a little at her silly, dreaming ways. Shadows and low land could not hurt a body; Burr-Head was healthy as if he lived on a hill. It was the poetry, she guessed, that made her so, twisting and tearing herself apart like that summer after Burr-Head was born. If

she had no books and no radio she could maybe be always contented as the cows and Lizzie Higginbottom.

For the moment she was glad that Marsh slept with his head on
her lap; she could not slip away and listen to the music as she had
meant to do. Sometimes the music she heard seemed like so many
tongues of the world calling to her, begging and crying the way the
wind and the moonlight and the flying leaves had used to do at
home. Not the world of which she read in magazines and papers, or
of the bright new cities in the north built of iron and tin and steel
where the young ones out of the hills went to work in offices and
factories. Since living near Burdine she had known many such who
had gone away; some to good jobs like Dorie's children, others to factories like Vinie; and none of them, she knew, had ever found the
world of which the music cried. The world behind the iron and tin
and steel, the same old world that tempted Azariah and the others
to go on until they died trying to learn the look and the feel of the
land over the next hill—and learning whether or not they could
reach the next hill.

Marsh roused and smiled at her. "That was a fine nap, Delph,
but Lord whyn't you push me off a your knees? I'll bet you're tired-
er than if you'd worked, an' it Sunday."

"I tried it an' you started plowin' th' mules enough to wake Burr-
Head," she said, and they both laughed, and neither noticed when
the hill shadow crawled to Marsh's feet. He was calling her stingy
because she insisted on saving all the money that had come from her
mother. He wanted her to buy a piano—she would like that so, and
Mrs. Elliot had said many times she'd like to teach her to play.

But Delph shook her head. She was saving the money for Burr-
Head's education, she said, and anyway she didn't want furniture—
now. She could not forget the flood. Many nights in winter she saw
the water as she fell asleep, and would lift wildly on one elbow, only
to find Marsh sleeping quietly by her side. There was another reason
why she did not want a piano, though she never spoke of that. Now,
when she went to the brick house she seldom touched the piano
keys as she had used to do, or maybe sit down and try to ripple out
a tune when Mrs. Elliot urged her.

Her hands were so big and brown and strong against the whiteness of the keys; and in their movements they were beginning to be

the hands of a farmer's wife. Their skill now was for washing and cooking and tending things; milking the cows and slopping the hogs when a press of work held Marsh late in the fields, keeping her garden free of weeds, gathering corn on bright fall days when it was more fun to be out in the fields with Marsh than working in the house. When she sang she thought sometimes of her hands; what had gone from them would maybe reach her voice.

Still, she didn't mind. Nobody ever heard Delph Gregory complain, not in nagging, scolding ways. She had a tongue too fiery for simple quarreling. Westover County had never heard a better calling down than she gave Sadie Huffacre the winter Burr-Head was a year old. Sadie had been telling for months that through the previous summer Marsh and Elliot's hired girl Vinie, before she went back to Cincinnati, had had such goings on. She, Sadie, had seen them once by the river and again in Hawthorne Town. Delph got wind of it through some careless remark of Katy's, and the next time she saw Sadie, which happened to be as she was riding to the store, she dismounted then and there and such a talking to as she gave the woman. Sadie had backed herself against the fence across from the store, and looked ready to drop through the ground, and only stuttered like a deaf mute when Delph dared her to say that it was true.

Most agreed that it was a spunky but risky thing for any woman to do. What if Marsh had been seen with Vinie—where there was a lot of smoke there was bound to be a little fire—and Delph would be the laughing stock of the county forever. But worse than that, Sadie would go behind her back and get even sometime or other if it took twenty years. Many wondered what Marsh thought about the business, but as he never mentioned it, and none dared question him, they never knew. In spite of the good going over Delph gave her, Sadie was, in a short time, able to laugh and pity the girl. It was pitiful for any woman to be so trustful of her man; in two months time Sadie was visiting Delph, for it was Sadie's boast that she never held grudges, and no one could make her mad for long—certainly not a young triggery-tempered thing like Delph Gregory.

The matter was forgotten more quickly than such matters generally were. The southern end of Westover County had plenty else of which to talk. The building and opening of a mighty flood proof steel and concrete bridge across the Cumberland, approached on the

Burdine side by a mile long sixty foot embankment and on the other by a tunnel through the river bluff, consumed no end of talk. The papers were filled with wars and rumors of wars, but mostly in countries that seemed far away as Mars. There was blacker trouble in the Harlan mines; tales were constantly coming from the rough unsettled Rockcastle country of hill men fled there from their deeds in the mining counties to the east. There was more talk of Roan Sandusky; every year more farmers came to consult with him on this and that. Not that he knew any more than he had ever known, but he had at Dorie's insistence and Emma's suggestion started a publicity campaign the year the prices went to the bottom. Roan and Emma and Poke Easy looked up all their friends and college acquaintances doing newspaper work in Kentucky, and since some of Roan's work was well worth writing about, articles with pictures of chickens, fruit trees, newly forested hill sides, members of 4-H clubs began to appear from time to time in various papers.

And since the pictures and the printed words impressed many people, especially the back hill men, a great deal more than their reality in the county had ever done, they for the first time in their lives saw lanky, tobacco-chewing Roan Sandusky as an important man, one with brains. His importance was multiplied when state and federal funds made it possible for him to have two assistants; one, a tall young man from Georgia, an expert in animal husbandry, an expert rifleman, and a man who feared neither the devil nor irate hill farmers when he insisted on inoculating their hogs for cholera or shooting their cows for TB—and so got along amazingly well. The other, however, was the one who gave Roan's office dignity, importance, and prestige. She was a tall girl with beautiful blond hair, beautiful eyes and a beautiful smile. There were women over the county who sniffed and said she put every cent she made on her back, and it was gossiped that even though Roan had found her in a big place like Louisville, she'd been raised in the backwoods of Wolf County where there were neither trains, busses, nor telephones, but the women's talk never troubled the men. Young Cow-Lick Meece from the other side of Kettle Pot Ridge, during the first month of her stay took twelve bulletins, one for each of the three separate trips he made on four consecutive Saturdays. Others of the young back hill men were little better and marveled continually how it was that a woman who looked as if she belonged in Hollywood had come to work in Roan Sandusky's dingy office.

And Roan sat sometimes with his heels on his desk and his head on his hands as old Reuben Kidd sat, and dreamed of the day when there would be no cholera or TB in hogs and cattle, or rickets in children, or pellagra in the old, or neglect of the trees; and when the people would grow grapes and drink wine instead of so much whiskey—and it such bad stuff at that. He talked sometimes of such things to Poke Easy and Marsh, and Marsh would listen and plan some day to be a member of the county board of education. More and more as Burr-Head grew he thought of the children he saw when some trading expedition or other business took him to the back hills; thin, bare-footed children with shoulder blades like wings hoeing corn on steep hillside fields that were never meant to grow corn. The children ought to be in school learning what ought to grow in place of corn, learning that life for a poor hill farmer could many times be made better than that of a factory worker in the north—especially when times were hard and work was slack.

Then work and Delph and the busy life about him would whirl his thoughts away. Elections reaped their annual harvests of bitter quarrels with some few deaths, and the great revival meetings coming shortly after saved the souls and restored to grace the ones left alive. And David Jonathan Fairchild saved many from the jail or penitentiary. Old timers like Reuben Kidd, listening to his nimble tongue, would nod and smile and say he was his grandfather through and through.

Already there was talk that, though young as he was and a bachelor, he should be the next county judge. Men still like to talk of his first case—three young negro boys, sons of a friend of Sober's down the river, had been caught red handed at midnight twenty yards from a farmer's smokehouse with six fat plymouth rock pullets in their hands. The prosecuting attorney as well as the jury had nodded and dozed while the witnesses testified; the men were guilty plain as day. When Poke Easy finished cross examining the witnesses, and building his plea of not guilty, even the young negroes themselves were certain of their innocence.

Still, the case of the young negroes was an easy matter. They were young; it was their first offense; chickens were cheap, and one of the negroes was as good a fiddler as there was in the county, and anyway the jail was crowded. Such had been the talk of most men when they learned that Poke Easy had taken the case of High Pockets Armstrong. The middle aged hill man had already killed two other men—back in his young days when he was hot-headed and wild. On one occasion he had been freed on the grounds of self defense, and on the other he had been sent up for eleven years, but it happened that then the penitentiary was crowded—Westover had its share and more—and the governor was just leaving office and so pardoned a lot of men the way they generally did, and High Pockets' pardon came while he was home snaking up logs to last his wife for firewood.

But this time it looked as if he'd be bound to go for life. Sadie Huffacre, as usual, was the first to get wind of the trouble. She came back from Hawthorne Town one day, telling of how High Pockets' oldest girl and her baby had come home from Cincinnati where she had gone two years back when she was sixteen. She had married soon after, and now she was home with her baby. She, Sadie, had seen them get off the bus, and the girl was pale and thin, not pretty and plump as she had been when she went away. Sadie had whispered the rest. She, Sadie, had walked right up to her. She had wanted to see the baby, learn if it were sickly looking, too. There was something red like a bad rash on its face, but Lord God that was nothing to what else she saw. There it lay on Lutie's arm with its brown eyes wide—the prettiest eyes—but Lord God they never moved or showed a sign of life when the sun came right on its face.

She'd looked at Lutie, but Lutie had said never a word, just turned and walked away, but Sadie could tell from the look of her that she knew she had a blind baby. And Sadie wondered if the girl knew what ailed her child. It only went to show that anything was liable to happen when a girl went to strange places and married a strange man she'd hardly known a month.

What happened next was common knowledge to Westover County. High Pockets had, on seeing his daughter and grandchild, left home and walked into Town sometime about midnight, aiming to catch the early morning train for Cincinnati. Men who saw the gun in his shirt and the shine of his eyes, knew where he was headed, and hinted that doing a thing in Westover was one thing—but doing it in Cincinnati was another. High Pockets thought it over and went back home.

About two weeks later on a warm rainy day in August while Marsh was looking over his cut tobacco for sign of pole sweat, Poke Easy came as he often did to talk of this or that. Not long after Caesar barked again, and Marsh went to the barn door to see who it might be. He saw soon coming up through the corn a tall thin man dressed in the usual blue shirt and overalls. He walked with the long free stride of a hill man, only more slowly than most as if he were tired or old. He carried a long hickory staff, and sometimes he would stop and stand with both hands on the stick, resting and just looking overhead at the corn, the heavy ears sometimes higher than the brim of his black felt hat. Marsh studied him, but when Caesar stopped his growling and ran to him with wagging tail, he called to Poke Easy, "What do you reckin High Pockets Armstrong is wantin' with me?"

At mention of the name, Poke Easy swore, mopped his face, and looked as if be would like to run away. "He wants me," he said, and came and waited with Marsh in the door while High Pockets came up through the corn.

High Pockets shook hands, gave each a brief "Howdy," then pulled out his jackknife, and began cutting the pattern of the twisted plaits on the bark of the hickory stick he carried. Poke Easy watched him uneasily, and Marsh hinted that he thought he'd better go see if Delph had anything she wanted him to do about the house. High Pockets hunkered on his heels in a stable door, and looked up at him with his sky-blue eyes, made bluer still by a week's growth of black whiskers and black bushy brows. "You needn't be runnin' away," he said. "My business it's no secret." He made a clean narrow notch in the hickory stick, then blew on his knife and whetted it slowly up and down one long lean thigh, looking fixedly at Poke Easy as he did so. "I reckin you know th' trouble that's overtook some a mine—bad trouble th' law cain't tetch."

Poke Easy nodded. High Pockets cut another notch in the twisted plait then said in his drawling gentle voice, "An' I reckin you know what th' Bible says. 'An' eye fer an' eye an' a tooth fer a tooth.'"

Poke Easy cleared his throat. "'Blessed are the merciful for they shall obtain mercy.' Christ said that. Recollect, High Pockets?"

The hill man's eyes made Marsh think of the blue stained glass in the windows of Salem Church. It was hard to think they were part of a living man, when he sat and stared straight ahead seeing nothing as he said, "I'd ruther burn in Hell till God goes blind than ask fer mercy in a case like this.—You can go so far with Jesus but not all th' way—an' when it comes to a toss up 'tween th' two I'll take God all th' time." He turned to Marsh. "Ain't that what you say? You look like a man that wouldn't let be done to yours what's been done to mine."

Marsh pondered and shifted uneasily from one foot to the other. "I think I'd try to keep mine by me so nothin' would happen t'em," he said.

"But if'n it did happen," High Pockets insisted, and bent forward and peered at him from under his hat brim.

"Aye, Lord, I don't like to think on it," Marsh said, and saw the hurt and the trouble in the old man's eyes, and pitied him.

High Pockets got up and stood whittling a time in silence before he nodded toward Poke Easy and said with his eyes on his jackknife, "I want ye fer my lawyer."

Poke Easy flushed and stared at the floor. "I appreciate your opinion of me, High Pockets, but—well—recollect this, that—well— I don't know what you've got on your mind, but in some places—for doin' some things—neither God nor I could keep you from goin' up for life—or worse."

High Pockets cut another notch and studied it as he said, "Don't be worryin' over that—I had Lutie write him a letter—invitin' him down—she didn't know, pore child. Saturday it'll be—he's a comin' with a truck—one he'll borrie to take her back in an' th' load a taters an' such I offered him—to come."

Poke Easy swallowed, and Marsh felt as if cold water were poured on his head. Neither spoke when High Pockets folded his knife, dropped it into his pocket and turned to the door. "I thought you'd mebbe like to be thinkin' on it," he said with a nod toward Poke Easy, and started down the lane.

He was half way to the road gate before Marsh remembered his duties as host and hurried after him. He begged him to stay for dinner, but High Pockets only smiled and shook his head. "Aye, I think I'd ruther walk about a bit in th' rain," he said, "an' then I'll flag a ride into Town an' walk on in home." He hesitated a moment, and then with the air of a child asking permission for some precious thing, asked, "I wonder would you mind if I walked about through your corn field?"

"Nothin' could please me better," Marsh said, and High Pockets smiled and said with his eyes on Poke Easy who had followed them, "It's might nigh th' prettiest piece a corn I ever seed—an' well—my days a walkin' through fields a high growin' corn in th' rain are mebbe about over—fer all I know."

The two men stood in silence and watched him walk down between the rows of corn. Marsh turned suddenly away with a something like a sickness clawing through his body. "God, it would be awful to be shut up—like he'll most likely be. Never so much as get a smell a th' rain—not even see th' sky."

Poke Easy nodded and looked after him. "It would be hell—an' for me, too," he said.

The days passed and many times Marsh while he worked or ate or played with Burr-Head would feel that coldness in his hair or sickness in his body and think of High Pockets, the blind baby, the sick girl, and the man who was to visit them. Later, he wondered if the young man ever knew why it was that when he drove into the garage back of the bus depot late on Saturday afternoon and waited there for High Pockets, so many came to look at him. Marsh did not go to Town that day; but others said that the man was young, hardly more than a boy, slim built with curly hair and shiny brown eyes like the blind eyes of his child, a pleasant-dispositioned man who smiled at a hill woman staring at him and asked her how old was the baby in her arms.

High Pockets came to meet him about the time of sundown and the streets were crowded with those who watched them drive away. No one ever knew exactly; some said one place and some another, but most seemed to think that it was at that little swag in the Rockcastle Road just before it turns up Honeysuckle Ridge that High Pockets choked him to death and broke his neck. It couldn't have been so very far out; for it was only a few hours until High Pockets came driving back with his son-in-law's body stretched neat and straight in the truck. Some said, though it was maybe mostly gossip, that though it was near midnight by then Estil Dick the high sheriff waited in his office and Cliff New the undertaker in his.

That year the date of the fiddlers' contest was moved from late October to mid September. High Pockets' trial was scheduled for the next meeting of circuit court, late in September, and he was one of the best fiddlers in the county. He won the prize that year; men said that they had never seen him fiddle so, from his head and from his shoulder with his fiddle talking like a live thing.

It was pretty well agreed that it was the last contest he'd ever see; the betting odds throughout the county were five to two that he'd be sent up, at least for twenty years. In the whole county twelve men could not be found for a jury who didn't know that High Pockets only did what he set out to do—still everybody felt that it was safer to have the trial in Westover. He'd have a better chance there than any place else. And all pitied Poke Easy, especially the older lawyers. They'd hate to be in his shoes, they said.

On the day of the trial Hawthorne Town was packed with people. Men sat in the courthouse windows, lined the walls and overflowed to the stairs and the upper outside platform. Poke Easy came looking more like a farmer than a lawyer, strolling in a little bit late, as if maybe he had just decided to come. It took the prosecuting attorney less than half an hour to prove High Pockets guilty of murder in the first degree, and the prisoner himself helped matters little by nodding over his whittling as he listened to the witnesses and thereby declared that they spoke the truth.

Poke Easy had no witnesses for the defense, so he called on God. Before he had finished the eternally just but never compassionate God the hill men knew was sitting in the room, and High Pockets had grown from a murderer and law breaker to a man who fearlessly carried out the word of God—because the laws of the land failed to do so.

The jury was out about fifteen minutes, and there was little tension in the room when they returned to read a verdict of killing in self defense. Marsh heard the verdict, and felt a burden lifted from his mind. It had hurt somehow to think of High Pockets never again walking down through his corn rows in the rain. And he was one of the many men who overflowed the saloons that day and drank to

Poke Easy's future as a great lawyer and to High Pockets who had upheld the laws by which Kentuckians in the old days had lived.

Many in Westover County wondered what would become of the sickly girl Lutie and her blind child. The girl died around Christmas time—of grief some said—but hardly a year had gone before High Pockets was bragging around about the way that grandchild of his loved fiddle tunes. Marsh saw him in Town one day, the summer Burr-Head was between three and four, and High Pockets was telling of how he had to fiddle him to sleep each night.

Then High Pockets put away talk of family matters to ask Marsh how were his crops and his calves—a question many asked Marsh Gregory that summer. More than two years back Marsh had taken John's advice and kept his cows and bought more calves. He'd make little money on the business, but he might as well grow corn on his corn land and clover and alfalfa on his pasture as sit still and wonder when he'd see another bit of cash.

So it was that he had continued to grow corn, and when there was a big-boned calf for sale, he had managed by hook and by crook to get it. There was one, a blaze faced Holstein steer he'd got from Wiley Davis for two gallons of honey; there was the clay colored steer he'd bought when it was three weeks old for a bushel of cow peas; there were Herefords he had swapped for chickens, and Green River Jerseys he got with tobacco plants; some he had taken in exchange for work with his mules or such, and several he had swapped for cider that fall the apple crop was good. The calves grew and fattened on the fine pasture he had, the clover and alfalfa hay, and the corn.

Now and then Perce or Roan or Poke Easy chaffed him about his calves. Fine as they were they'd hardly pay their way to market. And Marsh smiled, called them his manure-spreaders, said they were improving his pasture fields, and let it go at that. What happened came on so gradually that he sorrowed a bit because he had had no great moment of triumph such as he had felt when it rained on his first corn crop.

He heard men talk in Hawthorne, say that cattle and corn were going higher, read in the paper of short crop predictions and dry seasons, listened to such talk over the radio, and went on buying a calf when he could get it cheap enough.

By early June, though there was little sign of a drought in Westover, the talk was that in Iowa and Kansas and other corn growing states corn as well as hogs and cattle would be scarce that year. And so it was that in early August—between Burr-Head's third and fourth birthdays—Marsh sold fourteen hundred bushels of his last year's corn at a dollar-fifty on the bushel, and in October when some of the young Holstein steers he had bought almost three years ago tipped the scales at better than a thousand pounds, he sold fifty-three head of cattle at slightly less than five thousand dollars. Though he had by mid July begun to feel the teeth of the drought, he pulled his cattle through on the hay crop he had harvested earlier in the season, and in the lower fields there was the promise of at least a two-thirds yield of corn—and by October corn was a dollar-sixty on the bushel.

There were many nights that fall that he and Delph sat late into the night figuring and studying price reports and predictions. In the Little South Fork country straying over Delph's timber lands were close to two hundred head of hogs. The problem was whether he should leave the hogs to winter on the mast and sell his corn, and sell the hogs next fall, or drive them in, fatten them on corn and sell them through the winter—for hogs were so high that few farmers killed any that fall.

In the end John decided the matter for him. He wrote to say that with hogs the price they were, it was maybe not best to leave them all winter in the woods, and already he had heard of a gang up from Tennessee changing the ear marks on some and driving them across the border. Marsh went for his hogs without delay, and men who saw him pass on his return trip said it was like the old days when the hog drovers went to Georgia.

In the end the hogs brought more than the cattle, and the whole of Westover County talked of Marsh Gregory's luck, and some of the hill people wondered in what sign the moon had stood when he was born. He'd been lucky through bad seasons and high prices, through a flood, held on through good seasons and no prices, and now he had stumbled into some cash. Yet, for all their wonder of his luck there were but few who failed to say that he deserved it. Any man who had shown the toughness he had shown deserved whatever he could get.

All through the fall Marsh felt the bedrock of his dreams firm and sure under his feet like the limestone below his land, for his dreams were never airy things like mare's tails in the sky. He could have paid off the mortgage that year, and might have done so, hard up as he was for many things, had not old Silas Copenhaver, chief owner of the bank, objected. With the way things were the bank was having a time finding investments for what money it had; in fact they'd be glad to double the mortgage on his farm in case he wanted a lot of cash for something—say buy up several thousand acres of hill land at less than a dollar on the acre. That would be a good investment. But Marsh shook his head, and agreed to pay within three thousand dollars of the end.

It seemed then that the winter evenings he and Delph spent together were the best he had ever known. They spent hours over nursery catalogues and farm machinery catalogues, and Sears Roebuck, and book catalogues that Delph had ordered. He needed fence and more machinery and another barn for his overflowing produce. He needed tile to drain that swaggy bit of bottom land, and he would like to buy about five hundred grape vines and set them on the far side of the pasture above the creek. He would like to have a real bathroom instead of the makeshift he had made at the back of the house. He would like a registered Poland China brood cow, and he would like a pony for Burr-Head. He wanted to buy Delph an Encyclopedia; she was always wishing for one, and there was a book he wanted for himself, but it cost more than twenty dollars—a history of thorough bred horses printed in England.

Burr-Head, sitting on the floor between them, would hear their eager talk and plans and feeling jealous and shut away, would get up and run to the map of New York City and beg for a story from Delph. He was almost four years old now, a slender child with cinnamon colored curls, that curled still when Marsh kept them cut short as any boy's. His wide gray eyes and his straight back were his father's and no mistaking, but there was a tilt to his head that came only from Delph.

Marsh would listen in silence while Delph told him a story of some place that seemed a mixture of heaven and fairyland; it irked him sometimes that Burr-Head loved the map of New York City better than that of fairyland, but mostly he laughed and didn't care.

Burr-Head cared for neither when he had the Sears Roebuck farm machinery catalog with its pictures of farming tools and horses or better yet a seed catalog with its unbelievably red tomatoes and great ears of yellow corn—that is when Delph was not around to tell him stories.

Though Marsh was held by all to be a modest man who, when others praised his crops or cattle, was apt to look uncomfortable and say that his success was mostly from a good wife and good land, it was hinted by some that anybody could get on his good side by a few words of praise for Burr-Head. Sadie Huffacre was constantly lamenting the fact that the Gregorys were so slow about having another child, Burr-Head would be rotten spoiled if they didn't look out.

It was disgraceful the way they showed him off and let him learn so many little verses and such; he would most likely die with water on his brain before he was ten years old. Still, on the Christmas before he was four years old, even Sadie had to admit that, though he was too little to be in any kind of program, he did uncommon well for a four-year-old child, to stand up before so many people and sing the Christmas song of the little black lamb that would be white.

But it was disgraceful the way Delph and Marsh and Dorie and Katy, home from college in Lexington, had carried on over him—and Mrs. Elliot, too. It was all foolishness. She, Sadie had only given him a red candy rooster from the ten cents store, but he came and thanked her so sweet like; she thought she'd give him a chocolate rabbit for Easter.

· 23 ·

THE MEMORY of Christmas Eve at school and the song he sang was for a time sharp in Burr-Head's mind, painted in clear bright colors like the pictures of God and Moses on the cards he received at Salem Sunday School. Then the picture was gone, crowded out and smothered away by the myriad events of his life on the farm. It seemed sometimes that he stood on a high hill, high as the knoll in the pasture by Solomon's pen, and from that hill he could look back and see his babyhood days. Many times when Delph spoke to him of taking naps or such he laughed and showed his squirrel like teeth and cried, "Pshaw, Delph, I'm not a baby anymore."

And Delph would look at him and smile and say maybe, "But even big boys like you take naps sometimes, Burr-Head," or some such thing.

But he would go laughing away, swaggering in stiff many-pocketed overalls exactly like his father's even to the Indian heads on the copper buttons and the strong smell of new cloth and dye. He would go stamping his feet so that the iron cleats on his heavy cow hide shoes might ring the way his father's rang. He had been proud as a king's son dressed in his father's robes, the night Marsh brought his first real cow hide farmer's shoes from Hawthorne Town, put together with many a copper rivet, strong leather loops in back, steel hooks for string instead of foolish holes. He had gone clumping over the house, and that night he sat upright fighting sleep and nodding by the fire, determined to put off the time of parting with his shoes.

Sleep had conquered him shoes and all. He had awakened to find himself in his father's arms with his mother walking beside them with the lamp in her hand. He had looked up to see the lamps; the one in her hands and the two reflected in her eyes, then fallen asleep again, powerless to fight for the privilege of sleeping with his shoes.

Maybe he knew that with such shoes he could never be a baby anymore, or maybe because spring came on with a rush that year and he must be out helping his father plow the corn ground, but whatever it was it seemed that when he had marched up that high hill of his memory, the two lamps he saw that night seemed the last things he saw in his mother's eyes. He had seen so many other things in Delph's eyes, had learned to look at them and study their lights and shadows because the slow glance of his father often went hunting there as it hunted in the sky. But now he was too big to sit in her lap, and gradually the memory of lying in her arms and seeing himself in her eyes, of watching them change like the river from blue to gray and back again, of seeing them laugh and leap and quiver the way the high hill clover fields lightened and darkened when clouds raced under an April sun, grew dim.

His world was high and deep and wide, too great to be centered in his mother's eyes. He was no longer a baby to stay playing in the yard. He must be out with Marsh, take a hand in the turning of the corn ground, sometimes riding Ruthie Ann who seemed old and gentle now. He must be squinting at the sun from under his hat brim, wiping his hat with a great red bandanna, must always be on hand to shove his hands into his pockets, clear his throat loudly and answer, "Yes Siree, Marsh," when his father said, "Burr-Head, reckin we'll make a hundred bushel to th' acre this year?"

When Delph came with a quart of milk for Marsh, a pint for Burr-Head and stacks of meat and cornbread he must be on hand to eat and drink and say to Delph, "Look at th' corn ground we've turned."

Delph would answer, "You're makin' out fine, Burr-Head." When Marsh had gone back to the plowing she and Burr-Head would linger a moment together. She would maybe say, "You're all sweaty an' covered with dirt, Burr-Head. Don't you want to come in an' be cleaned up?" or "Burr-Head wouldn't you like to play in th' yard by me a little while? I'd turn on th' radio."

Mostly he would answer with a toss of his sweat dampened curls, "Pshaw, Delph, I can't leave th' plowin'," and go running after his father.

Delph would sometimes follow a step or so but stop when he went running on. She would turn then and go back, more slowly than she had come, and sometimes Burr-Head would turn to find her standing still a distance down the corn rows, just looking after him. Other times, if the press of her house and garden work were not too great, she would tempt him past his strength, "Come in out a th' hot sun, Burr-Head, an' I'll tell you a story."

They would go together then into the living room and sit in the cool green light that filtered through the morning glory vines. They would sit in front of the empty fireplace with the maps that Emma had sent before them on the wall. While Delph talked Burr-Head was still, looking sometimes at the maps on the wall, but most often into his mother's eyes, talking eyes they were, where all the stories seemed to move and live. In her eyes he saw the sea and ships, finer than the pictures she showed him in books and magazines, and there were cities he could hardly see, bigger and finer, more wonderful than heaven and Hawthorne Town together.

He would listen with round shining eyes, sigh with happiness when a story was done, and whisper, "An' is it true like you say, Delph? I'll go there some day?"

She would nod and study him and smile. "Aye, Burr-Head, you'll go. You'll do an' see a lot of things before you die.—You'll go to a college like th' one where Katy's goin' now—an' you'll learn so many things, how to be a great doctor or a chemist like Sam, or maybe an engineer like that Sloan boy from Salem."

Burr-Head always forgot just what was an engineer, and would smile and say, "An' when I come down th' Greenwood down grade I'll play 'Jesus Lover of My Soul' on th' whistles th' way that Sil Marcum does."

Delph would answer in patient explanation, "No, no, Burr-Head, not that kind of an engineer. Recollect I told you, one like th' Fitzgerald boy from Burdine.—He's laid out bridges and railroads all over th' world."

Burr-Head would remember again, and his eyes would darken and quiver with dreams. It would be wonderful to run a railroad train and make the whistles sing, but building bridges like the Fitzgerald man was a stranger more wonderful thing. He knew because Delph said it was.

When Delph had no more time for stories he would go running away, sometimes back to his father, but often calling Caesar for a voyage of discovery. They would go sometimes by the river, and sit in Marsh's flat bottomed skiff. They would sail under the trailing willow trees past the sycamores, down through the crooks and the bends of the Cumberland, down to the Mississippi. And down the Mississippi they would go, seeing cotton fields on either side, just as Delph had said, and past the Mississippi lay the ocean. It was endless and forever changing like the sky, so Delph had said. Sometimes storms rocked the boat, and he and Caesar were hard put to escape with their lives.

One hot afternoon in July they were overcome by wild black savages found on islands in the ocean as Delph had said. Burr-Head escaped with nothing but his skin and shoes, and ran pure naked and screaming for help. But at his backyard fence he thought he heard voices and peeped through a screen of hollyhocks, and saw Mrs. Sadie Huffacre stringing beans and talking with Delph under the shade of the box elder tree. The fear of being caught without his clothes grew suddenly greater than his fear of the savages, but the path through the corn to the river stretched long and hot for him to go naked, his return unhastened by wild black men at his heels. So he slipped to the barn and found an old jumper of his father's in which he walked sedately past Delph and the visitor. The woman had looked at him through the holes in the jumper with her lips pinching tight together, but Delph had only smiled to see him go marching by without his clothes.

"You'll have to tighten up on him one a these days," he heard the woman say, and then his mother answering. "I had enough of tight raisin' when I was growin' up without passin' it on to my own," she said. And Burr-Head was glad she never talked to him and Marsh in such a low hard voice.

Delph, he knew, was mad at the woman, not at him. So a few days later when he went up to the school with his father to see that Ezrie and the children were all in proper order, and Violie, least of the Huffacre girls, slipped around the house corner at recess and teased him with a crooked finger and a, "Shamie, shamie, I've heard Burr-Head Gregory goes without his clothes," he smiled at her and cried, "Look out for Solomon. He's a bad wild bull," and ran with a mighty roar and butted her hard in the stomach. She lay a moment and looked at the sky, too surprised to cry, and then she wailed with a mighty screeching that brought Ezrie with Marsh and half the school on the run. "Who hit her?" Ezrie asked in his big slow voice.

"Nobody. Solomon butted her," Burr-Head said, and smiled at Perce's Little Lizzie, ten years old and Burr-Head's sweet heart.

Little Lizzie smiled back, then switched her braids and caught Ezrie's sleeve, for she was a good little girl, never afraid of the teacher. "She said Burr-Head went around naked an' made a 'nawful face an crooked her finger, th' great big thing on little Burr-Head," Little Lizzie said, and Burr-Head felt himself growing tall in the children's eyes. He had vanquished a foe, much larger than he and older.

But as he and Marsh were going home he grew small again, felt like Sexton's new baby that blubbered and cried. His father said a few words about boys who fought girls, even when the girls were big and strong. He walked slower and slower, lagging behind his father and looking at the ground, and when Marsh turned about to see the effect of his sober, halting words there was no Burr-Head, only Caesar looking mournful.

Marsh glanced among the lock thick cedar trees by the road, called once, and when there was no answer walked on. Caesar watched him out of sight, and then went sniffing among the little cedar trees until he found Burr-Head weeping belly downward under one. Caesar licked his neck until Burr-Head lifted his head, and then he licked his cheeks and chin. They went then to their favorite spot, the top of a high sheer crag above the road where Marsh had forbidden them to go. The top was thickly screened by cedar trees, and mock orange bush, so that they could sit there and look over the country and down to the Cumberland with no danger of discovery. They sat a time and watched the river and Aunt Dorie's house on the next hill, but mostly they looked at the sky.

It was filled with high white flying clouds, and Burr-Head knew the reason; it was Saturday in heaven and the clouds were going to the county seat market town driving white sheep and white cows and white hogs to the city he could not see. But it was there. He knew: Aunt Dorie had taught him the days of the week in heaven, told him of the country there. When the sky was still and deep without one single fleck of cloud, it was Sunday then in heaven with the clouds all gone to church.

Burr-Head studied the sky and wrinkled his brows over heaven as he did sometimes in Sunday School when Delph taught his class and talked of heaven. He saw it then; bright like Hawthorne Town on Christmas Eve, and flashing with red and golden light like the brick house windows when the sun went down. The streets there were made of gold and all day long the people sang the way his mother sang, and no one there was ever sleepy or tired or in pain.

Still, that heaven for all its beauty and Delph's delight in it was empty and cold against that other heaven he had found one day. It was last year he thought summer when he had found it, the summer before he sang that Christmas song at school. He had gone visiting Mrs. Elliot, all dressed up in a red tie exactly the color of one Marsh had, and a new blue shirt and blue overalls exactly like Marsh's. He had stayed with Mrs. Elliot, picking out first one note and then another on her piano, and then he had heard the children come shouting out of the school house for morning recess, and he had wanted Little Lizzie to see him in his new red tie.

Mrs. Elliot had taken him to school in search of Little Lizzie. But she was not playing lady visitor in the playhouses with the other little girls or jumping rope. They found her in a fence corner with her head against a post crying and crying. Ezrie stood behind her and shifted from one big foot to the other, and three of her brothers leaned on the fence and looked sad. "Captain Harlan died last night," one of her brothers said to Mrs. Elliot, and another one patted Little Lizzie on the shoulder and said, "Ah, honey don't cry over that little runty speckled pig. He'd never ha been any good anyhow."

But Little Lizzie had cried on and Burr-Head had sat on the ground and cried, until Mrs. Elliot said she thought she'd better take him to his father working at pitching up hay in an upper field. Little Lizzie came along, for she wasn't any good in school, crying the way she was.

They found Marsh all in a lather of sweat and mad because his pitch fork was loose on its handle. It was a good thing Caesar ran before them or Mrs. Elliot and Little Lizzie would have caught him swearing, but as it was he only mopped his face and grunted when they came up. Burr-Head ran to him and caught his knees and wept like a river and Little Lizzie ran and caught his arm and began crying all over again, and Mrs. Elliot sounded none too happy when she told him of Captain Harlan, the speckled runty pig.

Marsh had stood and studied them and stroked his three days growth of beard. "Was he a well behaved pig?" he asked Little Lizzie.

"Better than all th' others," Little Lizzie sobbed. "He was never big enough or strong enough to be much mean. An' when I'd scratch him on th' side he'd lay down an' bat his eyes an' now—," but she fell into such a fit of weeping she couldn't even talk.

"You'd ought to be ashamed, you two," Marsh had said, "cryin' over a good little pig that's gone to heaven."

Burr-Head lifted his head and studied him, and when Marsh nodded slowly and Mrs. Elliot nodded, he knew that he had heard the truth. Marsh wiped his neck and slung more sweat from his forehead, then looked out over the little mounds of clover that he was raking into big ones. "Your little pig's in clover now," he said, "an' when he sickens a clover all he has to do is walk into a cornfield an' help himself to corn. An' Lord such corn as there is in heaven, sixteen feet tall with th' ears so heavy they fall right off for little pigs."

Little Lizzie had dried her eyes and Burr-Head laughed, and they all followed Marsh when he took a short cut over the hill, then back through the cornfields to the tool house to get his pitch fork fixed. Mrs. Elliot came with them, and they all walked together, each going down a row of corn. The first of the silks were showing, pale green and fine like bundles of silk, and overhead the wide plumed tassels waved. They came to a place where Delph had planted crenshaws and pumpkins, and their wide yellow flowers were bright through the field. Mrs. Elliot stopped and pondered with her chin caught between her thumb and finger, and then she turned to Marsh. "I guess Captain Harlan is in a place something like this, don't you think?"

Marsh considered and pushed back his hat. "A good bit like this," he finally decided. "Of course no man on earth can grow such corn as grows in heaven, an' there th' punkin flowers are wide across as my two hands, an' th' punkins—Lord, th' angels that wrestled with Jacob can hardly lift 'em. An' of course up there," he went on after a time while he stood swinging Little Lizzie's hand, "th' fields are all divided differ'nt. It's like this—this field where we're standin' now, it's summer, th' corn's too green for a little pig. Well, next to th' summer there's another one—different with th' corn hardly shoe top high. That's spring—not good for a little pig either. He goes on, a twistin' his tail an' a squealin'. He's hungry now. Th' next field he comes to, th' corn's all cut, Just th' fodder shocks, nothin' in that field but th' angels' cows. But he runs on—he can smell it now an' he goes a gruntin'. Pretty soon he comes to a field where it's fall. Th' angels are cuttin' corn—th' highest stalks an' th' biggest, whitest ears. They throw down one for him, an' he starts eatin' away. His sides get bigger an' bigger. He don't squeal anymore. He just grunts once in a while an' bats his eyes—an' then he goes back to a clover field—white clover with th' blossoms big as th' red that grows here—an' he goes to sleep—for he picked a clover field in spring.— Now, Lizzie, I'll bet you're ashamed you cried."

And Little Lizzie smiled and Burr-Head laughed and Mrs. Elliot looked at Marsh until she caught his glance. They smiled and their eyes were like hands touching across the heads of the children.

They all went on together and found Delph busy with dinner getting in the kitchen. Burr-Head never knew the reason or maybe there was none, but for some cause he did not talk that heaven over with Delph as he did most things.

Now as he stood on the limestone ledge he thought of that heaven for a time and smiled on Captain Harlan, but soon the sky glimmered in his eyes and he was tired of searching. He went hunting then until he found a long straight stick. He took the stick and laid it on his shoulder, and then he found a large shag bark hickory leaf and laid it on his head.

He crept stealthily back to the high rock until the toes of his brogan shoes were over the edge. He could look down and see his mother working in the garden, while in the farther field his father and the mules looked small in the waist high corn. "Indians," he whispered to Caesar, and dropped on his stomach and drew his gun, first rolling a pebble down its side for the shot that he knew had gone into the old gun in the attic, as Delph had said. He was not Burr-Head but Azariah, six feet four inches tall in fox skin cap with the tail dangling wide between his shoulders and his deer-skin hunting shirt down to his knees, and he was ready to kill the Indians, the bear and the deer and the panthers creeping up on him from all directions.

When he had killed his fill of game and explored the country from all angles he was suddenly conscience stricken by his lazy good-for-nothing ways. The hill shadow would soon be touching the river, and he had not helped Marsh with the plowing since noon.

Through the summer he decided he would rather work with Marsh than play, especially during the hay making when there was such a deal of riding to be done, and Sober Creekmore, 'black pappie,' came to help. The hay that year was bountiful and hay making was a busy time. Many were the nights that Marsh and Burr-Head did the barnwork after sundown and came to the back kitchen porch tired and hungry with Burr-Head walking proudly in front of his father, always the first to push his hat back, sling imaginary sweat from his forehead with the back of one hand and say like his father, "Lord, I'm hungry. Supper ready, Delph?"

The meal would be scarcely finished before he would be nodding, fighting the one great enemy of his days—sleep, like a monster always lying in wait for him, sneaking up to grab him at the most unhandy times and places. He liked to sleep in church, but while driving home in the wagon from Hawthorne Town or when visiting Mrs. Elliot, and especially after supper, at such times sleep was a thief stealing great chunks out of his life.

It was fun to run barefooted in the dewy grass, chase hop toads and fireflies and answer the whip-poor-wills calling from the river hill. He wanted to hear the katy-dids sing, and sit with Marsh and Delph on the front porch stops in the cool of the evening and listen to their talk. He would sit sometimes in the early summer darkness, and see them close together, the white blur of their faces and the darker blur of their hands. Delph sitting with her arms about her drawn up knees, and Marsh near her on the step below. And it seemed to Burr-Head that on nights like that when they sat together their voices were softer then, and they seemed different from the busy daytime Marsh and Delph.

But he seldom heard their talk and Delph's low laughter. Most always in summer he fell asleep, usually on the grass under the box elder tree, though one hot sultry night he was awakened by his father's half-glad, half-angry curses, and his mother's hugs and tears to learn that he was in the spring house. They might have gone hunting him all night had not Caesar gone sniffing at the door. Marsh had given him something of a lecture for scaring Delph so, and though Burr-Head knew enough not to sass his father, he felt that sleep was the guilty one, not he. He had slipped into the cool dark place to hear the little bull frogs talk among themselves, but he was scarcely settled before sleep snatched him away.

There were so many things to learn and do and see that naps in the day time grew to be an ever more irksome business. He always awakened cross and hungry with a suspiciously angry feeling that somebody had done something or something had happened while he was away. Once he missed a thunder storm, slept right through the thunder and lightning and only awakened when the rain had slacked. He had been fretful the rest of the afternoon with disappointment, for better than anything else in the world he liked thunder storms especially when they were loud and wild and the lightning seemed to race right through his hair. He liked the smell of the sudden wind that would come whistling through the corn, and the sight of the black thunder heads foaming and tossing over the valley, the prickly feel of the first big warm drops and the smell of the sun-heated limestone rocks in the rain. Delph would go dashing about, maybe jerking clothes off the line or bringing apples and beans in from their drying, and there was always a rush to the barnyard to see that the youngest chickens were safely huddled under their hens. Caesar would go running in circles and Marsh would rush in from his plowing; and when all that was done there was the fun of listening to the rain and knowing that everything was safe and dry.

Sometimes when she was in a mighty press of work like just before a rain, Burr-Head would help Delph in the garden. He knew all the things in his mother's garden, and though Mrs. Elliot's flowers had had their pictures taken and put in a Louisville paper, and strange cars were always stopping to admire them, he liked his mother's flowers better. Sometimes when he and Marsh were in the farther fields they would see growing down among the corn a clump of bright blue corn flowers or a red old maid strayed from her sisters. Marsh would plow carefully past the flower and say, "I see we've run smack into Delph's garden." Nights sometimes he would wink at

Burr-Head as he said to Delph, "You have th' travelinest flowers, Delph. We found some poppies clear on th' other side a Solomon's pasture."

Delph would wrinkle her brows and ponder, then smile suddenly with remembering, "Oh, did it bloom? I never went back to see— but once when I was passin' I saw th' spot, there's a big gray limestone rock to one side. I thought some poppies would look pretty growin' there—an' it would be sort of fun to come up on 'em unexpected like. So I stuck some out there th' first rainy day—but I never went back to see."

And Marsh would maybe suggest as he had suggested many times, "Delph, wouldn't you like a real flower garden? I'd fence it off an' plow an' manure it better than th' garden even. You could have all your flowers together so a body could see em. An' not go trampin' all over creation when people ask to see your flowers."

But Delph would laugh as she always did, and answer, "Law, I hate flowers all together in one piece, so pious like an' stiff in rows."

And so the flowers and the herbs grew scattering here and there with wild blue iris planted in spots by the river and the big purple iris on the river hill, and wandering Dorothy Perkins roses blooming on a back field fence. The tansy, dill, peppermint, catnip, sage, horseradish, and fever weed were always being found in scattered corners and unexpected places.

Burr-Head learned the flowers as he learned the vegetables— knew their smell and which the bees loved best, the ones that loved the sun, and those that loved the shade like pansies, and the four-o-clocks that would bloom only in the afternoon shadow. For a long time the wonder of a poppy's opening lingered in his mind. It must have been late June when for some reason he never remembered he was out early while the fog lay thick on the river and all the leaves were heavy with dew. He had walked out among a band of poppies scattered through the cabbage rows, and while he stood marveling at the newness and the strangeness of the world when it was neither night nor day but only blue, something had struck him on the chin. He looked and hunted and saw a yellow poppy flower opening slowly like an unclosing hand, and its petals were not smooth but wrinkled like cloth that has been packed away for ironing.

He had hunted again to find what hit him on the chin, and while he looked he saw the gray-green prickly case of a fat poppy bud burst and go flying away while a red wrinkled poppy leaped into wideness then continued more slowly to widen still more. He stood silent a moment, filled with the wonder of the life in the poppy flowers, and then he had gone flying to Delph, busy with breakfast getting in the kitchen. So great was his excitement it had taken some moments to tell her, and even then she learned more from his shining eyes than from his tongue which in moments of stress behaved like Marsh's tongue. Delph had shown proper excitement but his father had taken the matter so calmly that Burr-Head had a moment's uneasy suspicion that maybe others in the world had already learned the poppy flowers were given to flying open, more swiftly than chickens coming from eggs. Though he tried many times, he was never again able to waken early enough to catch the flowers in their opening, but must content himself with hunting the freshly opened ones, those with wrinkles on their petals.

Then suddenly summer was gone and the poppy stalks were dead. Fat fodder shocks stood in place of the high growing corn, and red and yellow beech and maple leaves floated down the river. The days shortened and sleep troubled him less and less. He never felt guilty at going to sleep after dark. Many mornings he would awaken and catch the dawn red handed in the sky. He would lie for a moment, waking to hear the whisper and rustle of the box elder leaves stirred in the dying night wind, see through the window the red flushed sky and the bottom lands blue in the dawn, and he would be strangely quiet about getting out of bed and maybe tiptoe to the kitchen and talk a time in whispers, awed still by the awakening world.

But the glory of red leaves flying in the wind, of bonfires in the evening, of hunting grapes and chinkapins, of stowing all manner of things away for winter, all were dwarfed and small before the crowning glory of his life, the first trip alone with his father to Hawthorne Town. He had never begged to go, knowing always that begging Marsh for anything was wasted breath.

There had come a morning when he was awakened by lamplight on his face, and there was Delph with the lamp in her hand, and saying, "But he's so little, Marsh, an' me not along. Let's not wake him."

After that the day had blossomed like the poppy flowers. He could hardly be bothered with eating breakfast but jiggled excitedly on his chair and asked so many questions that Marsh was forced to speak with more than his usual sternness, when he reminded him to give proper attention to Delph as she told him to be good and not stray from his father in the Saturday crowd.

Only one little trouble marred the goodness of Burr-Head's world and that was in the morning as they drove away. Delph and Caesar came to stand in the barn hall and watch them off, and they looked sad, he thought, as if they would be lonesome while the men were gone. Delph kept patting and smoothing his overall knees and fiddling with his shirt collar and whispering things about being good as if he were a baby still.

Then they were driving up the hill, beating the sun across the high pasture, going down the Hawthorne Road and there was no time for wearisome thoughts of his mother at home. The sun stood high and hot for October when they drove into Hawthorne Town, past the cannon bristling public square where the fountain played and on to the strip of lawn behind the court house where other teams and cars were gathered. There, they left the mules and went walking briskly over the town. Marsh Gregory was a busy man with much to attend to on a Saturday market day. Now and again Burr-Head would find himself hanging back, maybe alone while his father talked to this one or that.

There was so much to see and hear. He wanted to linger on the court house lawn and hear blind John Duncan's fiddle play and watch a little darkie dance. He wanted to stop and count the strokes when the clock on the court house tower boomed out the time, and he wanted to stop and hear the hill men play and sing in the saloon on Maple Street. It seemed he could never have his fill of staring at the railroad men in peaked caps and funny overalls like rompers, who like others in the streets had come to do their Saturday's trading. He wished he could talk to the soot blackened miners with carbide lights screwed in their caps, up from the eastern end of the county, and there were tall lean hill men with hound dogs at their heels strolling through the town, or whittling by the fountain or on the courthouse steps.

He could have done such things. There was no danger of his getting lost. Many in the town knew him and would call, "Hey, Burr-Head," until he turned and waved. While Marsh was busy in the stores or bank or at the school superintendent's office, he, Burr-Head, could have gone looking over the town. But Burr-Head stayed with his father; more than anything else he wanted the people to know that the wide-shouldered gray-eyed man with his red-gold hair and red-brown beard, and his overalls whitening at their knees was his father.

Men looked at Burr-Head in friendly fashion and patted his head and asked him if he thought he wouldn't be president some day, and Burr-Head would smile at their silly talk. He knew the president well; his name was much in the mouths of all people in Kentucky that fall, and he had a pretty voice that Burr-Head heard sometimes over the radio. He knew he was a great, important man but nothing to compare with his father. He could not manage a mean strong bull like Solomon that no other man in the county save Poke Easy could handle, and he could not grow the corn his father grew; three ears of it from last fall hung now in the bank where Marsh took his business, and today more than one man said they'd never heard of such luck as Marsh had with his calves. Marsh when they talked so would only push back his hat and scratch his head or grunt out something about land good for clover, but Burr-Head would stand and look up at him, and both his chest and his eyes would get bigger and bigger.

Still, he was glad when the afternoon was almost gone and it was time to go back to Delph. Now and again through the afternoon he found himself thinking of her, and when he saw a hill woman in a bright blue bonnet like one Delph wore in the garden he walked up to her and peeped under the brim of the bonnet, hoping a bit that the woman was something like Delph, but she wasn't. Nobody was. He always remembered that day in Town, for as they were driving home some hurt inside him came like a tearing but he never knew exactly what it was. The sun went down when they were only a few miles out of town, and the twilight came on blue and cold. The sundown was blood red in the west, but overhead the sky was deep blue and green with one wide pale star. A cold little wind came out of the north, and Burr-Head turned up his jumper collar and snuggled against his father. There was a smell of winter in the air, and when they passed the old Burgess place where nobody lived, the chimney sweeps were cutting great circles in the sky, and crying above the big rock chimney.

Marsh drove down the road by Higginbottom's place where Little Lizzie lived, and there she was by the front yard gate. She stood on tip-toe and reached for the cosmos flowers above her head, and broke them off and laid them in her tucked up dress. "Hello, Little Lizzie," Marsh said, and stopped the wagon.

"Howdy," Little Lizzie said, and her voice sounded small as if she talked from a good piece away.

"What'a th' matter, Little Lizzie?" Marsh said.

"Nothin'," she said, and broke another flower and laid it in her tucked up dress.

"There'll be no frost tonight, so you needn't cut your flowers," Marsh said, then he turned and said in a louder voice when he saw Perce come walking across the road from his barn, "Howdy, Perce, did you give Little Lizzie a spankin'? She won't talk to me or Burr-Head."

Perce said, "Howdy, Marsh," and walked slow across the road, and came and stood with his foot on a wagon wheel near Burr-Head.

"I was tellin' Little Lizzie she'd no need to cut her flowers, for there'll be no—." Marsh stopped and when he had sat a time fiddling with the reins he asked in a different voice, "What ails you an' yours, Perce?"

Perce cleared his throat and Little Lizzie came to lean on the gate, but she never smiled at Burr-Head. She didn't seem to know he was in the wagon. She looked at her father with her eyes big and watery bright when he said, "Recollect, Marsh, I was tellin' you th' other day that Joe—soon's corn cuttin' time's over—had gone to Detroit."

Marsh nodded. Perce cleared his throat again and his words came slow. "Well he wrote today—joined th' navy an' headed for San Francisco an' th' ocean. Three years," Perce said, "an' him hardly eighteen."

Marsh pushed back his hat and studied the sky. There were more stars now. "There's Ray doin' well in college an' plannin' to farm in this country.—You've got three more comin' on. It's—it's not like Joe was your only one—or your oldest."

"He was so lively in his ways," Perce said, and his voice was old and full of something like Little Lizzie's voice.

Burr-Head pulled his sleeve and looked at Little Lizzie as he said, "Th' ocean it's mighty fine—th' waves an' th' storms, an' th' biggest boats." He heard Marsh turn abruptly on the wagon seat, and he felt Perce's eyes falling down on him.

"An' how might a little shaver like you know about th' sea an' its ships?" Perce said.

Burr-Head was still for a moment. He didn't know why, but for some reason it seemed like telling tales to say what he finally said, "Delph told me."

"Oh," Perce said and took his foot from the wagon wheel and Marsh drove rapidly away. Once Burr-Head looked back and waved to Little Lizzie, but she never saw him. She stood and leaned on the gate, with the flowers spilling from her tucked up dress. He forgot Little Lizzie then when Marsh was driving down across the pasture hill. Marsh had never hugged or kissed him as if he were a baby or a girl, but tonight when they turned over the hill and saw the lights from their windows, yellow in the dark valley, Marsh caught him suddenly and drew him tight against him, so hard it hurt. He felt the thudding of his father's heart, and his deep slow breathing.

· 24 ·

MARSH LEANED on a briar hook and struggled with his foolish mind. He liked clean fence rows, but a wild rose in June was a pretty thing and smelled almost as good as fresh red clover hay. Still, he frowned at the wild rose, flaunting its pale pink petals against the gray limestone of the wide rock fence.

He remembered last spring. He had cleared his fence rows on a showery day in June, and then as now the troublesome wild rose had taken a good ten minutes of his time. He had decided to wait until the thing stopped blooming, but the rose as if in defiance had bloomed until July, and when at last the petals were shed he had hardly noticed it. He hung the briar hook over the fence and turned away. He guessed that by next summer he would most likely be wasting time over this same rose.

He stood a while and watched his cows graze in the lush thick clover. He knew he wasted time, but the watching of his herd was a luxury he would allow himself in odds and ends of time like this. It was Memorial Day for Salem Church with dinner on the ground, and services and singing beginning at ten o'clock and lasting through the day. Down at the house Delph was packing the baskets of food she had prepared. Marsh, with an hour or so to spare before starting time, had come to the upper fields on pretext of looking for weeds in the clover, cleaning his fence rows, and relieving Delph of Burr-Head.

But Burr-Head wandered with Caesar, and Marsh had done little but walk about and look at this and that. He started leisurely across the field when he heard Solomon bellow and Caesar bark from the screen of vines and young locust trees by the Solomon pasture below the high knoll. The fence was high and strong; the child nor the dog nor the bull could come to harm. Burr-Head knew better than to tease Solomon, but so strong was the feeling of pleasantness that seemed settled on Marsh like a dew, that he did not lift his voice in calling or even frown.

He climbed the high knoll and stood by the pasture bars and looked a time at the ivy chained chimneys of the brick house, showing a little above the pear and apple trees. He looked down at the bottom lands where his house was little more than a roof in a sea of green shrub and green vine. He thought of Delph, the way she would sit sometimes by the fire last winter and smile and plan how it would be when he paid for the land and they moved into the brick house. She would do thus and so to one room and that to another. She would maybe use the money she had for furniture. There seemed little chance that Burr-Head would need it in college. Next summer he would start to Cedar Stump and Ezrie; last winter Marsh in addition to ordering government bulletins and seed catalogs had collected a few catalogs from colleges. He had just wanted to see what they were like, he had said, though he knew it was useless to try to hide from Delph that he was beginning to plan for Burr-Head.

Last winter Mr. Elliot had planned to move nearer a large lumber mill he owned in Georgia, for the timber around Burdine was mostly gone, but through the spring he had changed his mind. His heart had been bothering him off and on; his blood pressure was higher than it ought to be. Not that he was scared or ever thought of dying, so he had explained to Marsh, but since he had lived in the brick house longer than in any other house he had ever known, he thought he might as well keep on living there. Marsh had offered no objection. He'd be glad to rent it for at least a few more years, but not too long. Delph had always liked the place, and he would rather fancy it himself—when he could afford it. Then Mrs. Elliot had come one day while he worked alone in the upper fields, and she had talked and smiled the way she did sometimes, said she hoped she could always live in this country and that, though she knew nothing of farming, she thought Marsh was a very good farmer, but some day Burr-Head would be a better one than he; already he knew which buds to pinch from the dahlias so that the remaining flowers might be twice as large. Marsh had listened with his chest expanding mightily. He could hardly remember when the conversation changed, or how it happened that when Mrs. Elliot suggested that she and Mr. Elliot buy the brick house, he had even listened. But listen he did, and with it there had come the thought of the stone house he would like to build.

Later in the week Mr. Elliot had come hunting him in the cornfield. He gave no foolish reason and excuses like Mrs. Elliot, simply said that since the building of the river bridge and the finishing of a through road that went all the way north to Detroit and south to Florida, the house with the many improvements that Marsh had made from time to time, had grown in his eyes. The price he offered for the house and garden, a strip of land to the road and a rough bit of river hill with none of the pasture and no tree of the orchard taken, would finish the mortgage and buy a strip of woodland just across the creek from his own that Marsh had long wanted. The thing was finished except for the signing of the deeds—and still Delph didn't know. For days he had refused to mar his sense of triumph in having a debt-free farm with thought of how he would tell Delph.

Solomon bellowed with a great roar of rage, and Marsh, glad to put thoughts of explanation from his head, hurried to the sound. He found Burr-Head and Caesar pressed against the high barbed wire crowned fence, lost in the drama of Solomon, who stood a few feet away and pawed and bellowed and tossed his head, especially for their pleasure it seemed, for when Marsh came he looked guilty, like a bully come suddenly against a man stronger than he. He turned and stalked away, and not until then did the guilty ones take notice of Marsh.

Caesar had the grace to look embarrassed and drop his tail and circle away a bit. Not so with Burr-Head. While Marsh stood pondering, aware that some good words concerning obedience were needed, Burr-Head reached into one overall cuff and pulled out a wilted sprig of wild delphinium. "Look at th' bouquet I picked for Delph, del—del—phee—nium," he said, and smiled and showed his teeth and wrinkled his freckle bespattered nose, as he returned the flower to the cuff of his overalls and patted it gently.

"You know a thing or two," Marsh answered, all in a maze of prideful wonder at the smartness of his child. Burr-Head not only knew the names of all the plants about, but knew also that his father would forget to scold when he showed him a flower he had picked for Delph. Marsh took his hand and they walked to the back of the field above the creek and across from the stretch of rough land he intended to buy.

Burr-Head teased to go down to the creek and hunt for minnows and mint and periwinkles, but Marsh sat on a flat limestone under a cedar tree. He took the broken arrow he always carried in his pockets, and drew lines and squares on the flat limestone. Burr-Head watched and forgot to tease. Caesar, feeling that he had shown contrition enough, came and sat by Marsh's shoulder, and wrinkled the brown spots above his eyes as he watched the building. "We'll need good big cellars," Marsh said.

"Plenty a room for my popcorn," Burr-Head reminded. The building of the stone house on the hill was a game he had played with his father many times.

"Never put popcorn in a cellar, son. Th' apples from that little Ben Davis you set this spring, they can go in th' cellar."

"Don't forget th' fireplace. I'll want a place to put New York an' Fairyland.—Marsh what kind a fertilizer do you guess they put on that bean stalk anyhow?"

"It was good strong bottom land on a crop a soy beans turned under," Marsh answered, and smiled a little in thinking of Delph's story. Jack's bean stalk always grew on Marsh's corn lands, but led, through some miracle which Burr-Head never questioned, straight to New York City where the giant lived and there were many wondrous things. Delph's mixing of the maps irked Marsh less than formerly. It seemed foolish to be afraid; to mind her whimsy, childlike imaginings.

"Don't forget a place for my little sister," Burr-Head reminded him.

"You've got no little sister."

"Dorie said I ought to have. She said I'd get so mean my hide wouldn't hold me if you an' Delph didn't get me a sister. I want one."

"We'll see about it," Marsh answered, and plans for the stone house—his way of telling Delph—faded while he sat and stared at the fallen red brown cedar needles, and thought of the night he had struck her, and she had cried out that she would never have another child. He wondered if she thought on all that sometimes and held it against him still. He needed children—now that the land was free of debt.

"Look, this is th' big back room where we'll test our seed corn," Burr-Head said, and pointed to a pebble outlined square.

"That's fine," Marsh answered and got up. "It's time for us to be home gettin' ready to go to Salem."

"I'm goin' to wear my overalls.—Marsh, why are some clouds big an' some little?"

"They're made like people, I guess. All kinds and sizes."

"But how do they grow so fast or get so little?"

"Th' wind—if it likes th' clouds it feeds 'em, but if th' clouds are bad th' wind blows their feed away an' makes 'em skinny."

"I'd hate to be a cloud.—Marsh, why does Maude when she gets up start with her front legs first, but Ivy, now she pushes up her behind?"

"That's part a th' difference 'tween a mare an' a cow."

"Marsh, why do bees like clover so?"

"For th' same reason that you like honey. Sing a little now so you won't ask so many questions. Recollect that song Delph taught you th' other night?"

"I'd rather be King George?" Burr-Head tilted his head and studied his father, and when he had decided that his father's words were suggestion instead of command, he pulled his overall leg and begged, "Marsh, you tell me that story about th' surprise."

Marsh grunted. "Aw, Burr-Head I'm no good at tellin' stories—not like Delph."

"Please, Marsh, just this once," he begged with another tug on the overall leg.

Marsh hunkered on his heels in a bed of white clover, while Burr-Head and Caesar dropped belly downward beside and lay and smiled at him while he talked. Prissy, grazing a few rods away, tossed her pretty horns and then drew gradually nearer until Burr-Head could have touched her on the nose; but while Marsh talked Burr-Head never noticed Prissy. "It's like this," Marsh began and pulled a clover flower and studied it, "there is a place in Kentucky called th' Bluegrass, an' Lord it is th' finest land, finer than this where th' bluegrass grows. Th' tobacco leaves are wider than a man's two hands spread wide an' thinner than tissue paper.

"But finer than anything are th' horses. Th' horses in th' blue-grass country have their names all set in books, an' their grandfathers an' grandmothers all th' way back through England to Arabia, I guess. They're not like our Maude. She's a good mare, but, pshaw, we don't know all th' blood behind her. But in th' bluegrass country they know th' blood behind their horses an' their mares. An' there when a fine one dies he can know his blood goes on an' they'll recollect him always.

"On one a th' big fine farms there is a mare's statue all in gold, an' it's on th' grave of th' finest mare that ever was. Her colts could run like th' wind an win races, an' her fillies could, too, but mostly they raised more colts an' fillies.

"Well, one a these days, Burr-Head, when you're a good bit bigger than you are now, I'll go away for a day, maybe two or three. An' in th' night while you're sleepin' I'll come sneakin' in back home, an' I'll unload th' truck in th' barn. We'll have a new fine barn then, fixed like a barn ought to be. I'll call you out to th' barn' early, an' I'll go openin' a stable door an' what do you reckin' you'll see?"

"A blue blooded filly from th' bluegrass country," Burr-Head cried. "An' when she's growed into a mare she'll have a colt for me."

There was more to the story but Marsh never finished. They heard Delph blowing the old fox horn she always used to bring them to the house, and both remembered guiltily that they ought to be home getting ready to go to Salem. They hurried across the field and down the hill, but paused a moment at the front yard gate to hear Delph's song of, "over th' hills of glory, over the jasper sea," rising high and clear and strong. Burr-Head listened and said, "I reckin that ole angel food turned out all right."

"You be good now," Marsh warned. Burr-Head was never bad when out with his father, but there were times while with Delph that a stern voice was needed. This morning had been such a time. Delph had just slid her eleven-egg angel cake into the oven, when Burr-Head decided he was Maude's second colt, Jule, and that the kitchen floor was a rough pasture with many rocks to be jumped over. Marsh had taken him away, and now was glad to learn from Delph's flushed happy face that the colt had not kicked the wind out of her cake.

She must start immediately with the dressing of Burr-Head. She was eager to see him dressed in his new white linen blouse, short dark blue linen trousers with large buttons like those of the children in Mrs. Elliot's fashion magazines. There were new slippers and new socks with dark blue bordered tops. He would, she knew, be the prettiest and the best dressed child at Salem Church, including Dorie's visiting grandchildren.

Burr-Head looked at the new clothing spread on a kitchen chair, and hastily swallowed the half of a deviled egg he had filched from one of the dinner baskets. He nodded to make the egg go down and said, "I don't aim to wear no drawers, Delph,—just overalls."

Marsh turned hastily away with a remark about shaving. He felt trouble in the air, and when it came to Delph and Burr-Head he could never make up his mind which side to take. Though, while he dressed upstairs his tolerance abruptly changed to anger when he heard the banging of the back screen door, and there was Burr-Head flying across the yard in nothing but his undershirt and it a short bit of nothing at that. Nobody had the right to treat Delph so. He dashed downstairs, forgetting that he wore no shoes. "He needs a good spankin'," he thundered to Delph as he strode through the door.

"He'll come back. Don't go chasin' him," she said, ruffled by the talk of spanking. "An' anyhow he'll never wear 'em. I'll maybe do well to get him to wear his new shoes," she added sadly, and turned and looked at the new clothes.

Marsh looked at them and then at Delph. He saw tears sliding down the corners of her eyes. He wished that Dorie or some woman would come and scold her for her foolishness. He had no heart for the business. He remembered the buying of the cloth in Hawthorne and the ordering of the paper pattern; the nights when she sat sewing and he had merely grunted over his figuring or government bulletins when she would say, "I just can't wait to see how he'll look. They're th' first halfway nice clothes he's ever had. An' please, Marsh, don't give him a convict haircut like you did before he sang that song at Easter."

In spite of his shoeless feet, he followed her now when she turned abruptly and started upstairs with a resigned, "I'll get him a clean pair of overalls, an' he can wear his new clothes Sunday."

"You need a girl, Delph, to fix up pretty th' way Lizzie dykes out Little Lizzie," Marsh said when they were on the stairs.

She stopped on the top stair and turned about and looked at him. "Would—would you mind?"

"Hell no, make it twins if you like."

She smiled, gay again, filling him with that old wonder at her nimble way of leaping from one mood to another. "I've always been afraid of a girl," she said. "What if she had your chin an' my nose? Wouldn't she be a sight?"

"My chin's all right. Th' trouble is your nose," he answered, and started to pull her nose in teasing, but caught her shoulders instead and pulled her down the stair; she smiled and did not draw away. Past the smooth braids of her hair just below his eyes, he could look to a window and see through that the rows of knee high corn marching away to the curve of the river. He felt her body against his own and saw his corn and knew that life was good. Delph was as he had always known she would some day be.

While he held her there on the stair, she seemed again the girl who had promised to marry him, with all of her his own, no part of her leaping away, flying over his head while her body remained in his arms. There had been times when he had felt that her body and her heart—the weaker part of it—were his maybe, but that the rest of her was like an unseen, unfelt wind that moved clouds a man could scarcely see. On summer nights it was a bitterness sometimes to lie with her and Burr-Head on the grass and watch the stars, hear her talk softly of the stars, tell the child that somewhere there were lights bigger and brighter and more beautiful than the stars. And though in all her words there was never a hint of complaining or of regret, he had thought sometimes that there was sorrow, the sorrow of one for another who is dead or forever gone away. He looked down into her eyes now, and asked, quickly to reassure himself, "You're not sorry, Delph?"

"You mean that Burr-Head likes overalls?" she asked, and buttoned the top button of his shirt. "Land, no. Maybe one of his seventeen little brothers and sisters will wear out that little suit."

"They will not," Burr-Head said.

They drew apart, and there was Burr-Head, looking guilty and jealous and sorrowful in the frilly white shirt and short blue linen trousers which he had put on so hastily that he must hold them up with one hand while he tendered the forgotten delphinium with the other. "I'll wear 'em," he said.

Marsh stayed upstairs and put on his shoes, and looked at Delph in wonder when a short time later she returned for the overalls. "It's not his fault," she explained. "I've no heart to make him wear 'em. He's heard Az's boys call Mr. Elliot's linen golf knickers 'drawers.' That's why he acted up so."

"You'll have to start spankin' him one a these days. He'll wear his suit now if you say so. I'll see to that."

But Delph only laughed, "Pshaw, let him wear his overalls. He'll be playin' today anyhow an' gettin' messed up with th' picnic dinner.—He'll not always be wearin' such clothes."

"Sure, he'll change. Soon's he starts goin' with th' girls he'll be spendin' all th' bull calf money he's savin' now on fancy shirts an' ties.—It won't be long."

Delph studied the clothing in her hands, and Marsh wondered how his light talk could have put such a stricken look in her eyes. "I guess he'll be out an' gone before we hardly know it," she said, and measured the length of the overalls against her skirt.

"But even while he's away in college, he can visit home," Marsh pointed out, but Delph turned away down the stairs and never seemed to hear.

She combed Burr-Head's hair and thought of other children. At first, in spite of her weakened body and Marsh's wish not to have a larger family immediately, it had seemed sinful and flying in the face of God not to have children when she lived with Marsh as his wife. Now, she wished that she had not in that weak moment of loving spoken of the girl she would like to have. She could never love another child as she loved Burr-Head. She thought of Lizzie and her empty eyes when she talked of her boy that had gone away. "Th' one that left us," Lizzie always said. She was cold and sick a moment, seeing Lizzie's eyes, and then she smiled; Burr-Head would be no common sailor gone for three years. No matter what he did when he finished college he would come home for vacations. They never got too far away for that. There was talk that Sam Fairchild, far away as he was, was expected home sometime this year—maybe in the fall.

Marsh called to know if he couldn't take Burr-Head and the baskets and wait for her by the river. She roused herself, saw the comb in her hand with a few of Burr-Head's twining red brown hairs caught in its teeth. Burr-Head had sickened of his mother's wool gathering ways and slipped away to the yard. There, with his fingers and some rubber bands he trapped bumble bees in the hollyhock flowers. Delph laughed and ran after him and took time to free the bumble bees. After that there was no time to plan on Burr-Head's vacations. Late as it was Burr-Head was not yet given his finishing touches and she had not combed her hair; and how Marsh hated to be late. However, today he did not quarrel, only smiled, called her Sally Thompson who was the slowest woman in the country, and while she braided one side of her hair he braided the other. And after all the rush across the river and up the hill to Fairchild Place they found the whole family including Angus, Dorie's visiting grandchildren, and Minnie Rakestraw, the hired girl who always stayed with them summers, all engaged in a breathless hunt for Dorie's glasses—at least one pair. Poke Easy had sickened of his mother's careless ways with her glasses a good while back and so bought her a second pair in case she lost the first; Emma had bought still another pair—and now all three were gone. Marsh went to the barn to see a new calf that had come during the night, for he was never any good at finding anything. He saw one of the old jumpers that Dorie wore about the barn hanging on a nail by the stable door, and sticking from a pocket of it were the horn rims of Dorie's glasses. He looked at the calf, then returned to the house; the hero of the day.

They were of course not late, though they found the church waiting and packed to overflowing; Memorial Day services at Salem would never begin without the Fairchilds, especially when the whole congregation knew that Dorie was home hunting her glasses. Delph went to her place in the choir while Katy and Dorie took the children to the bench where Fairchilds had sat for the last hundred years, held now by three of Perce's boys, sent there by Lizzie who had feared that some strangers might sit there and never know the place was meant for Dorie.

Since the house was already packed to overflowing, so that by his staying out he would not be setting a bad example for Burr-Head, Marsh went with others of the men to sit on the yew and cedar shrouded stones of the graveyard. He liked it there. The mournful sighing of the great white pines did not sadden him, no more than the myrtle-wreathed stones or wild rose and ivy-covered graves. The old fear of death that had once hounded him was lost.

When some neighbor died, usually one very old or very young, he would pause in his plowing or whatever work he did, wait until the tolling of the church bells died, and then plow on, untouched by any horror of life and birth and death. When he thought of men dying he thought of grass, the myriad separate blades of it that grew and died with other blades silently taking each vacant place, so that a man walking through the same fields year after year would never know that blades of grass had died. Men in a way were like the grass. They came from the land and to the land they would return; all science and progress and prosperity could not change that, no more than progress and prosperity and laziness and neglect and heedless governments and poverty stricken renters could destroy the land. The land might be impoverished, blown away, or washed in rivers to the sea but some day it would rise again as stone or mud or lie forever as ocean floor—whatever happened the land would endure.

He leaned against the stone of a man dead eighty years and watched thunder heads froth in the sky and heard without listening the intermittent conversation of Poke Easy and Roan Sandusky and other men gathered there. They mentioned some young boy dead of typhoid fever, and Marsh frowned in thinking of the dead child's careless parents. He made Delph and Burr-Head keep themselves inoculated.

He wished the men would be silent. He wanted to listen to the singing and the organ music which was pleasant when mixed with the pine trees. Delph had sung one solo and soon she would sing another, and he wanted to hear it with no interruption. He left the grave yard and went to stand by a vine covered window where he could see Delph as she sang.

He had wondered many times of what she thought when she sang, "And he walks with me, and he talks with me, and he tells me I am his own, and the joy we share as we tarry there—." In that as in the other songs she sang in church there was a richness and a mystery that led him to think at times that maybe her mind was less on some pale Christ with wounded hands than a living god of a man who could lead her to all the vague splendors that her life with him would always lack.

He marveled sometimes that she could please people so, could sing even in the biggest church in Hawthorne Town where there was a pipe organ, and with it all betray no vanity or pride as other women might have done. If praised she would only say, "What woman with half a tongue couldn't sing for her neighbors in some country church or county-seat town?"

Delph sang on, and the song held him so that he hardly noticed when a car drew up with a soft, scarcely audible purring, and a man got out and came and looked and listened with him by the window. Marsh caught a glimpse of well fitted, white-coated shoulder, and did not waste his time with looking. Some city man, a stranger to the country, had heard Delph's song and noticed the cars about, and stopped to learn what quaint thing the yokels did.

"That girl, the one singing, is beautiful," the stranger said, and his voice was soft and slow like a hill man's voice, but his words were those of a man who has lived a time in the north or east.

Marsh nodded, and knew that when the man got into his fine, soft-purring car and drove away, he would carry with him for many a day that picture of Delph. The old dark paneling of the pulpit walls, the Dorothy Perkins roses banked in red masses below her feet, the deep blue of the delphinium and clear yellow of poppies on the Bible stand above her head, the flickering pattern of light that filtered through the vine latticed window, the rows of upturned listening faces; all were no more than a background for Delph. There was her strong slender, deep-breasted body, the dark glint of a shining braid as she moved her head, the slow lifting and falling of her lashes, and then her eyes, blue and deep and shadowed by many things; the organ music and the roses, some smothered fire of gaiety, some gleam of hunger never satisfied, touched by a bit of sorrow now maybe as if she thought sometimes of the dead for whom she sang. "She is right pretty," Marsh said after a time, and turned then and looked at the stranger, for Delph had finished her song.

But he could see only his back, the long straight back of a six-foot man, and above the white linen suit his hair was dark, darker than Delph's. He continued to peer and search between the trembling leaves, and he seemed too interested and too eager for a stranger passing by. He found something and for a long moment he did not move his head, and, though it would have been the quivering shadows of the leaves, Marsh thought that his long hands trembled a bit, in the strange uncertain fashion of hands unused to trembling.

"Tell me," the man said after a time and in a whisper for in the church Brother Eli prayed, "is that one, Katy, there in the end of Dorie Dodson Fairchild's pew?"

Marsh, too, looked between the leaves "Yes," he said.

"And the children?"

"Th' two in kind a fancy clothes, they're Dorie's grandchildren from Detroit, but th' one in overalls with one shoe in his lap an' th' other on th' floor that's Burr-Head, Marsh Gregory's boy."

"The woman that sang is Delph Gregory, the boy's mother, isn't she?"

"Yes.—How come you know her?"

"I don't. I just saw her and from the way she sang, I guessed.— Where is her husband, Marsh Gregory?"

"I'm Marsh Gregory."

"Oh." The man turned and looked at him, and Marsh could hear Delph saying something she had said of another man a long while back, "an' his eyes were blue like corn flowers, an' his hair was black—an' he could see so far—."

But that man was dead a hundred and fifty years, and he had worn deer skin jeans, not tailored white linen. There were hill men and hill men, many tall with black hair and blue eyes, and their eyes deepened like Delph's eyes by black lashes and black brows, and maybe many of them had the same something in their eyes that touched Delph's songs. Then his foolish thoughts were gone; the puzzle finished and he was holding out his hand as the man extended his. "You're Samuel Fairchild, I take it. I've heard a lot about you—but, well—you don't look much like your brothers."

Sam nodded and smiled. "People used to say I took after my mother's side of the family. You know, from the back hills near your wife's home."

"You seem to know all about her," Marsh said, and started back toward the grave yard.

"That's not strange," Sam said with his easy hill man's smile. "No matter where I am, old Reuben Kidd always manages to hunt me up and send the *Westover Bugle*. Then, too, for the last three years I've seen a good bit of Emma. She's a great one to describe things and tell all the news—showed me Delph's picture and Burr-Head's and Solomon's and told me—oh, a lot of things."

Marsh continued silent, but Sam never seemed to notice, and after a moment or so went on to explain that he had intended to wait until fall, but Emma had been asked to take her vacation in late June and early July, and had wanted him to drive her down, for she was no hand at driving.

"Dorie'll be glad to see you an' Emma," Marsh said, and wished that Sam had not come home. He wished that Delph had not stood alone when she sang.

The men gathered in the graveyard knew Sam at once and greeted him as if he had gone away only yesterday instead of almost fourteen years. "You've hardly changed," Perce said, and slapped him on the shoulder as he added, "Well, Boy, I'm still waitin' for that good cheap fertilizer an' experiment farm."

"I might do something in that line yet," Sam said, then looked out over the country. "From the look of things you don't need such things the way you used to."

"We get along, but there's plenty a room for improvement," Roan said, and smiled with one corner of his mouth and spat with the other. He and Sam had met quite simply, as if there had never been between them either great dreams or great hatreds.

"Things have changed," Sam went on, and he continued to stand in the graveyard and sweep his eyes slowly over the rolling acres of corn and wheat and tobacco and pasture land.

And Marsh watching him saw something lost, and knew that a mind and a strength beyond that of most men had been taken from the country when Sam left it. He understood now why Dorie grieved for him more than for the others who had gone away. He with his hill man's eyes and body seemed to belong here, not away east in cities. He wondered what Delph would think of Sam, and the rest of the day seemed wasted, worse than wasted.

He listened to songs and sermons, talked with his neighbors, ate various foods that women took from the mighty dinner spread on the ground, and shoved into his hands. But always he watched Sam; saw him greet his mother and his family, saw Katy bring him to meet

Delph, saw Delph smile with no flustering and no embarrassment and offer him a piece of her angel food cake, watched Sam help himself and heard him say, "I know it's good, because I read in the paper last year that it took a prize at the fair."

"Not this same one," Delph said, and they all laughed, and no one, not even Burr-Head, stealing pieces of chicken and bits of cake for the dogs clustered down by the fence, noticed when he came away.

He knew he was a fool. Delph was no worse than others of the women; Dorie alone seemed in no wise overwhelmed by Sam's homecoming. While Katy and others clustered about him offering him this and that to eat, Dorie heaped a platter with choice pieces of all possible foods, and brought it to Roan and Marsh and Poke Easy who sat together, a little apart from the crowd. "I don't know as any of you deserve anything to eat," Dorie said. "But buck up, my boys. Maybe there'll come a war an' you all can line up fifty farmers from another country an' shoot 'em down, an' then you can come home an' all th' women will make over you, th' way they are now with Sam."

"Don't be foolish, Maw," Poke Easy said.

"His work's got nothin' to do with it. They hardly know what he does."

"But it's got a fine important sound, an' they can see his clothes an' see his car. Lord, such a car—worse than Joe's—like he was bawlin' to th' whole world he had money enough to buy a car. No wonder Emma decided to stop off in Lexington for a day to see an old friend that was visitin' there."

"Aw, Maw," Poke Easy scolded. "It's not his job or his car or his clothes, people—women anyhow—from all I've ever heard just naturally take to Sam. Recollect how you've been pinin' your life away wantin' to see him all these years."

"I've had precious little time for pinin', an' anyhow did you ever hear me say I wanted him to come home? I hated to see him go away for good, but I never begged him back."

Poke Easy got up. "Well, he's here, an' Sam or no Sam I'm goin' over to Flatrock to look at Sol Ping's hogs. Want to go, Marsh? We'll try ridin' that young team a mine."

"He can't go," Dorie said. "You'll be sundown gettin' home, an' who'll do th' night work for Delph?"

"Sam," Marsh said, and strode away with Poke Easy.

They rode the young team to Sol Ping's farm, a distance up the Long North Fork in the hills. Poke Easy promised to buy the hogs, and when they started home for the afternoon was better than half gone. But when they came to the head of a deep, apparently uninhabited hollow, Poke Easy went to a vine shrouded rock house and bought a quart of moonshine, and after that they rode more slowly.

The drink was strong in Marsh's mouth and fiery in his stomach. It seemed he could not get his fill of water, but must stop at every trickle of creek or spring for a drink. Poke Easy drank liquor only, and quarreled with Marsh. It was dangerous to drink strange water when there was so much typhoid about, he said, and Marsh was not inoculated.

Marsh drank still more deeply from the next spring, and conscious of Poke Easy's worried eyes, said as he wiped his mouth, "I've never been sick a day in my life, an' I don't aim to be."

Poke Easy lifted the fruit jar, drank and frowned at Marsh. "You're not like yourself today," he said. "Don't let that brother of mine, Sam, my mother's only son, make a fool out a you. He'll be gone one of these days—I guess."

· 25 ·

"THE CORN is laid by. The winter wheat is cut. The trees in our orchards promise heaviest yield in years. Cedar Stump School opened last week with Ezrie Cutler back as teacher. Canning and pickling are the order of the day."

Delph sat by the kitchen table, and wrote among the jars of cooling jam and little pickled gherkins. She looked at the prickly gherkins, and thought that in winter Marsh liked nothing so well as a plate of beans and cornbread with pickled gherkins. She felt something sliding by her nose, and heedless of whether it be sweat or tear, she wiped it away and wrote again.

"There is little change in the condition of Marsh Gregory. He is now in his third week of typhoid fever. Your correspondent is thankful for such kind neighbors. We thank the neighbor men for bringing in his hay and laying by his corn, and Sober Creekmore and Samuel Fairchild for looking after his cattle. The women are kind to come and help, and Mrs. Elliot keeps the correspondent's child.

"The clover hay this year is finer than—." She heard Marsh's shriek, and fat black Emma's troubled soothing. "There, there, you're not in burnin' oil. Look, there's that mornin' glory vine. Whoever saw a mornin' glory vine in th' oil fields Ah'd like to know?"

Delph clenched the table when the cry came again, then slowly her fingers dropped away as the voice changed to senseless, broken mutterings. Dorie came to the door. She looked at Delph, and her eyes were kinder than her voice as she said, "Don't set there lookin' like th' ghost of some white-livered woman. You'll have to learn to take it like anybody else."

"But it's been so long—three weeks an' th' fever not left him."

Dorie poured herself a sip of coffee, and waited a time before speaking. "You might as well know, Delph, this—what he's been through is only th' beginnin'. He's got it bad. There was Randal Dick, he lay in fever seventy-three days, an' he was a man bigger an' stronger than Marsh."

"Did—did he get well?"

"N-o-o. He went when his fever broke. But he was one thing an' Marsh is another.—Lord, Lord, Delph, don't be a cryin' an' a buryin' him 'til he's dead. Why don't you go up an' see if you can't maybe help Sam an' Sober in th' hay? It'll do you good to get out."

"I—I hate to leave."

Dorie sighed and set down her coffee cup. "Delph—you might as well know—it's no fault a yours, but did you ever in your life take care of anybody when they were sick?"

"N-o-o. Aunt Fronie would never let me learn—she said I was too fidgety—but—." She sprang up and looked at Dorie with jealous angry eyes. "That's not sayin' I can't at least help to look after Marsh. I'm older now—an' stronger. But neither you nor Doctor Andy'ull hardly let me go about him." She whirled and started toward the door, but stopped when Dorie said, "Delph," with the same note of command in her voice she used sometimes with Katy or her grandchildren.

She took Delph's bonnet hanging on the kitchen wall and held it out to her. "Delph, this is one time in your life you've got to be sensible. Just because it's your man that's sick is no reason why you, a girl that knows nothin' of nursin' anybody let alone a typhoid patient, can take care of him. Right now Dr. Andy's lookin' all over th' country for a nurse, any kind, either trained or practical, that can manage a typhoid patient like Marsh. An' when she comes you'll not be tip-toein' about him ever' five minutes an' then comin' back to th' kitchen to cry. An' you'll not be sayin', 'Marsh will have a fit if I don't at least put up some pickles an' make a little blackberry jam.'— I didn't say anything this mornin'—but, Delph, you've got to see you can't be heatin' th' house up with cannin' an' goin' on just because you think it's what he'd want you to do."

Delph stood and listened, her face pale and the pupils widening in her eyes, until the eyes seemed black instead of blue; and over all Dorie's words she nodded with slow heavy motions of her head. She continued to nod as Dorie went on, "From now on you've got to be sensible an' always recollect that Marsh is th' one to think on. It would be better for him an' you, too, if you'd stay with me or up at Elliots. Comin' down th' stairs fifty times a night an' walkin' around over him—it's killin' you an' doin' him no good."

Dorie shoved the sunbonnet into her hands, and she took it and went out the back screen door, taking care to close it gently. Sudden noises sometimes threw Marsh into a frenzy of screaming. After looking about to see that no one watched, she slipped through the iris beds that bordered the stone foundation of the house, and went to stand by a window thick with morning glory vines.

In the last two weeks she had stood by that window many times. She stood still, careful to touch no leaf or flower, and betray the fact that someone listened there. She heard quick, hard breathing, less like that of a man than of some angry wounded animal, fighting even as it died. She smelled medicine and antiseptic and some other odor that Dorie said was the typhoid, though for her it seemed the smell of death.

She listened a long while. She hoped to hear a calm word or a regular breath to prove that the thing on the bed was Marsh. There were times when the man with red eyes and sunken cheeks and fever-wasted body did not seem like a man—or anything that belonged in her life. Each setting sun seemed less the ending of another day for him than a deeper folding into all the mystery and the majesty of death which now enshrouded him. She could not in the ugly, pain-wracked body see Marsh any more as he had been than she could see flowers that had bloomed on a drought-bitten melon vine. She stood now with bowed head and clenched hands and thought of Marsh, but he was never there behind the vines. Laughing, he was as he walked across the yard on a morning in spring to begin the plowing; frowning over a government bulletin, braiding her hair and flirting with her from the corners of his eyes, playing with Burr-Head by the hearth on winter evenings—but never that screaming skeleton there on the bed.

She moved a step or so away and stood staring at her clenched hands when she heard words from behind the leaves. The words were thick and guttural, and somehow filled with a pain the fever did not bring. "Get away, Delph.—Delph, don't take ever'thing I've got, now. Delph, don't make him—."

The voice died in hoarse heavy breathing, and she leaned nearer the vines—listening. She had heard such words at other times. Sometimes they ended in a scream and she would rush away to spend long moments in the cool darkness of the spring house, trying to still the quivering in her hands and throat and heart. She had seen sickness—at least had heard of the ways of fever, it could make any man say foolish things. Dorie had told her that. She had held her and soothed her the first time Marsh talked so. But Dorie had never understood that her terror was not all for Marsh's sickness. Every silent meal, every questioning glance through that hard dry summer, all the plans that he had held away from her as if she were a stranger had come sharp in her memory, and taken new significance from his senseless talk.

He was so afraid of her—had always been afraid. Now, he screamed more against her than all the gruesome, ugly dangers he had gone through in his oil field days. Many times she had wondered with a hurt that never died, why it was that when they were married he never told her of his dreams and plans, had discussed them with Dorie, but never with her; if she could have had some hand in the shaping of her life on the farm it would maybe have never seemed so ugly as it had used to be—before Burr-Head. She bowed her head and thought of many things, the years of work that was sometimes drudgery, the never having, the pretending, and the smiling; most of it was done because of him. Not because of duty. She had never thought of that, but only of Marsh—he was a part of her—or had seemed to be.

He screamed again; she turned and with her bonnet dangling from her shoulders, ran through the yard, across the road and up the hill. She was out of breath when she came to the grove of trees by Solomon's pasture, and could do no more than fling herself under a walnut tree and stare at the sky. The sky wavered like a country seen through rain-wet glass; she heard blood pound in her ears and her hard heavy breathing, and felt the heat and the sweat of her body after the long hot run in the July weather; but none of such things could quiet her thoughts or shut out the sound of Marsh's screams and cries. She tried to see the sky; it was high and clean and beautiful, withdrawn from all the pain and ugliness of earth. She wondered why it was that in the slow life of a farmer's wife there must be so much hurt and wonder, and this always walking in the dark.

She heard Solomon bellow from his pasture, and lifted on one elbow and sat listening. She had never tried to drive the wild strong bull, but had always thought she could. Maybe if she went running into his pen and drove him to the barn, the work and the constant danger would make her forget, for at least a little while.

But she looked quickly in the opposite direction when she heard Sam call to her from the other side of the grove as he came up through the clover field. She sat up and smoothed her apron over her knees, and watched him as he came. Though he wore the rough blue cotton clothes of a working man, he looked very tall and very straight and walked with an easy, springing stride that marked him as being no farmer. He stopped a few feet away by a walnut sapling, and studied her a moment with some trouble in his face, and his eyes gentle as Katy's when she fed a sick lamb. "Delph—I know it's none of my business but you can't help Marsh by running around in this heat."

She drew a long sobbing breath and sat hugging her knees as she asked, "I guess you saw me come runnin' up th' hill, an' thought I was crazy?"

"I saw you run, but I didn't think you were crazy."

She hesitated a time, then asked in a low voice, "You know how it is—then—to run with your legs—just because—because th' rest of you—well, there's no runnin away from your head, ever,—but sometimes you'd like to try."

He came nearer and sat with his back against a small tree a foot or so away. "I used to—a long time ago," he said, "gallop a horse to some church in th' hills five or ten miles away, that is when I was a boy in school—and it all, I guess, just because I wanted to leave something or find something new—maybe."

"On windy moonlit nights in fall, I guess," she said. And when he nodded and smiled at her, she wondered as she had wondered at other times how it was he knew so much. He understood without her telling things she had never tried to explain to other people—not even Marsh—because she knew they could never understand. Because of all his years away, and his studies, and his work, so different from anything in her life, it seemed that he should have been a stranger, more so than Joe, but he somehow never was, not even at that first meeting in Salem churchyard.

She had thought at first it was maybe because he looked the way he did, like hill men of the old days: tall and slender and brown, with his blue, blue eyes, and his hair black as a coal, and his gentle, drawling voice, slower, except in moments of enthusiasm, than her own. He was a lot like Katy, a great one for talking when the notion seized him and interested in all things. He was friendly as Poke Easy, but not so blunt in his ways. Still, there was in him a dash of something that made him entirely different from the other Fairchilds; not so much his laughter, Katy laughed as much as he, and Poke Easy was gay enough, but there was in Sam a streak of nonconformity that made it seem sometimes as if that silly, wishful side of her had overflowed and touched someone else—and that someone else was a man she had heard of since she was a little girl and had dreamed sometimes of knowing, and when she did meet him it was as if she had known him always.

Since Marsh's sickness she had seen a good bit of him, and always he was kind like Dorie, trying in many ways to ease the burden of her trouble. Today, in spite of all her fear and misery, she had to laugh when he told her of his first tuxedo; the troubles he had had with his shirt and his tie, and how when he went calling on his girl to take her to the dance—the reason for all his finery—she hardly knew him, but made him wait an hour while she changed into another dress, one that matched his get-up better, the girl had said. And she had been so mad she'd hardly danced with him all evening.

Delph listened and smiled when he unashamedly went on to tell of how he had gone in debt to buy it. "When I was in high school I always wondered how it would be to have a whole new suit at one time. But when I was a senior and graduated I got one. Then when I was in college I wondered how I would look and feel in a tuxedo so I got one. Once when I was in Bermuda I wondered how it would be to have some English tweeds—they cost a lot of money, but I bought three suits. Now, I even have tails and a high silk hat—I wondered how I'd look." He laughed. "And it was all because when I was little I didn't have any clothes.—I've hardly bought a necktie in three or four years. Mostly Emma's influence, I guess. She was scandalized by my wardrobe—but I'm still not ashamed."

Delph laughed, too. "You're like me," she said. "When I was little, Aunt Fronie always said she didn't want th' neighbors to think she didn't do right by her niece—so I had a lot of clothes—nice sensible ones, but never what I wanted." She gave Sam a speculative glance, and seeing that he understood, went on. "Now, Marsh fusses at me sometimes because I don't dress up more, but, pshaw, I don't care, not that kind of clothes. But I would like to have a real little bathing suit, red or black, th' kind your mother or even your sister Emma would die to see me wear—an' Marsh would faint. An' then—I guess it was because all th' people that belonged to our church were sinners if they danced—I've always wanted a w-i-ide, long-skirted, red silk dress—real red, red as a black gum leaf in th' fall—an' with no sleeves an' not much shoulders an' no back—hardly anything but a little front an' a lot of skirt. I would wear a red flower in my hair, an' my slippers—." She paused to consider the matter of the slippers, and Sam eased his back against the tree, and pointed to a thunder head.

"Silver for your slippers like the edge of that cloud," he said.

But Delph was not so certain. "I don't know about silver slippers for a red dress. Now if it were blue—I'll make it blue—a bright blue like th' sky fresh after a rain, an' on th' skirt I'll have bands of red, th' bright shade to match that kind of blue."

"If it would change like your eyes," he said, "they—." He stopped and sat confused, as if he had remembered that she was Delph, the farmer's wife.

But Delph didn't mind; many had praised her eyes; and Sam seemed more like a friend or a cousin whom she had known as a child, and even though he had been gone away for a long long time, he was just as he had used to be. "Your eyes are like that, too," she said. "Th' kind they used to say in th' old days, 'th' wind blows through'; I'll bet you can't tell lies either or keep people from knowin' you don't like 'em so well—th' trouble I'm always havin' with people like Sadie Huffacre." And she turned and smiled at him and studied his eyes, fixed now on the sky.

"It's worse when they learn you like them—too much," he said, and got up. He stood a moment looking down at her, before he said, "Delph, please, soon as my back is turned don't be crying and running through the heat and eating your heart away.—He wouldn't like it, I know."

Her throat hurt, and she wished he wouldn't go away. He was so gay and happy in his ways; he, more than anyone else, made her feel that everything would be all right. "I don't aim to cry," she began, bravely enough, but her throat kept tightening as she tried to go on, "but there isn't anything—that can change it. He's maybe—maybe layin' there a dyin'—an'." Her eyes widened and darkened; she sat a moment looking up at him, then dropped her head on her drawn up knees, and cried as no one but Marsh had ever seen her cry—and that was a long time ago. Marsh couldn't get well. She knew he couldn't. She tried to see some life for her and Burr-Head past his death, but it was like looking into a dark, empty, soundless room.

Sam dropped to the ground beside her; she felt his hand on her arm, and heard him say, "Please, Delph—please don't cry." He said that and a lot of other things. Gradually, she found herself listening as he said, "You're young, Delph. You could do anything you want to do, or be anything you want to be.—It may seem hard advice, but try to look through th' trouble, Delph. There's always something ahead—till you die."

She wiped her eyes on her apron and sat very still, trying to hold all his words in her mind, see past the ugliness and pain of death to the life she had dreamed of back in the Little South Fork Country. Sam remained with her, and not long after Poke Easy came, and scolded her for the traces of tears he saw on her cheeks; said she was foolish worrying after Marsh, a man tough as ground hog hide. He'd pull through, never forget that, he said, and glanced at Sam, still sitting on the ground. It seemed to Delph sometimes, or maybe she only imagined it, that there was a coldness between Sam and Poke Easy, or rather on Poke Easy's side alone; she could not imagine Sam's being cold to anyone, he was too smilingly indifferent to most things for coldness.

Today he smiled lazily at his wide shouldered brother, and wanted to know if there were any work he wanted done. He and Sober had Marsh's corn, tobacco, and hay under fairly good control. Poke

Easy grunted and didn't know, and seemed to hesitate before he said, "Maw said that if I saw you to tell you to hunt up Delph an' keep her from goin' out of her mind—but I notice you've already done that.—Sober said tell you he'd be out of spray by noon, an' he'd have to have arsenic before he could mix another batch."

"That's simple," Sam said, and got up, brushing twigs and the sticky walnut leaves from his clothing. "Delph and I will go to Hawthorne for some. Won't we, Delph?" And he caught her hand and pulled her to her feet.

Delph hesitated. She would like to ride to Town with Sam in that long blue roadster that looked as if it would go like the wind. And because she wanted so much to go, it seemed unfair to Marsh. But when Sam insisted, teasingly reminded her of Dorie's command, she went, and in spite of Poke Easy's disapproving eyes, and questioning looks from neighbors met on the road, she was, in only a little while, glad that she had gone. Sam drove slowly and talked of tobacco, and the diseases that sometimes attacked its leaves. Men would never learn to cure them through bacteriology and botany alone; chemistry was the answer. He told her then of his plans for such work as a boy, and sighed a little with his eyes when he went on to say that he had, instead, decided to have a try at research in munitions.

"But you're not too old to do th' other yet," she reminded him, "work on an experiment farm, or have one of your own, or maybe go huntin' all over th' world for certain plants that won't take some diseases, an' learnin' why, an' tryin' to make others th' same way, like men I've read about in books," she said.

He nodded toward the road and smiled his swift bright smile that made him seem a young boy instead of a man older than Marsh. "It's never too late for anything is it—eh, Delph? There's nothin' like doing what you want to do—when you're certain you want to do it."

She watched a black lock of wavy hair tumble on his forehead, then one quick hand flipping it away. "Th' trouble is, I guess," she said, "is bein' certain what you want to do."

"So, you know that, too," he said, and drove a good piece in silence before he added, "but then when you do know, it's worth all the wasted time and trouble—and disappointment—it took to find out. Let's drive right on through Hawthorne and go till we find another town where they sell arsenic. There's no hurry. If we get hungry we can buy hamburgers and hot dogs. Did you ever eat a hot dog, Delph?"

She smiled a little ruefully, "Every year before I went to th' Fair back at home, Aunt Fronie always made me promise never to eat any such 'trash,' she called it. An' now Marsh always says it's foolish to spend money for such—once I bought some bologna sausage just to see what it was like an' Marsh he almost had a fit, trash, he called it, too—an' I guess it was silly to buy it when I had chicken an' ham an' beef an' such at home—but, you know in some books, th' new ones that Mrs. Elliot gives me to read—th' poor people are always eatin' things like hot dogs an' bologna sausage or pork an' beans.—You know, I've never in my life had a taste of canned pork an' beans."

Sam laughed, his gentle kind of laughter, that always seemed as much at himself as at her. "We'll have to have a picnic," he said, "on bologna sausage and pork and beans."

Delph nodded and agreed, and that afternoon when they brought Sober his arsenic somewhere around four o'clock, she wondered a little guiltily where the time had gone.

The day she picnicked with Sam was the beginning of a strange way of life, like a long sleeping, often black with nightmares of fear and the shadow of death, but shot through sometimes with dream-like moments of seeing and of understanding a man who should have been remote and different to herself, but never was. And through him she saw herself, the Delph she had used to be in the Little South Fork country; and now that Delph seemed neither strange nor sinful because she had thought at times of running away from home, had never promised God she wouldn't dance or do other things upon which the God of the Little South Fork country frowned. Others in the world had been the same at least once. There were moments when the sweetness of finding the echoes of herself and of having another find the same, seemed too precious for any moments not spent with Marsh. And she would go abruptly away, maybe to stand by the window with the morning glory vines.

Twice each day she went and sat a time in Marsh's room, and that was all she saw of him. Dr. Andy had found a middle-aged nurse in Lexington; a woman experienced in typhoid and strong enough to manage Marsh. When in her presence Delph always sat stiffly on the edge of her chair, feeling a stranger in her own house, anxious to do as the woman wished, but hoping always that Marsh would speak to her or she could talk with him a bit—at least enough to make her know that he was Marsh, her Marsh. But Mrs. Redmond discouraged such things, with a "Really, Mrs. Gregory, you irritate the patient," and Delph would feel her ineptitude and go away—to Sam.

The long skeleton under the sheet that through some miracle continued to breathe and scream and ask for water seemed no more than some piteous, slowly breaking link between life and death. True, the fever raged less fiercely. There were hours when he lay like one conscious and watched the flickering shadows of the morning glory leaves with wide gray eyes touched by nothing except the changing patterns of light. Sometimes he would speak and the words were those of a man in his sense, but the voice was low and hoarse like a voice from the sky or underground.

Then a fiercer flame of fever would come and he would be mad again and raving. Now, at such times if Delph were by, she would refuse to go away when Dorie and the nurse insisted, and take no heed of the women's complaint that she could do nothing, except kill herself with the agony of the watching. There were moments when she watched and seemed to see the fever like a monster tearing Marsh from his body. It drove him to inhuman cries and turnings and writhings so that the women sent for Sober, who slept now in the barn, to come help in his holding. Delph would run, thinking as she ran that no matter how swift her feet, she might return and find the sunken face still; its deep gray eyes fixed on some point past the quivering shadows of the leaves.

There could be no strength in that wasted shriveled body with scarcely breath enough to speak above a whisper. The strength for the insane screams had a ghostly quality, as if the fever, having taken all there was of life, now borrowed from death to prolong the agony. Delph's mind would run in countless, endless circles through sorrow and pity and angry rebellion against the ways of life and death; Marsh who had fought so for the life he wanted must now fight the bitterest battle of all for the thing that every man could have—death.

She wondered at the nurse and Dorie and Dr. Andy and the neighbors who came day after day, stood a moment by the yard gate or at the door, and went away saying always, "He's puttin' up a good fight."

"Maybe he'll pull through," she would sometimes hear one say, and then another answering, "Aye, he's weak. When th' fever goes, he'll go."

She watched Dorie as she watched Marsh through the hours. Dorie's face was the same as when she had watched the lower corn blades curl through the drought of that first hard summer. Apart from any sorrow or fear as to what the outcome might be, Dorie's eyes were filled with the admiration she had always held for fighting, struggling things, be they plant or human. Often when the fever was fierce upon him, Delph would look into the older woman's face for comfort—and never find it. Dorie's face was that of one who watched a battle or a storm. It was as if all life lay in Marsh and all death in the fever, and the drama of the fight between the two was a something that held Dorie and the people of the countryside.

Delph saw no battle. She saw only the tortured passing of a life. Evenings, while she sat the little time allowed with him she could feel death, touching not only the thing on the bed, but herself and her child and all the life about. Dorie would see her sitting so, with bloodless face and clenched hands, and say, "Delph, you'd better take Sam—he's waitin' out there to row me over th' river—an' see that ever'thing's all right in th' barn. An' then I'd go up to th' brick house, pore child, you're worse than nothin' here."

And Delph would go, no longer troubled with guilt at leaving Marsh. He never knew her, never would; the lingering ways of his death seemed cruel—and she would wish that he could be out of his fever and pain and fear. She and Sam would walk together to the barn, light the lantern and look at this and that as she and Marsh had used to do; and in his ways in the barn he made her think of Marsh, stopping to separate a flock of hens crowded foolishly close together on the roost, making certain that everything was locked and tight, stopping in the dark to listen for sign of mice or rats, stroking Maude's nose a time or so, and speaking a word to Jule, Maude's second colt.

Nights while he waited for Dorie they would sit on the back porch steps or on the grass under the box elder tree, and talk of many things. Delph would listen in the darkness to his soft, easy hill man's voice, and find again the world she could not see when near the skeleton on the bed. Sam could drive away the ugliness and the pain, and she would find herself young again and strong, able to dream and plan, and see Burr-Head grow into the man she wished him to be—someone hungry for the taste of the world, like Sam.

Sam no longer mentioned Marsh, no more than any of the neighbors asked her how he was. They knew—maybe better than she. Nor did Sam talk always of things he had done and seen; more and more he talked of what he would like to do, and Delph would listen and wonder sadly why it was that Marsh had never talked to her of his plans as Sam talked; they would maybe have seemed as bright and as worthy as Sam's now seemed. Sometimes he stood away and laughed at them as he sometimes stood away and looked at and laughed over the self he was. Other times he was serious and moody, a little regretful, she thought.

One night while they sat under the box elder tree saying little, he suddenly asked with a sober note under the banter of his talk, "Delph, you have the reputation of being a wise young woman. What would you say to a man if he quit a good job in these hard times for no reason at all, except to do something he wanted to do— and would maybe if he did it never have any money again as long as he lived?"

Delph wrapped a grass blade around and around her finger and studied the stars. "I'd say it all depended on th' man," she said after a time. "With some I'd say they ought to stick—but well, with a man that didn't take th' job for th' money, or th' name, or anything, I'd say for him to strike out after what he wants."

"But, Delph, why in God's name would any fool take a job for anything but the money or the name or because he liked the work so well he couldn't quit it?" Sam asked in a curiously eager voice, and moved closer over the grass.

She smiled. "Mostly, I guess because he wanted to see how it would be to work in a munitions plant, see if he could hold his own with all th' other chemists, or maybe th' work was dangerous—an' he wanted to be certain he wasn't afraid, or maybe he wanted th' money—then—or maybe he was just foolish, wantin' to see what he could do."

"You know an awful lot, Delph," he said, and put his hand over her hand lying on the grass. "My whole family—they never knew. And Roan my best friend never knew—at least enough but what he hated me for the going. But you know, and don't hate me because I seemed to go like all the rest, after money and a good job."

"An' now that you know you can do it, you don't care about it any more," she said, and felt his hand over hers, and knew she ought to draw away, but did not. After all he was like an old acquaintance or a cousin—and then she knew she lied in her heart, for when he said, "How do you know so much, Delph, about me?" she stayed to answer, though she knew she ought to go away.

"Just from thinkin' how I'd be," she said. "Always since I've been big enough to sing in church I've wondered if I could sing for people that knew what singin' was.—An' when I bake a cake that wins th' prize at th' Fair I wonder if I could have learned to do other things, more with my head I mean, an' won prizes in college. An' when people in Hawthorne Town nod an' wave to me or invite me to their houses I wonder—if in a city or in any place where th' people are different from th' ones here—if they would like me there— or if maybe I wouldn't feel more at home with them, somehow, an'— but pshaw, I'm always wonderin'. It's silly."

"It's not silly.—I guess I'll wonder about a lot of things till I die."

She turned about and studied him, but his face was no more than a white blur in the darkness. She was glad of that; he could not see her talking eyes. "But you never stopped with th' wonderin'," she said.

"No," he said, and lifted her fingers from the grass, "not always, but over some things I've done nothing but wonder. I'll always want to know—don't try to run away when I ask—but what became of that girl, you told Emma about her once and Emma told me—and never knew she told me—that girl in the Little South Fork Country? She could have gone away; her man would have followed then. I know; it was the fall that prices dropped to the bottom, and even Poke Easy wrote to say that he was thinking of going with Joe."

He waited and when Delph continued to sit motionless and silent, he whispered, "Please don't take it wrong, Delph. Don't answer if you don't want to—but I always wondered."

She felt his hand strong and warm on her own and forgot his question in thinking of one of her own. "Tell me, Sam—were you thinkin' of me then—wonderin'—why?"

"I told you once I always read the *Westover Bugle*. I used to read the things you'd say, about farming or the weather or the health of the neighbors, and sometimes you'd mention me, the way you mentioned the rest of our family or anybody else, and I could see that you never thought I'd let the county down or my mother by going away—when they all thought I ought to stay and help her raise the younger ones and manage the farm. You never hated me, or envied—and so I wondered.—There was no sin in that," he said.

"I'll tell you then," she said, and pulled her hand away and locked it with the other about her drawn up knees. "I couldn't have any man comin' to me like a whipped dog—takin' my way because he'd failed at farmin'—through no fault of his own. But he'd never ha' failed—but there was once—one night—he seemed to think he had. I guess maybe I saw how much it meant to him—an' saw maybe that he would never leave it—or maybe I couldn't stand to see him—feelin' that he wasn't any good.—But, pshaw, what does it matter? It's been a long time ago," she ended hastily, and sprang up and ran to the house; and avoided Sam for three or four days. But Dorie kept flinging them together.

· 26 ·

SOMETIMES WHEN Marsh lay in a seeming stupor, Delph would be conscious of his searching eyes as she went away. Often, when the nurse was resting and Dorie or Emma tended him, she would bring him a young ear of corn or a bough of half ripened apples or a cluster of tobacco flowers. She never attempted to talk with him, but tried to show him in that wordless way how things were doing. He would look at the thing she brought, smile faintly with his eyes, but say no word and never try to lift his hand for reaching. "He's savin' his strength, th' best patient I ever had," Dorie would say, and add when it seemed she spoke to the empty room, "Pore man, it always seemed anyhow that most a th' time you could plow ten acres a land easier than you could say six words."

Sometimes Marsh heard, and often he did not. In either case he never answered, Once, he smiled a little under his closed eyes when heard Sadie Huffacre say from the other side of the window that his seeming disconcern for all that went on about him was a bad sign. He knew most of the life about him with no asking of questions. Times, when he returned from some long voyage into the nightmarish land of the oil fields or the dreary waste of life that had been his childhood, he had only to look at the morning glory vine to know the hours or the days that the delirium had claimed him.

Sometimes he would see a morning glory flower, freshly opened and beaded with dew. The next time he saw it, the flower would be gone with a brown seed pod in its place, or again a bud would be a flower, or the pale green tips of climbing tendrils that when he went

378

away were even with his bed, now rose almost to the top of the window. He saw the earlier leaves grown brown and fall, and seed pods grow plump, turn gray and burst with a scattering of the small shining seed. Now and then an uneasy wonder would come to make him think that maybe he would never see the seed spring up as other morning glory vines. Yet, he seldom wasted his life on fear and wonder.

He knew the battle he fought. The fever was like the drought and the flood and an early frost, something that came and could not be changed, but he would live and it would pass as the drought had passed. He was patient. When conscious he never moaned in pain or cursed the consuming fire of the fever. He struggled, not for the privilege of drawing breath for some long vague period of years, but thought of foolish things, like walking up the hill again to see the sunset, or hauling wagon loads of corn on a clear December day. He seldom thought of his life; he thought of Delph and Burr-Head and his cows grazing in the clover fields, and how good it was to begin the spring plowing in a fine April dawn, when fog lay on the river, and the smell of the earth and of blooming plum trees hung about him as he plowed.

Most often he simply lay and watched the passing of the days. He knew morning and noon and afternoon and twilight through the changing patterns of yellow-green light above his head. He knew sunrise from the crowing of the roosters and twilight from the mockingbird that sat in the trumpet vine and sang and sang as if the songs were seed for a harvest of song. He was proud of the mockingbird. His was one of the few places about that could boast a mockingbird, and the only one to have a hummingbird. The hummingbird never sang but it was a pretty thing to watch. It came mostly to the trumpet vine which was a little distance from the window, but sometimes, early, when the corn rows lay still in the white fog of the morning, the hummingbird would come to his vine, and hang spinning above some purple flower.

There was a whole life in the morning glory vine. He liked it when there came a sudden summer shower, and he could watch the slow falling of drops from the heart shaped leaves, and think that maybe some day he could get cool again from standing in the rain.

Sounds from beyond the morning glory vine told him many things. He knew milking time, and Sober's time of returning from the fields, and the days that Caesar and Burr-Head were careless and left the sly Prissy to roam in the pasture. Then would Delph go calling, and her long drawn cry of, "Suke, Prissy, S-u-u-uke," would come faintly down through the twilight, and was a pretty thing to hear, better than the mocking bird or the katy-dids or the whip-poor-wills crying from among the little cedars on the hill.

There was a time of day that he liked best, and that was dusk when the nurse went away to have her supper, and Emma left him to feed Sober in the kitchen and he was alone. Marsh saved himself for that time of day, struggled steadily against the rising night tide of delirium until his child had come and gone. "How you comin' Marsh?" Burr-Head would ask in a whisper from the other side of the morning glory vines.

And he would answer in a whisper, too, "Fine, son, fine."

"Still buildin' that stone house?"

"Yes.—There's not another rock needed on th' big chimney."

Burr-Head would sometimes linger by the window, silent, crouched on the grass with Caesar, or other times he would ask questions in a soft whisper. The questions were sometimes answered; often they were not. "Marsh, th' clover leaves they fold their hands an' shut their eyes when th' sun goes down, but th' sunflowers now, they hang their heads. Why is that, Marsh?"

"They're sleepy, son."

"Marsh, where does th' corn pollen go?"

"Into th' silk—it makes seed."

"How?"

"I'm busy, son—tryin' to think about th'—back north room."

"I'll sleep there an' see th' lights from Hawthorne Town, won't I?"

"Yes, son."

"Let Delph sleep there, too. She likes th' Hawthorne lights better than th' sunset."

"Delph likes th'—sunset, too—an' th' stars."

"But she likes th' lights better. I heared her say so to Sam when me an' her an' him went to th' high knoll to look at the sunset.— Marsh, how is Broadway?"

"Delph will—have to tell."

"She don't know. I heared her ask Sam."

"Maybe she'll tell you—sometime. Run along—now, th' stone house—I need to be."

Burr-Head would listen a time and then go away. Sometimes he sang as he walked up the hill, unafraid of the early summer darkness, "For he has gone to fight th' foe of King George upon th' throne." Marsh would be alone except for Caesar stirring under the window, whining a little at times with a soft pup-like cry. Almost every night Poke Easy came and stood a time in silence on the other side of the vines. Roan would come sometimes and say, "Don't let 'em make you think you're goin' to die, Marsh. You'll live to plow sixteen hours under a hot June sun in knee-high corn for many a day." Mr. Elliot would come and look at him; Brother Eli came to pray for him; Dorie read him a letter from John—he was to call on him in case of need; and men from miles around would come, farmers in heavy brogan shoes with sweat stained hats in their hands would tiptoe awkwardly up to his bed and look at him, and then go away, silent as they had come. And their eyes were sorrowful when they looked at his wide fields of dark rich corn.

Sam no longer paused by the window. Delph came less often than in his early sickness; and she no longer brought fruit or flowers or ears of corn. Sometimes he would think of Delph and Sam; wonder what she saw in him, why he seemed finer to her than other men. Still, he seldom tortured himself with foolish imaginings. Most often he would only wonder if Delph wore her white sunbonnet, lined with blue, and tied with a blue bow under her chin. He hoped she did not. In that she looked prettier than when she sang in church.

Nights when she came to sit a time by the foot of his bed, he would look at her sometimes, find her face haggard in the dim light from the low lamp flame, see the torture in her eyes, and be glad that Sam was home. He, Marsh, had caused the sorrow and the torture in her face through his careless ways and stubbornness, just as he had made the faint thread of scar on her forehead, and caused her the long sickness after the coming of Burr-Head. That first summer it was because of him she had worked so in the fields and garden, peddled in Burdine, churned and worked from summer daylight to summer darkness. He owed her so much. If Sam could in any way make pleasant the little time she spent away from him, he, Marsh, should be grateful. Sam only told her stories, talked to her, told her of things from away. He would reason so in his saner moments, but in his delirium he sometimes begged for her—and she was never there. Both Mrs. Redmond and Dorie agreed that it was best she stayed away—most likely Marsh would not have known her at such times, and she was an unhandy person to have around in case of sickness.

Other times Marsh would think of the brick house, and wonder if Delph knew that it was to be sold. He feared that Mr. Elliot with his booming tongue had let her know. He wanted to tell her himself—in his own way. Nights, he wished, when he could wish, that she would smile at him or come to his bed, or sing a little. But Delph when near him never smiled and never sang.

The morning glory vine made other buds and others flowers, and slowly Marsh grew less conscious of bud and flower and leaf. The vine was only a greenness that promised a never-brought coolness. There seemed more life in the room. There was another woman in white, but she was dim and of little account like Mrs. Redmond. He knew Delph's eyes, and Dorie's voice, and black Emma's hands, and the rest were mostly shadows and echoes flitting between the morning glory leaves. Once, he roused to hear Dr. Andy's voice and his dry sharp cackle. "His fever's goin' down. It'll break one a these days." And Dorie saying, "Yes.—It's got to break." And Delph's voice, hollow and strained, "that, that's th' worst time?" And Dr. Andy's cackle again. "Buck up, girl. It's all bad time." And one of the nurses saying, "Really, Mrs. Gregory, wouldn't you be more comfortable outside?"

Sometimes he heard Katy's quick light steps, saw her flying yellow hair, and knew that tobacco cutting time was maybe past, else Katy could not have left the hired hands and come away. That would mean late August, almost time for the Fair. He wished Poke Easy could take Jule and Solomon. One night he tried to tell him, but he could not make his whisper carry through the morning glory vines.

He knew he was no good for talking. Still, he could see and understand. He liked to look in Katy's eyes. They showed many things, sorrow, and a fear of death, but stronger than those was hope with no resignation. He could not say that of Delph's eyes; in them there was sorrow, but stronger than that was the waiting—waiting even in sorrow was waiting.

At last the promised coolness came, slowly as if his feet and his hand trailed in an ice cold flood. Then gradually the morning glory vine changed to a green ice mountain that crushed and froze and ground him down; he was ice against ice sinking slowly into ice like earth. Most things were dim and faint and far away behind the green ice mountain.

He wandered through the Rockcastle Country where all the trees were tall and fine and green, but there was a coldness in the air, and snow sifted through the leaves. Delph was lost and he was hunting her. Burr-Head came calling and crying through the trees, and Sam carried him away, hid him behind rows of cold white lights. He wandered and wanted to plant a crop of corn, but he had no heart to cut the fine tall trees. He saw a high mountain crowned with pine trees, and below it there was a holly bush thick with berries red as blood. He wanted to climb up the high dark bluff but there was Azariah with his blue, blue far seeing eyes, and his hair black, long down to his shoulders, and Azariah stood frozen faced and silent, looking past him to a country he could not see; and he turned away and did not climb the mountain.

Sounds from another country would sometimes call him away, Burr-Head piping through the pasture fields, "for he has gone to fight the foe of King George upon the throne," the mocking bird at sundown; the ringing of the school bell, and then another day there came the church bells. There was Big Salem and Little Cedar Stump, the Burdine bells, the cracked bell of the Golden Lily Colored Church; all rang and rang, and when their ringing died the room was very still.

The church bells rang for him he knew. They asked all people in the countryside to pray. They prayed for him as they had prayed for Garfield long years ago, when Garfield lay shot and dying. He had heard Dorie tell it. Garfield, he was a president, and he had died, but he, Marsh, was a farmer. The church bells they might ring for him, but they would never toll for him.

Up at the brick house Delph stood by a window and listened to the bells. She was alone in the room, an upstairs room above the garden, opening on a wide view of the valley and the farther hills. Sometimes, she looked down at the asters and dahlias and other late August blooming flowers, but mostly down into Marsh's corn lands, or up past the river bluff and into the farther hills. There was something sad about the earth and sky today. The leaves were green, it was summer still, but the air was cool with no wind; and the sunlight sickly white and little warm, falling like a dead thing out of the deep, cloudless, blue-green sky, with the shadows dark and sharp.

The leaves of the trees by the window and the yellowing iris leaves in the garden glittered as if painted with ice. Maybe they looked that way because they knew they were going to die. They died gaily with no pain, dressed in bright red and gold, and for a moment before they died it was the lot of some of them to be lifted above the valley and whirled against the sky. They died—and all things died, and maybe it never hurt so if sometime in their lives they could have that one moment of glory, of feeling themselves lifted above all ugliness and sorrow and misery, and knowing the feel of the sky.

Marsh, she thought, had known more of the sky than most men. The sight of a clover field in June or the smell of his ripening corn could make him forget so many things, the mud, and the work, the ugliness and pettiness of life in a river valley. He had never wanted her pity; and with her sorrow he would not have it now. The church bells rang again, and she hoped Burr-Head never knew why they rang.

The hill shadow touched the river, and still she sat and looked into the valley. Mrs. Elliot came, and some of the neighbor women came, but she sent them all away. When Dorie or Dr. Andy or any one of the nurses watching by Marsh sent word to her that it was time for her to come and watch him while he died, she wanted to be alone. They would pity her and comfort her and never know that she had borne the pain of his dying through weeks and weeks, and the hardest part of it was gone—now. There was only so much sorrow, and she had spent that when she watched Marsh wither and change like a corn plant through a drought. She would sit by the hideously pitiful thing on the bed, but it would never know her, or speak, for Marsh was gone a long while ago.

June, with the Memorial Day and then the beginning of Marsh's sickness were back in some dim, long gone time; she had lived the whole of a life since then—learned and found and dreamed and suffered more than in all her other life together.

It was late afternoon with the shadow creeping up the hill across the Cumberland when she heard a man's feet coming down the hall. She turned away from the window and waited, knowing it was Sam; she knew his feet, light they were like a dancer's. Dorie had sent him to tell her. She called, "Come in," when his feet stopped by the door. He opened the door, closed it, and walked a few steps into the room before he looked at her. He hesitated, then came on with great eager strides, his hands reaching for her, and his eyes hunting her eyes.

"You've come to tell me," she whispered, and cried in his arms with her head on his shoulder. But through her grief she felt his arms; and they were not the arms of a cousin or a childhood friend, but those of a man with a man's heart and a man's body. He was silent, holding her tight against him, as if she were the one dying, and he would with much holding never let her die.

She felt his face on her hair, then heard him begging, "Delph," in a scarcely audible voice, but with a wild, wild calling under the voice.

"You don't have to say all th' things you have said—not any more. I'm not afraid, an' I'll be brave—now," she said, and drew slowly away and smiled up at him, a slow sad smile, but sad for a sorrow worn by many tears and tired.

"Delph," he said again, and stood holding her, just holding her as if he didn't want to speak or move, and looking down into her face, caressing it with his eyes.

She tilted her head and studied him. "You look tired," she said.

He nodded. "I was always one to find waiting hard."

"You—you've been waitin' down by th' house all day?"

He nodded again, and the black forelock trembled above his eyes. "Most all day I sat under the box elder tree." His face twisted, as if he might have had a sharp memory of watching something die. "Don't think hard of me, Delph—please. There've been others watched and waited, too, for lots of things—that never mattered so I never hoped or wished—I just thought on ahead, I think. Then when Dr. Andy came and said—the worst was over—I knew there was no need to wait—any more, ever—for anything.—They say he is an uncommonly strong man." He bent and kissed her on the mouth, gently took her arm from about his shoulder, turned sharp about and left the room.

Delph stood and watched him go; and her arms dangled loose and limp by her sides like those of a wooden doll.

She was standing so, looking at the nothingness beyond the door when Mrs. Elliot came, running and calling up the stairs. Delph listened in silence while the woman laughed and cried and babbled. She had just talked to Dr. Andy. It was amazing the way Marsh's heart had reacted to his treatment and the treatment of a specialist he had called down from Lexington. There was no reason now in the world why Marsh with proper care shouldn't get well. Maybe the prayers of the people had helped. She just couldn't, couldn't believe it, and Mrs. Elliot started to cry, but screamed instead.

Delph had fainted.

She revived soon, and found herself in a room, oddly familiar not to be her own. After a time she remembered; the dark wood paneling, the flowers that made her think of spring. The room where Burr-Head had been born and where she lay while he almost died; and where when he was better she had knelt by the window and watched the road and smelled the orchard bloom, and dreamed for him—and for herself. Maybe he had only been the excuse. Oh, God, but she was such a fool.

Dorie heard of what had happened, and came laughing and filled with talk, telling her not to be ashamed of having showed such a weakness as fainting. Even she had fainted once, a long time ago, but over some little nothing it had been, not a great thing like Marsh's turn for the better. She had to laugh at that. It only went to show that a body could never tell—not even when the chances were one in a million as they had been for Marsh.

Delph lay and looked at the ceiling, and tried to listen to Dorie's talk. She could feel that old forced smile on her mouth like some familiar mask that she had taken off for a little time, but now must wear again—for always and always. "It'll seem strange to talk to him again—an' find him like he used to be," she said, when she noticed after a time that Dorie was silent, maybe expecting her to say something.

Dorie shook her head impatiently. "Lord, Delph, I never saw a woman like you. I've heard Marsh laugh lots a times an' say you'd ruined many a pretty flower bud just from pullin' it apart to see what color it would be—an' I can believe it. When he was in th' fever you had him dead an' buried, an' now you've got him settin' up in bed, discussin' th' primary elections, I reckin. He's not well, but he rallied after his fever broke—that's th' main thing. He can't be doin' but precious little talkin' for days, an' you mustn't be expectin' it." She glanced about the room. "Where is Sam? I thought he came up this way."

Delph nodded. "He was th' first that told me."

Dorie beamed, and was led into a long monologue in praise of Sam. Since Poke Easy's coming to live at home, and more and more as he demonstrated that he could both manage the farm and take a hand in law and county politics, Dorie was too contented with her world to hold any bitterness for Sam. Though she scolded now about his expensive car and his carelessness with money, she showed little anger, talked of him more as if he had been a lovable but spoiled child. "He was always a great one for seein' what he wanted an' goin' after it," she said, and added musingly, "I've been wonderin' lately what he set his head on now. When he came home he was supposed to take a month's vacation, but th' next thing I learned he'd asked for three months leave of absence—an' now from th' books he's readin' I wouldn't be surprised if he struck out on some work of his own."

"He'd like that," Delph said, "always to go huntin' down th' things he wanted to find."

"He wouldn't be goin' about th' country," Dorie corrected, "maybe stuck in a laboratory an' experiment fields closer than Marsh sticks to his farmin'."

"He'd still be huntin'," she said, and got up. She couldn't lie still in bed any longer, trying to recross in a few minutes all the country it had taken her so many painful weeks to cross.

Dorie studied her. "You look kind a peaked, Delph. You ought to try to take things easy now—while th' nurses are still with Marsh. In a couple more weeks you'll have to be gettin' back into harness—dryin' an' cannin' an' fumin' around, tryin' to catch up on your work. Now, when you can rest easier in your mind on Marsh, I think if I was in your place I'd make Sam—he wouldn't mind—take me around a little. Whyn't you have him drive you into Hawthorne to a picture show tonight? Some kind of silly, foolish somethin' would do you good."

Delph turned abruptly away and said with a sharpness she had never used with Dorie, "I don't went to be drivin' into any picture show—or or—goin' any place with Sam."

But Dorie only smiled, too happy at Marsh's improvement to have anything more than high good humor for all the world. "Pshaw, Delph, you're just tired an' cross as a cat. It all goes to show you need somethin' like that—you've got to be patient now—in a few days you can be talkin' to Marsh. You mustn't even go about him tonight, but all th' time you can be thinkin' he's gettin' well." She smiled teasingly and stroked Delph's hair. "You may not notice it—you're married, but I'll bet there's many a woman that would give her eye teeth to be drivin' around with Sam.—Not just because he's my boy—but I do think he's one a th' best lookin' men in th' country, takes after his father in his winnin' ways an' he's got th' looks of th' men on my side in th' old days." She stopped and a calculating look came into her eyes while she counted something on her fingers, but after a time of trying she gave it up, and explained that she had always intended to figure out the kinship between her and Delph. There was some connection from away back between the Costellos and the Dodsons, but it was so far back, all the way to Azariah, maybe, that she could never get it straight, but some rainy day she and Delph must get together and figure out their cousin-ship.

Delph listened and smiled, and wished for nothing except that Dorie would go and she could be alone; she didn't think that ever in her life she had wanted so much to be alone. She wished she could take a long lone ride down a lonesome pine ridge, or go anyplace where there were no people and no one to see. In order to hasten Dorie's going, she put on her bonnet and made some excuse about having to go to the store; and when Dorie continued to linger, warn her not to go lest she faint on the way, she had a moment's terror that she would break into wild screaming laughter or senseless crying.

However, when Dorie had gone at last she only stood on the back porch and stared down into the valley; but when Myrtle the cook came with some talk of what she would fix for supper, she dashed down the backstairs, caught up a split basket on the back porch and ran down the road toward her own house. She wondered why she ran or where she would go to be away from people, and when she came to the barn lane she turned and walked through the corn field, remembering with a rush of thankfulness that through a strip of the corn she had planted late beans. She could pick the beans and have an excuse for staying alone until full dark came.

She walked down the rows of yellowing corn and pulled the little goose craw beans and dropped them into her tucked up apron. The afternoon shadow lay thick on the field, and the air was cool touched with the promise of fall and of winter. She had not worked long when she heard Burr-Head behind her calling, "Delph, you're droppin' all th' beans on th' ground 'stead of in your apron," and he ran up to her, his hands filled with the plump green beans.

She took the beans from his outstretched hands, and he looked into her face and asked, "Sick, Delph? You look peaked. Myrtle said I'd mebbe better hunt you. You didn't look so well."

"No. I'm all right, Burr-Head."

He ran away to look at a pumpkin a few rows away, but came back soon and looked at her and asked again, "Sick, Delph?"

She shook her head.

"There's water in your eyes, Delph."

"It's this little cold night wind."

"You dropped some more beans, Delph."

"It's no matter.—There's lots of beans."

She walked on to other hills, but soon he was with her again, tugging at her dress. "Oh, Delph, come an' see this whoppin' big punkin."

She followed him to the great pumpkin, watched in silence while he smiled and patted it and said, "Punkin, punkin what a 'nawful fat thing you are," and the way he smiled, his eyes like Marsh's eyes when he looked at his corn.

She pulled a sticky bean leaf from her skirt and looked at it as she said, "Burr-Head, what—what do you mean to be when you are older?"

He sat on the ground with one arm over the pumpkin and pondered. "I can't ever make up my mind," he said, and wrinkled his nose and laughed. "I don't know but what'll mebbe be a corn farmer like Marsh—but I'd like to have a lot a pretty milk cows like that man up by Burdine—an' I'd like to grow a lot a grapes an' make a lot a wine like Mrs. Elliot says they do in France—an' oh—so many things I don't know." He lay back on his arms and studied the sky with narrowed eyes as Marsh often did. "I want me some blue-blooded horses from th' bluegrass country—an' I'd like to have a lot of pretty sheep an' goats like Mrs. Elliot says they have in Switzerland—an'—." He looked from the sky into his mother's eyes, then sat up suddenly, saying all in a breath, "But, pshaw, Delph, I'll be livin' with you an' Marsh an' my little sister in th' stone house till I'm big as Dorie's Poke Easy."

"Stone house?"

"Pshaw, you know, Delph, th' one we'll live in when Elliots buy th' brick house, you know th' one Marsh has been a buildin' in his head. Don't you know about it, Delph?"

She shook her head and smiled. "Suppose—you tell me?"

"You know, with a big cellar an' chimneys, up where he planted th' black locust trees by Solomon's pasture. It'll have a great big fire place, wider than two rows of corn, an'—Delph, you look sick as all get out. Your eyes shine like a sick cow's eyes." He got up and whacked the earth from the seat of his overalls as he had seen Marsh do. "Let's go up to th' Elliots, Delph. You've got your aporn full a beans anyhow."

"I brought a basket. I'll fill it full. You run on."

"But it's nigh supper time."

"I know—but I don't think I want any supper—now."

He hesitated about going, and stood pulling a bean now and then or digging in the soft ground with the toe of one shoe. "D-e-elph, don't you like th' stone house? It's goin' to be mighty fine—when we build it."

She smiled and patted his shoulder. "Sure I like th' stone house, Burr-Head. Run on to your supper now."

He called Caesar and walked away through the corn, but now and then he stopped and looked back at her and waved, but the last time, even though he called, "Goodbye, Delph," she was looking straight overhead at the sky and never saw or heard him.

She walked on and gathered beans, but most fell on the ground. It didn't matter where the beans fell. Nothing mattered; it didn't seem to matter much that she could never dream again for Burr-Head or plan how it would be to live in the brick house. The stone house would be thick and strong and solid, ugly; never the brick house with stained glass in its parlor windows, a graceful winding stair, and fireplaces of marble and tile, and windows from which she could see the cars go by. She stood on tip-toe to reach a high growing bean, and as she pulled it away she saw between the rustling blades of corn the wide reach of the sky, high and deep and blue, shut away as if the narrow corn leaves were a prison through which she must always see the sky—and the world.

When the twilight deepened she went to stand by Marsh's window. She stood a time behind the morning glory vine, its leaves were beginning to brown now, and after putting her ear close among the leaves, she heard breathing, light it was, no louder than a baby's breath, but regular—strong somehow through its weakness. In the kitchen black Emma, preparing some broth for Marsh, smiled at her, and Mrs. Redmond the big nurse was more cordial than she had ever been. She sat a time with her on the back porch, and talked between sips of her after supper coffee. "You know," she said, "experienced as I am, I couldn't see much chance for him. Sometimes it even seemed a sin for him to linger on—and suffer—and you eat your heart out through all those weeks—almost ten it's been."

"It seems like that many years," Delph said, and thought that time, the house and days and minutes of it, was the poorest measure for life of all.

She went back to the brick house, and that night wrote Fronie and John of Marsh's miraculous recovery, or chance for recovery, and filled the letter with words of gladness.

The night and the following days were endless reaches of gray time, empty of everything except a kind of waiting that made all things, be it eating or singing to Burr-Head, seem less the doing of a thing than a means of living through time while she waited. And why she waited, or for what, she never knew, nor did she ask herself.

There was one day, for a little while, a time when she forgot to wait and lived instead. She and Mrs. Elliot were on the upstairs back porch making crepe paper dresses for the school children to wear in the Arbor Day program, when Myrtle came to say that Delph and Mrs. Elliot and Burr-Head had a caller in the front hall, and she was not supposed to say who it was.

Both Mrs. Elliot and Delph wondered who it might be, and rushed about to tidy their hair and pull crepe paper from each other's clothing. Burr-Head ran away before Delph could comb his hair, and in a second was shouting up the stairs that it was nobody but Dorie's Sam playing make-believe.

Delph walked slowly down the hall and down the wide front stairs, taking care that Mrs. Elliot should always be in front of her. There was Sam in the hall, looking tall and strange and handsome in an immaculate white linen suit and a blue tie that matched his eyes. He stood with his hat in one hand and a box of candy in the other and waited at the foot of the stairs. He bowed to Delph and to Mrs. Elliot. "My mother, Mrs. Dorie Dodson Fairchild, who lives on the next hill, sent me to entertain you ladies—you all were very lonesome, she said." And he bowed and smiled a playful mocking smile that made Delph want to cry.

But she smiled and said, "Good afternoon, Mr. Fairchild," and curtsied as she had been taught to do by her mother when a very little girl, and so did Mrs. Elliot, and they all laughed, Burr-Head most of all to see the grownups play at being people they were not.

Mrs. Elliot felt that the occasion demanded at least tea in the front living room. Much to Burr-Head's delight they all sat in the wide shadowy room and drank tea from Mrs. Elliot's best and thinnest china, and had beaten biscuit topped with cherry preserves.

Now and again Burr-Head looked at his mother and wondered why she sipped her tea so slowly, and why she ate none of the beaten biscuit and cherry preserves, and only nibbled at a piece of the candy Sam had brought—beautiful candy wrapped in gold and silver paper.

Then he, too, forgot to eat his candy when Mrs. Elliot played the piano and Delph sang, not the songs she sang in church, but nicer ones—some she had learned from Mrs. Elliot. He always liked to hear his mother sing; she said so many things and he could hear so much, sometimes there was the heaven of the little speckled pig, or again there was the sea with ships and storms, but today he thought the song was neither heaven nor the sea, but sad like the night when Little Lizzie picked her flowers.

He wanted to cry and wished for Marsh, and when Delph would not sing the song he wanted, gay and filled with tra-la-la-las, he slipped from the room and ran down the hill and to the window by the morning glory vines. He whispered softly through the leaves as the nurse had told him he must always do when she caught him one day calling and calling and Marsh did not answer. That was days ago; since then Marsh had never answered, and the last time he had tried two days ago the nurse had sent him away. Today, he forgot Delph, the nurse, and everything and everybody when an answer came through the morning glory vines. The voice was weak, but it was Marsh's all right. "Well, son—tell Solomon to quit his bellerin'—an' carryin' on—tell them mules a mine—they'd better set their heads for work—an' tell that Burr-Head a mine—he'd better start bein' good.—I'll be onto 'em all—pretty soon."

Burr-Head jumped up and down, and Caesar the fool began such a barking and running in circles that there was noise enough to wake the dead. The nurse was out the door and after him in an instant and Burr-Head ran away to the garden gate, and stood swinging on it, ready to run if she kept coming after him. He was half afraid of the big woman in white. He waited while she went back to the house, and was sneaking again to the window when she poked her head around the house corner. She was smiling and motioning him to come to her. He edged gradually nearer at first and then he ran when he understood what she wanted of him. If he would promise to be very quiet, ask no questions or try to make Marsh talk, and if he washed his hands real clean, he could go sit five minutes by his father—and above all things he must not cry.

"I'm no girl," Burr-Head said, and washed his hands and went swaggering in to see his father. But at the door he stopped, and Mrs. Redmond had to give him a little push. "Just look at his eyes," she whispered. "You'll find your father there."

Burr-Head nodded and swallowed, remembered he was no girl, and kept his eyes on his father's. He wouldn't have known the man on the bed was Marsh. He was so long and thin, and he was white, sickly white like a potato sprout grown in the dark, and the bones of his face and his hands looked like sticks and rocks ready to cut through the skin.

He wanted to run away, but he walked on up to the bed, and when Marsh did not lift his hands from the sheet to pat him on the head or whack him on the shoulder as he had used to do, but only whispered, "I guess—I ought to ha' waited—to make 'em bring you in," he was certain he was going to cry.

Then he looked hard at Marsh's eyes, and knew that everything was all right. He wouldn't cry, but give him time and he would answer properly as man to man. He thought of Perce; he had driven into Hawthorne Town with Perce and Little Lizzie several times this summer and one time Perce met a man who had been sick and he said—. He wished he could spit as Perce spat. He couldn't do that, but he did run his fingers through his hair the way Marsh did and say with a little swagger, proud he had remembered, "Well, right now you look holler-eyed as one a Wiley New's cows after a hard cold winter—but, pshaw, you'll fatten up with a little good grazin'."

His father shook a little and the sweat came on his face, and Mrs. Redmond said, "I made him promise to do everything but not to make you laugh—I never thought of that," but she smiled at Burr-Head as if she didn't much mind.

Burr-Head knew he was not to say anything more, so he was still, just looking at the man on the bed, and little by little he found his father. They'd shaved him too close was one thing made him look so strange—especially for a Thursday—his shave looked more like Sunday morning in church—and his hair was cut too short, but it was colored still like a red sandrock flecked with gold.

He asked no questions, and though he felt the nurse's eyes burning a hole in his back, he couldn't help it when Marsh asked one. "What's Delph doin' now, Burr-Head?"

"Singin' to Sam," he said, and whispered because his father whispered.

"Where?"

When he asked that Burr-Head knew his father was all right. His eyes were narrow black the way they were when one of the mules kicked or a bolt worked loose in the cultivator. "Up at th' brick house with Mrs. Elliot," he answered. He wanted to tell him about the tea and the box of candy and the crepe paper dresses for Arbor Day, but the nurse was right behind him, pulling on his shoulder. "Your five minutes are gone, Sonny," she said.

He walked away, looking back over his shoulder at Marsh, but Marsh stared at the ceiling and never seemed to know he had a Burr-Head. Once out of the house he went running back to tell Delph of his visit with Marsh, but stopped when he came to the orchard fence. Sober and Caesar were driving home the cows, and as Delph wasn't singing now—just playing the radio, he guessed from the sound he heard, he ran after Sober and Caesar.

And in the brick house Delph and Sam sat alone in the living room. Mrs. Elliot had for days been so taken up with the problem of making Little Lizzie look like a silver maple tree and one of the fat little Sexton girls a willow for Arbor Day that when she had finished her tea and played a time on the piano, she made her excuses and returned to the green crepe paper.

Delph, after a moment's painful silence, went to the next room and turned on the radio. When the music came she wished she had not, a waltz it was, one of the old ones filled with the sound of violins, bringing visions of long wax candles burning in great ballrooms where women whirled and bowed in wide-skirted dresses, tinted like acres of flowers, and the men were tall and handsome, graceful and gay, sure of themselves and of the world—like Sam.

She turned and he was there, bowing again and saying with that gay smile that made her want to cry, "Shall we dance, Cousin Delphine? It is within the proprieties, for cousins to dance."

"Yes, Cousin Samuel," she said, and they danced in the wide hall where the coming twilight gathered like blue dust in the corners.

"Close your eyes, Delph," he said.

"You are th' one to close your eyes—an' I will wear my blue, blue dress trimmed with red, an' th' red rose in my hair an' th' silver slippers, too, I guess. An' I am not Delph th'—."

"Don't cry, Delph, please don't cry—always remember that in this world you can forget anything—anything—always remember that—even yourself."

"But th' neighbors an' God—Fronie's God—an' th' God Poke Easy made for High Pockets.—I don't want Burr-Head to have a God like that.—What if when he grows up—."

"Don't think about the neighbors and God, Delph—not while you're there and I'm here."

They danced in silence again, and Delph remembered that other dance—a long time ago it was—and the violins then had cried of the wider world and all the mysteries it contained—and now they cried because there was no world—could never be—had never been—the only world there was was not in cities or the sea or multitudes of people. It was—"The next number will be—." Sam snapped off the radio with one hand and held her with the other. "Imagine for just a little while we're—we're in a square dance, Cousin Delphine, waiting for the music to begin, and there are many others watching us and we—."

"The music would begin; we would dance and the dance end. They always do," she said, and slipped out of his arms, and turned on the radio.

The music was a march now, a wild strong thing, like the winds and foaming water set to time. Delph listened a moment, then twisted the dial, and turned abruptly away. "But I thought you liked marches and parades and bands and such," Sam said.

She nodded. "I do—but not today, somehow," she answered and talked on, rapidly as if afraid a silence might say more than her words. "You see it makes me think too much of things, foolish you'd maybe say. But well—I hear them sometimes over the radio like this, their music I mean. Parades I'd like to see with drum majors high steppin' in th' funny hats they wear, an' see th' others beat their drums an' hear th' bugles blow, an' see their uniforms, bright red an' blue I know they wear like men in th' old days wore to war—an' horses, oh I'd like to see a lot of fine cat walkin' horses." She stopped and stood confused, twisting her hands. "Oh, even a fool would know me for crazy."

"You're not crazy, Delph," he said, and took her hands. "I wanted the parades too, and so when I could I went to see them in the cities here and in foreign countries. It was always either too hot or too cold or raining, the sky never blue as it should have been. The uniforms never fit so well as they ought, and some of the men and most of the women you see go walking by were never meant for parades. The flags look old and tired—they never blow in the wind as they ought, but tangle and twist or maybe hang straight down, and the horses are never so fine as the ones you've seen in fields— and finally you get tired and walk away."

"But still I'd like to see—have all that knowin' for myself."

"And I guess if you were in one, marching in time to the music,—I never was—there'd maybe be something else you'd want, maybe a real war to go walking to, or maybe you'd just be tired of the walking.—Anyway, Delph, it's better, I think,—I think they're finer if you never see them, just sit and listen to the music and imagine how they must be."

"Your eyes don't speak with your tongue, Sam."

He pulled her hands together and pressed them under his own. "I have to say something, Delph. You can't live always eating your heart away with wonder, the way I used to be. Please take my word for it, and let me comfort you."

"You took nobody's word for it. You went out to find yourself an' learn how th' world is—like anybody would like to do."

"It's different with a woman, Delph. My mother, I think, has more fun out of our going away and doing this and that than any one of us has ever had. She was talking the other night of how of late years she was glad we'd gone—and how—Delph, please, look at me, my eyes are not lying now."

"It was different with your mother," she answered after a moment in a low voice, almost a whisper. "She had children that were a part of her—if I gave birth to a dozen I'd never have one that was a part of me. Burr-Head he—." She stopped and looked at him with her hungry, empty eyes. "If I could have just one that would seem—when it got older—to be a part of me—an' not go flyin' away like Burr-Head—so different when they're little boys from what they were when they were babies. An' every year he'll go farther away an'—". She pulled her hands away, straightened her shoulders and smiled at him. "It's time I went to see Marsh now. He's able to know me again."

"Yes, Cousin Delphine," he said and smiled. "I thank you for a very pleasant afternoon. . . . I maybe won't be seeing you soon. I'm going for a horseback tour of the mountains."

"I hope you have a pleasant time," she said, and wished he wouldn't try to smile, and wondered why she did.

They shook hands at the door, but he lingered a moment over her hand and asked, "May I come sometime before I go east to tell you goodbye, Delph?"

She hesitated. "Cousin Delphine, you mean to tell goodbye."

"No—I want to see Delph again—please."

"Delph will see you again—maybe," she whispered, and turned then and ran up the stairs.

· 27 ·

THE FALL that year was a farmer's fall. October brought high-skied, windless days when the valley lay filled with yellow dusty light that seemed less air and sunshine than some special manifestation of that particular fall. For Marsh each day was something more than hours of a life, but was like a stay in some well earned paradise where his life and all the life on his land was fine, beyond his dreams. He had never known a vacation, a time when he was neither working nor looking for work, but since Dr. Andy and all the neighbors as well as Delph reminded him continually that he must take things easy, he did no extra work that fall.

Sober and other hired men had cut the corn and dug the sweet potatoes, and he had ridden to Hawthorne Town in Elliot's car and attended to this and that so that the most pressing of the work was done. There were whole days when he did little except the barnwork; and that left long free hours for walking about in the fine fall weather with Burr-Head and Caesar. Sometimes they gathered hickory nuts and walnuts that grew on the rough land above the creek. Other times they crossed the creek, and went to a forgotten stretch of worn out meadow land where the wild rose pips were red in the sage grass, and in the corners of rotting rail fences the clustering vines of bursting bittersweet made clouds of deep orange flame.

He and the child would go walking back to the house, their arms burdened with many things. They would leave their loads on the empty hearth and go to the kitchen and Delph. There, all the enchantment and the essence of the fruitful fall seemed gathered in the jars and crocks that Delph filled with jellies and ketchups and preserves and pickles, and through the house there was the smell of fruit and spices and of cider bubbling into apple butter.

Marsh would call as he had always called when he entered the house, "Home, Delph?" and she would answer as she usually did, "Here, in th' kitchen, Marsh."

He and Burr-Head would go to stand in the kitchen door, and Delph would turn and smile at them, push a sweat dampened curl from her forehead with the back of one hand, and say, "Havin' a good time, you two?" and then turn back to her work.

Burr-Head would go running away to rake leaves in the yard or hunt chinkapin on the hill, but Marsh would linger in the kitchen door, and hunt with his eyes for some kitchen work he could do, and if there were a pan of pears half peeled or short core apples to be cut and cored, he would sit by the kitchen table and do the work—just to keep him there by Delph. But most always she would smile or laugh a tight little laugh and send him away. "I'll manage," she would say. "Th' Lord knows you've got a little somethin' good comin' to you now."

When she had spoken thus a time or so he would go to do some fiddling work in the barn, maybe, or simply to walk over his corn and pasture lands and plan crops and work for the coming year. The plans tangled sometimes in his head, while his mind went back to Delph in the kitchen. He wished she would leave the canning and the pickling and come walking with him. He wished that in the evenings when he lighted a fire in the fireplace against the early cold, she wouldn't just sit staring into the fire or reading books that Sam had loaned her or suggested that she read—so she had said. Still, when he spoke to her, she always smiled and listened to whatever he had to say, and then next day she never knew what it was he had said.

He knew she was tired, worn with all the weeks of worrying after him. The circles under her eyes and the sudden thinness in her cheeks were proof of that. Now that he was well and walking about he was ashamed and sorry for the way he had acted during the last part of his sickness—when he was well enough to sit up in bed and fret and fume over what was happening on the farm, and reckon in his head how much his sickness had cost him. There were days when the never being allowed to eat enough of the few little things that Dr. Andy permitted him to have to kill the wracking pains of what he had been certain was certain suicide by slow starvation, had made him impatient and cross as a fretful child.

The thought of all that money going to a nurse—six or seven dollars a day—when nothing ailed him except a bit of weakness had caused him to dismiss her, much to Dorie's disgust, a long time before he was well.

The whole burden of his tending had fallen on Delph. Still, no matter if he yelled for buttermilk six times within an hour, she had never complained. It was strange to find her patient and so kind, and when he apologized and pitied her for having such a husband as he had done almost every day, she had only smiled and said, "Pshaw, Marsh— it's better to be here busy with you than just wanderin' around like I was all summer. Not even livin' at home." And that old lonesome look would come in her eyes, and with it she was so far away.

He would think sometimes of Sam, and ugly wonders and misgivings would come into his head, and he would hate himself and try to think of other things. It was pure sin to notice little things that meant nothing; there had been the one day that Sam was home after a three-week horseback ride through the mountains. It was foolish to remember it so, that all that day Delph had sat breaking late cornfield beans on the back porch. He was just getting able to walk a bit then, and every time he came to the back porch there she was with her hands and her lap filled with beans, but her eyes on Dorie's house. And he was somehow glad that Sam never came to see them, but drove on to a camping trip with Roan in the Rockcastle Country—and he hoped that when he came from there he would go straight on and back to his work where he belonged.

But more than anything he wished she would help him plan for the stone house he was going to build; be Delph again talking with her hands and her mouth and her eyes. He knew the loss of the brick house hurt, and he was sorry that she had learned of it by accident through Burr-Head, and not as he had planned. Still, when he had explained how it was, she had listened in silence with lowered eyes—until he had wondered half angrily if she had even thought on what he was saying. And when he asked her what she thought, she had answered in a quiet voice that told no more than her lowered eyes, "Yes, it's th' sensible thing, Marsh."

And now on the evenings when they all climbed up the hill together to see the sun go down, and he and Burr-Head paced off the dimensions of the stone house and planned where windows and chimneys should be, Delph usually sat on Solomon's fence and never seemed to know what he and Burr-Head did. She never seemed to know what the stone house really was, and how terribly much life held for him that fall.

Though he had mentioned it but little, he had hoped at times that she would maybe plan as she had used to do for many things, and see the day when he was able to drive his team into Hawthorne Town as a great day in their lives, worthy of many plans. He wished she would get a new fall dress for herself to wear on the day they all went together to the town. He had Elliot's money in the bank, and all that remained to be done was have old Silas Copenhaver count the interest due on the remainder of the mortgage, and he would pay it all then, there in the bank with Delph and Burr-Head looking on. Burr-Head was too little to know the taste of a mortgaged farm; and that was where a great lot of the goodness lay. Burr-Head would never remember that once he had lived on a mortgaged farm.

He had planned the day for late October, and on the evening before as they all walked up the hill to look at the sunset, he kept hoping that Delph would say some thing of what she planned to do tomorrow in Town. He would wear his good suit instead of overalls, and maybe have their dinner at the Hotel Hatcher instead of at the little restaurant on Maple Street. Delph would like that.

But she never seemed to remember what day tomorrow would be, and was silent as they walked to the top of the high knoll where the slender trunks of the walnut trees stood straight and black in the red light. Better than almost anything Marsh liked these nights in fall when he could stand and watch the sun go down and dusk fall blue in the valley, and feel the rising night wind, sharp against his face.

Delph stood a moment with him there, and then as if eager for something higher, she climbed to the top bar of the Solomon Pasture fence and sat and looked into the west.

Marsh forgot the sunset and went to Delph and leaned his shoulder against the fence, and tried to shape in words all the things he wished to say. When he looked at her, staring away from him, her eyes on the sunset, but the heart in her eyes beating for something beyond the sunset and past the clouds, he felt a weariness and a loss and a sense of failure. She was Delph and he was Marsh. They had been together in the long fight for the land, in drought and flood and heat and cold, through sickness and poverty, through quarrels and the ecstasy of love; and she was Delph and he was Marsh, the same as the shy strangers meeting over Azariah's grave.

He looked at her and thought of so many things, and all the while she looked away from him. He wanted to bring her nearer, make her see that he knew how much she had given, make her know that some day she would be glad of their way of life and proud of him. But as always the thoughts remained thoughts; the gratitude was both hurt and burden and there were no words. He straightened his shoulders and said, "Delph, you oughtn' to get in th' habit of climbin' on Solomon's fence."

He waited, and then again: "Delph, you've picked a bad place to sit."

She suddenly turned her head and looked down at him, her face puzzled as she tried to think what he had said. "Oh, yes, I'll be settin' a bad example for Burr-Head climbin' on Solomon's fence like this," she said, and sprang to the ground. "I'll bet you've been talkin' about th' house, an' I never even heard—wool gatherin' as always, I guess."

"Nothin'—I was just aimin' to show you how big I thought th' cellar ought to be—recollect I'll need a big one when my grapes come in an' we start makin' all that wine," he said, proud that she had at last noticed. He walked away, and with Burr-Head and Caesar following at his heels, counted the cellar off in paces, marking a corner with a stone or tree, drawing a line with his shoe heel for the stairs or a window.

Delph stood with her arm about a sapling and watched him with a fierce desperation in her eyes, that caused her to nod slowly over each least thing he did. She would put her mind on Marsh and Burr-Head and the stone house and never, never let it go wandering away again. Maybe a thing too big to be forgotten—ever—could be crowded out and choked to death, just as Bermuda grass if left to grow could in time choke a young shade tree. She wished she could feel sin and sorrow or pray for the blackness she knew was in her soul, even though she couldn't feel it. She wished it were that hard dry summer come again, and she had to work from daylight till dark with never a pause for rest—she could maybe sleep then at night. Not lie with wide hot eyes wandering hour after hour through the darkness, hear Marsh's strong regular breathing, and think—and think—of how she had felt when she had learned he would get well. And then heap sin on sin by thinking past him to how it might have been, and hold still the memory of a bit of brightness and laughter and gaiety—and dream—like a warm live thing in her heart.

She saw herself sometimes and marveled at that self of her that could work and smile, and talk to the neighbors, and make no sign of that something like a grindstone grinding slowly through her head. She clutched the little tree, and was proud of the lightness she could put into her voice when she called to Marsh, "From that upstairs window there, right above your head, you can look down an' see how your hired men are tendin' th' corn."

"I'll be with 'em until I'm so old I'll need two walkin' canes," Marsh answered, and he and Burr-Head continued to tramp and measure and plan until the falling darkness hid the corner stones. They started home then, and passed the brick house where the tips of the chimneys were faintly silvered with the white rising of a harvest moon. As always Delph paused by the back garden gate and looked into the garden where the chrysanthemums and late-blooming cosmos and marigolds glimmered through the dusk.

Marsh watched her as she leaned on the gate, and felt a guilt and a hurt as he said, "You can have a whole acre of flowers up by th' stone house."

"Pshaw, I wasn't thinkin' a that," she said, and turned away.

They walked on, but the spicy scent of the flowers followed, sharp in the frosty air. Delph stopped and looked up at the sky, and back toward the flowers and said, "I wonder will it frost tonight. I maybe ought to tell her."

Marsh, too, looked at the sky, and so did Burr-Head, and Caesar sniffing at old rabbit tracks, paused and studied the rising moon. "I'd not tell her to cut 'em for another night or so. Maybe it'll turn warm an' they can live a week or so," Marsh said. He, too, hated this cutting of the flowers, the foolish ones that only bloomed to die, and never lived to make their seed.

They turned down the hill and Caesar pricked his ears and Burr-Head said, "There's a car turnin' in up at our pasture gate."

Marsh listened, and said, "It's Sam—I reckin," and wondered why he did not drive over the bridge and home and not come bothering him—and Delph.

Delph said nothing and went on down the hill. "He's comin' down to see us, most like," Marsh said. "It's no more'n common manners to wait for him."

"You wait—I'll go on an' start th' fire in th' livin' room—an' take Burr-Head. His sleep is catchin' him," she said, and he thought her voice sounded low and strained somehow as if she were sick or afraid.

He heard her feet go on down over the rough road, and then Sam's car stopping at the top of the hill. He waited and Sam came down to him through the darkness. He saw his long body like a smudge of deeper darkness coming toward him, and when Caesar barked Sam was the first to speak. "That you, Marsh, up walking around?"

"You didn't expect to come and find me still in bed, I hope," he said, and after that it was easier. Under the darkness and with the easy farmer's talk they had as they walked down the hill, Sam seemed no more than another one of the Fairchilds home for a visit.

They talked of many things, the fine harvest of fruit and of corn, the good tobacco curing weather the fall had brought, the coming winter, and of Roan's land in the hills. "He said for you to be certain and stop by his office tomorrow," Sam said. "That was mostly why I came by, to tell you that. He said you'd been talking to him of buying a few sheep. He knows where there's a couple of yoes for sale—cheap, he said, and good as there is in the county."

"Thanks," Marsh said, and the talk then turned to corn and clover and alfalfa.

"I always meant to ask you," Sam said as they neared the front yard gate, "but you were too sick. How did you fertilize that clover in that little field? I could tell it was fertilized in strips, and I wondered what you had used."

Marsh frowned and was glad of the darkness. Sam knew too much, understood so many things. He was not a farmer and he had lived most of his life away; still, he could come and see a thing such as that small fenced off square of clover, and know the thought behind it and understand the world it might contain. He tried to speak lightly, brush the business away as if it were a nothing with which he sometimes fooled his time instead of a great love for which he would have given a great deal to have a more complete under- standing. "There were ten strips, measured in square feet, an' before I took sick I meant to cut it an' weigh th' yield an' figure th' fertiliz- er costs," he explained, and went on after his usual halting fashion to tell of the ten strips of red clover, one fertilized with lime and phosphate, one with phosphates only, one with triple superphos- phates, one neither treated nor inoculated—it was a long story and meant nothing except that he was trying to find the best and cheap- est way of growing the best clover.

Sam listened with more interest than politeness, interrupting to ask questions, but when Marsh had finished he was silent a time before he said, "Marsh, you ought to have been a scientist."

And Marsh answered, "Maybe you ought to have been a farmer—I mean th' kind you used to think you'd mebbe be."

"I've wondered," Sam said. He glanced toward the squares of yellow light that came from the living room where Delph had led the sleepy Burr-Head. "I guess I'll always stick to commercial research— now," he said.

"You make good money in that kind of work, so I've heard. That's somethin'," Marsh said.

"People seem to think it is," Sam answered, and his stride lengthened and quickened so that Marsh could hardly keep up with him as they went down the walk toward the squares of yellow light. But he stopped a moment on the stone terrace by the door and asked abruptly, "Delph hasn't gone to bed has she? I just wanted to stop long enough to tell her and Burr-Head good-bye."

"Pshaw, no. Sometimes she's up half th' night readin'.—You leavin'? I thought you had a longer stay," Marsh said, and was more pleased by the prospect than he wished to be.

"I've changed my mind," Sam said, and they walked into the liv- ing room together where Delph stood by the mantle with her back to the fire.

She was silent a moment, standing stiff and still like a woman made of glass who could remain a woman and unbroken only as long as she was still. Then Sam was going up to her, holding out his hand and saying some commonplace words of greeting that any other man might have said, and Delph was smiling with her head bowed a little over his hand, and Marsh wished he could see her eyes. He heard her say, "I guess you'll be leavin' soon," and Sam answering, "Yes. I decided I'd better go back to my work."

They sat a time by the fireplace and talked of little things, but the talk was slow and disconnected and there were long whiles of silence when the ticking of the clock and whispering of the fire seemed loud. Delph talked less than either of the men. She sat frozen faced and silent, looking sometimes at the fire, sometimes at Sam. Marsh saw the stricken look in her eyes, and knew why it was there and through his anger and his sorrow comforted himself with some words he had heard from John a long time ago. "She's got a mind like an April wind."

She roused only when Sam arose and said in a strained awkward way, strange for Sam, "Well, I must get home and try to get ready to leave about noon tomorrow."

"Your mother'ull hate to see you go," Marsh said.

Sam smiled at that. "Not so much as you'd think. Emma and I have been begging her to visit us in the east this winter. She can leave the farm with Poke Easy and you two. She'd maybe stay two days."

"That would be fine for her," Delph said, and stood and pinched little pleats into her apron. She thought of Burr-Head, sleeping on the cedar chest. Once, she had planned that he should some day live in a strange place near a city. Now, she knew he never would. He wasn't her child. He was Marsh's child. He would be a farmer, too. But then it didn't matter. She would have been old by then, a graying farmer's wife gone to visit her son, not Delph to try her strength against the city.

She raised her head and Sam was smiling at her, holding out his hand to say goodbye. She moved her head so that her face was in shadow. She wondered if she cried. She knew there was a crying in her heart. Then she was reaching blindly for his hand and saying, "Goodbye, Sam," and he was gone, and Marsh was walking with him through the yard and up the hill.

She waited with only her hands folding and unfolding her apron, the rest of her was still while she listened for the sound of his car going away over the hill. A cold night wind blew through the door and she thought of the winter. She would be alone day after day while Marsh worked in the barn or in the fields. Burr-Head would be with him and Caesar, too, and she would hear the ticking of the clock and lonesome sound of passing trains; see the flat stretch of bottom lands, black mud under gray rain or untouched reaches of snow where leafless corn stalks whistled in the wind. And always she would think—and think—and remember. This couldn't be the last time; all of him that she would ever have or see. It couldn't be.

She ran to the door, but stopped when she saw Marsh standing in the square of light that fell through a window. He stood straight and still with his feet spread a little, his hands clenched in his over-all pockets and a hard anger written over his mouth and his eyes. "You needn't cry for him," he said, and came across the porch.

"I'm not," she said. She knew the hurt behind the anger in his face and felt heavy with a sense of guilt but with it all could feel no sorrow—or shame. She went back to sit by the fire, sitting crouched on the edge of her chair and staring into the flames.

Marsh came and stood and warmed his back, and looked at her. "You've already got all th' neighbors talkin'," he said in a low flat voice.

She clenched her hands and saw her tears splashing on them like slow drops of summer rain. "You—you oughtn' to hold that against me, Marsh. I—never believed it when Sadie told tales on you."

A coal dropped from the fire onto the hearth, and he ground it out with a long heavy crushing of his shoe heel against the stone, a grinding sound it made for such a little coal. His lips were thin and flat and white against his teeth, and his eyes like narrow bits of black stone in his face. "Maybe Sadie tells th' truth sometimes," he said, and stalked away to make his last round of the barn.

Delph sprang up and stood calling after him, "Please, Marsh, please," but he walked on, and after a time she sat crouching by the fire again and staring at her hands. She was sitting so when he came from the barn a good while later.

He came and leaned his elbow on the mantle, and in a moment said with his voice kinder than it had been, "We'd better be goin' to bed, Delph."

"I'm not sleepy," she said, still looking at her hands.

"You'll get sleepy when you go to bed. We'll want to get an' early start in th' mornin'."

"For what?"

"Delph—don't you recollect? Tomorrow's th' day I finish payin' th' mortgage."

"Oh," she said, and got up and picked up the lamp, then set it back on the mantle. "Marsh—you go on to bed. I think—I think I'll read upstairs in bed—th' way I do sometimes when I don't want to keep you awake."

He walked away in silence, but stopped at the door of their bedroom when she said, "Marsh, if you don't mind—I think—I think I'll just stay at home tomorrow. I've—got a sight a work to do."

He turned about and looked at her, but he could see little of her face. The lamp was on the mantel just by her head, and as she stood, looking not at him, but at the floor there were shadows on her mouth and on her eyes. "You know I mind," he said, "havin'—a wife that thinks she's too good to ride with her man in a wagon. When I was sick you were plenty willin' to—." Delph had turned away from him and stood leaning her forehead on the mantle. Her shoulders looked strange, not like Delph's shoulders, but tired and bent, as if they belonged to some worn out old woman. He had an instant's picture of ten thousand different things those shoulders had done—mostly for him. He wanted to go to her and say the things he thought of saying while she sat on Solomon's fence, but he knew he never could. There would be a tomorrow and Sam would be gone. "There'll be another day, Delph," he said. "Things will seem different then. Let's go to bed now."

"There'll be a lot of other days," she said, and he left her there with her head leaning on the mantle.

It seemed a long while before he heard her go upstairs. More than once he lifted on one elbow; he thought he heard a smothered sobbing but it was so low he couldn't tell. He lay and watched the square of light from her window above his own glimmer on the dead leaves in the yard until he fell asleep.

Sometime in the night some sound awakened him. He lay and listened but half concernedly, filled as he was with the thoughts of Delph that came sharp in his mind. He heard it again, Caesar's eager whine by the backyard gate as if he would follow something. Marsh lay a time, and when the dog continued to whine he got up, drew on his shoes, and went to see if there were prowlers about, though Caesar knew enough to bark at prowlers or would-be chicken thieves instead of stand and whine.

It was an eerie time of night, he thought, near moonset time with the valley black as pitch, but the top of the hill on Dorie's side of the river shining like silver. He went down the back porch steps, walking slowly so as not to stumble in the dark. Caesar came sniffing at his feet and his hands, then circled away toward the gate, whining to follow something through the cornfields.

The night was warm for October with a warmish wind out of the west and the few stars low and dim like stars in a summer sky. He stood by the back gate and listened with Caesar, but could hear nothing except the dried box elder leaves rustling in the wind, and the soft swish of the little cedar trees on the river hill. Somewhere, far away, maybe as far as the high hills back of Burdine, he heard the thin mournful cry of a hunter's horn calling hound dogs in as the moon went down.

Caesar pricked his ears and whined again, and Marsh reached for his head in the darkness and patted him. "Too bad when a farmer's old dog gets a taste a huntin' fever in th' fall," he said, and groped his way back to the house, but Caesar did not follow, only stood whining by the gate.

In the kitchen he stopped at the foot of the stairs and stood a moment, of half a mind to go to Delph. She slept lightly as Caesar and most likely she had heard his whining and the hunting horn. He called softly, "Delph," but when she did not answer he went back to bed.

· 28 ·

BURR-HEAD awakened him, bright eyed and eager for the trip to Hawthorne Town. Marsh quieted him with a sh-sh-sh-ing for he knew that Delph would never awaken so early; the morning was still more black than blue. But Burr-Head bounced and jiggled on the bed, until Marsh got up and tiptoed shoeless to the kitchen and built a fire.

He dressed Burr-Head, and though it was hardly light enough for walking, he and the child went to the barn to feed the mules and wait until Delph should waken. They stood in the barn hall and listened to the crunching sound of mules feeding, and watched the coming of the red autumn dawn. The light warm wind still blew out of the west and rustled the yellow blades of the late garden corn, and high in the east one star hung large and pale above the river hill.

"I like it now, don't you, Marsh?" Burr-Head whispered, and Marsh nodded, soothed in spite of all the misery in his heart by the feeling of security and achievement and peace that his great well-filled barns gave him in autumn. It was good to smell the clean hay and new corn and think of the winter, know that however hard it might be, he and all that looked to him for keep would be safe and warm and fed.

"I want to see th' sun rise," Burr-Head said, and they climbed in darkness to the haymow and crawled over the high mound of hay to a small eastern window. There, they lay in silence and watched the round red sun roll over Dorie's chimneys. "I guess Delph will be up now," Marsh said, and slipped down the hay, but stopped when he felt something by his foot. He reached and drew the object into the

410

red light and saw a book, a pretty thing bound in red leather, filled with curious pictures of people like those out of fairy tales, and in a strange language—German he guessed it to be. "That's one a Sam's books," Burr-Head explained.

"How—why is it up here?"

"He used to read to us here in th' hay—on rainy days when people thought you might die—but I knowed differ'nt. He'd read an' we'd all eat apples, him an' Delph an' me.—Sometimes I'd get tired an' go away. Poetry, I think it was. Then he'd just read to Delph." Marsh left the book on the hay. He explored and found another one, and left it also. When Burr-Head said, "We'd better take 'em back to Delph," he only answered slowly, "We'll leave 'em there."

Burr-Head came reluctantly away. "He thought a sight a that red one, he said. It's old an' come from over th' ocean. He'd read it an' Delph would laugh so."

"If he wants it he'll come."

"Mebbe I can tell him goodbye. I wisht I hadn't gone to sleep last night, when I heared his car.—I hope he comes again."

"He will—most likely—but we'll be gone to Hawthorne Town."

"But Caesar won't bite him an' chase him away. He likes Sam."

"Delph, she'll be here."

"Oh—I thought she was goin' to Town. But she can tell him goodbye for me."

"Yes—she can—tell him goodbye."

Burr-Head looked up at the haymow in the direction of the pretty book. "Sam liked Delph. Maybe he left th' books on purpose for her."

"Yes—maybe he did."

Burr-Head looked into his father's face, studied it a moment and seemed to find something he had never seen. He turned away and did not speak of Sam again.

Something in Delph's face made him want to be good. Her eyes were big and she looked tired, and all through breakfast she hardly said a word, just passing food to him and Marsh, asking Marsh if he wouldn't have another hot biscuit or a little more coffee or a bit of plum jelly, and Marsh always shaking his head. When he was getting ready for the trip to Town, he washed his face so carefully and scrubbed his ears so well, that when Delph examined him as she always did, she smiled at him out of her big sad eyes and said, "You're a clean child, Burr-Head."

He wished she would come to stand in the barn hall and watch him and Marsh drive away, but she hardly lifted her head from the dish washing as they went out the door. They climbed in the wagon and Marsh gathered up the reins, but lingered a moment, and looked back toward the house before he drove slowly down the lane. He stopped at the big road gate and said, "You hold th' reins, Burr-Head. I—forgot somethin' back at th' house," then he jumped from the wagon and hurried away with long strides. He found Delph as he had left her, rubbing a plate round and round in the soapy dish water and staring at the wall. She looked up like a startled wild thing when he spoke to her from the door. "I—I forgot to ask you, Delph, was there anything you wanted from Town?"

She considered a time with her eyes on the dish pan before she finally shook her head. "N-o-o. I don't guess I need a thing—but you ought to buy some shirts for yourself an' Burr-Head."

He studied her face, and after a moment said, "You look peaked, Delph.—Why don't you get out while we're gone, go up to Perce's, say."

"I get tired of Lizzie's talk," she answered, "but it would be nice to walk about in this pretty weather. If it wasn't Saturday I'd visit th' school."

He fumbled with the broken arrow in his pocket and would not look at her as he said, "It'll be such a fine day—this weather won't hold much longer—you could hunt hick'ry nuts over by th' creek— or pick wild grapes for jelly. Th' vines by Solomon's pasture are fairly purple, an' th' other day Sadie Huffacre was tellin' me she'd like to pick some if I didn't mind.—Th' jelly would be nice this winter— I'm even beginnin' to like such things."

It hurt the way her sad eyes brightened, proud as always when she could do something to please him—but never proud of him. "I'll pick 'em as soon as I get th' work done."

"Don't work hard at it. You need a rest. Play along an' take your time. But—wait—wait till about noon, say. It'll be warmer then."

"That'll be nice," she said. "I'll not bother with cookin' dinner. Caesar an' me we'll have a picnic up where th' stone house will be."

"Oh, Delph, I wish you'd gone with me," he said, and caught her shoulders and kissed her quickly on the mouth.

He felt better as he ran back to the wagon. Delph would be all right. Sam might come to tell her goodbye, but most likely he would never find her, picking wild grapes in the pasture. It was better that way; she with her foolish whims and fancies had to be watched sometimes like Burr-Head.

Once he had topped the hill, he cracked the whip and the wagon wheels spun faster. He drove between the rolling fields of shocked corn and pasture and tobacco land that bordered the road to Hawthorne Town. It was good to look at a field of fine shocked corn, and know that no matter how large and straight and heavy the ears of corn, he could raise as good or better. Once, he had wondered if he could grow corn, fine corn.

It was good to have men wave and call, "Aye, Lord, I never thought after last summer th' day would ever come when you'd be drivin' by." It was good to meet the men in Hawthorne Town; see their gladness on finding him well and able to come to Town, hear their talk of crops and cattle and land, have some ask his advice on this or that, find admiration in most eyes, and spoken recognition of what he had done from not a few. Silas Copenhaver gave him the paid-off mortgage and praised him for being clear of debt, but he knew the moment was not as fine as it might have been. He wanted to get out of the bank and have a drink in some saloon; but he couldn't do that, not with Burr-Head, so he only sat still in his chair and tried to make a little conversation. "I've been lucky, I guess. I'm built like an ox—an' money from Delph's timber an' sellin' th' brick house, all that helped a sight."

"Call it luck if you want to," Silas said. "You've had your share a trouble. I'll always recollect th' time I saw you in th' store when that boy there was three or four days old. You looked like a mule driver fresh from a two weeks spree."

Marsh nodded and studied his hat. "Things did look bad—then. Delph so low, an' my house an' all my bottom lands under water— but Delph an' Burr-Head pulled through—an' all my neighbors they were mighty fine."

Silas studied Burr-Head's curly hair. "You have been lucky in a way—your wife, I mean. My wife was sayin' a while back when folks were beginnin' to think you'd never live that Delph must be one more woman—bear up so well under all that sickness an' trouble an' see that your farmin' went on."

Marsh's eyes brightened. "Did you ever see her vegetables an' canned goods an' cakes at th' Fair—an' that flower garden up by th' brick house, she had a bigger hand in th' makin of that than th' Elliots?" He remembered that Delph had never liked to be praised for such things—work that any dumb-witted hired girl could do as well, she always said.

He left the bank soon after, and outside in the street he thought of Delph, and the day was empty and dull. He stood now on the high hill of his life, but he was all alone. Delph had never felt the burden of debt on their land, had never cared for the goodwill and admiration of the county seat town, and in her eyes he had accomplished nothing—less than nothing, he guessed.

Still, some of the lost goodness came back to the world when Burr-Head teased to be taken to Roan's office and see a drop of Prissy's milk under the microscope. Marsh, though no dairyman, was rather proud of the milk production record of his county,—and his was among the best. He and Roan had worked much together, had schemed and plotted and planned on ways and means to increase the cream content and decrease the bacterial count of a cow's milk. Marsh had succeeded beyond the others, and he was proud that he could feed and breed and tend cows able to produce such milk.

Today he watched Burr-Head's clumsy, squint-eyed efforts to look into the microscope, and thought how Delph would like to see him now. But they would tell her tonight. He smiled a little with his eyes in thinking of the evening; they would sit by the fire and talk and plan. She would say as she always said when she had failed to come to Town with him, "Pshaw, Marsh, you ought to ha' made me gone. I didn't know you'd all have so much fun," and she would nod and smile into the fire and the shadows of the leaping flames would cut across her eyes and tremble on her hair.

• • •

Delph walked over the rough land above the creek and gathered grapes. She worked slowly, stopping now and then with her hands filled with the frosty purple bunches, while she lifted her head with listening and looked in the direction of the Hawthorne Road. It was a Saturday with many cars going by, and the sound of their passing came to her in a faint droning and humming like that of circling bees. Now and then she glanced toward the sun, and when it stood almost overhead she left the creek side and went to gather grapes by Solomon's fence. The split basket was filled now, but she continued to heap more on, and never noticed that many fell to the ground.

Sometimes Caesar trotted up to her, but when she did not pat his head or speak to him, he would lift his brows and study her, then go away to chase rabbits or lie in the sun. Solomon, grazing in the upper corner of the field, came near the fence and looked at her with his angry eyes and pawed and bellowed and lashed his rope-like tail. But when Delph only glanced at him a moment and continued to pick grapes on the other side of the fence, he tired of watching her and stalked away to the lower side of the field.

Though it was near noon, and Caesar showed plainly that it was time to go home, Delph, when Solomon had gone, climbed to the top of his fence where it crossed the highest part of the hill. She settled herself on a post and looked out over the country. Toward the east there were the rows of marching hills, not sharp against the sky today, but filmed with haze and fading into a deeper and deeper tone of blue until earth and air seemed one. She looked overhead at the sky, high, and calm, and blue, holding so many things beyond it; frost and winter and dull dark days—and other things worse than the silence of snow or the drip of winter rain from the eaves. She shivered and pulled her apron over her knees and sat crouching by the post as she had crouched by the fire.

Now and then a red or yellow leaf would come drifting over her head; a squirrel came near and studied her then scampered away over the leaves, and a covey of quail lifted out of Solomon's pasture with a loud whirring, but she noticed none of such things. Sometimes she looked at Fairchild's Place, the bit of roof and the chimneys that could be glimpsed between the leafless trees in the backyard, now and then she twisted about on the post and glanced toward the short strip of Hawthorne Road past the brick house, but most often she was still, studying her drawn up knees.

When the short shadow of the post had started to point east instead of west, a car whirred softly up the Hawthorne Road, through Marsh's pasture gate, and stopped by the orchard fence, Caesar ran wagging his tail and barking, and Delph leaped from the post and ran through the grove of walnut trees toward the car. But when she reached the open pasture, she turned abruptly back and ran to wait among the trees.

She watched Sam get out of the car, pat Caesar on the head, look quickly over the field, find her at last, and then come striding up to her. She saw his proud dark head, bare, with his black hair flashing in the sun. She watched his long legs come swinging over the grass with the easy hill man's stride that all his living away had never changed. She watched his face as he walked nearer, tired it was with all the light laughter gone from his eyes. Then he was there and taking her hands, just holding them and saying never a word. "You oughtn't to have stopped," she said, when the choking in her throat would let her speak.

He shook his head over her foolish ways. "You knew, Delph, I couldn't go away until I was certain you were—all right."

"I'm all right," she said.

He tossed back the black forelock that was always tumbling over his eyes. "You know you're lying, Delph. Neither of us can ever be all right again—ever, not after—."

She jerked her hands suddenly free and sprang away and stood with her back to a walnut tree. "Don't remember anything, Sam. We're what we've always been. We've got to be all right. We've got to be." She tried to smile, and failing, straightened her shoulders and lifted her head until the yellow sunshine falling on her face made the shadows of her lashes like dark fringe across her cheeks. "We—we—don't be so miserable, Sam. Recollect once you said, a body could forget anything, anything. Recollect that? You've got your work an' all your life away an' I've got—." Her voice she knew was loud and shrill, empty as the look in Sam's eyes.

She made no move to draw away when he came and hemmed her with his hands against the tree, and talked to her in his husky voice that quivered sometimes, and other times was dull and dead like a clock ticking out words. "You know you can't forget—ever. That day I talked to you, I didn't know. I'd never tried—not this. Just little things, like forgetting all my family here, and forgetting the hills so I could live always away, and forgetting the smell of the wild iris by the river, and forgetting that once I had wanted to do real honest to God research, not this eternal hunting for what I'm paid to find, and forgetting that someday I'd be old with nothing to show except that I'd held down a job like millions and millions of other men and made a little money like millions and millions of other men—all my life I've been forgetting, Delph—and now I can't anymore. It's not as if there was any need. Everybody else takes what they want in this world. Why shouldn't we?" His hands were not against the tree, but around her, and when his storm of words was spent she dropped her head on his shoulder, and stood quiet in his arms with her hands against his breast.

She never moved or gave a sign she heard when he went on in eager whispers, "Can't you see, Delph? You know and I know we belong to each other. We'd be blind not to know. All we'd ever need would be ourselves and a little earth and a little sky in a land where there's hills something like here. We could live in another state or in Switzerland or France or Italy, any place you'd say.—I can always get in any country a job like the one I have now—you're important when you figure out ways for war—but not when you work out ways to make plants grow and live, but someday we could do that together." He bent and kissed her lightly on the forehead, and begged again in rushing, hungry whispers, "Delph—I'd never say a word if you belonged here—but you don't. I know. They're shaping you like they'd shape a cedar tree. You were never meant for the ones that love the having of things or the holding. If you were happy, Delph—it wouldn't be so hard. I could stand it for myself but—. There's my car and there's the road. By night we'd be so far away."

She lifted her head and looked at him. "We're crazy, Sam," she said in a low toneless voice, "but we'll be all right, give us time. It's just some foolishness mebbe that runs in our blood, for I've heard it said that in th' old days when men heard th' wild geese go flyin' over, they'd start then on their long hunts an' never wait till spring an' summer time—. They never thought of such things then, I've heard it said. It was only in th' fall in th' face of a hard cold winter that they wanted to go away.—I can see how that would be, crazy they were with th' wild geese callin' an' th' last of th' leaves comin' down.—I've always been a little crazy, I guess, but," she smiled a brief sad smile, "I've always lived by th' laws laid down by th' ones that were sane—an' mebbe if I live long enough I'll forget that I ever had one thing in my blood an' another in my head." She caught his coat lapels and shook them a little. "Please, Sam—go on, now—it would always be like that. I'd always be lookin' back knowin' an' knowin'—it's sinful to talk on such, Sam."

He shook his head. "There's no sin, Delph, in the wild geese flying over.—Maybe one gets penned away or crippled with a broken wing, but when he can he goes with the others—he doesn't stay back.—You can't live all your life wanting and wanting; the older you get the smaller this place will be. You'll sicken more of the gossips and the small talk of the neighbors and the always being watched, and—Lord, how well, I know."

"You can't tell me. I know—but I'll live on an' be a part of it—like I was. I'll work so hard I'll never know—I've always worked to fill my days—be busy so you can't sit still an' wonder or think of th' next twenty year—be tired so you can go to sleep an' I'll work an' I'll sleep an' I'll sing in church—an' when I'm old." She stopped and whispered the word and looked at him with wide darkening eyes. She choked and then went on after one slow nod of her head, "An' when I'm old—I won't feel or think or want—or wonder then—so much.—I won't even remember then that once—everything hurt th' way it does today—that talkin' sky an' th' way th' walnuts smell, an' th' grapes, too. All this mornin' while I picked them—I thought how it would be to carry them home—this afternoon—an' watch th' shadow creep across th' valley—an' sit so still pullin' them off th' stems—but I can do that, Sam.—Oh, I know I can. Oh, Sam." She flung her arms tight about his neck, then jerked them away and rushed toward Solomon's fence.

He started to follow her but stopped. She stood pressed against the wires, watching him with her wide dark eyes, like some mortally wounded animal, trapped and powerless to fight with anything except its eyes. "You're strong, Delph," he said.

She shook her head, and kept pushing him away with her eyes. "You're th' strong one, Sam—if there is such a thing as people bein' weak or strong, or bein' good or bad.—I couldn't go with you no more than I could fly—an' I can't forget you no more than I can be sorry or ashamed for—but I can forget. I know I can." She clenched her hands and stood with their nails digging into her palms. "Go on, Sam, please. It'll be a lot to know always that there's someone in th' world like you. Goin' after what you want an' takin' it gay an' never tied by—."

"Gay?" he asked and came a step nearer.

"Don't wait any longer. Th' neighbors they'll be seein' that car an' comin'. But, oh, Sam, please, please I don't want to see you walk away like a whipped dog. An' when you've gone hunt what you want to find, don't stick by that good payin' job just because it's sensible—an' have your fun—an' listen to music an' dance an' read poetry—an' oh do all th' things I'd like to do—don't ever live by your neighbors an' this God like ours—please."

He caught her wildly beating hands, but she shrank still nearer the fence and begged him with her wild, wounded eyes to go away. He tried to speak, but when she struggled with her hands as with her eyes, he turned and walked rapidly away.

She stood clinging to the fence and watched him stride across the field, leap into his car and drive away. She continued to stand with her eyes on the road, her mouth open, and her head tilted with listening when the car was hidden by a down dropping curve in the road. But the faint thread of sound kept constantly breaking; and though she leaned farther and farther from the fence with listening, there came a time when other sounds of the road and of the world smothered it.

She climbed then to the high post on which she had sat and stood upright, but could see nothing more than a cattle truck going down a gray stretch of road. She stood a time staring at the road, and gradually noticed that Caesar was barking, the short loud barks by which he announced day time visitors. He had, she thought, been barking so for a long while.

She turned slowly on the post, for the top was scarcely larger than her two feet. She saw soon down among the shrubs and grape vines by Solomon's fence, the moving pinkness of a woman's dress. Delph studied the broad fat back as the woman hastily reached for a bunch of grapes; in a moment she knew it for Sadie Huffacre's. She was still a moment, dazed by a sense of loss and a foreboding of some ugliness and misery, greater than any she had ever known; and while she stood Sadie turned and looked at her. She saw her loose wide mouth, too eager, like the mouth of a starved animal, and her greedy pale blue eyes filled with the same mocking silence and the knowing that lived in the sky. Like the sky, her eyes seemed to say, "Always and always I will live with you, Delph, be over you and watch and hold you to the ways of a farmer's wife."

She stared at the eyes a moment longer, felt no fear and no shame, only that wild madness at being trapped and tied, bound for a long torture that would end only when she died—maybe in fifty years. She looked up at the sky, then down at Sadie. She was between the two and so were Marsh and Burr-Head. She drew a long sobbing breath and looked toward the road; Sam would be miles away—now. It would have been kinder to Marsh had she gone with him—and now the two of them would be flying up and down the little hills—and the wind would tumble the hair above his eyes, and he would look at her and smile and say, "There's always something ahead till we die, eh, Delph."

Sadie came a few steps nearer, and she couldn't think for wanting to be away, out of this trap and away from the ugliness of it all. She had an instant's picture of fat black Emma, laughing she would be and with no time for the gossip of white women—and black Emma was there, not far from the lower side of Solomon's pasture.

She sprang from the post into the field with no bothering to look where she jumped, or caring to remember that when Caesar barked Solomon had come stalking and lashing his tail to see what Caesar was about, for now as ever he hated the dog. Her feet came hard against a rough steep spot below the fence, she swayed and tried to right herself but fell sprawling, her hands plowing through the rough ground and a stone grinding into her face. She heard Sadie scream and Caesar bark, and Solomon bellow, just by her head, it seemed.

She circled away, and Solomon circled, too, his eyes on her bright red apron—she'd felt this morning that she needed to wear a bright red apron over her faded blue dress. She tore at the apron, then stopped. She was wasting her time; she could never get it off.

Sadie screamed again, and Caesar leaped, snarling and howling against the fence, but Solomon noticed nothing except the bright red apron. She hesitated another moment, and Solomon circled nearer. If she ran, he would be after—it wouldn't be easy to climb the fence here with his horns just by her back; but it was a long run to the lower side—and she might not climb it then.

Sadie screamed again, she came to sudden life and knew that she must get to the fence near Sadie. Sadie was a human being; she loved Burr-Head; she wouldn't do anything to hurt him—and if she could talk to her—make her see—Sadie screamed as Solomon leaped for her in a mad plunge. She sprang sideways, heard the tearing sound of her dress on his horns, circled around him and back toward the fence. The ground was steep, and one of her ankles felt strange as if she had maybe twisted it when she whirled away from Solomon. She ran a step or so and fell, then struggled up again, and heard Solomon's hooves beating beside her, too close to try to climb the fence.

She circled again, plunged forward and up again and felt the fence wires with the tips of her fingers. Her lungs were filled to bursting, and there was no air in the world. Sadie ran to her, and Caesar crashed against the fence, fighting to climb it with his frantically beating paws. Solomon would kill her if for no other reason than to get to the dog whose head was almost by her own. "Go away—you fool," she gasped.

She tried to climb but Sadie's hands were fluttering behind the wire, pulling at her, lifting, hindering more than they helped. She saw her wide pale eyes, blind with terror. She was still then, knowing there was no use to waste her breath with climbing. "Sadie, if I don't—make it over—don't tell—."

There was pain and screams like great birds fluttering above her head. She wanted that breath the screams had wasted; she wanted another moment of living more than she had ever wanted anything. She had to tell Sadie that she mustn't tell anyone—ever—make her promise not to tell. She didn't want Marsh hurt or Burr-Head hurt; she wanted them safe in the stone house—Sadie must run and leave her—never let anyone know that she had heard and seen. She wouldn't scream. She stood upright and clutched the fence, and still the screams flew past—nothing left of her but screams and eyes. Her breasts and stomach were bloody pulp soaking through her dress. She saw the blood, beads on the fence wires and stain on Sadie's hands and Caesar's paws. She tried to whisper, but there wasn't any breath. She felt her body torn and her backbone seemed to grind into the fence. Her head jerked backward and her eyes filled with sky; there must be something more than this in the sky, some sense of victory, some promise of fulfillment, or foretaste of glory, not just blue fading to darkness. Maybe the world was built on hunger, maybe there was no fulfillment, no glory, no greatness, maybe the ones who lived never knew they lived—an empty sky above an empty earth and darkness through it all. Oh, but Marsh must be safe and Sam must be gay.

• • •

Marsh and Burr-Head ate in the little restaurant at the end of Maple Street. The place was filled with its usual Saturday crowd, a gayer crowd than common; corn and tobacco prices were good, the local harvest heavy, and farmers and cattle buyers were glad. They ate and talked and laughed, their noise mingling with the sounds from the men and mule and automobile crowded street. One of Quarrelsome Sexton's boys sat in one corner and played a guitar, and sang with loud tipsy gusto: "Shady Grove my little love, Shady Grove my darlin'," and somewhere up the street blind John Duncan played his fiddle while a little darkie danced. Burr-Head begged to go hear the fiddle play, and Marsh, deep in talk, let him go. Young Riley Lee from over by Salem was at his table wanting to know what Marsh thought of cedar fence posts—if it would be better to buy steel and do away with the cost of digging holes. "Cedar's better than steel if you've got th'—." Marsh began and stopped, annoyed by the loudness of his voice. His words seemed loud as if he talked against a room full of sound, but the place was quiet, still as if all the close-ly crowded men were dumb.

He glanced from Young Riley's face to the door, but it was filled with the heads and shoulders of tall silent men. And many of the men stood with their hats in their hands. The fiddle from up the street came clearly now, two quick cries of shriekin' laughter, and then one little sound like a half note, and the fiddle, too, was silent, and the beating feet of the little darkie tapped once and then were still.

Marsh turned and looked at young Riley Lee, and though he had not moved, his face seemed far away, and the face was different, looking first at Marsh and then at something behind him in the door, as if the something were a sign or a signal or a dumb man talking with his hands.

Marsh looked at the door again. The heads and shoulders were drawing away, leaving a lane like an empty road from nothing to him. He waited and tried to think, and in a moment remembered Burr-Head. Something had happened to him—he could never tell

Delph. Delph would never forgive him. He sat waiting and the man-bordered lane remained empty, and no man dared come to him. The silence in the room deepened; he heard the heavy breathing of the men, and somewhere a horse neighed and a mule's feet pawed in the street.

No one moved or spoke and all eyes were kept carefully from his eyes when at last a man came through the door. The man was Poke Easy. He looked very tall and very straight, and he no more than the others would look into Marsh's eyes. Marsh pushed the table from him and arose and asked, "Burr-Head?"

Poke Easy shook his head, and Marsh could not understand. Dorie's children were never ones to lie. "Come outside, Marsh," Poke Easy said, and he followed past the silent men into the crowded silent street. He saw Roan and Tobe and Perce and Reuben Dick. They were his friends and they were waiting for him. He knew them, knew their faces, but they were strangers now. They looked at him with pity, and no man had ever pitied him.

He felt a familiarity in the silent pitying faces, and he seemed to have walked backward into his oil field years—a long way back. He was one in a group of men who stood by a heavy boiler fallen on its side. He and the other men had been moving the piece of machinery, inch by inch with oxen and block and tackle up a steep hill. A cable was broken, and a man lay with his legs up to his thighs under the crushing rim of one heavy iron wheel. It was a moment, the first one, when the man did not scream, had seemed to feel no pain, drowned as it was by the understanding. He knew, lying there, that whether he lived or died he would never be a man, the same again as those who watched him. The man knew that though agony might pass and sorrow and regret, the change from what he had been to what he now was would not pass.

And now the scene was come again, and Marsh was there, but not one of the men who watched. He looked at Poke Easy and asked, "Delph?" and this time Poke Easy did not shake his head. He wanted to run, he wanted to break something with his hands, he wanted to ask if Delph were in pain, but while he stood, helpless, changed from what he had been, like the man with the cut-off legs, the men who lined the streets made a lane for him, and he walked between the silent people with his eyes on Poke Easy's back. It seemed he walked a long way through the old narrow streets of the town.

They passed the square where the fountain played, the drops were silver against the empty sky, and the fountain spray was the only thing that moved or made a sound. The boys playing by the cannon stood open-mouthed and stared at him as he walked by, and the men in the crowded street by the courthouse made way for him in silence. The hill men bared their heads, and in the eyes of a stoop shouldered woman with a fat baby in her arms he saw tears. When he had walked a space he understood the bared heads of the hill men. He knew that Delph was not in pain.

They came to the one hospital of the town, and Poke Easy turned and said, "Maw's there. She came—with her. She said to come to her. Don't go—to Delph."

"I want to see Delph," he said.

"Wait—you can't see her. I mean—Solomon, he—."

"Solomon?"

"Yes—Sadie did what she could—but not soon enough. She's here in th' hospital, too."

Marsh brushed his hands across his eyes, and it was strange to feel the coldness of his fingers. His hands were never cold. "I want to see her."

Poke Easy walked again, and there were girls in stiff starched white, and there were men, he had known them yesterday, but they were strangers now. And they, too, looked at him, and one man older than the others said, "I don't think you ought to go, Mr. Gregory."

He answered nothing but followed Poke Easy to a room at the end of a long hall. He paused by the door, angry with the hospital. Delph would want a room in front where she could watch the people in the street. He remembered then, and watched a nurse open the door. It seemed to take her such a time, awkward and fumbling with her hands, but then few women had the light skillful hands of Delph. It was her hands that had pulled him through that first hard summer. "I want to go by myself," he said when Poke Easy and the nurse followed.

It was a small room with a chair and a window and a bed. The bed looked long and high and wide, or maybe it was only that Delph looked strangely small. He knew it was Delph in spite of the sheet with its spreading stain of blood. There was her hand, not meek and folded on her breast, but tossed away with the fingers showing past the edge of the sheet.

He walked up to her and took her hand and drew it from under the sheet. In it there was a faint warmth and there was grape stain on the fingers. She wouldn't like that now, for tomorrow she was to sing in church and when she sang she hated work-stained hands. He remembered and laid the hand gently back upon the sheet. And it was strange to see it stay as he had laid it, cupped and empty like a wind blown leaf. The emptiness of it worried him, the slightly bent fingers had an expectant look as if they waited for something. He wished he had a flower. He wished he could see her face, but the sheet above her face was dark with stain, and he knew she would not like for him to see her so. She had flushed each time he had looked at the small scar he had made on her face.

Still, there was her hair. He pulled the sheet away, and saw the little loosened tendrils, stirring softly when he moved the sheet, and the hair was alive and soft and warm still to his hand. The nurse and Poke Easy came again, and Poke Easy said, "Please, Marsh," and the nurse said, "Now, Mr. Gregory."

He felt guilty and embarrassed. He shouldn't have done that. Maybe it was against the rules. Delph wouldn't like it. She was always saying, "Marsh, I want Burr-Head to grow up an' learn how to act with all kinds of people in all kinds of places." He had never hardly been in a hospital, and here he was acting all wrong. "I'll just sit," he said. "I—I won't move, but I want to stay—a while, yet."

The nurse brought a chair and he sat by Delph. He sat straight and still with his hat on his knees. Sometimes he looked at her hair and sometimes at her hand and sometimes out the window. He saw buildings and a block of sky and a square of grass. The grass worried him. He thought a time and remembered. He had thought of the grass when his neighbors died; men, he had said, were like grass. He wondered why he had ever bothered with thinking of such things. Death was nothing, an emptiness like the sky. He could measure death no more than he could measure the sky, and like the sky he would always live with it.

He saw the shadows of buildings fall long and thin across the grass, and he remembered that once he had loved the twilight, for that meant milking and barn work time. For him there would never come another barn work time. He could not go home and leave Delph. Before he had a foot of land, he had seen in her eyes something like that place there in the valley, and now he couldn't see it anymore. He couldn't see anything. He had always wanted his work and his life and Delph to be one thing—and they were.

He saw twilight fall and the shadows die and still he sat. Dorie and Brother Eli came and tried to talk with him and each he sent away. The twilight deepened, and her hair was a blurred spot of deeper darkness against the sheet, and he could not see her hand, and he wished that the daylight would linger always and that he could sit and never go away. He got up and turned on the light, but it was hard and bright; he was afraid it shone in her eyes, used as they were to lamplight and firelight only.

Full dark fell and he heard Katy sobbing in the hall. She was the youngest of Dorie's children, but when trouble came Dorie sent for Katy. Delph had loved Katy like a sister, and she didn't want to hear her stand out there and cry with a quivering, broken crying, the way Delph had cried last night.—He remembered last night; it was a long time ago, Sam had come to tell her good-bye—and then Caesar had stood whining and whining by the gate.—He knew he must go now. There were things he must straighten for Delph that could not be done in this room. Foolish she had been, little sometimes in her head like a child, and her mind like an April wind.

He turned on the light again. He stood by the bed and looked at the hand a long while, then put it carefully under the sheet. It was cold now. He glanced guiltily at the door, then smoothed her hair again, drew the covering gently over it, and came away. He closed the door softly, thinking that she would not mind. Delph had never been afraid of the dark. She had never been afraid of anything.